MERIDIAN

ANDREW
CERONI

outskirtspress

DENVER, COLORADO

This is a work of fiction. The events and characters described herein are imaginary and are not intended to refer to specific places or living persons. Other than factual, geographical, or historical information known or available to the general public, names, characters, places, and incidents are used fictitiously, and any resemblance to actual persons, living or dead, events, or locales is entirely coincidental. The opinions expressed in this manuscript are solely the opinions of the author and do not represent the opinions or thoughts of the publisher. The author has represented and warranted full ownership and/or legal right to publish all the materials in this book.

MERIDIAN
All Rights Reserved.
Copyright © 2000, 2016 Andrew Ceroni
v3.0

Cover Image by Andrew Ceroni

Outskirts Press, Inc.
http://www.outskirtspress.com

ISBN: 978-1-4787-7322-1

Outskirts Press and the "OP" logo are trademarks belonging to Outskirts Press, Inc.

PRINTED IN THE UNITED STATES OF AMERICA

ALSO BY ANDREW CERONI

SNOW MEN

For my son, Andrew-Michael

"...in an infinite universe, anything that could be imagined might somewhere exist."

Dean Koontz
Dead and Alive

CHAPTER 1

Nags Head, The Outer Banks
North Carolina

Tony Spencer pushed his feet off the sand, bobbing gently with the greenish-gray water lapping at his shoulders. He reached up to pick off a few pieces of seaweed sticking to the back of his neck and tips of his curly black hair. The sky above was an azure blue, the sun directly overhead, and the westerly Atlantic breezes soft against his face. Exhausted as he was from lack of sleep, this day was still a delight.

He glanced to his right. Tony Jr. was grinning from ear to ear, floating in the water some twenty yards away. Barb was yet another fifteen yards south, also watching Tony Jr. when she caught her husband's eyes beaming in her direction. Her lips creased in a smile and she nodded and waved. The sojourn at the beach was a pleasurable time for all of them, a welcome respite.

"Dad, this is great!"

"Yes son, it sure is. You want one of those someday?" Spencer had noticed Tony Jr. eyeing a cabin cruiser sailing on the near horizon... stark white against the water and sky, an American flag flapping lazily off the stern, a real beauty. It had been out there for an hour or more, not far off the beach. It motored slowly northward.

"Oh yeah, for sure!" Young Tony said with an admiring chuckle, still staring at the boat.

Labor Day weekend would soon be over. While the holiday meant vacations for so many Americans, its passing for Tony was perfunctory these days. Having resigned his position with the Agency two weeks ago, he now had all the time in the world. Not even a smidgeon of thought had crossed his mind about future employment. No, he had far more important things on his mind. Darker, more sinister things.

The tale he'd heard months ago from his fellow agents in Europe was incredible, preposterous, although they'd sworn it was true. Their story eventually consumed his attention until he knew he had to verify it. With the approval of Langley Center three weeks ago, he'd flown out to Denver to trace that story to its origin. What he saw shook him to his core, gripped his soul like never before. Even seeing it with his own eyes, he failed to come to grips with it, to comprehend the reality of it. The images stalked him nightly in the hot sweat of waking dreams, terrifying visions. Mostly the eyes.

When Spencer returned to Washington and advised management of his decision to leave the Company, they were furious. Spencer was too deep into the *project* to just walk away now. Livid, they demanded Spencer consider the impact to an operation that had such serious national security consequences. But their entreaties fell on deaf ears. Tony's very faith was now teetering.

Driven to resign, he still couldn't believe it. Now, the term "believe" was a very brittle concept for Tony Spencer. What did he, what could he, what should he, believe? Would prayer help?

Really help? Nightmarish visions hounded him from each night's agonizing darkness to the leaden gray of dawn.

Waking each morning in feverish sweats, he knew he had to somehow expunge these thoughts, the very knowledge, however true, from his mind. And today, an afternoon at the beach with his family, immersed in the cool, comforting waters of the Atlantic, he imagined for a fleeting instant that he might soon be free of his fears.

On the Hatteras Sport Fisherman, its engines shut down and now drifting south, four fishing poles were slung from their steel cups in the frame, but no one paid any attention to them. Men moved busily about the boat, forward and aft, some wearing shoulder holsters under their shell jackets.

"It's a go!" The captain shouted down from the flybridge.

The diver flopped clumsily in his flippers out of the cabin and sat on the transom, his back to the water. One of the crew handed him a large plastic bag filled with seawater, then his more fragile tools. He nodded to the men and tipped backward into the ocean. Swimming downward to about 25 feet, the diver read his watch compass to take his bearings, turned, leveled off, and swam toward the shoreline.

Squinting against the bright sun, Spencer looked at his watch. He decided to give it another twenty minutes or so before waving his family to their towels for a picnic lunch on the beach. They could catch some rays. He wanted to make the most of this last day, a refreshing break before young Tony headed back to school.

Eyes skimming the water just in front of him, he saw the domed translucent float rising to the surface, drifting toward him. He saw another, then another. All were washing in warm waters toward the shore.

He recognized the danger immediately, but before he could

even shout a warning to Barb and Tony Jr., his right leg shrieked in pain. Like a carpet of needles had brushed against his leg and then sunk all at once into his flesh. Following immediately came the even deeper sting, as though something punched into his calf.

"Arghhh! What the... "

Spencer's muscles cramped severely. He tried to yell... but he suddenly had no air. He couldn't breathe, his vision blurring. Instantly nauseous, he vomited, clutching his stomach. The pain swept up his leg, the whole right side of his body convulsing in agony.

Spencer's heart pounded in his chest. Struggling to keep his head above the surface, as if cinder blocks were tied to his ankles, he gasped for air, but gulped water into his lungs instead. He heaved again, gripped in shock, his eyes glazing. His muscles totally crippled, his body dead weight, Tony Spencer slipped below the surface. The entire episode took only minutes.

Tony Jr. often saw his dad flip down to skim along the sand below. So, at first he took no notice when Spencer went under the water. But too much time had passed. Now his father's head was still just below the surface, his hair floating, and Tony grew alarmed. This was different. Something was wrong.

"Dad! Are you okay?" the boy shouted. "Dad!"

"Dad!" he screamed again, racing toward his father with everything he had, fighting the rolling waves. Finally reaching Spencer, he yanked hard against the weight and the pull of the water. Grappling to keep his dad's head above the surface, he began towing him to shore. Barb, facing to the south away from them, saw none of what was happening. Then, his father gasped and coughed up water. He was alive!

"Dad! Dad, do you hear me? Dad? Tony reached the shallows and dragged the body onto the sand, cradling his father's head in his arms. He looked around wildly. "Somebody, anybody, call an ambulance, please!"

But there was no one else. The beach was empty. Hearing her son's shrieks, Barb turned to see them and swam frantically toward shore.

Spencer looked up, retching as water streamed from his mouth. His eyes seemed frozen, staring beyond Tony. "M… Marie… Ma…"

"Dad, what?"

"Mar… Mary…"

"What?"

"Marie… Maria… Dean." His eyelids lowered and closed.

Barb came running toward them, saw Tony's condition, then jolted to her beach towel and scrambled for her cell phone. Breathlessly she described the scene to the 911 operator, then returned to young Tony's side and pulled her husband into her arms. There was no movement in Spencer, but he seemed to be breathing… but with breaths ever so shallow. She couldn't know that her husband's circulatory and neurologic systems were failing.

Nags Head is a small town and the response was swift. In minutes, Barb heard sirens. An ambulance swerved off the road and plowed through the dunes toward them. Two med techs pounded across the beach with a stretcher. An older man, wearing a suit, walked as quickly as he could, his street shoes struggling in the sand.

"We have him, Miss. Your name?" The paramedics went right to work, hauling a heavy, limp Tony Spencer from her arms and onto the stretcher.

"I'm Barb Spencer. That's my husband, Tony. What happened? Will he be alright?"

"Well, you'll have to follow us to the hospital, Ma'am. We

don't have any spare room. Mr. Chapman's with us... we were coming back from Manteo when your call came through."

"Who?"

"The county coroner."

"Ohhh... Tony, we've got to get to the car. Hurry!"

A minute or so later, the ambulance bounced off the beach and back on the roadway. Sirens wailing, it raced to the hospital.

"Whaddya think, Mr. Chapman?"

"Too soon, guys. It doesn't look good though." Chapman examined the swollen, angry red lesions on Tony's right leg. "Jellyfish. Probably Portuguese Man of War." Hearing a faint mumble, he lowered his ear to Spencer's lips.

"Mary... Ma... Marie..."

"Yes sir?"

"Maria... Dean..." His eyes rolled back and the head lolled sideways as he lost consciousness. The young med tech looked at Spencer, then Chapman.

"Hallucinations. That's a tough venom. Although the area of lesions doesn't seem large enough... well, I'll get a much closer look at the hospital."

As the ambulance backed into the emergency room dock, Spencer drifted in and out of consciousness. His pulse dropped still lower. Emergency room staff grabbed the gurney and rushed Spencer into the building where the on-call physician waited.

It was too late. Spencer's life systems had collapsed. Fifteen minutes later, behind a curtain in an exam room, after two attempts at defibrillation and in the presence of Doug Chapman, Dr. Eisernmann pronounced Tony Spencer dead. A nurse slowly, steadily pulled a sheet over him. Tony's body was lifted onto another gurney and wheeled out to the elevators, heading to the basement morgue. Chapman followed.

Barb Spencer and Tony Jr. burst through the emergency

room doors. Barb quickly saw the gurney and pushed Tony Jr. into a chair, bolting forward to block the gurney in the corridor. Chapman waved off the med tech, allowing the desperate wife to reach over and rip the sheet off. Tears streamed down her face.

"Tonyyy!" She sobbed, seeing her husband motionless, pale, his eyes closed. Barb began to tremble uncontrollably, her face bleaching marshmallow white. She clutched her husband's arm.

"Nooo! Tony!"

Beads of sweat appeared on Barb's face. Chapman reached over to grasp her hand. Like ice. Barb Spencer's eyes suddenly spun up into her head, and she slumped sideways, collapsing onto the tiled floor.

"This woman is going into shock!" Chapman yelled. "Get her into a treatment room! Now!"

Two nurses and a med tech scooped Barb up and carried her into a treatment room. Young Tony shook his head, his face wet with tears. The boy slid off the chair and onto the floor, curling into a fetal position. He shook violently.

"Somebody, now dammit... help the boy!" Doug Chapman shouted, frantic. As young Tony was lifted from the floor, Chapman finally turned away, shaking his head, and pushed the gurney to the elevator.

In the basement morgue, Doug threw on the flood lights and wheeled Spencer into an open autopsy well. He pulled off the sheet and, with a long-handled Q-tip, lifted Spencer's eyelids. He nodded to himself, obviously agreeing with what he observed. Moving to the right leg, specifically the calf muscle, Chapman leaned over to get a closer look.

"No. Not enough. No way. Not large enough," he mumbled to himself in a clinical monotone.

Chapman drew a blood sample and placed it in the mass spectrometer. He threw the switches and the machine hummed for the toxicology analysis. Minutes dragged by before the graph began to etch its way across the screen. The toxin was indeed Portuguese Man of War venom, hydroxytryptamine. Nasty stuff.

He examined the toxicity graph, his eyebrows rising. "What the hell? No way… impossible!" Chapman shook his head, frustrated. He must be missing something.

Doug walked to the metal counter behind him and pulled open a drawer. He slipped on a headset light and grabbed his magnifying binocular glasses before stepping back to the gurney. With the floodlights, his headset lamp, and the binocular glasses on, he began a close, detailed search over the lesions left by the stinging cells of the jellyfish tentacle.

Scanning the surface of the epidermis on Spencer's calf, his eyes widened. He shook his head in disbelief. With the magnification, he saw it. Saw it clearly.

"Oh, my God." Chapman backed away in sudden shock and horror.

CHAPTER 2

Weeks Later, McLean
Northern Virginia

John Tanham frowned at the man sitting across the booth. He shook his head and glanced down at his cigarette. A long gray ash broke off and missed the ashtray, disintegrating on the wooden table. One sweep of his hand sent the remnants drifting down like ashen snow to the floor.

He turned to the window. The pavement shimmered from the day-long rain, reflections dancing under streetlights that had switched on early in the sullen evening sky. The showers were now slowly waning, as was the rush-hour traffic that poured out of Washington, D.C. in a daily deluge between four and seven p.m. Tanham crushed out the half-smoked cigarette and picked up the iced mug of beer without looking at either one. He was distracted by the question before him.

"John… hey! Come on."

With an effort, Tanham brought his country club-tan face and piercing blue eyes around to meet O'Donnell's stare.

"John…?" Phil O'Donnell's voice rose. The muscles in his

face twitched. He was more than a tad aggravated at Tanham's seeming indifference. The man seemed to have fallen off the edge of the planet.

"John, we've got dead people on the other side of the pond, a pissed-off station chief in Berlin, and a bunch of German spooks who want to know how badly their electronic warfare programs have been compromised! And, who the hell knows what the KGB, I mean, the SVR, will do next. Or when or where they'll do it! We need to develop some answers!" O'Donnell ranted.

Phil O'Donnell's voice rose above the tavern chatter. More than just a few disapproving faces turned his way, distracted from their happy-hour drinking. O'Donnell swiveled in his chair to meet their gawking eyes, baring his teeth in a menacing smile. They shook their heads in disappointment and returned to their conversations.

"Spooks, damn spooks! The whole place is filled with spooks!" Phil lamented in a brash whisper.

Sully's Grill and Tavern *was* filled with spooks. Just off Chain Bridge Road, a couple of miles west on Route 7, it was less than four miles from Langley Center. As the local watering hole, it filled quickly every evening with "good old boys," the self-styled defenders of western democracy. These were the warriors of the shadow wars... lifting presidential power to great heights, influencing politics in foreign nations, toppling governments, removing or more accurately, *terminating,* any obstacles, and raising new regimes. And as it served the national security interests of the United States, it was all for God, motherhood and apple pie.

Nevertheless, Sully's Grill was a classy place, from its polished mahogany walls to the padded leather chairs. The spot was almost sacred actually... to the spooks, that is. And, those present expected a modicum of discretion, even from O'Donnell who had a reputation for a big mouth.

"Spooks and snake-eaters. I'm surrounded by them all damn day, and I gotta put up with it here too. Gees." Phil turned back to Tanham. "John, seriously, I apologize for the tone, but we've got to write an ending to this thing. And fast."

His voice sank. "At least, well, STALKER *did* work. Without STALKER, we'd have never picked up on Laszlo to begin with. But what to do now? We could continue to localize him, grab him, make a believer out of him, what?"

Tanham broke his silence. "I agree. The project is in danger of compromise. This guy Laszlo knows way too much. He's got to go." Tanham turned back to the window, now streaked with rain and glittering jewel-like from the passing headlights.

"And if I know Bill Nordheimer, he's gonna want to crucify the guys that got us into this. If any of them are still alive. As the senior Resident for Europe, he's got more than enough power to do it too."

"Okay, John, tomorrow's Thursday, the third of October. The Director's got to make a recommendation to the Security Council at eleven o'clock. We need to line up our ducks. You know damn well that if the House and Senate intelligence committees get wind of this, we can scratch the intelligence budget for the next four years!" O'Donnell's face contorted in disbelief at the potential for disaster.

Tanham nodded, his eyes drifting past Phil to the room beyond, distracted by movement. Several patrons sitting near the entrance had turned all at once as the heavy wooden entrance door swung open behind them. A damp swirling wind swept through the room. The scent of rain was heavy.

A man stood in the open doorway, backlit by the tavern's neon lights and random flashes of lightning. His trench coat glistened wetly, but his face was in shadow. He paused, his eyes sweeping the room, an ominous presence hanging over his broad shoulders. Finally, he shrugged, shaking some of the rain from his coat and letting the door swing shut behind him. Stepping briskly toward the bar, he left a trail of water on the hardwood floor.

"Good evening, sir. What can I get you?" the closer of the two bartenders asked as the newcomer moved up to the counter.

"Hi Georgie, make it a boilermaker," he replied, smiling. "A pale ale and a shooter of Jim Beam, please."

The man's gruff voice emanated from deep in his chest. He wedged himself closer between the stools to reach the shot of whiskey that appeared in front of him. As he picked it up, rivulets of water drained off his drenched trench coat onto the shoulder of the young man next to him. The bartender grimaced at the sight and turned away. He pulled the spigot to fill the iced mug with ale.

"Hey! Dammit! Watch what you're doing!" The burly young man on the next stool raised his hand to the shoulder of his blue cashmere sport coat.

"Gees, I'm sorry." the newcomer apologized. "I'm soaking wet... all this rain and..."

"I don't give a shit about the rain, old man!" the man bristled.

"Look, I'm sorry. It's only water though." He picked up his bar napkin and tried to blot the young man's shoulder. "Let me buy you a... "

The man in the sport coat rose slowly from his stool, thrusting his tree-trunk chest forward. He smelled of way too much liquor. His large hands pushed his wavy black hair back from his forehead as he inched toward to the older man.

"Well, see those damn coat racks over there! This is a six-hundred-dollar sport coat, and it's gotta be dry cleaned! You're an idiot! Got that, an idiot."

The heads of a few patrons turned toward the bar. Tanham

peered through the yellowish light of the tavern, eyeing the situation. O'Donnell caught Tanham's movement and turned to look as well.

The newcomer's eyes narrowed. He spoke again, but this time no longer sympathetic. "Look, I said I was sorry. Let's leave it, okay? And, I said I'll buy..." Again, his words were cut off in midstream.

"No, let's not leave it! But why don't you leave, you know, just get the hell outta my sight? You old bastard. You're oblivious!" The young bull's chest puffed as he leaned forward.

The newcomer quickly sized the man up, a piercing gleam in the dark slits of his eyes. He lowered and shook his head, then abruptly shoved the younger man. The young bull lost his balance, staggering backward. He bumped clumsily into a neighboring table, causing the patrons to grasp their glasses. Despite his apparent age, most saw that the older man had tremendous strength. The room turned silent.

"You... asshole!" the young man barked, clumsily righting himself. He reached for the long neck of his beer bottle. The bartender swung around, opening his mouth to shout, but before he could utter a word, the young man's arm whipped forward, bottle in hand.

"J.T.! The kid's drunk! Don't you break this place up!" Though the bartender shrieked at Brannon, it was the snorting young bull he glared at.

"Whoa!" J.T. Brannon's hands moved with a blur. The polished steel blade of a dagger appeared from nowhere, glinting in the pale light. The blade entered the loose sleeve of the man's sport coat and slammed into the wooden bar, pinning the arm. The bottle clattered to the floor.

"You prick!" he shrieked, tugging futilely on the fabric and tearing a longer gash. An angry glare spread across his reddened face. In frenzy, the young man's arm darted under his coat.

Brannon saw it. In one smooth, practiced motion, his right hand grasped the man's wrist, then slid forward, bending the man's hand inward and wrenching the pistol away. Brannon pushed the barrel under the man's chin. The muzzle dug into the white flesh of his throat. Brannon scowled, drawing closer.

"Enough! You nasty little bastard! Where the hell do you think you are, Dodge City?" he snarled, shoving the man's head back and over the bar with the muzzle.

"Stop it! J.T., let him go! Please!" the bartender shouted, his hands gripping the bar.

The assailant froze in place. He whimpered, glancing toward the bartender and back to Brannon. He raised his left hand, palm forward.

"Okay, okay... look, mister, I'm sorry! You're Brannon? J.T. Brannon? I didn't know! God, I'm sorry..." He strained to see the revolver under his jaw, then closed his eyes in humiliation. A warm fluid dripped onto his shoe and puddled on the floor. He shook his head.

"God ain't got nothing to do with this just yet... unless you've got some burning desire to go meet Him. It shouldn't matter *who* the hell I am. You've got one damned nasty attitude, you little shit. Try to bash my face, cut my throat with a bottle, and all over a little rain water? Then draw a pistol yet? Way out of line. You're a newbie in the field operations school, right? Shame on you."

Brannon frowned, and glanced down. A smile broke across his chiseled features. "You know, Mr. 007, I do believe you've gone and pissed in your pants."

J.T. stepped back, eased the hammer back down with his thumb. "So, I tell you what, let's say *you* leave, *you* get the hell outta my sight. Go home, change your underwear, and sober up."

Brannon set the gun on the bar as his left hand jerked the dagger out of the wooden counter. It quickly disappeared. "You can pick up your revolver from Georgie here tomorrow. Go on, get outta my sight... go home and think about saving your energy for the real bad guys."

"Yes sir." He sniveled, backing away, his palms out and down. Eyes downcast, the young bull rushed out of the bar, rubbing the sliced fabric on the sleeve of his sport coat. He never looked back.

"Georgie, sorry, but I have this thing about not eating beer bottles. Damn young bucks today. I don't know where they're coming from anymore."

The bartender sighed, nodding, relieved things hadn't gone further.

"Fix the gouge and put it on my tab, okay?"

Brannon's palm curled around the mug of ale in front of him. He downed it in one long gulping swig. A slight smile twitched at the corner of his mouth. He winked at the bartender, backed up and turned toward the door. He was gone in an instant. Astonished faces of patrons and the empty beer mug, still frosted, were all that remained.

J.T. paused on the stone steps outside the tavern, letting the cool mist fall on his face. Reflecting, he shook his head and made his way to the car.

"Shee-it. You see that?" O'Donnell muttered, turning his head back to Tanham.

"Yeah. Brannon." Tanham twisted in his seat to watch the dark-green sports coupe pull from the parking lot. "Dumb-ass kid should've known better. Too much booze. And of course, Brannon's way too fast. Too fast, too strong, too lethal. He's nuts himself. Everybody knows that."

John returned from the window. "So, back to where we were,

Phil. Look, we can't deny squat on this one. The Army took care of that long ago. And, they documented every damn detail too, the stupid bastards. What they did to Laszlo was outrageous. They stole almost a year of the guy's life… broke his hands, fingers, nose. Injected him with truth serum. And we accuse the Russians of brutality in their Siberian gulags? And, you're right about the Germans. They're going to drill themselves into the ceiling. That is, *if* we tell them. We've got to do the right thing on this. Dead men considered too. If the project even appears tainted, then Laszlo's gotta go. Terminate him. It would be a righteous sanction." Tanham leaned back and downed the last of his beer.

"Okay, good. We're counting on you to help fix this, John. All of us are counting on you."

"Phil, I know we're on a very fast train here, but I'll make sure we remain the drivers."

The waiter paused by the table and refilled their mugs from the pitcher. Tanham raised his in the air. "So, gentlemen, here's to us and the table dust. C'mon lads, bottoms up."

"Fast train and we're the drivers, eh? You still think Laszlo's demons come from that train crash?" Phil smirked.

Tanham had read the interrogation records front to back. He did indeed consider the horrific death of Laszlo Csengerny's parents in a train crash in southern France as the psychological vise that first squeezed, then twisted the mind of the man they all wanted either dead or in custody.

"I'm going to talk to Doc Kriegel in the morning. Pete Novak's my choice to go. I'll give confirmation to you, then brief Novak… with Kriegel's concurrence. We can't tell Novak everything. The National Security Council caveat on this is just too heavy. And, he might not be able to handle it anyway. Remember Tony Spencer? What happened to him? Well, Spencer couldn't handle it. But then, Novak's different. Cool-headed. He's well-liked, a rising son. Non-controversial. We'll get him over there no later than day after tomorrow."

O'Donnell's teeth sparkled in smile. "And a good bag-man if it comes to that too, right? See? John, I love it when you use your gray matter."

"You know, Phil, sometimes I think you have got to be dense. You saw what just happened at the bar. You know Brannon's rep. J.T.'s killed more men than Bayer's has got aspirin and the Director gave him the National Intelligence Medal for doing so 'Word is, J.T. thinks of Pete Novak like a brother."

"Hey look, I just…"

"No, you look. Phil, you screw with Novak – you're screwing with Brannon. I don't think you want to do that. If J.T. heard what you just said, he'd shove you up on a meat hook, gut you, and dress you out like a ten-point buck. Pete Novak's no bag-man, no scapegoat. Anyway, we don't need one. We need to localize this bastard Laszlo and stop him. Put a bullet in him if we have to. He's too dangerous and the project is too critical. Novak's a good shot. And Phillip, I'd watch my words if I were you, unless you want to have a come-to-Jesus session with Brannon."

CHAPTER 3

Fischergasse 2, Dörnigheim
Germany

Dörnigheim, east of Frankfurt and on the northern shore of the Main River, is a dank, clammy little urban area on the very best of its cloudy days. The faded brick street of Fischergasse is at its center. Bordered on each side by tall, weathered apartment buildings, the thoroughfare is a habitually wet and shadowy one. At the loveliest times of the year, these environs are a damp and uninviting place.

Laszlo Csengerny's apartment just off Fischergasse had never witnessed a ray of sunshine streaming through its narrow windows, only the watery light of street lamps switching on in premature nightfall. That was fine with him. He relished the dark. He hid in it. Hid from the demons always in pursuit.

And, he hid from both the Russian SVR and American CIA agents now hunting him. On the run, he knew he had to leave the apartment. Soon. Like now. Laszlo considered trains to be his best option. Trains were the most common, innocuous form of travel in Europe.

It was 2:00 a.m. In a cold sweat, Laszlo had coiled himself into a knot on the bed. As distant from vibrant, pulsating city life as it could be, his murky apartment still failed at shielding him from the bad dreams. If… they were dreams. Though the air in the room was tepid, he shivered from utter exhaustion and a horrifying dread he could not escape.

The creatures usually entered from his closet, so it was now closed with boxes stacked against it. Their long, clawed hands seized him in their clutches on several occasions, tearing his flesh into bloody welts, but they'd never managed to take him. The knife kept always under his pillow had saved him from that.

Laszlo's nightmares were always either of the demons continually seeking him out or of the U.S. Army's horror of an interrogation camp at Unterwössen in the Bavarian Alps. It was pointless to think about which condition was worse as both emanated from a reality deep in the blackest gloom of his ravaged psyche.

Struggling as best he could, his eyes wouldn't stay open. He pulled the covers up and over him for protection. The new layer of warmth soothed him. His vision gradually blurred.

Bit by bit, Laszlo was engulfed in the surreal world of a reality long past. His eyes blinked open and shut. He was in the cell. He could feel the rough wool of the blanket of the cot. The yellowish plaster walls flanking the small room grew clearer.

The nausea gripped him. A grid of light from the steel-barred window slowly tracked its way across the floor, crept up the blanket, and burned through his eyelids. He heaved sluggishly to his side.

On the wall, the large black numbers on the clock read 7:30 a.m., although he could no longer hear its hourly chimes. His ears were filled with a dull ringing. He glanced around the room… sparse, menial quarters, a metal cot with a thin mattress and the clock. No chair. No toilet. He knew very well the cell wasn't meant to be comfy. He'd been incarcerated in the camp at Unterwössen, in the Alps southeast of Munich, for longer than his dull memory could recall.

Rolling onto his back, he let the morning sun fall across his face. The dime-sized birthmark under his right eye disappeared into a bluish swelling that bloated the side of his face. The eye itself was swollen shut. A crust of dried blood stained his lips where a raw, jagged split had ruptured. His jaw throbbed in pain.

Laszlo pushed himself up to the edge of the mattress and eased his arms through the sleeves of the olive-green shirt. He struggled with a few buttons before giving up. It was useless. At least one finger on each hand was broken, and he had no reason to expect any splints. He leaned backward and pulled on pants of the same color.

"Ohhh." His side throbbed at the effort. The shallowest of breaths ached with searing flashes of pain. His ribs were covered with bruises. Above his left kidney, abrasions were still oozing blood. At least there were no injections last night. And so, the demons of his horrifying nightmares hadn't returned either. For that alone he was thankful.

He rubbed his abdomen, failing to notice the sound of a key turning in the door lock. The heavy door swung open and slammed into the wall behind it. His eyes opened wide. Laszlo fell backward onto the cot at the sight of him. A hulk of a man crossed the threshold of the doorway, then walked in a casual gait toward the prisoner.

The sergeant's eyes glittered as he spoke. "Good morning, Kurt, ah, excuse me, Herr Messerman. Or perhaps today it's Louis Montesson?"

The camp's chief interrogator paused, rubbing his chin.

"Then again, perhaps you really are Laszlo Csengerny, eh? Well, whoever the hell you are, how the hell're you doing? The lieutenant and I were just talking about you. We think we're just about there. So waddya say, Laszlo? No sodium pentothal last night, huh. You liked that, didn't you? Your demons didn't make a call on you?" The sergeant laughed derisively.

"Now Laszlo, old chap, you're gonna work with us today on this, aren't you? We're about finished with all this." With that, Rory swung his black boot into the prisoner's left knee.

Laszlo doubled over. The sergeant's right fist followed, smashing down on the prisoner's swollen right eye. Rory paused, wiping his hand on his pants. He then sent a strong left uppercut plowing into the base of Laszlo's nose.

"Ahhggg!" Laszlo fell at Rory's feet. "Please don't!"

The interrogator was untouched. Rory reached down, hauled the prisoner to his feet, and viciously delivered another crushing blow to his stomach. Laszlo lurched forward. The interrogator grabbed a fistful of hair. One final, heaving blow to an already cracked lower rib sent the prisoner to the concrete floor, wailing in agony. Laszlo landed with a crumpled *thump*. His moans for mercy resonated down the corridor.

Outside the entrance to the containment building, the younger of the two guards glanced at the other. He shook his head in dismay, shuffling his feet on the coarse boards and vainly trying to drown out the sounds from inside. His eyes glassed over. A tear escaped, streaking down his cheek.

Enough was enough. The young corporal, flushed with anger, swiveled on his heels to the door behind him. His right hand unsnapped the holster's retainer strap and gripped the butt of his Colt .45 pistol. Before he could take a step, the other guard spun about and grabbed his wrist, his eyes demanding restraint. The corporal struggled to pull free, but soon reluctantly nodded compliance, his face red with emotion. He stared at the floorboards as sounds of the brutal beating continued.

Finally, the door to the cell creaked open. Rory stepped into the hallway, dragging Laszlo by his right foot like a limp rag doll. Laszlo's face scraped against the floor, blood oozing from a pulpy right eye. The sergeant turned into a small shuttered room, lifted the prisoner to a chair and strapped him with rope. He switched on the tape recorder sitting on a small table against the wall.

"Laszlo? Mr. Csengerny? Let's take it one more time from the beginning, shall we?" Rory reached across the table and slapped the prisoner. His open hand struck the bruised right eye and swept across the man's fractured nose. Laszlo howled.

"Okay, Laszlo, let's see… if I remember correctly, you had a troubled childhood. Your mommy and daddy died a long time ago? Right? And some years later, it was those dirty rotten communist meanies who turned you into the disgusting bastard you are today. Now, isn't that correct?"

The interrogator paused, his irritation notching upward at the prisoner's lack of response. "Answer me, dammit!" Rory bellowed, curling his right hand into a fist. He drove it into the man's right cheek.

"Ahhgg! Please! Yesss! Yes, it's true! I've told you this over and over… what more do you want?" Laszlo sobbed, unable to hold his head erect. He slumped over, but forced a recovery.

"Ah, that's better." Rory replied, "Now then, you came all the way down to Trieste to join Uncle Sam's Army, right? You wanted to be a soldier? But we know now that you were working for the Russians, and you were gonna hurt us just as bad as you could. Weren't you?"

Rory leaned back in his chair, snickering. "You know, Laszlo, it's sweethearts like you that keep guys like me in business. The

Cold War just keeps getting a whole hell of a lot colder. Isn't that right?"

"Yesss, I suppose. But, I've told you all of this before." He whimpered, his head bobbing, weaving in and out of consciousness. The room swirled around him, illuminated only by the pale light of a single bulb. His brown hair was matted with blood.

Hearing footsteps approaching in the hall, Rory rose from his chair. He smirked at the battered Laszlo, then stood smartly at attention. The lieutenant turned into the doorway. He scanned the room and noted the prisoner, then nodded to the sergeant. Rory retrieved the towel soaking in a water pail under the table and rubbed it across Laszlo's face. The cold water removed the fog in his aching head. Laszlo slowly began to regain some composure, but blood clotted in his still-open left eye prevented him from focusing fully. He mumbled something incoherent.

"Rory, you have everything we need?"

"Yes sir."

"Good. Take the recorder and tapes over to my office. Give me a few minutes here with Laszlo."

"Very well, Lieutenant." Rory picked up the machine and disappeared through the door.

The lieutenant slumped into the chair and pulled himself toward the table, all the while watching the man wobbling in the seat across from him. "Laszlo, can you understand me?"

"Yes." With a heavy heave, Laszlo took in a deep breath.

"All right. You've been here nine months. You finally confessed your role in espionage against the United States. We caught you and your cohorts fairly early on and therefore the damage was minimal. So, your time with us is drawing to an end. This could have been much shorter and a lot less painful if you'd cooperated with us earlier. You know that, don't you?"

The prisoner leered back at him, turned away and then nodded in agreement.

"I know what you think of us. Do you really imagine though that if you were one of our agents, captured, sitting instead in a torture chamber in Moscow Center, you'd be having it easier?"

Laszlo's eyes lowered. "No."

The lieutenant smiled briefly. "Damn right no." He shrugged. "In any case, we've decided to release you. Pleased?"

"Yes."

The lieutenant leaned closer. "Okay. Then tell me, Mr. Csengerny, after all your games… who are you really?"

The prisoner squinted back. "You keep me here for almost a year, beat me senseless, break my hands, and you don't know that yet?"

The lieutenant just stared back.

Laszlo shrugged, "The answer is, I wonder about that sometimes myself."

"Let me rephrase. I'm not talking about your identity here. We're quite certain of what you believe to be true in that regard. Sodium pentothal solved that issue for us. No, there's something else, perhaps only a tangential issue to our clinical staff here, but important to me none the less." He paused.

"And?"

"Fact is, we've never satisfactorily explained the psychological origin of these demons that haunt you. Your… nightmares. Granted, that's not been the focus of our examinations, but it's still unresolved. You endure hellish nightmares about these creatures, shrieking about demons night after night. You claim they visit you here. More puzzling is that even under administration of sodium pentothal, there is still an apparent reality… your claims have remained consistent. These monsters come crawling into your conscious mind from somewhere deep in your psyche, from somewhere in the reality of your past. That remains a mystery. I would like to understand it better. I'd like to know what you yourself believe. Talk to me about it. Please."

"There is no answer. I don't understand why I have the nightmares. You've all told me I'm psychotic, I'm crazy, and that the beasts don't exist. They can't."

The lieutenant's eyes drifted. He grimaced. "You have streaks of blood soaking through your shirt. Both shoulders. Rory do that?"

"No."

"Then, what is it?"

Laszlo was silent.

The lieutenant reached over and pulled Laszlo's shirt open and away from his shoulders. Deep, bloody gouges ran across his upper chest, the flesh torn raw. "Good God, how did this happen?"

"They came for me."

"When?"

"One night ago. I woke up when they were trying to pull me from my cot. They clawed my shoulders, my ankles, trying to jerk me from bed, to take me."

"Take you where?"

"I don't know where."

"Laszlo… the creatures, it's not possible. Nothing could have breached your cell without us knowing."

"They did. They were there."

"How? There's no way…" The officer paused, shaking his head. "We'll get the wounds treated. You should have said something before this. Look, what I'm trying to say is there's a door in your mind that you haven't allowed us to enter. Only you have the key, Laszlo. I want to understand."

"Why?"

"I want to understand the insanity of the paradox, what appears to be true, yet the impossibility of it."

"Oh, bullshit." Laszlo's mind was clearing; the bleeding somewhat abated. "They're my nightmares, my damn demons. You're releasing me. So, why bother with this?" He scrunched his eyes.

"Mr. Csengerny, you're an amazingly intelligent man, an IQ almost off the charts. And yes, the staff is convinced your ability to reason logically is impaired. I myself am not so certain about that." He rasped, clearing his throat. "No, there's something else. Something deeper... hidden. It concerns me."

Laszlo managed a weak chuckle. He shook his head. "You're... concerned? Well hell, lieutenant, maybe they'll become your nightmares! I mean, if it concerns you so much." Laszlo laughed, then shot a look of stern defiance.

"I see. Well, I'd assumed this might be pointless." He pushed himself to his feet, walked to the door, and turned. "It might be best that I don't determine the real truth in this." The psychiatrist suspected that something of the darkest origin had manifested itself in Laszlo, a glimpse of hell. He shook off a shiver. "Oh, and by the way, Mr. Csengerny, if you end up here again, you'll never leave. Not alive, that is. You should understand that."

"I do."

"Rory," he turned to the sergeant now standing in the doorway. "Have him sign the papers. Any resistance, call me. Tell the dispensary to clean him up, patch up the injuries on his shoulders, and prep him for release. Make sure all the medical reports are packaged and shipped to Walter Reed with a duplicate to Medical Command. I want his ass out of here by Friday and turned over to the French in Marseilles. Laszlo's going to love French prisons."

The lieutenant stared back at the battered Laszlo and

reconciled his failure to gain an answer. "He's loony anyway. All this demon crap, screaming at the top of his lungs every damn night. I'm sick of that and sick of him." He glanced back at Rory. "And Sergeant, tidy up a bit in here, will you?"

"Yes sir. Have a good day, sir." Rory smiled, rubbing his chin as the officer's footsteps faded to silence. Grinning, he approached the prisoner.

Palms on the table, Rory moved his menacing face a mere inch from Laszlo. "Well, how about that, ole buddy? 'Looks like you'll be leaving soon. I'm depressed all to hell about that. You see, I think it'd be a lot cleaner if we just put a bullet in your head and dropped your sad ass in the Adriatic Sea. But then, the lieutenant is a gentler man. Guess what else? Laszlo, I've always admired that birthmark of yours. Indeed, I have. So, let's see if we can pretty it up a bit, just for old time's sake."

Laszlo opened his mouth slightly in anticipation. Rory's hands groped behind his back, felt the wooden chair, and raised it. He stepped to the side of the table and swung the chair around with all his strength. The chair smashed into Laszlo's shoulder. The impact shattered fragments of wood across the room and knocked him to the floor.

Rory stared down at the battered form. Shaking his head and laughing, he stepped over a splattering of blood on his way to the door. He sauntered down the hall, rubbing his knuckles.

Laszlo's head shook back and forth. He moaned, taking short, panting breaths, trying to gather himself.

Rolling over to his back, his eyes blinked and opened. It was the apartment in Dörnigheim. He stared at the ceiling, wiping the sweat from his forehead. He cried, trembling.

"They will never leave me, never."

CHAPTER 4

Hauptbahnhof, Frankfurt
Germany

T he wooden doors to the *Hauptbahnhof*, main train station, burst open, slamming into red brick walls. Laszlo leaped from the passageway. He dodged several automobiles and scurried across busy Düsseldorf Strasse to Taunus Strasse. He ran hard without looking back, his arms and legs pumping in tandem, drawing curious glances from onlookers relaxing in the street cafes. He skittered around a corner and stopped abruptly.

He pressed himself against the wall, gasping for breath. As he wiped his dripping brow, he glimpsed movement to his left and turned to face a dark figure. The guard standing in front of the *Deutsche Bundesbank*, German Federal Bank, had spun slightly on his heels and was staring directly at Laszlo. The guard's hand slipped beneath the flap of his uniform jacket. They faced one another for several moments.

Finally, Laszlo managed a smile and nodded his head in greeting. He stepped away from the building and in a casual stride crossed the street to the Taunus Gardens Park. A cobble-stone path angled off to the left, skirting the gardens. Well into the calm of the park, he hopped over onto the grass and leaned against the thick trunk of a tree.

His chest heaved, his lungs straining for air. Had he made it? He gathered the courage to peer back through the park toward the train station. He was surprised to see no unusual motion, no men frantically searching for him, just the meandering crowds of lunch-time window shoppers. He'd lost them! Hard to believe it, but he'd lost them.

Just minutes earlier in the basement men's room of the train station, he'd thought he was done for. The man had him by the throat. Probably CIA, not the Russian SVR. He didn't smell bad like SVR... those bastards never bathed. No, he was certain the man was CIA.

But then a second man jumped at them from the doorway and grabbed the first. Laszlo eased a few steps away while the two scuffled. He caught the flash of a knife in the bright fluo-rescent light and bolted, scrambling up the stairs and darting for the north entrance. Now, here he was in the park, blocks away. What next?

They were onto him. No doubt about it. How they could be, he had no clue. But he knew he couldn't go back to Dörnigheim and the apartment. If they had a surveillance team here at the train station, then surely they had the apartment covered as well. He could easily guess why the CIA wanted him. But then, the man in the station obviously had no intentions of detaining him. No, he meant to kill him.

Laszlo had to assume the CIA meant to terminate him with extreme prejudice, no matter where, no matter how. His for-mer SVR brethren would be more cautious. Laszlo and what he had uncovered were far too important to them now. Only

Laszlo knew the startling details relayed by the American traitor, the double agent, Yezhovich. Dr. Jon Yezhovich had given him everything.

He couldn't stay in Frankfurt. This was as good a time as any to leave. Laszlo knew that his quarry lay elsewhere, across the Atlantic. He would find it there and he would destroy it. Destroy it, no matter how valuable to the Americans or even the Russians. He could not let the beast survive.

Laszlo recognized the unmistakable tan of the Mercedes taxi cab turn the corner onto Reuter Weg. He stepped out onto the sidewalk and hailed it. To his relief, the driver saw him and swung the taxi to the curb. Laszlo jumped into the back.

"Good day. Where to?"

"East Park. The parking lot. My car's there. You know that place, East Park?"

"Yes… a 10-minute ride."

Lost in his thoughts, Laszlo noticed nothing of the short ride to the large park at the southeastern edge of Frankfurt. The city would soon be blanketed with surveillance. There was no question about that. But to his favor, at this moment neither the CIA nor SVR had any idea where he was. Most of the cash he had was on him. That too was good. Nevertheless, he knew he had to act quickly before the huge intelligence machinery of both adversaries swung into motion.

It was imperative he leave Frankfurt and now. But to where… Amsterdam, Brussels, Luxembourg, Paris, perhaps Basel? What would be safest? Paris? It would be Paris. It was the best bet, only a seven-hour drive on the Autoroute. He could put a lot of distance between him and them.

In minutes, he was in his small blue Fiat near East Park, looking over the gray waters of the lake. Very few people were out today, the weather too cool, dreary. Laszlo reached down to pull the maps from the glove box when he jerked up abruptly. It was impossible to miss the blaring horns. Across the lake was the huge rail switching yard of *Frankfurt Öst*, Frankfurt East.

The long black hulks crept through the yard, freight cars rearranging into a different mix of trains for the next leg of their journeys. His hands clapped over his ears. His eyes squeezed shut. He hated those damn horns! They were a trigger for images he never wanted to see again. They sent him on a journey to places he didn't want to go. He strained to push himself deep into the seat to block out the horrid memories. The horns always managed to bring back the sad, dark memories of those terrible days long ago.

Overcome with emotion, Laszlo could no longer distinguish between the whistles and horns of the Frankfurt East train yard from those now rushing into his mind from the past. The haunting overwhelmed him.

"Nooo," he held his head, whimpering. The visions crept into his mind like a movie on a theater screen. He knew the horror of it so well. It had plagued him with nightmarish dreams for so many years. His head thumped against the seat back.

After the accident in France took the lives of his mother, Katka, and father, Semmi, the railroad sent an agent from Paris. His job was to answer the questions and ease the suffering of immediate family, in this case, Laszlo's grandmother, Margo. The man related the story to her exactly as the investigators had tried unsuccessfully to piece together the evidence or rather, the lack of it. The dead bodies of the crews and track men had been recovered from locations where they were supposed to be. They were where they should have been. There was no explanation. The tragedy should not have occurred.

But the railroad man had witnessed these horrible anomalies before. Trackmen knew it all too well. It was the work of the demonic gremlins of railroad legend. They occasionally struck terror on remote, lonely stretches of track, leaving no evidence of their presence. At a total loss for explanations, the accident investigators had spoken of this probability themselves.

In her despair, Grandmother Margo in turn explained it to Laszlo. He could feel the images forcing their way into his mind. In the dark fog of his dreams, it was choreographed over and over again. His memory replayed itself on his mind's screen for viewing. The vision proceeded as it had always done.

His parents' train began the rapid descent from mountainous grades and entered a long tunnel exiting into the Garonne River valley and the rail switching district of Montauben. At one end of the expansive valley, in the village of Villemur, freezing rain had begun to fall hours earlier. The tracks were now coated with a thick glaze. The entire village and surrounding area had been transformed into a virtual ice palace.

Tree limbs, thick with ice, blew back and forth in the storm's black wind. They struck each other, sounding like the heels of a million shoes clicking sharply on a pavement. Phone, telegraph, and electric lines, looking like a giant spider's web, were soon too heavily burdened and snapped away from their junction boxes. Temperatures continued to drop, mixing the rain with sleet, erupting with torrents of snow. The switches for the north-south and east-west intersecting lines of track lay in Villemur. Those switches needed to be clear of ice and snow for a safe crossing.

In the surrounding forest, they were already dancing in mad frenzy before they wreaked their terror. Before they took the lives of his parents. It was here that the beasts went to work.

Laszlo could see the headlamp beam of the southbound freight's lead locomotive shining down the track. The long, straight, narrow mounds of snow on the rails shook with increasing tremors of the approaching trains. The ice began to crack in fine hairline fractures that spread outward along the track.

At the same time, the Nice-Bordeaux Express steamed from the East at full throttle toward the Villemur station's switches and obliquely intersecting tracks. Where was the track crew? Why didn't the trackmen throw the lever to send the express train onto the parallel siding where it would roll safely along the side of the yard and into cushions of snow?

Instead, the demons played out their grotesque evil, the investigator told his grandmother. The two steel goliaths drove fiercely toward one another like serpentine messengers of some dark legion. All sound was drowned out by the pounding thunder of the train cars colliding and breaking apart as the Nice-Bordeaux Express struck the southbound freight just forward of the engineer's cabin. The crumpled locomotive instantly derailed, rolling onto its right side and burrowing into snow and ice with thunderous momentum.

The passenger train's engine climbed up and leaped over. An immense, muffled detonation sent jagged shards of thick steel bursting in every direction. Steam, flame, and debris shot across the Villemur yard. Heavy steel rails split from their ties and swung violently from under the derailing train cars. In the express train, the center sills of the cars, their spines, broke apart.

The cars then disintegrated. Floor plates erupted and enormous wheel-truck assemblies were propelled upward and into cabins, gutting them and sparing no one inside. Thousands of spikes ripped out and launched into the air as deadly projectiles. Boxcars careened like prehistoric behemoths in every direction.

Laszlo shrieked in his waking dream as he saw his mother and father ripped apart. Trumpeting blasts of the colliding trains echoed throughout the frozen village of Villemur. It sounded like the end of the world. The demons reveled in the evil they had crafted.

With painful effort, Laszlo slowly lifted his head. The despair on his face turned to a sullen, angry look. He struggled to refocus. His cheeks were stained with tears... tears for his parents, tears for the horror that had so violently taken their lives and now plagued his own. This gut-wrenching grief followed him wherever he went, as did a seething hate for those he held responsible. A day of revenge, of settling up, would soon come for him.

Laszlo's ultimate destiny was the destruction of those demons. This was his only reality. And he would not let it slip from him. Yezhovich had showed him the way, and he had seemed unusually eager to do so. He had given him the directions to the exact location in the United States and also the facility's closely guarded access codes. The Americans would not be able to stop him.

"I will destroy them!" He wailed, pounding the dash. Laszlo turned the ignition key and the Fiat's engine turned over. In his coat pocket was a passport, one of several. His new identity would be Andreas Romburg. With renewed determination, Laszlo jammed the gear shift into first. The Fiat sped from the parking lot and headed south for the autobahn that would take him west from Frankfurt across Germany to the French border and the Autoroute to Paris.

CHAPTER 5

Langley Center
McLean, Northern Virginia

The next morning arrived too soon for everyone. The rain was gone. The abundance of moisture left behind a heavy fog that blanketed the Potomac valley up to McLean where the majestic river dwindled to a narrow stream by the front door of Langley Center, the Agency's headquarters. Outside the glass, steel, and marble headquarters, the CIA looked like a posh corporate retreat nestled deep in the forest, owned by some Fortune 500 company.

Inside however, things were anything but quiet. The air buzzed with activity, today more so than usual. Something was up. The morning staff meeting schedule had been compressed personally by the Director of Central Intelligence, the "DCI" himself, and all the way down the food chain.

Things had started popping long before then. Pete Novak, an up-and-coming Deputy Assistant Director for Special Programs in the Operations Directorate, was startled awake at 4:30 a.m. by the beep of his voice messenger. He had been sound asleep in his colonial brick home near George Mason University in Fairfax County. His hands fumbled on the night stand until he found the right button, then rolled over to reach the phone, settling it on the pillow.

"Mr. Novak?"

"Yes?"

"Sir, hold one, please." The Operations Center controller spoke crisply, passing Novak on to the Duty Officer.

Pete could tell from his tone that the DO was exhausted from a long night of crisis calls. "Sir, I'm calling to notify you that you're scheduled for a meeting this morning with the DepOps, Dr. Douglas Kriegel, at 8:30 a.m. in Dr. Kriegel's office."

Pete was then advised that he would skip the shuttle to Capitol Hill. His meeting with the House Permanent Select Committee on Intelligence would be canceled for him by the Center. Further, he was to first get a "heads-up pre-brief" with John Tanham, Chief of European Operations, in time to be in Dr. Kriegel's office at 8:15 a.m. There were no apologies, no pleasantries, *no hope we didn't wake the kids*. 'Just do it. The DO wished him a nice day and signed off.

Pete yawned and raised his head off the pillow, peering through the dark shadows of the bedroom. He brushed back his sandy brown hair. Rubbing his eyes, he glanced over his shoulder at Sarah. Sound asleep. Years of calls in the middle of the night had taught her to block them out. Company wives with husbands in operations had told her to find a way to do so. His eyes lingered on her for a moment. She was a beauty, even asleep with her hair disheveled. The curve of her hips under the sheets distracted him, but he knew work was waiting.

Novak slipped gently off the bed and stepped quietly through the dark into the bathroom. He closed the door without a sound. Ah, he loved working for the Company at moments like this.

Okay, so he'd have to forego the Cheerios, leave a little early at 5:00 a.m., catch a doughnut and coffee near Tysons Corner. Fact is, he'd just about fly up to Langley on Chain Bridge Road this time of the morning. Absolutely no traffic. It's the little things in life that count, Pete, my boy, he chuckled to himself as he set the razor down on the sink and patted his face dry.

Novak left his brief meeting with a bleary-eyed John Tanham at 7:50 a.m. Tanham had really been no help at all. All Pete learned was that he'd be on a plane to Europe within the next 24 hours… there was a bit of a crisis that needed cleaning up. One that could be embarrassing to the Company if left unattended. This had the smell of a *Special*. No subject now; details to follow. He'd be told only enough to do the job. That's what specials were like, and, of course, he'd been named, by whom he wondered, to work this one. "Some personal crusade for the DCI," Tanham had said. "It's truly an honor to get the opportunity to work this. 'Be the man to fix it. You understand, Pete." *Uh-huh, right*. There was some allusion to maintaining security of a project that not even Capitol Hill knew about, but Tanham was too vague for Pete to make any sense of it.

At 8:26 a.m., he was whisked into Doc Kriegel's office by Joyce Cowan, Doc's attractive and highly competent executive assistant. She ushered Pete to one of two small burgundy leather sofas offset by a glass-topped coffee table. Kriegel was already seated, browsing through the various satellite imagery pics and text of the morning's Presidential Briefing. Preparation of the PB was a daily event, and the cars filled with briefers had already left on their run to the White House.

Doc looked up over the edges of the folders with his bifocals, smiled, and rose to shake Pete's hand. Kriegel was a big-shouldered man. Three years of weight training for Ivy League football had determined the size of his suits for years to come.

He wore a closely cropped mustache, a beard, and a pin-stripe Wall Street suit.

Doc Kriegel cut a figure… a Harvard man, cum laude, both undergraduate and graduate. Then there was his attendance at the School of Government and a "piled higher and deeper" PhD to boot. He was well respected by the intelligence community as well as among Washington's political elite on the Hill, which was no small feat. Doing well in one circle usually meant being on the outs with the other.

Kriegel wielded tremendous position power as *the* underwriter of Company covert operations throughout both hemispheres. Many at Langley were betting he'd rise to be the next DCI if he continued to balance all the pins so effortlessly. Pete was certain he would do so and apparently, so was Yevgeni "Zhenya" Primakov, the Russian SVR chief who, of all things, sent Doc a birthday card each year. Zhenya always planned ahead. The card was a laugh for Doc, though not so much for the agency's counterintelligence staff.

After pleasantries and some coffee, Kriegel looked at Pete with discerning eyes and proceeded with the briefing. There wasn't much he could tell him. For one thing, Pete wasn't cleared for all the details or history, nor would he be. There wasn't enough time and it wasn't necessary to do what Pete was being tasked to do. The central file was classified TOP SECRET Codeword, Compartmented Level 7, *Must Know* access level. That meant only those with not only a *need-to-know*, but an absolute *must know* requirement were cleared for access.

This was serious stuff. If Doc Kriegel said he didn't need to know, then Pete accepted that he didn't need to know. What he objected to, however, were the instructions to step onto the Bonn Station's turf and "take over." Pete as well as everyone else in operations knew Bill Nordheimer wasn't the type to let

someone just stroll into his corral and take over. That's how Wild
Bill got to be *the* Resident for Europe.

Nobody pushed Wild Bill around – not the Russians, not the
Hungarians, Czechs, Germans, not Mossad, and certainly not the
Company "wanna-be's" in the FBI. But, Kriegel didn't like what
he was hearing. Doc wasn't one to entertain objections once he'd
made a decision. He leaned his thick six-foot-three-inch frame
forward in the leather sofa, placing his coffee cup down on its
saucer. Pete eyed it, the gold trim and Company logo.

Kriegel didn't miss it. "Ah, one of the perks when you're
Deputy Director for Operations at CIA, the premier intelligence
agency in the world," Kriegel said, smiling. "I'm told Primakov
uses stoneware. No class." He smiled, motioning to the china
service and cookies on the table between them. Yes, Doc was a
piece of work. His presence seemed to engulf the room.

"So, as I was saying, Pete, you're going to be my point man
in this. This is the kind of thing they trained you for at West
Point, remember? You'll be speaking *for me*. If it comes down
to it, remind Nordheimer of that. He'll understand. Bill learned
that very well when he was back here years ago, wearing your
shoes. Don't be afraid of him, Mr. Novak. It's black and white."

"Ah, no sir, it's gray. And I learned that for myself, not from
what they try to indoctrinate. It's all gray."

"Mr. Novak, I'm talking about power. And, you'll be the
extension of mine. Besides, what about the code, Pete? Duty.
Honor. Country. Come on, it's got to be black or white, or all
those cadets in the long gray line don't graduate. It is now and
always has been that way with the West Point elite. That system
doesn't just grow generals, Mr. Novak, it grows senators and
presidents. Isn't that so?"

"Sir, with all due respect, I'd wish you'd leave this West Point
shit alone."

"Or what?"

"Or, sir, I'll have to…"

"Okay, okay. Enough, I surrender! Now get off your butt and come over here, for goodness sake!" Kriegel laughed. He slapped his knees and thrust his palms out conceding. With a broad smile creasing Doc's face, he said, "Pete, how are you really doing?"

Doc grabbed his nephew in a bear hug, patting his back. "Pete, I continue to hear good things about you. You're doing so very well," he said, with almost a father's pride. "You'll have this job someday. Please, sit down and finish your coffee, son. Look, I know this doesn't sound like a plum of an assignment. It's tough on me too, not being able to give you all the details. But there's no time to get the NSC approvals. Believe me when I tell you this matter has the complete attention of the President. We have what looks like a crazy on the loose over there, this Laszlo character. He may have compromised what is our most sensitive, closely held… I'll tell you what, I'll bend the rules a little and have a background paper from the STALKER surveillance file ready before you leave. Read it on the way over. I can't impress upon you how close-hold that information is. So, read it, then shred it. You'll then understand some of our urgency. We've lost men, some very good men, in this operation and I don't…"

"Lost… men? Intentionally? As in, killed?" Pete interrupted, his face was no longer flushed from the verbal bantering.

"Intentionally? Oh yes, and I…"

"Over there, or over here? Is the SVR regressing to old KGB modus operandi?"

"Well, this thing going on now… it sure does look like the old KGB. Problem is, we don't really know who's been doing the killing. My money is on this fellow, Laszlo. In fact, there may be much more to this fellow than we've already seen. If what we've discovered at Walter Reed Medical Center is valid and our medical experts are correct in their analysis, then Laszlo's past may come to impact our future. There's enough scientific evidence now that he just may be the most dangerous entity on the face of this planet. But, I can't elaborate on all that now. It's another story. You might need to help us there, too."

"What? I don't understand what you're saying, Doc?"

"I've already gone too far, Pete. It's just that we can't afford for this thing to get any worse than it has. That's why I want you to go over there and set things back on track. It's a mess. What I'm saying is that if anybody over on the Hill gets even an inkling of what's behind all this, it'll be... horrendous."

Doc took a deep breath and went on. "I'd like to say it can't get worse, but that's not true. You know morale here at the Center is still in the toilet. Pete... read the file. You'll get another brief when you reach Frankfurt. Dig up some facts. Localize the target, but low-key it. Bring me back some answers. The Director needs a status report and he doesn't want to wait until hell drops below 32 degrees for it. Bring this to closure, and minimize the damage. Go over there and do the best you can, as fast as you can."

"Doc, you said *target*?"

"Absolutely. That's what this Laszlo is right now. A target. Stop him. Shoot him, kill him if that's what it takes. Keep that in mind. Our assessment is that's he's highly skilled, very dangerous and mentally unstable to boot." And, as I mentioned, there might be even more to him than that, but we can't go there in this conversation."

"Like what?"

"I can't tell you. We know now that it's far more now than radical assumptions by our often eccentric science staff. Read the file, Pete, and get some sleep. How do you think you'll go over?"

"Probably Delta, tomorrow morning,"

"I'll call Wild Bill and pave the road a little for you. Give the girls a kiss for me?"

"Sure. Thanks, Doc." Pete rose, shook his uncle's hand and was engulfed in another brief hug before heading out. In the outer office, he picked up the phone and called his own, one floor down.

"Molly?"

"Yes, sir?" Molly responded crisply. She was the best secretary he'd ever had. A genuine sweetheart.

"Molly, I need a ticket to Frankfurt for tomorrow. Book me a morning flight out of Dulles, mid-morning if you can swing it. See if you can get me the non-stop on Delta or Lufthansa. Leave the return flight open."

"Yes, sir. I'll have it in the top drawer of your safe first thing in the morning. Anything else, sir?"

"That's it for now. Thanks, Molly. Bye." Pete walked out into the corridor and jumped into a waiting elevator.

He looked at his watch. He still had to pack. Time would be tight. His head spun imagining the things Kriegel had said he wanted to tell him, but couldn't.

CHAPTER 6

Fairfax, Virginia

In the Metro area's suburbs of Fairfax County, clattering sounds from Sarah Novak's kitchen poured out the window into the crisp autumn afternoon. Recipe cards and a Julia Childs cookbook were strewn across the granite countertop. Sarah was distracted by the never-ending issue of dinner, and when the phone rang at 3:45 p.m., she picked it up absentmindedly. "Hello?"

"Hi, Sarah. 'Hope I'm not interrupting, but is Pete...?"

"No, he's not. And, I'm trying to get dinner ready." An instant frown furrowed Sarah's smooth brow. Brannon. Right at dinnertime too. Her voice was more than stern.

"Okay, I'm sorry. I was hoping..."

"Hoping? Hoping for what, J.T.?" Sarah interrupted again. She could feel her frustration rising. No longer distracted by thoughts of dinner, she moved from the counter and glimpsed out the bay window into the back yard. The girls were chasing each other around the towering silver maple.

"You're calling a little early, aren't you? What in the world makes you think Pete would be home now, anyway?" "

"Oh, so he's not home, then? Look, I'm sorry. I'll call back later, but I really need to speak with…"

"And, I really need to get dinner going, J.T.! Don't you think Pete should be allowed just one iota of peace away from Langley?" Her voice rose.

"Ah, please forgive me, Sarah, I didn't think…"

"Didn't think? Well, that's about par, isn't it? Look, give us a couple of hours together. You know – Pete, his wife and his children… together? I swear you get more time with him than we do! Give us a break, will you?"

Whoa. Talk about bad timing. Brannon's face flushed. His mouth gaped but no words came. Sarah unloaded on him out of the blue. "Sarah, I apologize for the intrusion. I understand. I do. I really am sorry. I'll call back when…"

"When? Later, much later, please! Bye!" Sarah stomped back to the phone set and slammed the receiver, simmering. She found it impossible to like him. Despite all of Pete's constant urgings to the contrary, what she'd heard from the other wives in operations left her no choice but to despise that man. Brannon was a killer, an assassin of the worst order.

They said he'd killed tens of men and in the most horrible fashions imaginable. How in the world could a man like J.T. Brannon be considered the hero, the patriot, he was? How could he be so endeared by the Company? What was even worse was that the girls loved him. They went nuts when he visited. Well, that brought his kind of evil too close for Sarah.

And… Brannon stared. She could feel his eyes following her, staring at her. It made her flesh crawl. The heavy metal spoon slid off the counter, clattering to the floor. Sarah blinked.

Pete pulled the Durango into his driveway at 4:00 p.m. It was a little early, but he still had to pack. The front door burst open as he shoved the car door wide. The girls scurried down the slate walk to the driveway.

"Daddy's home!" They ran to the car and grabbed hugs as he stepped out.

"Mommy, Daddy's home!" Susie, ten years old, had her mother's blonde hair, which swung about jubilantly as she jumped up to steal a kiss. She grabbed his briefcase and clasped his left hand in hers, dragging him toward the house.

Joanna, six, hung on his sport coat, then dropped and clung to his right leg, impeding his long stride. Sarah met him at the door to free him from his darling escorts. As the storm door closed behind him, the girls ran away giggling, chasing each other around the side of the house and out of sight.

"Boy, you're home early, doll. What's the occasion?" She led him to the kitchen and stuck a cold glass of fresh cider in his hand.

"Oh, thanks, honey… that looks good. Hmmm. Get this at the grocery store today?" He took a long swig, and sank into a chair at the table.

"No, the fruit stand on Ox Road. The cider's right off the presses. So what's up, new hours?"

"Right," he smirked. "No, I've got an airplane to catch in the morning. Europe."

"Where?"

"Honey, you know, I can't…"

"Okay, when're you coming back?" Sarah pouted.

"Don't know that either. 'Couple of days, I think. I'll get a message to you if it looks like it's going to be longer than that."

"Nothing dangerous, I hope," she sulked, but Pete only frowned back. "Well, just have Molly call to keep me posted. Oh, and tell her to keep that gorilla of yours at the zoo." Sarah growled.

"If you mean J.T., Sarah, I don't appreciate it." He shoved his hands in his pockets, scowling.

"Pete, I've tried, I have. But I've had it with him. More and more, you and I are like passing strangers. No time together. None." She placed her hands on her hips.

"That's not J.T.'s fault."

"Well, the gorilla's called here already! We haven't even had dinner!"

"Sarah, knock off the gorilla crap. I don't knock your friends. J.T.'s more than a colleague to me. More than a body guard. I like him. I like him a lot. If you'd only take some time, talk with him. Get to…"

"I've told you, I just don't like the man. 'Just because you don't see it doesn't mean I gotta like him! I'm so tired of all this, Pete. 'Tired of the CIA, tired of the trips to who knows where, tired of the secrets. And, I'm very tired of J.T. Brannon."

"That's enough!" Pete's fists clenched as they slammed down onto the table.

Sarah paled.

"Knock it off, Sarah! I don't appreciate that, and J.T. doesn't deserve it! If you had any inkling at all of the hell he's been through… way beyond the call. He could have been killed a dozen times for this country. I don't know where you get this." Pete collected himself.

Sarah looked like a scolded child and, in truth, he was as stunned at his outburst as she was. He lowered his voice.

"Look, Brannon's one of the good guys. He's a friend. The girls love him. Give him a break once in a while. He would throw himself in front of a truck for you or for any of us."

"He's a body guard. He's supposed to protect you. I've heard the stories about the secret operations, cold-blooded assassinations. J.T. Brannon's lived nothing but violence. And, he's creepy.

46

He scares me."

"Come on, honey. Creepy? When has J.T. ever done anything to scare you?"

"Sometimes... he stares. He always seems to be staring at me. It makes my skin crawl. I don't care for the man at all," she insisted.

"Well, the bottom line is that this man is my friend. His friendship with me doesn't require you to like him. But please treat him like a human being and call him by his name, J.T.!" Sarah jumped at his sudden shout.

"Okay, all right, J.T., whatever. For goodness sake, Pete, I don't have to be nuts about him just because you are?"

"The girls like him too. They *love* him."

"Of course they do. They'd fall in love with anybody who sneaks 'em M&Ms every time he visits. Look, I'll give it a shot. If Brannon's your friend and guardian angel, then I'll try to like him, try to care for him. I'll even feed him occasionally. He likes bananas, right?" She smirked. Pete glared back.

"Gees. All I'm asking is for you to give the man a damn chance, that's all. If you need help, anything, when I'm gone, I want you to call him."

"Okay, I'll call him... *if* I need anything. Go up and change. Pack. I'll work on an early dinner, something special. Okay, hon?"

Pete stood looking at her, his hands back in his pockets. He loved this woman. He liked J.T. and saw genuine goodness in his character. He couldn't see why in the world Sarah found J.T. so repulsive. Because he was a semi-retired assassin, not exactly brimming with talk-show-host personality? The rumors, the trained killer stuff about Brannon were way over done. Pete shook his head and stepped toward her.

"Okay. Thanks." He grabbed Sarah's waist and pulled her to him. He drew her closer and kissed her deep and long, his hands sliding below her hips. Her hands reached back and caught his wrists.

"Pete, the girls! For goodness sake, honey, you need to be more careful around the house."

He cracked a smile and disappeared jogging up the stairs. Sarah turned to the refrigerator with a quizzical look. Men. Her loving husband sometimes drove her nuts, not to mention Brannon. She knew in her heart that she could try harder with Brannon. Maybe she would.

Dinner was great. By eight o'clock, Pete was stretched across the bed watching the news, his bags packed and leaning against the bedroom wall. The phone rang. He reached over to the night stand to pick it up. Sarah was already on the downstairs extension.

"Oh, hellooo, J.T.! How you doing this evening? By the way, you big hunk, I'm sorry for flying off the handle today. Just a crazy moment, I guess." Her voice dripped sweetness, slathering it on for Pete's benefit.

"It's for you, Pete-honey," she drawled into the phone. "It's Jayyy Teeeee!" A click and she was gone. Pete smirked and shoved himself up on the bed.

"Hey, buddy, how ya doing on this fine autumn night, eh? What's up? I'll see you first thing in the morning, right?"

"Yes, sir, we're still on. Say, how about ringing me up on your encrypted phone, sir?"

"Now?" Pete asked, puzzled.

"Yes, sir, if you can. I'll get on mine in 60 seconds." J.T. sounded anxious.

"Okay, buddy. I'll be there.

Pete hung up the phone, swept down the stairs, and flew out the front door to the SUV parked on the sloped driveway. He unlocked the door, reached in and flipped the phone on. He then threw the switch to go secure. He pulled the receiver out through the door, the cord spiraling behind it. It was cold out, almost Halloween. Pete shivered, shifting his weight from one bare foot to the other.

"You read me, sir?"

"That's a 10-4, old buddy. Five-by-five'."

"What's your 10-20?"

"My 10-20 is the damn driveway outside my damn SUV, and I'm damn near freezing, ole buddy. Now what's up, J.T.? Why all the cloak-and-dagger stuff this fine evening?"

"Sir, we're good for just about three minutes, assuming worst case with the guys at Ft. Meade. They break encryption like this as easy as thin bone china. Good ole NSA... No Such Agency. The reason I'm calling is, do you still have time to climb out of this STALKER special? Is there any way you can get them to tap someone else?" J.T. was obviously concerned.

"Partner, just what the hell do you know about STALKER? And, how in hell do you know, how much do you know... about my trip? Dammit, J.T., I'm sure your intentions are good, but this sounds like a security problem." Pete was dumbfounded. His mouth hung open while his mind searched for an answer.

"Sir, please, we don't have time for this. Still with me?"

"Yes."

"Great. There's a bit of a war going on in Europe. The SVR, maybe the Hungarians and who knows who else. We've got dead people, but no details. Please stay out of it, sir. This one's not for you. It smells really bad. Is there some way...?"

"Just a minute, J.T., look, this is not new news. I've been briefed by the DepOps himself. We have three dead people in the field, and I think I'll get..."

"No, sir. Four dead. Four. Three in Europe, one here. I'm betting on it, Mr. Novak," J.T. spoke matter-of-factly.

"Here? In the States? Who, where... how do you know that? I don't get this. Gees!" Pete was thoroughly frazzled.

"Tony Spencer, sir. Apparently, you're replacing him on this job. This operation is not new, and you're not the first from Langley Center who's been tasked to assist the Europe Center on this. Something big, heavier cloaked than anything I've ever seen before and I've seen a lot. Tony was the first to go over. He and I have been in at least 20 deadly situations. Tony covered my back, and I covered his. Good man."

"And?"

"He died last month down on the Outer Banks near Nags Head. Very weird, and I don't like it. So, as far as I'm concerned, there's four dead men. Take my word on it, sir."

"But then, he came back. This Tony Spencer came back. How do you connect his death with what's going on over in Europe? How'd he die?" Novak felt his stomach tighten. He knew in his heart that J.T. was just looking out for him, but the apparent security breaches were unreal. Pete seemed to know less than anybody and he didn't like it.

"Sir?"

"I'm here. Go on." Pete leaned against the car, and cocked his head, listening intensely as Brannon continued.

"Tony died in the Atlantic off Cape Hatteras. That's the report. They say he drowned after being stung by a jellyfish. A damned jellyfish! That's bullshit. This guy was a piece of work. Tony would make it back to shore if a shark tore off one of his legs. One tough sonofabitch. I don't believe it for a minute, Mr. Novak."

"Did he have family? What did they say?"

"That's another story too. Barb won't talk to me. I went down for the funeral. She was a mess. Tony Jr. too. Nice kid. Anyway, she would hardly look at me. I called her a couple of days after I came back, and she just hung up on me. I called back, but she must have taken the phone off the hook. We were good friends, very good friends. No, it's more than grief. The story spooks me. He supposedly died in his son's arms."

"And, the other three? Who were they, Headquarters staff or Nordheimer's folks?"

"I'm not sure yet, but so far the word is they were ours. Somewhere in the Covert Operations Directorate. Rumor mill says it's something new. They're calling it the JOG Squad."

"The what?"

"JOG Squad. Joint Operations Group… something like that. I don't know what it is, nor does anybody else. The word is though that they're real bad asses. And, they have sanction authority. They can kill. I'll need to follow up, very cautiously too, if this stuff is that close-hold. Is that what you want me to do?"

"I'll talk with you tomorrow, J.T."

"Okay, sir. Bon nuit." He was gone with a click. The only thing left was the cold October night.

"Bon nuit to you too, mon ami."

Pete looked up at the night sky as he shut the car door. A new moon hung low in an inky black sky glittering with a million stars sprinkled across it. A meteor streaked above him in a sudden, short burst of light.

"Oh, what do the stars portend? Caesar asked." Pete whispered the words and shivered again, listening to the ring of them. He glanced up at the house and saw Sarah at the bedroom window, staring down through the curtains at him in his pajamas, no slippers on his feet. He couldn't see the features in her face, but as she turned away he could feel her concern.

CHAPTER 7

Langley Center
McLean, Northern Virginia

J.T. turned the black GMC Yukon out from its parking place near the Dome, the Company's auditorium used for award ceremonies. It purred through the lot to the front steps where it idled smoothly. He paused, then turned off the ignition. Brannon reached into the glove compartment and pulled out a black leather-covered Bible with gilded pages. He had taken it years ago from a room in the Watergate Hotel, compliments of the Gideons.

He turned to the Gospel of John. It was one of the few things J.T. Brannon considered worth reading. Every minute or so, he glanced toward the entrance to the building. J.T. couldn't quote chapter and verse, but he believed that just about all he had ever done in his "business" truly was for God, country, motherhood, and apple pie. And pretty much in that order.

Reflecting like this did make him wonder. He'd endured 28 years in field operations without a scratch, that is, until six years ago. That's when everything unraveled. That's when he was brought 'in from the cold' forever. A mission in the Middle East intended to neutralize a pending terrorist attack by the Palestinian PFLP terror group against an embassy of a western ally went bad. Very bad.

The PFLP's attack was thwarted, but the confrontation and ensuing pursuit of the surviving Palestinian commandos through two North African nations left five Company field operatives dead and four more severely injured. On the other side, the PFLP lost 14 front-line commandos. Indeed, no small coup for the Company, but its success was tarnished by the blood-letting of its agents. Five men were dead, and two died later. J.T. was one of the two lucky survivors.

Brannon's body had taken no less than six rounds, three to the upper chest, three more in his left calf, all but severing the muscle. He had been left for dead on the floor of a burned-out safehouse in south Cairo. In their frantic escape, the terrorists left him for dead without wasting another shot.

Egyptian security found Brannon, did some emergency patch-up, and flew him to Rabat, Morocco. The "damn leg" wasn't right to this day, as evidenced by a slight, ever-present limp. More importantly, J.T. was finished in operations. Every radical terrorist group in the world now knew who he was. George Habbash, the PFLP's ultra-radical chief, had personally put a $500,000 price tag on Brannon's head.

Now in more mundane assignments, he still hoped for payback. A chance to settle the score. As it seemed now, that opportunity would never come. What really bothered him was how, after being so good for so long, he had been caught with his ass hanging out. He never saw it coming. What had he missed?

The PFLP commandos came bursting in behind them in an area his team had already cleared. Their full auto weapons blazing, the pungent reek of cordite explosive, the pounding thuds

53

in his chest. That's where his memory blurred. The whole affair had a stink to it. He felt... betrayed. But by whom?

On one lovely spring day in 1978, the axe fell. The Company's personnel chief told him it was time to retire. But just at the moment he was to be kicked out to pasture, Pete Novak stepped in. Novak saw something in Brannon... values, a code of integrity, loyalty, and determination, that he believed the agency should find a way to hold on to. So, Pete insisted Brannon be retained as his security escort. Brannon quickly accepted his position as bodyguard to Pete Novak as an appropriate arena to demonstrate the deadly skills he had developed over the years. He knew he owed Novak, something he would not forget.

Brannon glanced toward the building as the mirrored front doors swung open and Pete walked briskly through them, near jogging. He was wearing the Company travel uniform – dark-blue blazer, gray slacks, white shirt, and burgundy tie.

"Sorry I'm late, J.T.," he called, "I took the milk run on the elevators. 'Didn't miss one floor!"

"No problem, sir. You'll make the plane," J.T. responded, closing the armored door with a thud.

He climbed behind the wheel and fired up the engine. The Yukon motored through the thickly treed Langley complex and exited the south gate onto Dolly Madison Boulevard. Five minutes later, they turned onto the westbound ramp of the Washington Dulles Toll Road. The big SUV accelerated smoothly, no stress for the large V-8 engine under the well-polished hood. Pete looked past Brannon's head into the rear view mirror, and their eyes locked. J.T. nodded his head, raising his index finger. They'd talk, but at the airport... outside the car.

The fiery colors of October foliage shimmered across the hood of the Yukon. Pete always enjoyed the scenery on the ride to Dulles. He'd like to catch a whiff of the crisp autumn air too, but that was impossible with bullet-proof glass. The windows couldn't open. Washington's weather peaked in refreshing glory in the fall. The sultry, wilting days of summer were now just a memory. Until next year, that is. Pete sank into the upholstery, mentally reviewing the objectives for the trip. He'd grown accustomed to avoiding attempts to chat with J.T. in the vehicle, distracting him from his work.

Brannon was now totally absorbed in his world, always training mentally for the real thing. He continuously checked the flow of traffic and sequence of following automobiles, up to ten cars both behind and several ahead. Those merging from entrance ramps were given a once-over as well. He was always looking for the one that didn't fit. The one whose occupants would have less than honorable intentions. Men who might come to challenge his skills.

"Well, whaddya know, there they are." About six cars behind and slowly moving up… a green Jeep Grand Cherokee, and two more cars back, what looked to be a blue Ford Taurus. J.T. could probably recite the license plates as well. These two belonged to the Company's Field Operations School.

Brannon then noticed a third vehicle cautiously moving up. Also suspect. This one was a burgundy BMW, 700 series. It was hard to be discreet in a big, gorgeous burgundy Beamer. That's why they let the students use surveillance cars like that – easy to keep track of the young agents-in-training. Keep them out of trouble, if necessary. In boredom, Brannon watched them maneuver for the next ten minutes. They changed out the lead car every couple of minutes in school-solution fashion, but maintained their position in traffic, hanging about eight cars back.

"Tsk, Tsk. Amateurs," J.T. mumbled.

"What's that?"

"Oh, 'looks like the school's out with us today, sir. They're still teaching classic A-B-C methods for vehicular surveillance. Kids' stuff. They're taking us out to the airport. They might break it off earlier. We'll see. Practicing. Terrible, really… gees, you'd think we were the FBI or something."

"Now, J.T., be nice. The boys and girls in the FBI are our colleagues in the great war against all things evil." Novak chuckled.

"Uh-huh. Yours, maybe, sir."

Brannon's eyes squinted into the rear-view mirror. Sporting a mischievous grin, J.T. gave the black Yukon a big push of gas. The five liter engine surged, and a clump of traffic was left behind. This sent the student surveillants into a tizzy, if they were students, that is. Brannon smiled as the traffic receded in the rear-view mirror. He grinned ear to ear, shaking his head.

Minutes later, the Yukon swung under the huge archway of the Dulles International Airport Terminal and whispered to a stop. Brannon pressed the rear gate release. He stepped back to retrieve the bags, then walked with his characteristic limp halfway to the glass doors. There, Pete turned and stuck out his hand for a firm shake. He appeared concerned.

"J.T., if you can break away without raising eyebrows, I'd like you to see if you can get the details on Tony Spencer. Go down there if you have to. Talk to his wife… anyone else, maybe the local coroner. That is, if you think you can slip away. Also, nose around discreetly and see what you can find out about this JOG Squad. Whatever the hell it is. You know, who are they, where are they, who they report to. See if you can identify who our dead are – field operations men or something else?"

"Okay, sir. That shouldn't be a problem. By the way, sir, this trip's on a Company bird today. I set it up for you. On your authority, of course. 'Safer this way. At least, until we know what's going on, who the real players are."

"J.T., I wish you hadn't. You're being a mother hen. You

know I can take care of myself." Pete frowned, attempting to conceal a smile.

"Sir, they're in place, waiting for you, bird and all. That's what these assets are for, Mr. Novak. And it is my job, you know."

Brannon's feelings for Novak went beyond a debt of gratitude. He liked Pete's family as well. Those girls were sweethearts. So, J.T. had made an irrevocable pact with himself to see to it that Pete Novak and his family lived long, healthy, and happy lives.

Pete's brow wrinkled. At that moment, a flash of burgundy went by, pulling in about six cars down from them. It was a BMW 750 li.

"I know you're just watching out for me. You're a good friend, J.T., but I'd like you to check with me on stuff like this. Okay, so where do I go from..."

"Take the two suitcases to the counter, sir, and check them. Then go directly through security down Concourse A. First door past the second men's room on the right. There'll be a baggage handler. Give him the ticket. He'll direct you from there."

"How can I check the bags? I'll need them!"

"Sir, these are duplicates. They're stuffed with gym towels. The real ones are waiting for you. You need to get out of here."

The passenger door on the BMW opened and an orange-colored, ostrich western boot reached for the curb.

Pete, smiling but still a bit confused, shouted, "Good enough for now, J.T.! Thanks for the lift. Take care of the business while I'm gone. Tell you what, I'll bring you back some real German beer, not that elephant piss you drink!" Novak turned briskly to the terminal doors toting the bags.

"Sounds good to me, Mr. Novak. If you need anything, don't hesitate to call me." In an instant, Brannon refocused. He knew the first thing he'd do when he got back to Langley was stroll through the parking lanes reserved for student exercises. That might be an interesting diversion.

"Got it. See you, J.T." Novak gave a broad farewell sweep of his arm and stepped through the portals, swerving toward the check-in counters.

"You check your six, you hear. I need the work," Brannon mumbled to himself as the terminal doors closed behind his principal. His face had paled a shade or two. He glanced up the lane at the burgundy BMW. It was pulling away from the curb. Looked like only one occupant now.

Brannon walked to the Yukon and looked back one more time before he got in, pausing briefly in reflection. "Check your six" was Company lingo, borrowed from fighter pilots, for knowing what or who is behind you. It referred to the six o'clock position on the clock when you're facing twelve. And this time, Brannon was deadly serious about it.

CHAPTER 8

Dulles International Airport
Herndon, Northern Virginia

Pete approached the Delta ticket counter. The ticket agent told him he was cutting it a little close, and needed to hurry to Concourse A for the flight to Frankfurt. Pete moved out, half running. He breezed through the security checkpoint, grabbed his briefcase as it came out of the x-ray scanner, and darted down a short hallway where the concourses split. He continued up the long cavern of Concourse A.

Just ahead was the first men's room. A minute later, he passed the second and picked up speed. There was the first exit door, on the right. Also there was a baggage handler, nodding to him. Pete approached, handing him the ticket envelope. The door pushed open, and he was ushered out the door to metal stairs that ran down from the concourse. He could see the back of a white airport utility vehicle underneath, its engine running. As he stepped off the last step, the driver opened the rear left door of the white Ford Explorer.

"Hello, sir. Let's go, chopper's waiting."

"Okay, coming," Pete climbed in.

The Explorer pulled away under the concourse, cutting across to Concourse B. They came to a halt in the shadow of the massive building, and Pete saw the white-striped outline of a large helipad, a red-white-and-blue painted helicopter in the center. On the side, big blue lettering shouted "Paradigm Modeling, LLC."

The chopper certainly looked commercial, but it had the distinct smell of a Company bird. The uninitiated would mistake the white pod under the nose for a camera or spotlight of sorts, despite the barrels of what looked like twin guns, also painted white, protruding ominously. 'Probably 20 mm full-auto cannons.

A crewman in a pale green flight suit jumped out and sprinted up to help him board. In just minutes, Pete was strapping himself in. Wide nylon belts held his two suitcases against the wall next to him. A black, ballistic nylon weapon bag slung over the outside suitcase was tied to the handle. The crewman saw him notice.

"The bags came out a little over an hour ago, sir. Mr. Brannon had them delivered."

"Yeah, I know. Thanks."

Pete thought to himself, *Well, the old bastard had to break into my trunk somehow. In the damn Company parking lot yet, and in broad daylight, in order to make the switch. That old 007's pretty good.* Novak slowly shook his head, still a tad uncomfortable with being manipulated by J.T. or anyone else. Novak preferred being firmly in control.

"Nice helicopter. Paradigm Modeling, huh? You guys on the New York or American Exchange? Or maybe the NASDAQ?"

"Oh, I wouldn't know that, sir. They don't pay me enough to buy stock."

"Well, thanks. Let's get on with it," They shook hands and the crewman reached out to swing the cabin door shut. He winked at Pete as he walked up to the cockpit.

Back over on Concourse A at Dulles, Chris Blanchard, a man roughly the same height and build as Pete Novak, stepped out of the second men's room just as Pete disappeared out the concourse door. He too wore a blue blazer, gray slacks, white shirt, and a burgundy tie. He also carried a briefcase and a big broad smile. Chris owned and operated Corona Arms, a gun shop for the sophisticated in Alexandria, Virginia. As a Class 3 dealer, he was licensed to trade in fully automatic machine pistols, scoped rifles, and exotic assault weaponry. His biggest customers were a few federal agencies, including the Company. Chris had been granted the added ability of trading in weapons that had no audit trail. Weapons which, according to their serial numbers, had never been manufactured, were never sold, and thus, were never purchased by anyone.

Chris was a long-time friend of Brannon's. He turned to his right and walked briskly. As he brushed past the baggage handler, still standing at the exit door, the ticket for Delta Flight to the Frankfurt Flughafen was discreetly slipped into his waiting right hand. He whispered to himself in perfect German, "Danke sehr. Ausgezeichnit." Thank you. Outstanding. Grinning, he continued down the concourse.

Six hours later, as the jet began its slow descent into Frankfurt, Chris would enter a restroom, stuff his blazer and burgundy tie into his carry-on, and apply a small mustache to his upper lip. The stewardesses would be too busy with food trays, seat backs,

seat belts, and crying children to notice. He would settle casually back into his seat. Even the woman next to him, on her
way to the old country to visit her brother in Stuttgart, would
not remember anything about him. Chris saw to that by buying
her several glasses of white wine. He would exit the aircraft at
Frankfurt wearing the gray suit top to his gray slacks, a new blue
tie, and a new passport. An hour and a half later, Chris would
board another jet back to the States, but only after grabbing a
beer, a damn good German beer, to quench his thirst.

"Pidgeon's boarded. He's off. It's taxiing to the runway," a
gruff voice spoke into a receiver in the middle of a bank of pay
phones at the end of Dulles Airport's noisy Concourse A. The
surveillant had missed the switch. The ruse had worked.

Inside the burgundy BMW, once again at curbside, the driver
brought the black handset to his mouth. "10-4. Return to base."

The same pay phone on Concourse A was again lifted, and
there was the jingle of another quarter. This time the call was
routed through the central switch at Langley Center.

"Hello," a male voice from the other end.

"Pidgeon's got wings. Up and away."

The only reply from the other end was a click and the return
of the dial tone. Moments later, the surveillant dashed out the
terminal entrance and flung open the front passenger door of
the BMW. It jerked away from the curb and sped down the exit
ramp.

On the helipad, the helicopter rose off the ground with a
roar, nosed out its direction, then accelerated rapidly. It broke
for the open grassy area. The chopper shot ahead, hugging the

ground until a row of trees loomed ahead, then jumped up and over, and climbed rapidly to altitude. Pete thought how, for any terrorist team attempting to ply their trade in the Capital, this nicely camouflaged gunship would be the kiss of death. It was fast, highly maneuverable, and could carry an entire assault team. The rate of fire from the pod's twin cannons was probably unbelievable. At least, Pete assumed that's what this baby was for.

He turned to the window and drank in the scenery below, the Virginia countryside in autumn. "Wow," Pete thought. In minutes, they were crossing the Potomac, and dropped altitude. The Andrews Air Force Base Control Tower was visible on the horizon.

"Hey, not bad, guys – thirteen minutes to Andrews! Sure beats going over the Wilson Bridge."

The crewman smiled at him, nodding in agreement.

"Andrews Tower, this is Falcon Three-Nine'r-Two. Request a straight-in on runway two-zero. 'Rendezvous with Special Air on the run-up ramp," the pilot radioed.

"That's a Roger, Falcon 39'er2. This is Andrews Tower, you're cleared for straight-in approach on Runway 2-0 and rendezvous with Special Air Mission Flight 711. Execute final approach," a young male voice in the tower came back.

Falcon 39'er2 banked, then ran straight, passing over the length of Runway 20. The gray, converted KC-135 Tanker idled at the end of runway's engine run-up area. The chopper settled to the ground just off its wing tip.

"Well, here you are, sir. 'Careful stepping down. We'll bring the bags along behind you, sir," the crewman bristled as he swung open the door.

"Are you sure there isn't another set of bags on that airplane too?"

"Sir?" The crewman's brow wrinkled.

"Oh, nothing. Inside joke, I guess. Well, thanks for the flight, guys!" he shook the crewman's hand. The pilot waved in acknowledgment.

CHAPTER 9

Andrews Air Force Base
Suitland, Maryland

N ovak glanced around the interior of the large jet and settled into a cushy blue leather captain's chair at a table for four just aft of the galley on Special Air Flight 711. The new pilot, a Lt. Colonel, stood stiffly in front of him in a tailored flight-suit. Pete looked up.

"Welcome to Special Air, the 1776th Military Airlift Wing, and Flight 711, sir. I understand we're going to Rhein Main Air Base today. Any changes? Flight plan changes aren't a problem with Special Air, sir."

"No, that's it. How long?"

"A little over five hours, sir." At Pete's questioning look, he continued, "Oh, we're not limited to commercial air routes. We beat the airlines by over an hour!"

"Great! Have at it!"

"Ah, we'll serve lunch or late breakfast, whatever you want, once we're over water. Okay?" the pilot took Pete's nod for a command, turned, and stepped briskly to the cockpit. The copilot had already fired up the turbofans and the converted tanker jet was taxiing into position.

A young crewman-steward approached and squatted in front of him. "Sir, your weapon is secured in the safe, aft of the cockpit. You may arm at your discretion, but you really might be more comfortable if you wait until we're close to reaching Rhein Main."

"Weapon?"

"What you requested, sir. Walther PPK, .380 ACP caliber, 3.2-inch barrel, checkered grips. There's three magazines and 21 rounds. Three holsters too, depending on your druthers — shoulder-holster, hip, and a nice ankle holster. It's all padded with fleece, really nice. 'Just let me know when you want it. Okay, sir?"

"Brannon, Brannon, Brannon," Pete murmured under his breath, nodding his approval.

Ten minutes later, as the sun sliced through the cabin window, Pete loosened the lap belt and reclined the seat. He reached under his seat for his briefcase. It was armored inside with Kevlar bullet-proof panels for use as a shield if necessary. He took out a half-inch-thick red folder.

On the folder's cover was a white square which warned, "TOP SECRET – SPECIAL ACCESS DATA – SENSITIVE SOURCES AND METHODS INVOLVED." The Subject line read: "STALKER PROFILE – File Number E-013."

Pete pushed himself back into the seat. Before he could open the file, the steward appeared with a cup of coffee and a small plate piled with butter cookies. He set them on the table next to Pete.

"This will have to hold you until lunch, sir. Can I get you anything else?"

"No, thanks a lot. This is great. Say, do you have a shredder, or do I have to tear this up when I'm done and flush it in different toilets?"

"Shredder's on board, sir. I can do it. Or, you can do it, and I'll witness the destruction certificate for you. Now or later?"

"Later… thanks. I'll grab you when I'm through with this stuff."

"Okay, sir. Your call." The steward turned back to the galley.

"Man, it doesn't get any better than this. Now, let's see what this is all about, fellas," Pete opened the file in his lap.

In McLean, a brittle fall wind blew through the trees. Leaves went soaring through the air in all directions, causing quickly moving shadows to dart across the tiled floor. John Tanham sat alone facing the glass walls in the first-floor cafeteria wing, sipping his coffee. He had that pensive, all-too-serious look he was noted for. The woods stared back at him in their fall splendor.

"Damn!" Already not in the best of moods, his coffee cup tipped, and the hot liquid slid over the brim and onto his gold-striped burgundy necktie. His hand jerked, spilling even more of the coffee onto his starched blue oxford shirt. He grabbed a napkin and patted the shirt and tie. The moisture disappeared, but brown stains remained.

Tanham's brow creased. He knew that the problem in Europe was bigger than Europe. Bigger than Bill Nordheimer too. Nordheimer couldn't fix it. And, it was certainly bigger than Pete Novak. Novak wouldn't be able to fix it either. Hell, maybe the damn thing couldn't be fixed.

Tanham couldn't remember ever facing a problem like this one. He'd never been so close to something this explosive. The only good news was that the project was so ultra-sensitive, access so tightly compartmented, that the risk of a leak had been virtually nil.

Then along comes this crazy Laszlo character. Nobody had yet found his leash, not even his Russian brethren. Worse yet, *Laszlo knew*, at least it looked like he knew, as impossible as it seemed. The most classified program since the Atom bomb? Tanham was certain of it. And then, some double-agent tripled back, maybe – one of theirs or one of the Germans? Unless the medical folks at Walter Reed were right about Laszlo's blood assay and the DNA contained in it. That would explain it too. And, that alone would make this a whole new ball game, one beyond the Company's wildest imagination. Tanham grimaced. Laszlo was undoubtedly very dangerous. A killer. And, he would most certainly kill again.

"Hey, John. You're lone'ing it too much, Bubba. Lighten up. You know Mark Bennis, right? Mark's been here a couple of months actually."

O'Donnell pulled out a chair, motioning to his companion. Mark Bennis, an analyst in operations, was at his elbow, a cup of coffee in hand. Tanham reached out and shook his hand as he sat. Bennis looked him over.

"Yeah. I think we met some years ago – you were working over on the Mid-East desk, weren't you, Mark? 'Doing pretty well too, if I remember." Tanham took another sip.

"That's right, Mr. Tanham. You've got a good memory."

"Well, not too tough to remember, actually. If I recall, things were really cooking back then... on fire. You guys did one hell of a job containing things. You still there?"

"Thanks for the compliment. No, I left a long time ago. I've been a floater in clandestine ops for years now, until Phil picked me up anyway."

"No kidding? Why'd you leave? You were doing really well in Mid-East Ops, weren't you?"

"Yes, I was. I was running the company's first-ever source penetration into the PFLP, an extremely high-risk source. I mean, this guy sat at the same table with George Habbash himself. He sat right next to the sonofabitch. Things heated up, got really tight. We couldn't afford to lose this source. I ended up making a couple of decisions in the middle of a crisis that turned out to be unpopular with the leadership, You know how that is. Bullshit. Pure bullshit."

O'Donnell frowned and turned to Tanham, "Well, Novak's on his way."

"Okay, who drove him? You've seen Brannon… where is he? I need to…" John's eyes left Mark Bennis and focused on Phil.

"Ah, no. I haven't seen Brannon. O'Donnell interrupted. "Not around here anywhere yet today. The guy's strange, seriously strange. Who the hell ever knows where he really is."

"Well, how do you know Pete's off? Molly get a call?"

"I don't… I mean, he's got to be up and away by now. It's almost eleven."

"Right. How much does Mark here know?"

"Everything. He's NSC cleared."

"Everything? How the hell did you manage that?"

"Good contacts. And, I had the time to make it happen. I've had Mark following the JOG around for some time now."

"Gees, Phil, the JOG too? I didn't know that. Why didn't I know? Isn't that dangerous?"

"I thought you left decisions on the JOG to me, John. But no, it's not dangerous, not really. Mark is more than just familiar with the wet operations."

"I see. All right. Well, look, I'm sorry to run, but I'm late for the DepOps post-brief, Phil. End-of-the-week recap, you know.

'Gotta go. You guys have a good one. Oh Mark, it was good see-ing you again. 'Catch you around the campus."

Mark nodded in response, eyeing him again. Tanham turned away, stopping only to deposit his tray on the kitchen's conveyer belt.

O'Donnell and Bennis watched together as Tanham walked through the cafeteria exit and disappeared.

CHAPTER 10

Vienna Township
Northern Virginia

Early morning sunlight filtered through the trees to glitter on the still dewy grass. It was 7:00 a.m. with the temperature a crisp 49°F. The musty smell of fallen leaves was everywhere as a slight breeze rustled the tree branches. With every gentle gust, leaves scattered like blazing snowflakes across the manicured lawns. Nothing disturbed their rush down the empty street. It was too early on a Saturday morning in Vienna, Virginia, for the neighborhood to have yet come to life.

The breeze carried the sound of a garage door opening in front of a small split-level house, pale blue with burgundy shutters. An abrupt roar like feeding time at the zoo in the lion cage shattered the peaceful scene. Leaves blew away from the opening as if swept by some giant broom.

With a deep-throated growl, the sloping hood and black grill of an emerald-green 1970 Super Sport SS-396, inched its way out of the garage and nosed down the driveway. She was fully restored and loaded – big white-letter Goodyear Polyglass

71

Wide-Ovals on Mag wheels, Hurst speed shift and linkage, headers, and dual four-barrel carburetors.

The car was Brannon's baby, his sweetheart. She gleamed from bumper to bumper. The classic Chevelle SS-396 boasted a hair over 400 horsepower with its bored-out block. J.T. kept an 80-pound sandbag in the trunk over each wheel-well just to hold the rear end down on wet roads or whenever he decided to clean out the pipes. The latter was a rare event, for he treated the sports coupe like a newborn puppy... with lots of tender loving care.

The Chevy throttled up the street in first and then second gear, stopped briefly at the corner, and swung south on Maple Avenue. J.T. switched on the radio to a *Golden Oldies* station and the bright sound of "Classical Gas" filled the interior. He smiled, turning up the volume until he could feel the throb of the bass line. He shifted the gears instinctively and moved into the left lane, cruising at 45 mph in third gear. Trees and sky flickered across the polished, humped hood as the car powered along. The engine's resonant, deep-throated rumbling flared out from the dual exhaust and echoed along the boulevard.

It was a pleasant morning spin. But even in what appeared to be just a Saturday morning drive, J.T. took the precaution to *dry clean* himself. He wanted no tails on him today. Brannon was an expert at it, winding his path through the streets to identify and then shake off any would-be surveillants. And at the same time, make it all look utterly casual. He glanced at the rear-view mirror. Nothing. After four traffic lights, Southbound Maple turned into Ox Road, Route 123 south.

After ten minutes or so, he passed the George Mason University campus and turned east off Ox Road onto Braddock Road. At the first light, the green Chevy turned into the University Mall complex and drove around it, weaving through the mostly-empty parking areas. After one full circle, he took the west exit from the mall, turning left and south, back onto Ox Road. Once more, he checked the rear view mirror. Good, nothing. He was *clean*.

Settling back into the seat, he cruised south through the hills of northern Virginia, past the sleepy village and marina at Occoquan, and then onto Interstate 95. Once there, he opened the Chevy up and let it bore down the highway for three fast but monotonous hours. He flew past Richmond, past the I-64 cutoff to Norfolk and its vast array of shipyards at Newport News.

He decided to pull off the interstate on Exit 11, just north of the North Carolina border. There he picked up Route 58 east toward Routes 17 and 158 south to bring him to the Cape's backdoor. The monotony of the interstate was behind him, and the fall countryside of the Atlantic coastal area came alive with sights. Brannon was caught up in the scenery, smiling at the little shopping plazas and neighborhood corners as he passed. Occasional cars flashed by, filled with families mostly.

He still had the radio on the station in Richmond. It was on but low, just enough volume to keep him company. Brannon wasn't a fan of blaring heavy metal or rap. It was too *crazy* for him, and there was the whole *drug thing* that went along with it too. It seemed to him as though everything was changing anyway... the music, people, values, the nation itself. He didn't like to think about that too much because he liked things the way they were. Time passed with the station fading in and out

His thoughts raced back and forth, his shoulders beginning to slump. Extended quiet times always brought him to this. The depressing reality of it. What did he have left now? The Company? Not really. He had... nothing. J.T. took a deep breath and opened his eyes to stare into the fabric of the roof. He tried to quell the wave of emotions sweeping over him.

Then again, in a way, times like this served to clarify his thinking. They crystallized his sense of purpose, and gave him hope. He did have *one* thing left, at least one. The one thing that was now his *raison d'*être was Pete Novak. J.T. knew in the deepest core of his heart that he would allow absolutely nothing to harm one hair on Pete Novak's head. And, at the cost of his own life, if it ever came to that. Somehow, the road ahead looked straighter.

It was going on two o'clock in the afternoon and a bank of low, gray clouds were moving inland across the sky. The smell of the salt water hung in the air. He was approaching the southern end of the narrow peninsula at Point Harbor where Route 158 took an abrupt left turn east toward Wright Memorial Bridge. The bridge was named after the Wright brothers and their world-famous flight across the dune hills at Kitty Hawk in 1903.

A large memorial and museum now stood in the very center of Kill Devil Hills, a stone's throw from the Town Hall. It was the only real curiosity on the Cape, but wasn't much of a tourist draw. People came to the Outer Banks mainly for the sand, the sea, the broad sky, and to be alone or with their families far away from the crowds.

As the Chevy climbed the long, gentle slope of the bridge, Brannon couldn't help but take notice. It was beautiful. Green-blue water shimmered in every direction, turned white-crested by advancing off-shore breezes.

The bridge at Point Harbor crossed the intersecting mouths of Currituck and Albemarle Sounds, connecting the mainland with the string of islands that made up Cape Hatteras and the Outer Banks. It was a long, sturdy bridge built to withstand the driving winds of hurricanes that often slammed into the Outer Banks and North Carolina in early fall.

After crossing, he turned south onto Route 12, Beach Road. Motel after motel passed on the right, their *Vacancy* signs swinging tamely back and forth in the light winds. Only a random car or two came his way.

Not a lot of folks down here this time of year, J.T thought. It was a pretty lonely place in the off-season. The last of the large crowds left a month ago with the end of Labor Day weekend. That thought brought him back to Tony Spencer. Tony died that weekend. Brannon still had trouble believing that his dear old friend was gone.

As he approached the little town of Nags Head, he began watching for their street. After a few blocks, he saw it, Windy Cove Road, and swung left toward the ocean. Just ahead on the right, he saw number 19. It was a nice beach front wood-frame building with two decks wrapped around the second and third floors, offering a wondrous view of the Atlantic. As his tires crunched onto the crushed shell driveway, he noticed the figure of a woman sitting on the rear deck.

It was Barb Spencer. She was facing out to sea. Her elbows rested heavily on a table, its umbrella folded down, flapping lightly in the steady breeze. She was looking out somewhere along the beach and either didn't hear or didn't care about the car now entering her driveway. She just sat staring at the sea. J.T. walked along the side of the beach house to the wooden stairs and stepped up them. He paused at the top of the steps. She finally turned her head.

"Oh, J.T.?"

"Yes, Barb, it's me. Please, don't get up. It's been a long time. How are you? How've you been? I just drove down, wanted to see you. I thought maybe it was time we talked. You know, I've been worried sick. I had to be sure you were okay, see if there was anything I could do." He pulled out a chair and sat across from her.

The look of her struck him like a pail of ice water. A chill raced through him. It had been some time since he'd seen Barbara, but the change was dramatic. She wore no make-up. Her once-cheerful, freckled face was sullen, haggard. Deep dark chasms encircled her eyes and gave them a sunken look. They were tired, expressionless eyes. Barb's brown hair streaked with gray fell to her shoulders in thick, unkempt strands. The faded denim dress and light blue shirt looked as if they hadn't been pressed.

She extended her right hand. He was shocked even more by how thin and weak it felt. He cupped it with both his hands. A gentle squeeze. He let go.

"J.T., it *is* good to see you. Thanks for coming. I'm sorry about last month. I couldn't face anyone. It's still so hard. I can't believe he's gone, that it's over. Thirty-two years together and it's over. 'Just like that. I… " Her eyes were heavy for want of sleep. He could tell she was struggling to maintain her composure.

"So, how are you doing? Okay?" Barb half whispered, forcing a weak, trembling smile.

"Oh, you know me, Barb. I'm always doing okay. I want to, I need to, know what happened. Can you… are you able to talk about it?"

"Oh J.T., I really don't want to. I know how much Tony meant to you, and, of course, you to him. 'Seemed like every crazy story he could tell had you in it somewhere. His eyes always lit up when he spoke of you."

"Thanks. Barb, what happened at the beach? Was it on the fourth?"

She stared at him for what seemed the longest moment, then spoke. "Yes, September 4th. We were all out in the water, swimming a little, floating. You know, just bobbing around. But Tony had changed long before that. He changed in a way I'd never seen before. He was so… different… when he came back from Europe that last time. Something had happened over there, J.T.

He wouldn't talk about it. But then, he never talked about his work." She paused, wiping her eyes.

"Please go on."

"You see, he would just sit out here on the deck looking up at the sky. Staring, day after day. Finally, he told me he wanted out. Of course, I told him to do whatever he thought was best. So, he applied for an early retirement. The Agency was reluctant. Some of them in Special Operations were quite angry. But, in the end they approved it." Barb turned her eyes past the deck's weathered railing to the sea.

"Tony retired?"

"Yes. You didn't know? Didn't he tell you?"

"I didn't even know he was in Europe."

Barb's eyes never left the sea. "Oh well, you know how *that* is. So… what was it he always said, *compartmented*, I think. He never would talk about those *black world* things, or whatever you call them. I felt lucky just to know what continent he was on. Sometimes you guys are something else."

"Yeah, I know. I'm seeing that myself more and more. Why'd he retire?"

"This is going to sound crazy, but I really don't know. He was shaken up by something. It had a grip on him, this thing in Europe. He'd suddenly had enough. But let me tell you, it was much more than that. Much deeper."

"What do you mean?"

"Tony came back from Europe six weeks earlier than I expected. I didn't even know he was coming back. He just suddenly showed up one day. He hardly said 'hello,' raced through the house like a madman, slamming doors, packing another bag and took off again. He wasn't here two hours."

"Where'd he go?"

"Denver."

"Denver? What the hell's in Denver?"

"You tell me. But that's where he went. He never called while he was out there. He came back three days later. Tells me he wants out of the Agency. That trip put the lid on it."

"My goodness. I don't get it."

"Neither did I. Oh, I was certainly glad to have him back. But that's when… the dreams started, nightmares, bad dreams. Every other night or so, Tony would get out of bed, drenched in sweat, walk around in the dark, and end up on the beach. He always ended up on the beach. He said he couldn't get past the bad dreams."

"This must have been terrible for you. What kind of dreams do you think he was having? Would he talk to you about them?"

"No. He did say that he wished he could talk to me or to somebody, anybody, about it, but he couldn't. He said no one would believe him anyway. Finally, early one morning, it had to be four o'clock, I saw he was gone from bed again. His pillow was soaked. I got up, looked out the window, and saw him sitting out here. Just sitting in a robe and staring at the sky. I brought him a cup of coffee and sat down by him. I started to give him a kiss and when he turned his face… J.T., I will never forget it. It scared the hell out of me…"

"What?"

"His face. My husband was in tears, sobbing like a baby, his eyes bloodshot. He said, 'Barb, I think I've lost my faith.' Then he got up and walked off the deck, down the beach. He didn't come back until almost noon. 'Just in a bathrobe. I thought he was really losing it, going insane."

Barb turned back to the sea. Brannon sat quietly pondering her words. Tony had 'lost his faith.' What the hell did that mean? Lost his faith in God? Not possible. Tony was a staunch Christian, a solid believer. What could shake a faith like his?

Brannon started to speak, but she interrupted, "J.T., like I said, despite his being so troubled about whatever it was, I wasn't sorry to see Tony leave the Agency. Not if that's what he wanted. I saw the chance for a new life, a different one, a happier one. More freedom for us. I was glad to have him back and all to myself... all to myself, now that's a joke." A sudden fury blazed in her eyes. She turned away once again to the ocean. "J.T., no more, I can't do this. Please understand. I just can't."

"Barb, what is it?"

"I can't talk about it! How he could, hell, maybe he was just away too long. Maybe he was always that way, and I just never knew. Never caught on. It tore little Tony up too." Her voice had risen sharply.

J.T. could make no sense of any of this. His eyes narrowed. What was she trying, or refusing, to tell him now? Maybe he himself was too afraid to understand.

"Barb, I just don't... "

"J.T., the bastard was with someone else. After all these years? Why now after all these years? I'm sick of thinking about it, thinking of them together. I can't even talk to him about it now because he's dead! Maybe someday she'll call. Wouldn't that be great? We could be one big happy family. Spend our holidays together – the women who've slept with Tony Spencer! Damn it! Why now?" Barbara turned her face to his. 'Seeking an answer. The sunken hollows of her eyes were now red and wet.

Despite the warm air, an icy chill shook his bones. Gooseflesh rose over him in a tingling wave. He gaped at her in disbelief, trying to comprehend. He shook his head from side to side. Finally he managed, "Tony? Barb, I don't believe it! That's ridiculous. How did you ever...?"

"J.T., I can't do this. Not now. I'm sick all over. If I had anything in my stomach now, I'd throw up. I miss him. I love him. And… I can't help but hate him."

"Barb, honey, that's just not…"

"You've got to go. Please. I'll call you in a couple of months or so. I will."

Barbara rose from her chair stiff as a skeleton. She walked to the glass siding door before turning back.

"I love you, J.T. You're the brother I never had. My dearest of friends. Please, believe that. But please go. You must. Please." She closed the door behind her, flipping the lock without looking, and disappeared into the darkness inside.

His eyes strained until they no longer could see her shadowy figure. He turned to the railing and stared out to sea as Barbara had done. Stunned. He raised his face to drink in the salt air. Brannon could see how she might find some solace there, might lose herself in the endless waves. He turned back, but there was no one. The door was still closed.

He shook his head, stuck his hands in his pockets, and took one last look up and down the beach. The wind was picking up. He squinted his eyes and leaned over the railing. Far down the beach to his right, he saw a lone figure walking slowly away, dragging a foot, kicking at the piles of sand. It looked like a boy.

CHAPTER 11

Nags Head, The Outer Banks
North Carolina

The Chevy growled as Brannon backed it out of the driveway. Instead of turning north back to the bridge, he headed south on Beach Road. After about six streets, he turned left and drove to the end of the pavement. He pushed through the brush and weeds to the first dune and saw him, not sixty yards away.

"Tony!"

The boy turned. It was Tony, no mistaking it. He had the same handsome face, the same lean build, and the same curly black hair. The boy stood staring, wondering who this intruder was who dared to violate his communion with the sea. Brannon stepped toward him, struggling down the slope as his shoes filled with sand. He stopped to yank them off, then raised his eyes to meet the boy's stare.

Tony Jr. was the image of his father thirty years ago. He looked twelve, maybe thirteen. His hands were at his sides, a seashell in each. The boy didn't know why, but the sight of the stranger filled him with anticipation. This was someone he knew.

"Tony?"

"Who're you?"

"I'm Brannon, J.T. Brannon. I… " He took a few more slow steps. Tony backed up. Only a few feet separated them.

"What're you doing here? Whaddya want? How do you know my name?"

"Tony, your dad and I were good friends. I walked you on this beach a long time ago when you were in diapers. I came to… "

"Who'd you say you were?"

"J.T. Brannon. Please call me J.T." He stepped forward and offered his right hand. Tony leaned backward but his right hand reached out and met Brannon's in a firm shake. The invisible barrier between them crumbled.

The boy's shoulders dropped from their defensive brace. He paused, listening to the sound of the waves breaking on the beach, his windbreaker flapping in the breeze. Tony dropped to the sand in front of Brannon. He pulled his knees into his chest and wrapped his arms around them.

"My dad's dead, mister. He's gone. So, why are you here? Can't you see my mom's had enough? I saw you on the deck. Please, leave us alone."

"What about your mom, son? What's happening with her? Can you think of any way I can help?"

"Help? How? I told you my father's dead. Buried. I don't know about her, not anymore, not really, I guess. We don't talk much." Tony's head was bent and his finger mindlessly traced in the sand. Brannon squatted in front of him.

"What's that? You should be helping each other now. You'll need to… to try to put this behind you. Your Dad would want you both to move on."

"It'll never be behind her. Never."

"Tony, what's going on? Tell me, son. I don't understand. But maybe I can help, in some way we just can't see yet."

"She hates him! Loves him and hates him. How's she ever gonna get over that? And, she hates me too!" Tony looked up, his chin on his knees. His eyes were misty. He turned his eyes to the waves breaking on the sand, unable to look at J.T., embarrassed by his emotions.

"Why? Why does she hate your Dad and you? Please, son. Tell me."

"Because I told her. I told her. I didn't know how it would, I didn't understand. Now she blames me too." He looked back at Brannon, searching for answers. A tear broke from his eye and trickled down his face.

"Tony, what? Tell me. Let's talk about it."

"She said Dad was cheating on her. He was gone so much. He'd found another woman to be with. But, I don't see how Dad... I don't know. She hates me too. Why? How could he?" He coughed, trying to hold back the tears.

"What? You think your dad was having an affair? Hey, that's not the Tony Spencer I know. He lived for you two. He loved you both. No son, that's not possible."

"Then, go tell her that! Yeah, go tell her that! You seem to know everything. I don't give a damn anymore! He's gone. She hates me. Who gives a... I... I miss him so much." Tony barked, finally letting go. His head dropped on his forearms. He sobbed, his shoulders heaving.

J.T. moved forward in the sand and put an arm around him. He patted his shoulder. Now Brannon felt his own eyes wet. It was his turn to stare over the expanse of ocean in front of them. A few minutes of awkward silence and Brannon watched the boy raise his head and rub his hands over his eyes and face, smearing the tears.

"I just wish it would stop. My dad's gone, and my mom too, really, even though she's here. I don't know what to do anymore. That's all."

"Tony, did you ever see your dad with somebody else? With some other woman?"

"No, no. I never saw him, but Mom said it explained everything. She said Dad had changed."

"What son? Tell me."

"My dad was going under. I didn't realize… " The conversation had now brought the boy to the jagged edge of his painful memory.

"Going under? The water? You mean the day he died?"

"Yes."

"He was swimming? How far out?"

"Nooo. No, he wasn't swimming. We spread out and we were just bobbing up and down, just past the surf where the waves were breaking. He just… "

"How deep was it?" J.T. interrupted, relieved now that the boy was talking. Brannon tensed as he visualized the scene and the death of this friend begin to unfold.

"Only about five feet, maybe a little more. That's all."

"Five feet! How'd he drown in…?"

"He didn't drown! Don't you know? He got stung! Jellyfish. He swallowed too much water. But I didn't know. I was closest, didn't realize… " Tony's head dropped again and he coughed a short cry.

Brannon was forcing the young boy to relive the horror of his father's death. Tony sucked in a breath and peeked over his arms, then continued, "His head went down. I didn't know. But I saw something wasn't right. I swam over to him."

"You swam, Tony? How far away were you?"

"Twenty yards, maybe. The top of his head, his hair was

floating in the water. I pulled him up, then pulled him to the beach, the shallow water. He was so heavy, even in the water. He coughed up water, some of it gurgled out of his mouth. My dad was alive! I had him in my arms." Tony was white as a sheet. His eyes again brimmed with tears. His grief was overwhelming.

"I'm sorry, son. I know you loved your dad."

"Well, he closed his eyes, and then said something at first that I couldn't understand. He said this woman's name over and over again. Not my name, not mom's. I just don't understand. Then he... "

"What name, Tony?"

"Maria... Maria Dean. Maybe it was Marie, Mary... Dean, I don't know. And he kept repeating it. At the hospital, the coroner said he must have been hallucinating. But I heard him. He was asking for her, Maria Dean."

"Coroner? Your dad made it to the hospital alive?"

"No, Mr. Chapman, the coroner, told me he was certain that Dad was already dead. I had him, but I couldn't help him. Nobody to tell me what to do. I screamed to my mom, but she was too far up the beach."

"Tony, was there anyone else around? Anyone on the beach, in the water, who might have seen what happened to your dad before you saw he was in trouble?" Brannon's mind was racing.

"No, not where we were. The beach was empty. There was a boat, but no, they were too far out."

"Boat?"

"Yeah, men fishing, I guess. But they were too far out. They couldn't have seen us."

"How far, Tony? What kind of boat?"

"Oh, what does it matter now, anyway? It's over. He's dead."

"I'm sorry. I just thought, I was looking for any way, anyone who might… " J.T. could see the boy was too distressed to dredge these details from his memory.

"It was a cabin cruiser. You know, sport fisherman kind of, with a flybridge and all. It was a nice one, 40 footer or so. I'd seen them trolling up and down the water all morning. They were too far out though, maybe a half mile. Fishing, it looked like. So what?"

"You said *they?*"

"Oh, three, maybe four guys. They were walking on the back deck. I saw some long poles, fishing poles. Look, I really didn't notice too well. They couldn't see. Boats like that, they have fish finders, sonar kind of, helps 'em find the schools of fish. They were probably watching that screen all day. They couldn't have seen what… " he paused,

"My mom, she didn't even get to, didn't… " Tony leaned forward on his knees and his hands reached out to J.T as he sobbed again.

"She didn't get to say good-bye?" J.T. quietly finished the sentence for him.

"Yes. It wasn't my fault. I loved him. But I couldn't help him. I didn't know what to do. Ohhh, Dad." He gasped for breath between the words.

"Of course not, Tony. No one blames you. It was already too late."

"She does! She blames me! Now she doesn't want anything to do with me."

"Why, son? Why do you say that?"

"I told you. 'Because I told her about Maria Dean. That woman, Maria Dean."

"I see. Come on, Tony. Let's get some lunch."

Arm in arm with their heads down, J.T. and young Tony walked to the car. They drove down the beach road without a word between them to the first open place they saw. Inside *The Seagull's Nest* they ate together but in silence, each lost in his own thoughts. It was obvious from his ravenous appetite that Tony felt better. He wolfed his food. The boy had gotten it all out, finally. It must have been an immense, crushing burden for him to carry all that inside for so long.

Afterward, they stood outside the double glass doors and shook hands. Tony insisted on walking home alone. J.T. agreed, but gave him his phone number. He promised he'd see him again soon. He leaned against the car and watched the boy walk up the road until he disappeared. J.T. genuinely liked him, not surprising because Tony Sr. and Barb were great people. If he'd been blessed with children, that boy was the kind of son he would've wanted as his own.

CHAPTER 12

Nags Head

B rannon glanced at the sky. Night was creeping in from the ocean. He checked his watch. *Five o'clock. Gees, time flies when you're having fun*, he mused, then strode briskly back into the restaurant. He waited at the cash register until the waitress came up, sporting ruby-red lip-stick and blondish-gray hair in a net.

"How can I help you, darling?"

"What county's this?"

"Dare County, darling. Named after Virginia Dare. You know, like I... dare you." She giggled, eyeing him.

"Thanks. Where's the county seat?"

"Oh, it's over in Manteo, honey, on Roanoke Island. Anything else you need?" Her hands slid down her hips onto the counter. Like a cat ready to pounce.

"Thanks. How do I get there?" His fingers drummed nervously. He edged back.

"Out of the parking lot, go right, straight south. Two miles down. You'll see signs on your right for Route 264. It'll run you right over the Washington Baum Bridge. *Baum*, that's *tree* in German, honey. Stay on it and you'll be in Manteo in less than ten minutes. Want me to come along – show you the way? It's dead around here this time of year anyway."

"No, that's fine, ma'am. I'm sure I'll find it. Thanks again."

"Don't mention it. Stop by again. I get off every day at seven. Okay?"

"You bet," he pushed his way through the doors, thinking, *Goodnight, and not on your life.*

Brannon found the bridge. He drove past the village of South Manteo as the road swung north. He saw the sign for Dare County Center, turned right on Twinford Road, and parked in front of a fairly new building. Lots of glass.

As he walked up the steps toward the entrance, a man stepped out, locking the doors behind him. His green jumper had his name, *Jack*, embroidered in yellow on his chest. He carried a large canvas bag.

"Say, Jack," Brannon took a guess.

"Yeah, how ya doing."

"Coroner's office in there?"

"Nah. Downtown. On John Borden Street, near the hospital. Who're you looking for?" Jack dropped the bag with a thump on the concrete.

"Well, I guess whoever the coroner is… a Mr. Chapman, something like that. They open today?"

"They were. 'Closed now though. You mean Douglas Chapman. Yeah, old Douglas gets outta there early enough. Then again, I gotta say he's in awful early too. About six a.m. most days." Jack wore about two days' worth of beard and smelled like ammonia cleaner.

"Douglas?"

"Douglas Chapman, the coroner. Little guy. Oh, it's Doug

really. I call him Douglas 'cause it irritates him, but he's okay, I guess."

"Know where he lives, maybe?"

"Nope. Over on the Cape somewheres. Ain't you the eager one? Best thing is catch him early in the morning. Before he hits the bottle is best. But you gotta get there real early for that!"

"Say again?"

The janitor stopped in mid-chuckley, his ears flushed. He looked down at the ground as he answered, "Oh, Douglas does do his drinking. On and off all day sometimes, so it seems. Don't get me wrong, mister, he's real good at what he does. He's a smart one."

"Okay, thanks. So now, Borden Street near the hospital?"

"That's *John* Borden Street. Not that it matters. You'll find it okay. Red brick building. Take care now. See ya around." Jack walked over to a beat-up red Ford pick-up in the corner of the lot. He threw the bag in the back, climbed in, and waved as he drove off.

"Dammit. Never planned on staying overnight, but it looks like that's what I'm doing."

Brannon acknowledged the darkening sky. It'd probably be pitch black within the hour. He climbed back in the SS-396 and drove back out to Route 64, turning north to Manteo proper. At a convenience store on the way, he picked up some shaving cream, a razor, a tooth brush, and some tooth paste.

Back on the road, he began to watch for a motel. Not half a mile down, the blinking neon sign of the Green Heron Motel beckoned him. The sign boasted 22 rooms and 13 efficiencies. It looked small, but it would probably do for one night.

After he woke the clerk from a late afternoon snooze, Brannon registered and went straight to the room. It was comfy, knotty-pine walls, seascape pictures, and a single queen-size bed. Good enough. J.T. closed the curtain and flopped down on the bed, pushing off his shoes with the toes of each foot. It felt good. Reaching over to the nightstand, he grabbed the phone.

"Yep?" he drawled. The desk clerk picked up the phone on the third ring.

"Give me an outside line, please," J.T. cradled the phone between his chin and shoulder as he unbuttoned his shirt. No dinner tonight... the burger and fries were still with him. The tone came through and he dialed, smiling at the old rotary numbers.

"Hello?" a female voice answered.

"Hi, Carolyn? It's J.T. How you doing?"

"Fine, J.T. You calling from home, lover?"

"No, I'm away on business. Say, Carolyn, I need a big favor, need it bad, honey. Can you help me?"

"Well, speak to me, big boy. I'm all ears. Or better yet, come up to see me some time," she gave him her best Mae West impersonation. "Excuse me while I turn down the TV, honey. Good romance movie on."

Carolyn Campbell tipped the scales at about two hundred twenty-five. Big girl, and a spinster. Her favorite hobby was chowing down on potato chips and cola while watching romance flicks late into the night. However, she was also deputy chief of personnel at Langley headquarters. Carolyn knew of and about, everybody.

Brannon had considered courting her about five years ago, but had chickened out. Since then she had ballooned up to the size of a sumo wrestler. Nothing lost there, though. They stayed good friends.

"Carolyn, I'm sorry to bother you. This is on the Q-T, okay? I'm trying to piece something together. Very important. I need to know who the guys were that were killed over in Europe last month. And, I need it fast. Can you do that for me?"

"J.T., honey, shame on you. That business is very hush-hush. I don't know if... "

"Carolyn. I wouldn't ask you unless it was vital. Please, can you get it?"

"I bet you need it by tomorrow morning, say seven o'clock," her voice dripped honey.

"Five or five-thirty would be better if you can."

"Damn, J.T.! You're sure pushing it." Carolyn was envisioning trying to roll out of bed at least by four. That would be the start of a bad hair day for sure.

"Honey, if it wasn't you and it wasn't so vital to me, I wouldn't ask. Please, help me."

"Oh, stop. I know that. Where do you want me to call you? Gotta number where you can be reached?"

"Carolyn, sweetheart, one more thing... "

"Yes, snug-ums? What is it baby-cakes wants nowww?"

J.T. knew by her tone that he was indeed pushing his luck. Resigned, he answered her directly. "I need any traces you can get on a *Maria Dean*. Maybe any derivatives, like *Marie Dean* or *Mary Dean*, you know. Company types, intelligence sources, and counterparts in the foreign services, whatever. Hit the Link Files. I know this is a lot, and please know I love you for it."

"You have any other identifiers on your lady friend?" Carolyn's tone went sharp.

"She's an investigative lead, Carolyn, not a friend. Try our Europe files, stick to central Europe."

"Okay. That it, darling?

"Yes. Thanks so much, Carolyn."

"You mean that's it until dinner? When you get back, right, lover?"

He knew that was coming. "You bet, honey. Pick the place."

They chatted for a couple of minutes and then said good-bye.

He sighed as he set the receiver down. This would cost him an expensive dinner in downtown Washington. She'd pick some ritzy French place, to the tune of about $300 or more. J.T. slipped under the covers. He was dead tired. In seconds, he was snoring.

CHAPTER 13

Nags Head
North Carolina

In the early morning blackness of the small motel room, the sudden loud ring startled Brannon from his deep, dreamless sleep. He sat up. His right hand groped in the darkness, searching for the receiver.

"Hello?" he mumbled, propping himself up on his left elbow and rubbing his eyes.

"Hey J.T., ain't you outta bed and got that pretty body of yours all showered up yet? Early bird gets the worm, you know."

"Carolyn, good morning. Thanks for getting back to me. What time is it anyway?"

"It's 5:00 a.m., you lazy hunk. And me here at the office already, doing all the work, huh. Come on, wake up honey, I ain't got all day! Today's gonna be a killer, thanks to you."

"Thanks again. Any luck?"

"Yesiree, you know I always come through, don't you? Here it is – number one, the three dead men are Bob Kaminov, Nick Potter, and Jon Yezhovich. It looks like all Ops types. I can't be sure if that's current though because every one of them was detailed about twelve months ago. New office, unit, or something." All business now, Carolyn's voice was crisp and matter of fact.

"Good. Okay. I know Kaminov and Potter. Both on the Russian desk. Yezhovich is a ringer though. I can't place him. What else can you tell me about him?"

"He's only been with us a year. But wait, no, I saw that he had an entry here for us back in 1974-75 as well. He's gotta be a contractor. Let me see, hmmm, yep, there it is in background notes. He's FTD, honey."

"FTD?" Brannon drew a blank. He was still too foggy to tap his own mental reserves.

"Come on, J.T., F-T-D! I'm not sending you flowers, sweetie! I'm talking *Foreign Technology Division*. You know those guys, J.T., techie types. High-tech, developmental stuff, the opposition's stuff, that is. FTD gets their hands on Russia's newest stuff, their leading-edge weapon systems. They test them, find the vulnerabilities, and figure out how to beat them. The whiz kids. You with me now?"

"Yeah, I'm with you. I know those folks. I just don't… how's Yezhovich fit in? Anything else on him?"

Brannon was now sitting up in bed, pen in hand, rummaging for some paper. His other hand felt inside the top drawer of the night stand. Yes, the Gideons saved him again. He pulled out the Bible, flipped open the cover, and started taking notes. He was reaching the outer boundaries of his luck with the Lord. He'd ripped off two Bibles in his sinful life.

"Well now, apparently Mr. Yezhovich has a Ph.D., so he's Dr. Yezhovich. Hold on, ah, metallurgy. He's done a lot of research on alloys, metallic composites, carbon fiber reinforcement in metal-plastics, metal composites at the atomic level, that kind of stuff. Very bright fellow. He had some trouble, but looks like that's all straightened out. His security clearances were still intact."

"What do you mean?"

"There was a reference to a security file. He was interviewed by our counterintelligence folks for his membership in NICAP."

"What's that?"

"Hmm… NICAP. The National Investigations Committee on Aerial Phenomena. The gist of it was that the good doctor was talking to people about things he shouldn't have been. But as I said, he kept his clearances so it must have turned out okay, a verbal admonishment maybe."

"NICAP? Strange. Got anything on them?"

"Not really, nothing substantive. There was nothing there except a file number reference, a counterintelligence file maybe. There was another reference to Dr. Yezhovich working as an analyst on some rather dated Air Force projects named *MAJIC* and *BLUE BOOK*. Ah, that's MAJIC with a "J", but that was it. That's all there is here. Enough?"

"Were there any linked files for those projects?"

"Yes, sketchy though. BLUE BOOK was a pure vanilla, public-releasable report. It was apparently an altered version of the sister classified project, black world – MAJIC."

"Altered?"

"Yes. But, I can't talk about it over the phone to you. The indicators are that it was. MAJIC, by the way, was *very* deep black. Yezhovich worked both projects."

"Carolyn, was there anything you saw that indicated the nature of the projects?"

"Yeah, but it's so weird."

"What?"

"Unidentified Flying Objects. UFOs – BLUE BOOK

anyway. Probably safe to assume the MAJIC project was too."

"UFOs?"

"Yep. Say, that's all I can see. You got enough, sweetie? 'Sounds like you've got a hot one here. I personally am not into the Loch Ness monster or flying saucers."

"Guess so. Puzzles me, though."

"Well, build your puzzles on somebody else's time, lover. I need to go to the restroom and put on some make-up. You want the rest, Maria Dean or whatever?"

"Oh, yes. Any hits?"

"Nope, not really. I checked everything. We do have a Marie Dee over on the Pacific Rim desk doing Economic Analysis. But she's 67, a widow, and she's filed for retirement. Any possibility there?"

"Doesn't sound too promising, but I'll keep it in the back of my mind. Carolyn, you're a sweetheart. I owe you big time. Thanks for… "

"You bet your sweet cheeks you owe me. Pay-up time's coming, lover. You take care and be safe now. Don't fight with the other boys. Love ya!"

He heard the click, and Carolyn was off before he could say good-bye. He placed the receiver back on the cradle and swung his legs off the bed.

"Time to get up, Captain Midnight," he whispered.

CHAPTER 14

Manteo, The Outer Banks
North Carolina

Brannon drove north through the dark to Manteo. His cold hands had a death grip on the steering wheel, the air damp and heavy with the smell of the ocean. The gray light of dawn was just brightening over the water's eastern horizon as J.T. turned off at Devon Drive, heading for the center of town. He saw the white concrete walls of a hospital to his left. The next street over was John Borden, and just as Jack had said, there was no missing the old red brick building.

Brannon parked the Chevy in the empty side lot and walked around to the front entrance. One of the glass doors swung open easily. It was dark inside; a tiled hallway stretched ahead. His ears strained to a faint echo down the hall… two men in a heated discussion.

Brannon approached cautiously, his eyes scanning the closed door of each office as he passed. The voices were louder here. At the end of the hall was an iron railing and a stairway down to a lower level. The sounds were coming from downstairs. He peered over the rail to the lower level and saw a dim light flickering on the tile floor. J.T. tiptoed down the metal stairs, pausing at every second step to somehow make sense of the garbled voices.

Two metal doors with glass windows stood guard at the bottom of the stairs. Behind them was a lab room with a lone, white-jacketed figure perched on a high stool. The man sipped at a mug. J.T. could smell coffee. On the wall, on a stainless-steel shelf, sat a flat panel TV. The images of Humphrey Bogart, Ingrid Bergman, and Claude Rains filled the screen.

J.T. couldn't believe it, six o'clock in the morning and this guy's watching *Casablanca*! He shook his head and abruptly pushed open the door. The man jerked around in alarm. Startled, he swung around on the stool.

"Who the hell are you?" he asked defensively. "Didn't you see the sign? We don't open 'til eight o'clock. What in hell you doin' here at this hour anyway?"

"No, I didn't see the sign. It's dark in the hallway. But if you're Douglas Chapman, Dare County coroner, then I need to talk to you. I'm J.T. Brannon. I apologize for the… "

"It's *Doug*, not Douglas. Now, what do you want?" he cut J.T. off mid-sentence.

Jack was right. Doug sure was sensitive about his name. He *was* a little guy, all of about five-foot-six, small-boned and stooped shoulders. He was balding but still sported some curly gray hair around the sides. Chapman peered over his bifocals at Brannon, waiting for a reply. His initial apprehension was gone, that replaced by obvious irritation.

"I'd like to talk with you about a death case you might have seen out here about a month ago. The man's name was Tony Spencer. He lived over in Nag's Head. He was a good… "

"Look, mister, I told you, we open at eight o'clock. Come back then." Chapman cut him off again, his tone harsher. He hesitated, then continued, "Better yet, let me see your badge now."

"Badge?"

"Yes, badge. What are you, FBI, Treasury, Drug Enforcement, what?"

Brannon didn't carry a badge in his line of work. And, he wasn't about to leave now, nor let the conversation go on like this either. Chapman was abrasive and Brannon didn't like it. He gestured to the TV.

"Say, Doug, you see old Humphrey there in *The Treasure of the Sierra Madre*? You know, there's a scene in it with the Mexican bandits?"

"Yeah, great movie, and I know the scene. I like old movies. So what? I told you… " Chapman looked stumped.

"Well, we don't need no steeen-king badges! Got that?" This time it was Brannon who interrupted.

"No badge, eh? Come on, why the hell are you guys back here, anyway? I gave you what you wanted, every damn thing I had. Ain't nothing changed unless you got some new news." Chapman stared at him, smiling

"What do you mean?"

"You're CIA, right? So was Mr. Anthony T. Spencer. I already gave your guys what they wanted… weeks ago. The whole report. 'Like I said, nothing's changed. The case is closed. The man is buried. End of story. So tell me, what the hell could you possibly want now? I'm very busy, and I don't like unannounced intrusions."

"Busy my ass." Brannon flicked a singular light switch and walked to the TV, hitting the 'off' switch just as Claude Rains was catching up with Humphrey and Ingrid at the airport. He turned to glare at Doug.

"Stop screwing with me. Yes, I'm Agency. And, yes, Tony Spencer was too. He was also a very close friend of mine, and

I want to know what happened to him. I don't give a shit what you told anyone else. You got that, Doug?"

"You're not connected with the other two? How do I know that?"

"Trust me. These other two, what were their names?" Brannon snapped at him.

Chapman slid off the stool and walked over to one of the lab tables. He reached up and turned on the overhead battery of florescent lights, flooding the lab room like a twilight double header at Yankee Stadium.

"That's over a month ago. I don't remember. The guy who asked all the questions was a *Mark...* somebody or other. I just don't remember. So, where's that leave us?" He leaned defiantly against the table behind him.

"Look, Doug. I'm not trying to hassle you. Tony Spencer was like a brother to me. We fought side. Special Forces. One tough cookie. An expert in hand-to-hand combat, black belt Tae Kwon Do. Tony could neuter a fly at a hundred yards with any hand-held firearm. He wasn't a man who would die easily. Help me with this, please. Doug, tell me about your work here. You a forensic expert?"

"I'm a medical examiner and coroner by degree and state certification. But I'm a forensic expert by experience. Why do you ask?"

"In my line of work, I've met a lot of men who do what you do. All varieties, all levels of expertise. Do you see a lot of crime down here? I thought this was mostly a vacation spot?"

"Mr. Brannon, that's correct. The majority of what I deal with here is what washes up on the beach. Or it's the remains of whatever doesn't spill through the Coasties' nets. But then, we also get... "

"What do you mean, 'whatever doesn't spill through the Coasties nets'?"

"Floaters."

"Come again?"

"Floaters, Mr. Brannon. Floaters." Doug continued. "Okay, let's say you're somebody who's fallen off of a fishing vessel, a tanker, or some cruise ship, whatever. You're dead now. And, you've been in the water for two or three days, afloat. Your flesh gets severely bloated. You take on the consistency of, well, kind'a like a nice vanilla custard. Along comes a Coast Guard cutter and scoops you up, or tries to. You see, by now, you don't stay in the net real well, you just kind of spill through it. Except for your bones, cartilage, and big muscles."

"Eh-heh, that paints a real pretty picture, Doug. Thanks for sharing," Brannon had an uncomfortable look on his face. Even with no breakfast, he felt his stomach churn.

"Sorry, I didn't mean to… "

"It's okay. Go on."

"I also get to work any of the occasional bad things that happen, even in a garden spot like this. Jealousy in the bars or on the beach that ends up in a stabbing or a shooting. Or somebody drives down from Richmond because he thinks it's easier to knock off a convenience store here."

"Is it?"

"Yeah. Not much of that stuff though. Generally, this is a quiet place. I get most of my challenges up in Richmond. I put my services on call to the coroner's office there a few years back. They ask me for forensic support when they need it, which is occasional. Unless of course, I'm tied up here."

"Doug, thanks. Like I said, Tony Spencer was one very tough hombre. He swam like a fish. I have a lot of trouble believing he just went and drowned in five feet of water. Not with his strength, his skills."

Chapman stood there looking for the longest time, not

moving. He brought his right hand up and stroked his chin. He crossed his arms and shifted his weight against the table.

"Mr. Brannon, I rode to the hospital in the ambulance with Mr. Spencer. I examined him closely. I don't believe it either."

"Then why…"

"Because there's no evidence I could present in any court of law to the contrary, Mr. Brannon. I'm sorry. Your friend Spencer was stung by a jellyfish, a Portuguese man o' war. They took him to the medical center in Kitty Hawk, and they couldn't help hi/m. Mr. Spencer's neural and cardiovascular systems had shut down. It was too late." Chapman eyed him and continued.

"In September, there's a lot of warm water still moving along the coast. These jellyfish… they travel in large groups and get carried up the Atlantic coast in the Gulf Stream. The waters here get warm, murky… just right for jellyfish. The whole tub is one big heat sink. They drift up here, congregate around the inlets. Then they spawn and die."

"But you said you don't believe it? Did you see the police report?"

"Yes. They found three or four jellyfish in the water, all relatively small. They were scooped up and put them in plastic bags. I got to take a close look too. They were all dead and it looked to me like they'd been dead a while, for half a day maybe. They were already in some state of decay."

"Already dead?" Brannon eyed the coroner anxiously. Chapman was holding back. Brannon was certain of it.

"Yeah, dead. But that in itself doesn't mean anything. They probably weren't, well, couldn't have been those jellyfish that killed him. I don't know what else I can tell you."

"Were there any other reports of jellyfish that day? Stings, anything?"

"No."

"Isn't that odd. From what you've said, about them drifting around in large groups?"

"Yes, it is odd. We should have had at least some other sightings. But still, there's nothing to support any other theory. What else?"

"Okay, tell me about jellyfish. The Portuguese man o' war." J.T. was prepared to suck Chapman's brain all day until he opened up.

"Those are the big guys of jellyfish. Their floats, the translucent parachute-like balls, are only about eight or ten inches across, but their tentacles can get as big as forty feet long."

"Gees! Forty feet?"

"That's right. They're not aggressive, but their tentacles are covered with stinging cells, nematocysts. Each of these stinging cells is like a trigger cocked and ready to go off. Mr. Brannon, a snake or a spider can only bite you in a single spot. A jellyfish hits you with a barrage of stinging cells all at once. They affect a large area. And, on top of that, it's a very difficult venom to deal with."

"How's that? I mean, what's it do to you, Doug?"

"Their venom is a powerful chemical, a tetramine toxin, specifically hydroxytryptamine. The chemistry is probably lost on you. Anyway, it results in stings that are extremely intense, like hot burning irons. You get bright red, inflammatory hive-like lesions all over the area of contact. There's immediate swelling. You get severe cramps. Your muscles become crippled. The venom is absorbed extremely fast, going directly into your circulatory and lymphatic systems where your blood and lymph actually help transfer the poison. Breathing becomes difficult. Your heart rate drops off. Next comes nausea and vomiting. You are emotionally upset, faint and disoriented. Finally, shock sets in. It's nasty stuff. When you consider that you're in water and trying to swim too, there's not much chance. This all happens relatively fast."

Brannon pulled one of the metal stools out from the table and sat down with a heavy exhale. He looked at his watch: quarter to seven. He propped an elbow on the table and looked at Chapman as the minutes ticked away. Chapman sat back down on his own stool. Brannon took a deep breath.

"Doug, you still haven't told me why you don't believe it either. I'm not leaving until you do. Tony, his wife, and his son mean too much to me. I've got to know, and you're gonna tell me."

Chapman looked like a man caught in the act by eyewitnesses and now was about to confess. After another long pause, he responded.

"Because, Mr. Brannon, there was way too much, too much of it."

"Too much of what?"

"Too much serum toxicity. Too much venom in him to be supported by the lesions on his one leg, his left leg, the calf, if I recall. There are no sea wasps around here that I'm aware of."

"Doug, what are you telling me? What's a sea wasp?"

"Sea wasps, *Chironex fleckeri*. They're the most poisonous living things on planet Earth. They're a box-like jellyfish. But they're only found in Australia, New Zealand, and Southeast Asia. That's a long way away. Their venom is devastating. They've killed hundreds of people in Australia alone. I don't have the statistics for New Zealand or the rest of Southeast Asia. But one large sea wasp has enough venom in it to kill say, oh, sixty people."

"You're saying a sea wasp did this?"

"No, I'm not. What I'm saying is that only a sea wasp's venom can kill with so narrow an area of lesions like Spencer had. Yet he had enough venom in his blood to kill twenty men his height and weight. My mass spectrometer... that's for toxicology analysis... showed that clearly. Irrefutable. You won't find that in the coroner's report, though. It didn't correlate with the lesion damage. It didn't make sense. But it was there… a boatload of it in his blood and I found it." Chapman glanced off to a far wall.

Brannon's mouth opened but nothing came out. His fist slammed down on the steel table with a thundering crash that reverberated through the lab. He glanced from side to side, seeking some way to vent the anger that swelled up in him. His eyes bore down on Chapman. He was about to speak when the coroner continued.

"Look, I first noticed it at the hospital morgue. I… J.T., come in here, follow me." Chapman motioned as he stood, heading for a door in the far corner of the room. Brannon trailed, seething.

"You walk with a limp. What's wrong with the leg, arthritis, gunshot wound?" Chapman spoke over his shoulder.

"It's an old war story. You don't want to know."

Doug opened the door and they stepped in side-by-side. It was a small, tight back room. He turned on the light and reached for the handle on one of three large white freezers. He groped behind some boxes until he found a small package. Chapman backed up to a small table that held a microscope and sat down, looking somberly at J.T. as he opened the package and pulled out four slides. He slipped the first slide under the microscope.

"Mr. Brannon, this microscope has 1400X power. With it, I can look into structures at the cellular level. This is a tissue sample from the epidermis, the *stratum granulosum*, a sort of middle layer of the skin, affected by the lesions on Mr. Spencer's left calf. Go ahead, sit down and take a look. Tell me what you see."

"What am I looking for?" J.T. sat and squinted through the lens.

"Just tell me what stands out. What strikes you as different from the condition of the surrounding tissue?"

"Well, there's what looks like a huge round hole, a tear or something."

"Good. It's not a huge hole, though. Remember this is a 1400X power scope." Brannon nodded as Chapman changed the slide.

"Now, look at this one. Tell me again what you see."

"For one thing, the tissue cells look different from the other one?" Brannon squinted again.

"Good again. That's right and that's okay. This sample is from the lateral head of Mr. Spencer's *gastrocnemius muscle*, the calf muscle. It runs from the back of the knee to the ankle. What else do you see?"

"I see the same thing, that hole?"

"Thank you. That's it. I could show you the other two slides here, but they indicate the same thing. They're both from the lower dermis, *stratum spinosum*, or the bottom layer of derma."

J.T. watched motionless as Chapman pulled out the slide, turned off the lamp, and returned the slides to storage. He shook his head in puzzlement. Not until they were back in the lab could he voice his questions.

"Doug, what do you mean? What do the slides tell you? I don't get it."

"As I told you, Mr. Brannon, Mr. Spencer had enough Portuguese man-of-war poison in him to kill twenty men his size. The presence of that amount of venom is in no way consistent with the area of lesions. In my off-the-record and never-to-be-mentioned-again opinion, that hole is how it got there. The hole, actually a circular perforation, extends all the way down through the derma and muscle tissue. It's too perfect. It is too perfect and too deep." For the first time, Doug cracked a slight smile in self appreciation of his forensic powers. He did indeed know his business.

"What are you saying? Spit it out, Doug. Layman's terms." The muscles in Brannon's jaws tightened. His shoulders hunched, and his fingers curled into fists.

"I believe this clearly was a homicide, Mr. Brannon. A very cleverly executed homicide. But I will testify in no court, nor will I ever mention it to anyone again. Tony Spencer was, somehow, in some way, injected with a huge dose of Portuguese man-of-war venom. That's not just what I believe, that's what I know to be scientific, medical, absolute fact. This is the first time in my 35 year career I have ever omitted clinical observation from a report. This case scares the hell out of me. It terrifies me to think of the possibilities."

"But how could...?"

"How could it get there? You tell me. That's your job, I guess. According to the reports, Spencer was already sinking in the water. Scuba diver? Is that too far-fetched? I don't know, but I've had time to think about this. A diver could carry the jellyfish, say, in a plastic bag filled with saltwater. But what do they say about even best-laid plans? The damn things had already died! There was enough life left in the stinging cells to do some slight damage to Spencer's leg. But this is too much science fiction to take to court without a whole hell of a lot more, like a solid motive and a suspect or two. Nevertheless, that's what I think your two idiot colleagues really came down here for. They wanted to be damn sure of what my medical determination would be on the cause of death, not to express the CIA's condolences at the passing of one of its own."

His eyes wide, Brannon's mind raced wildly. How could it happen? He pictured a scuba diver, a diver using a re-breather tank so no telltale bubbles would rise to the surface, and approaching Tony through the inlet's waters. A diver could carry plastic bags of jellyfish and, of course, a syringe, a spring-loaded injector with enough cubic centimeters of venom to kill, and kill quickly. But approach from where? No, no, it just didn't make sense.

Then, through the angry fog engulfing him, J.T. heard young Tony Jr.'s voice. In his mind's eye, he saw the sport fisherman cruiser the boy had described trolling up and down the coast. They were there, just off the beach. The image struck him like a bolt of lightning, a flash of sudden light and instant understanding. *All day long,* Tony had said. Men on the deck fishing, or something else. No, those bastards were waiting for the right moment. Brannon's eyes glittered with rage.

"Shit! Fucking assholes!" Brannon shrieked at the top of his lungs. He pounded his foot into the tile floor.

"Sonsofbitches! I'll kill 'em… every one of them!"

Brannon's right fist repeatedly slammed onto the steel counter beside him. The lab echoed with his fury. His left hand swept a metal lab stool off its legs, sending it clattering, smashing across the floor into the wall. His right fist exploded through the small wooden door of cabinet above him. He turned back to Chapman, his face bright red and chest heaving.

Caught off guard by the sudden display of violence, Doug backed into the lab table behind him. A tray of test tubes shivered, then fell. The glass tubes spilt out into beakers and shattered on the steel countertop and across the floor. Chapman's bifocals slid down and teetered on the end of his nose. His mouth hung open in surprise. He didn't know what to expect next, and he gripped the lip of the counter behind him.

"These, these colleagues of mine. Doug, you didn't let on to them?"

J.T.'s voice no more than a low growl. He eyed the coroner cowering before him and tried to get a grip on his anger. Brannon relaxed his clenched fists and held his hands out reassuringly, palms down. The knuckles on his right hand were red with blood.

"It's okay, Doug, it's okay. I know this wasn't your doing. Did you, did you tell them what you just told me?"

"Hell no! Not on your life! I probably shouldn't have told you either! This damn thing just sticks in my craw. Then again, I don't want to end up a floater either. The Coast Guard's got enough to do. Look, J.T., whoever did this is very smart and has all the resources necessary to pull it off. They wouldn't think twice about doing me in either if it seemed necessary or just damned expedient."

"Doug..."

"Mr. Brannon... J.T., it's 07:30. This building will be filling up soon. I don't think it would be a good idea for anyone to see you here. You need to leave. Please"

Brannon approached him, his face still flushed. The passion had not yet left him. Still terrified, Chapman's first reaction was to back up another step. J.T. extended his hand, struggling to speak through his intense emotion.

"Doug, thank you. Thank you for everything. You're quite a guy. I'm going to take care of this in my own way, and in my own time. These bastards, whoever they are, will pay dearly, damn dearly. You can take that to the bank. Thanks for leveling with me."

"Your hand's bleeding. Take this." Chapman tossed him a towel. J.T. snatched it in mid-air, smiled, and turned toward the lab doors. He spun around on his heel.

"Oh, and look, here's my card. Call me at home if you ever need anything. It's the top number. If it's an emergency, use the second number. But Doug, that's a last resort, my 'hello' phone at the agency. Don't hesitate to call me, I mean it."

"Thanks. I, I understand. You're certainly a different sort,

J.T., different from the other two, I mean." They walked in silence to the lab's double doors where they shook hands again.

"Do you know where I can find the harbor master down here?"

"Harbor master? Sure, J.T., but you'll have to go back over to the island and drive north. He's up in Colington Harbor across from Kill Devil Hills. Name's Captain Brent Mason. A big, burly character, good-hearted though. Say, please don't tell him I sent you. You never know, huh?" Chapman managed a weak smile.

"Don't worry, Doug, I have your best interest at heart. And thanks, that's on my way back north. Doug, you take care now. Remember, if you need anything…" Brannon waved and jogged up the stairs as fast as his gimpy leg would take him.

He paused, sitting behind the wheel of the Chevy as sunlight poured down over Manteo and streamed through the alleyway, filling it with a warm glow. He stared out the windshield at the brick wall, jingling the car keys in his hand, mulling over Chapman's revelations.

He kept coming back down the same logic trail. The Russians never had the guts to kill someone here, never inside the USA. They knew we would retaliate too fiercely, hurt them too bad. Nor had they even shown any penchant for precision assassinations, *wet affairs*, as it was known in the business, anywhere in the world, for the last twenty years.

So who would dare? But, if he expanded the possibilities to include the Company itself? At the thought, Brannon shook his head. As Chapman had already figured out, they, whoever they were, had to have both the brains and the resources. The Company certainly filled those criteria. But what about motive? Why in the world kill Tony Spencer, one of their own, a loyal troop? Why, and after he'd already retired? Why would they consider Tony's leaving them so dangerous as the only option was to kill him? What was it that drove Tony to leave the service? Lose his faith? And, what could it have to do with Europe and, of all places, Denver?

He went over it yet again, reviewing every angle. Who else? There was no one else. If Pete Novak hadn't asked him to come down here, he would have come anyway. He was driven to do so. Tony's death had a rotten smell to it from the beginning.

It was the same foul stink of his near-fatal encounter in Egypt with the PFLP terrorists who had come out of nowhere. A Déjà Vu of horror... and possibly betrayal? The answers to his questions, the explanation behind all the confusion, were probably somewhere in Europe. Pete Novak was likely heading straight for it.

CHAPTER 14

The Outer Banks
North Carolina

Brannon reached under the Chevy's dash and pulled on a band of Velcro. The smooth, dark butt of a semi-automatic slipped into his hand. He bent around the steering wheel and strapped the ankle holster to the inside of his left leg. Cradling the pistol lovingly in his palm for a moment, he slipped out the magazine. He spun it around to ensure it was fully loaded, then snapped it back up the grip, slid it back in its leather sleeve and he pulled his pant leg back down over it with a sharp tug.

The pistol was a Walther PPKs, .380 ACP caliber, seven rounds. This had suddenly become a new ball game. Brannon was suiting up to play ball, hard ball. His opponents were not yet on the open field, but he'd find them. Oh, he'd find them. He turned the ignition key, revved the engine, and the SS-396 roared like an angry dragon. The green beast burst out of the lot and flew toward Rte. 64.

Just a tad after 8:30 a.m., he crossed the bridge from Kill

Devil Hills onto Colington Island and followed the signs to Colington Harbor. The harbor master's office was not hard to find. It was an old wooden lighthouse watching over the protected waters of the inlet. As Brannon entered the office on the first level, a large brute of a man in a white wool turtleneck turned to face him with a broad smile.

"What can I do for you, young fella? I'm Brent Mason. Like some coffee?" He spoke with a jolly chuckle in his voice and held a steaming mug of coffee.

"Thanks, I'll take you up on that. Just black, please. I need to ask you about a boat that might've been down here over Labor Day weekend. You keep a log?"

"Have to keep a log. It's the law. We talkin' about a *boat* or a *ship*? And tell me, why do you want to know?" Mason pulled a cup from a shelf and held it under the spigot of the coffee pot. Here you go."

"Thanks. Look, Mr. Mason… "

"That's Captain Mason. But please, call me Brent," The harbor master broke in, still smiling.

"Okay, Brent. My name's J.T. Brannon. I don't have a subpoena, no court order. I'm not the FBI, but this is a matter of life and death. You're the only one I can see who can help me. I really need to know about this boat."

"I see. Life and death, huh? You own a boat, a ragtop or stink pot, or maybe even a ship, Mr. J.T. Brannon?"

"No, Brent, and I'm dead serious. This is vitally important. Will you help me?"

Captain Mason leaned back against the big desk and looked Brannon over, still smiling and sipping his coffee.

"Okay, Mr. J.T. Brannon, you're a land-lubber. You found me way down here. Now that's something. You keep this just between us two and I'll see what I can do for you. What's the boat you say you're looking for? The name and registry? Who's the owner?" Mason moved to his desk, set his coffee down, rubbed his hands together, and reached for a pen and pad.

"Well, I don't know specifically, but… "

The harbor master plopped into his chair and twirled the ball-point pen. "J.T., how do you expect me to help you if you can't even…?"

"I know. I'm sorry to bother you with so little to go on. But I know where it would've come from, Brent, and when it would've been here."

"Maybe that'll work. Tell me what you know. Shoot." Mason looked up at him briefly, then reached into a lower desk drawer and pulled out a large black log book.

"It would've been here over Labor Day weekend. The way I figure, she probably left, uh, sailed, on the 4th, maybe the 5th. But the 4th's more likely. She would've been from northern Virginia. She was a cabin cruiser, had a flybridge. I'd say at least 40 feet or so. A sport fisherman, a nice one. I don't know what else I can tell you. Does that help any?"

He opened the log book and thumbed through page after page of scribbled entries.

"Let's take a look. Hmmm, okay, let's say the 3rd through the 5th. Northern Virginia. We had the *Star Catcher*, nope, she's out of Philly; the *Added Expense*, nuh-uh, she's from Bayville, Delaware. I'll just skip a lot of the boats I know from around here, the Carolina's and such. Nope, doesn't look too promising. Ah, J.T., what about Patuxent, Maryland? Is that close enough, or does it have to be Northern… "

"Patuxent? Yeah, that's great, maybe even better! You have something?" Brannon was at the Captain's desk in two steps. He craned his neck to read the scrawled notation. Yes, Patuxent. He didn't need to think twice about it. The good thing about

Patuxent was that, unlike being in a marina slip or moored somewhere up the Potomac River, you were already down at the southern tip of the Maryland peninsula. It had immediate access to the lower Chesapeake and the blue water of the Atlantic. You didn't have to sail all the way down some river to get to the Bay. Yes, Patuxent was perfect.

"Yes, we do. Lookie here, the *Moon Shadow* out of Patuxent, a Hatteras fiberglass sport fisherman, 42-footer, a nice big one. Whaddya think, J.T.?"

"*Moon Shadow*. Who's the registered owner? Brannon inched around the desk, sipping his coffee, and leaned over Mason's shoulder.

"Oh, I wouldn't have that here, just the skipper's signature. And, hell, I can't even read that myself. Let's see, yep, they bought a lot of gas here. 'Paid for everything in cash."

"Is that unusual?"

"Not really. A lot of folks with enough money to own a Hatteras that size carry around a wad of money when they're on a long sailing. It's not uncommon."

"Brent, is there any way to get the name of *Moon Shadow*'s registered owner?"

"Well, since it's you, J.T., you know, somebody I've never met before in my life and will probably never see again. I guess I just gotta do it for you! Right?" Mason's laugh was deep and hearty. He picked up the phone.

"Hey, Jennie? Captain Mason here. How about ringing up the skipper of the *Jackie Mae* for me, Commander Gary Allen. They're in the harbor today. Would you do that for me, darling? Thanks."

Jennie rang back in less than a minute. The harbor master explained what he needed, the Coast Guard commander readily agreed to his friend's request. But the indices search would take several hours. The two chatted for a few minutes, Mason thanked him and hung up.

"Did you get all that, J.T.? Commander Allen will run all that down and give me a call. Do you want to wait or can I get back to you? If you give me a number I'll try to let you know by tomorrow or so. Will that work?"

"I guess that'll do, Brent. I've got a lot to do, and it's a long drive back. You'll call me tomorrow?"

"Day after at the latest. Tomorrow's gonna be a busy one, first day of the week and all. Got my rounds to do. Don't worry, Mr. Brannon, we've gone this far. I'll get it to you." He stood, shaking J.T.'s hand as they walked out.

"Brent, I really appreciate this. Talk with you soon. Take care now."

"Ah, big boys and their toys!" Captain Mason murmured, watching the green Supersport tear out of the parking lot, scattering gravel around behind it. He smiled and shook his head.

The drive back up I-95 seemed to take no time at all. Consumed by his thoughts, Brannon didn't even turn the radio on. He whipped past the exit to Occoquan and Route 123, heading straight north to the I-395 Expressway. He shot over the 14th Street Bridge into the city of Washington.

A few minutes later he swung the Chevy into a parking slot on 17th Street in front of a gray marble building. He went through the glass doors and down the hall to a door that sported the glossy image of a black, red, and yellow flag. Over the door, large white, emboldened letters read: *Deutsche Tages Schau* – the German Daily News. The lights were on inside, but when he rattled the metal handle, it was locked. It was Sunday, almost two o'clock in the afternoon.

Brannon cupped his hands and peered through the smoked glass. A young woman in blue jeans walked through the inner office and stopped when she noticed him. She warily opened the door a crack.

"*Wir sind geschlossen…*" she then repeated in English, "I'm sorry, but we're closed," but spoken with a heavy German accent. Brannon reached out as the door closed and held it. Her eyes bore down on him.

"*Entschuldigen, aber ist Herr Schneider noch da?* 'Excuse me, but is Mr. Schneider still in?'

"Yes, Mr. Schneider's in his office. Come in please!" Her blue eyes opened wide, surprised at Brannon's use of German. She respectfully nodded. The door opened wide and her voice was suddenly gentler.

"*Vielen danks.*" J.T. stepped inside.

The woman glanced up and down the empty hall with a fair degree of caution, then closed and locked the door.

CHAPTER 15

Montreal
Quebec, Canada

The *Quebec L'Autobus Express* was a misnomer. The route was a milk run. Bus stops at every mile marker. Laszlo was content with the monotonous ride south. It gave him time to rest. He made it by the very skin of his teeth. For the first time since leaving Frankfurt, he could relax. His elation at eluding capture had faded into exhaustion.

He knew it wouldn't take long for the CIA to pick up his scent. They would most certainly enlist the assistance of the Royal Canadian Mounted Police, their Counterintelligence Division. But with so many possibilities, at least for the next few hours they would be relatively clueless as to his whereabouts.

Laszlo yawned, pushing his head deeper into the seat's coarse fabric. He'd slept very little on the flight from Paris, and had even expected arrest when he landed in Montreal. But the CIA's intelligence machinery must have been caught off guard and energized too slowly. That was the only explanation for his slipping through their grip.

He figured that the SVR would become resigned to accept their losses and back off. He was well off the Russians' operating turf now. Continuing to track him in North America could be very hazardous for them. The political risks far outweighed any possible gains. Other than notifying their Rezidenturas in Montreal and the Washington embassy to be alert, the game of running down Laszlo was now probably over for the SVR.

On the other hand, Laszlo knew very well the CIA could ill afford to give up on him. They'd missed their best shot at wrapping him up in Europe. In the bahnhof. Not only would it be more difficult to localize him now, but they also knew he was getting dangerously close. But only Laszlo himself knew how close he really was, how much he really knew.

By now the CIA would be forced to assume the worst. They would kill him at the first opportunity to protect their deep black project. So black in the revelation of a high-technology breakthrough that the Americans believed it would change the face of warfare on the planet forever.

His fatigue gave in to the soothing motion of the bus's wheels. It was like the rolling of a ship on a river. Laszlo drifted into a light sleep. His body was grateful for the rest. But as was more often the case than not, his mind crept slowly elsewhere, prompting the images that always came floating up out of his memory.

His head lolled against the seat cushion. His lips parted into a smile as he strolled under a summer sun at the historic park in Budapest. The fragrances of blooming flowers and the leaves of other greenery filled his senses. This time the demons were in another place. He drifted.

Laszlo's eyes opened suddenly at a rough jostling and his REM-sleep dream quickly faded. The man seated across the aisle had leaned over and nudged him at the sound of the bus driver's announcement.

"Messieurs and mes dames, all departing at Ste. Martine, please come forward." The speaker on the ceiling crackled. The bus jerked to a stop, the door hissing as it opened.

"Monsieur, I'm sorry to wake you but I didn't want you to miss your stop." The man offered apologetically as he rose to depart.

"Oh? Thank you." The cobwebs left Laszlo's head. He wiped his eyes and sat up. He saw the sign over the driver's seat flashing for Ste. Martine.

"I'm okay, but thanks. My stop is a bit further on... St. Antoine-Abbé." He laid his head back, still somewhat stunned at the abrupt awakening.

"Okay, mon ami. Have a safe trip. 'Bye." The man disappeared out the door.

"Next stop, Ste. Clothilde."

The door closed. It was followed by a short blast of the horn as the bus lurched forward. Once again, Laszlo settled in the seat. He closed his eyes. The quiet hum of the passengers speaking in both French and English droned out the noise of the engine. His vision once again blurred to the exhaustion overwhelming him. His lingering fatigue carried him quickly back to the twilight of sleep.

Blind to the blur of countryside passing in the windows, he was in and out of a dreamy state all along the journey, despite the occasional rough bump in the road. Hazy visions dimmed in the clouds of his dreams, time flowed into time, and Laszlo's smiles crinkled his lips. His head slumped to the side and bumped the window as the bus made the U-turn at Ste. Clothilde. His eyes creased open. He yawned, stretching out his arms.

"Messieurs and mes dames, all departing at Ste. Clothilde,

please come forward." The speaker on the ceiling crackled again. The driver drawled the words in obvious fatigue. The bus halted abruptly, the hissing of the door again filling the cabin as it opened.

"The next and last stop will be in approximately forty minutes… St. Antoine Abbé." Three passengers exited down the stairs, only a few remaining on the bus.

As the bus pulled ahead, Laszlo leaned back into the seat cushion. Barely awake, his mind wandered once more while the bus rolled down the Route 209. The sun was peeking in and out of the clouds, warming his face. He breathed deeply and settled into the seat as the dream in the park resumed.

A softly uttered moan escaped him as the bus lurched violently. A white Chevy Blazer, also heading south, roared past the bus and had swung abruptly in front it. The driver slammed on the brakes, sending passengers and luggage flying.

Laszlo jerked awake, bewildered. He struggled to identify his surroundings… no longer in the park. No longer in Budapest. No longer in the old times. He shook his head, slouched back in his seat and rubbed the sleep out of his eyes. He stared out the window.

"Messieurs and mes dames, I apologize for that idiot driver. Such fools. Well, we are now entering the city limits of St. Antoine-Abbé. I will make a final stop in the town center and then return the bus to the station."

The driver slowed the bus to a crawl and stopped at an intersection. As it moved forward again, Laszlo sat up in his seat. A smile inched across his face. He was getting closer to the demon by the hour.

CHAPTER 16

Special Air Mission Flight 711
Over the Eastern Atlantic

T he steward leaned over and gently shook Pete's shoulder. Pete stirred. He opened his eyes and strained to see in the dim light of the cabin. The sunshine once beaming in from the window had long disappeared. He leaned to the window and saw the tops of white clouds below illuminated by moonlight. Raising his hands to rub his eyes, the red folder on his lap slipped to the floor. Pete turned to the steward standing over him.

"Oops! I'm sorry. Thanks for waking me. How long, uh, what time is it?" he bent forward to retrieve the file.

"About 7:30, sir. We're over the Channel now, about an hour out of Frankfurt. We'll be passing over the French coastline in a minute or so, just north of Calais."

"Seven-thirty! I must have really slept."

"You did, sir, and I didn't want to wake you. Five and a half hours in the air, and a five-hour time change going to Frankfurt. I thought you might need the sleep. I hope I didn't ..."

"Oh, no. Don't worry about it. I'm just surprised I could sleep that long."

"Thanks. Sir, would you care for some coffee, cookies or something, before we start the descent to Frankfurt? Oh, and do you want me to shred that report for you now?"

"I'll take you up on the coffee and cookies, but give me about ten minutes to go over the file one last time before we shred it, okay?"

"Sure thing, sir. Coffee's coming right up."

Pete flipped on the overhead reading lights and leaned back into the seat. He opened the red-covered folder again and skimmed for a final look. The brainchild of the operations directorate, the STALKER program utilized every possible methodology and hyperlinked database technology to identify a set of highly reliable indicators. These were indicators that would lead to uncovering deep-cover foreign intelligence operatives. The pony-tailed software wizards they brought in to do the job had done well. They combined a series of interlocking matrices linked to various databases provided by the Company's own analysts as well as from friendly western intelligence services.

From an analysis of correlations in the information, hypotheses were formed, programmed into a software application, and loaded onto the Company's mainframe system. Finally, actual data was plugged in. The resulting massive program summarized the experiences of numerous intelligence services in unearthing deep-cover agents, illegals, moles. It included all the indicators that could be realistically gathered... the tradecraft used by the opposition service in initial placement of the illegal, handling and servicing of their spy, factors that had led to the initial discovery, customs file data, and defector information where it could be credibly relied upon. But STALKER's biggest coup was the analysis of data from post-mortem analyses of espionage cases discovered too late after damage had already been done.

A little over a year and a half ago, STALKER had identified an old, grandmotherly woman, an unlikely intelligence courier to be sure, who was traveling into Germany every four months. She was servicing an illegal Russian agent operating under the nose of the Germans in a ministry-level department. For almost a year, the Company watched and patiently waited. This strategy was politically risky, but it paid off handsomely.

The old woman eventually led her surveillants to who was now believed to be the SVR's most cherished mole. He had gained access to something enticingly big. He had been tentatively identified as an operative of the SVR's Second Main Directorate, Eighth Section – Illegals Apparatus.

The mole was operating in Germany under the cover name Kurt Kalmbach and living in a small second-floor apartment in Dörnigheim, a small, outlying suburb to the east of Frankfurt on the Main River. With the full capability of the STALKER program's database and a surveillance command post assembled in Dörnigheim, the illegal's true identity had been determined. He was positively identified as a Hungarian working for the Russians who had been arrested by U.S. Army Military Intelligence (MI) in Trieste, Italy.

Pete set the coffee cup down. He flipped the pages to the target profile itself. STALKER identified Laszlo with an existing Army intelligence file of some two thousand pages. The man's history read like a gloomy medieval novel. The details had been wrenched from his mind, pieced together during nine months of solitary incarceration and savage beatings in a U.S. Army MI interrogation camp secreted in the forested mountains of Bavaria, south of Munich. The executive summary in STALKER summarized nearly two thousand pages of interrogation text in only two and a half pages. It struck at the core of Pete's emotions.

Laszlo was the son of well-to-do parents, Dr. Semmi and

Katka Csengerny. Both were killed in a tragic train crash in southern France. The child was one year old. His grandmother, Margo Csengerny, raised him through his early years. The boy was terrorized by nightmares of gruesome demons who he believed killed his parents and who would be coming for him as well.

Months of intensive psychotherapy had no beneficial effect. About the time Laszlo was turning eleven, his grandmother was at the same time becoming too infirm to care for him properly. The 'State' stepped in and assumed custody. He was placed in a state-run children's home where he did somewhat better initially.

He was extremely gifted, in fact brilliant. Socially, the youngster was impaired. The boy terrified other children and even the staff with his screaming nightmares and tales of demons. As a makeshift solution, they gave him his own room in the attic, but in the middle of the night his wild shrieks still echoed down the halls of the building, unnerving everyone.

Laszlo felt so desperately out of place, so unwanted. One late spring night, under the wet fabric of a light drizzle, the boy packed some clothes and slipped out of the home, never to return. They never saw Laszlo again. The rest is fuzzy speculation until the time of his arrest by Army MI.

Bouncing around throughout Eastern Europe, SVR 'spotters' took an interest in his wandering ways. Laszlo was eventually vetted, recruited and trained by the Russians. His first handler directed him to move to Trieste, Italy, and apply to enter the U.S. Army Alien Enlistment Program that offered eventual, naturalized citizenship. Laszlo coerced two accomplices to assist him with threats against their families in Hungary. In a sweep by MI agents, Laszlo and his accomplices were arrested. The other two men confessed, were given just months of jail time in Italy and deported. Laszlo, an extremely intelligent and devious man, however resisted. He was flown to a secret intelligence camp in the Bavarian Alps at Unterwössen.

Interrogators noted Laszlo's horrific nightmares, especially after injections of sodium pentothal. Placed in isolation, his nighttime screams were far from the ears of other prisoners. Nine months of brutal interrogation eventually forced his confession and then he too was jailed in an Army detention facility and eventually deported back to Italy.

Laszlo reinitiated contact with his SVR brethren and a classic insertion operation moved him with several sets of identity documents through several countries, three towns, numerous jobs, and two planned, back-to-back marriages and divorces. He was eventually back in business in Frankfurt five years later. In an incredible turn of events, Laszlo had discovered something so astonishing that the Russians were drooling in amazement. Ironically, it was the SVR's own courier who unwittingly led surveillants to Laszlo.

A routine surveillance took a deadly turn two days ago. After some kind of confrontation in Frankfurt, three Company men were on their way home in body bags. Details were scarce. Langley Center assessment was that Laszlo was the killer, though it was equally possible that a SVR counter-surveillance team may have been too determined to protect their investment.

Bill Nordheimer has admitted the situation is unstable. The DCI was livid. The Company had tried to communicate discreetly with its SVR counterparts without involving the White House or Kremlin, but so far Moscow was being tight-lipped. Without admitting to anything, the SVR had at least agreed to a truce. And now, here was Pete Novak on a plane to Germany to try to clean up the mess.

Pete shook his head. He didn't like it. Though handy with a variety of weapons, he had never been trained as a field agent. He didn't regret that for a moment. This current predicament reeked of the old violent, gory days of the Cold War. Pete's expertise lay in analysis. He was gifted in determining the crucial factors upon which an adversary's decision making apparatus would pivot. In this arena, Company superiors told him he was brilliant.

He had done so well indeed that young Novak was thrust into the upper strata of the Company far ahead of his contemporaries. Still struggling with his own style and his vision for Company operational priorities, he nevertheless impressed all of those in the community with whom he worked. Pete reached up to dim the overhead lights and swallowed the last of his coffee as the steward marched down the aisle.

"Sir, we're approaching Frankfurt and Rhein Main Air Base. If you look out the left window, you'll see a long winding string of lights – that's actually the highway by the Mosel River. Look hard and you can probably see the river, that dark line next to the lights. That big cluster of lights you see to the north is the city of Koblenz."

"Thanks. Pretty, isn't it?"

"Yes, sir. Sir, we need to shred that document now if we're going to. May I?"

"Oh sure, here it is. Thanks for everything. You've been great."

Pete stood to stretch. He quickly sat back down as the plane dropped altitude for its approach to Rhein Main Air Base. In minutes, they were on the ground, taxiing to the terminal. As the aircraft pulled into its parking slot, the young steward came down the aisle carrying Pete's overcoat and a small bundle.

"Mr. Novak, here are your things. The bags will be loaded directly into the limo. Would you like to arm yourself now?"

Pete started to say "No, leave it on the plane," but caught himself. Brannon's words echoed above the diminishing roar of the jet engines and rammed like hot irons into his brain, *Watch your Six!* If J.T. was concerned for his safety on this trip, then maybe he should be too.

"Ah, okay, let me have the shoulder holster. Say, nice DeSantis slant-rig holster."

"That's right, sir. The best."

Pete took off his jacket and laid it on the seat back, then put his arms through the soft suede shoulder loops and slipped it smoothly over his head. With his right hand, he unsnapped the release button on the holster, and with practiced ease, pulled out the Walther pistol, jerked the slide back, and locked it. The cold metal-to-metal sound caused the steward to blink. Pete examined the empty chamber and cleared the weapon's breach, then released the slide, ramming back into the breach. Pete took a magazine from the steward and jammed it in the butt of the Walther pistol. He pulled the slide back once more, chambering a bullet, and with a satisfied click, the pistol was ready to fire. He released the cocked hammer with his thumb, gently lowering it back to the closed position. Last, he flicked the safety release, ensuring it was locked. He looked back at the steward and held out his hand for the extra magazines. The steward's eyes were wide, amazed at Pete's sure handling of the pistol.

Pete stepped on to the gantry into the chilly night air. He set his briefcase down on the metal platform and took a deep gulp of air. His frosty exhale blew away in the brisk wind. The roar of jet engines assaulted his ears. The ramp area was brightly lit.

Rhein Main was a busy air base any time of day or night, the hub of U.S. Air Force operations in Europe. In the distance, across several pairs of runways, he could see the international airport, the Frankfurt Flughafen, which shared runways with the air base. Pete picked up his briefcase and looked at his watch. The pilot appeared behind him, carrying a nylon hang-up bag.

"Precisely 8:43 p.m., local time, sir. Your car will be here in a moment. They're over at the passenger lounge right now. I hope you enjoyed the flight, Mr. Novak," the lieutenant colonel extended his right hand. Pete switched the briefcase to his left hand and shook the pilot's hand firmly.

"I did indeed. Thanks a lot. It's good to know you guys are on our side!"

"Well, thanks. That's always good to hear. By the way, we'll be in town a couple of days before we head back. If you're still here and need to get back, just have somebody give Base Operations a call. We'll hold the plane for you as long as we can. Enjoy Germany. *Aufwiedersehen!*" The pilot clambered down the stairs, waving his hand over his head.

"Thanks. I may take you up on that. And, *aufwiedersehen* to you too!" Pete stepped cautiously down the stairs.

A black Mercedes raced across the ramp toward the jet. The car screeched to a halt in front of the gantry. A man in a dark overcoat leaped out of the front passenger's seat, leaving his door open.

"Mr. Novak, sir?"

"Yep, that's me. You Bill Nordheimer's folks?" Pete stepped off the gantry, glad to feel the ground under his feet again.

"No, sir, Frankfurt Consulate. RSO, Regional Security Office. Mr. Brannon... "

"Here we go. Okay, I know, Mr. Brannon, Mr. Brannon." Pete bent over and climbed in.

"Sir?"

"Nothing. Thanks a lot. I appreciate the service. Where is Mr. Brannon taking us now?"

"As soon as I get your bags in the trunk, we'll take you to the Frankfurt Intercontinental, over on Wilhelm-Leuschner Strasse. Nice place. You'll like it. That's where Mr. Br... "

"Where Mr. Brannon wanted me. I know." The armored rear door closed with a solid *thunk*.

The streamlined limo sped out of the Rhein Main front gate toward the autobahn access road. It roared up the ramp, accelerating quickly into traffic on Autobahn E-4 north to Frankfurt. Pete watched from the back seat as the speedometer neared 145 kilometers per hour.

"Say fellas, what's the rush? How fast are we going anyway?"

"No rush, sir. We're doing about 145 kilometers an hour. That's only about 85 miles an hour. We're just keeping up with traffic, Mr. Novak. Over here, if you don't do at least 80 on the autobahns, the Germans will run right over you."

"'Only 85 miles an hour... I see. No problem. Thanks."

The man with the overcoat in the right front seat spoke, turning his head slightly. The man reached back, handing Pete a small piece of paper.

"Mr. Novak, you've got a phone back there. If you want to call Mr. Nordheimer at home, here's his number. He's on the Consulate net."

"Thanks." Pete grabbed the black phone. He heard three rings before the receiver was lifted.

"Hello?"

"Yes, hello. Bill? This is Pete Novak."

"Hey, hi Pete. How's the flight? You must be up front, I don't even hear the engines. Look, we're all set up for you. My folks will meet you in an hour and a half or so right at the flughafen's concourse gate and take you over to the hotel. Got you registered in the Steinberger Hotel on Kaiserplatz, really a nice place. Anyway, I'll see... "

"Bill, that's why I called you at home. I'm already here, in Frankfurt. At the last minute, I took advantage of a Company flight that was already scheduled. Saves a little money for the budget guys this way, you know. I'm in the Intercontinental. I hope I didn't cause you any trouble."

"I see. No, no problem. What's next, Pete?" A pregnant pause. Nordheimer finally spoke.

"Well, when would you like to see me in the morning?"

Another pause. "Oh, about eight o'clock. I'll have the coffee on, unless of course you're planning on bringing your own. We'll pick you up, ah… seven-thirty or so in the lobby." The tone reflected Nordheimer's displeasure.

"That's fine, Bill. See you then. Good talking to you. Goodnight." Nordheimer's phone clicked off somewhere between *Good* and *night*.

"Well, that's a great way to kick things off," he muttered under his breath.

"What's that, sir?"

"Just thinking to myself."

CHAPTER 17

Vienna
Northern Virginia

The engine whined as the green SS-396 shot across Teddy Roosevelt Bridge from Washington into Virginia and onto I-66 West. It was near three o'clock in the afternoon. Brannon was starved. He'd missed lunch, so he'd concentrate on getting an early dinner. He knew his friend Schneider at the German news bureau would follow through for him. Pete would be warned.

With a notice to Pete taken care of, J.T. needed some time to think over the weekend's revelations. His tires squealed around the exit ramp and onto Nutley Road, which fed into Maple Avenue, just minutes from home. Downshifting into third, he cruised up Maple, letting the big V-8 cool down.

The Chevelle Super Sport crept into the garage purring like a tiger. Brannon climbed out and stretched. He hit the wall switch, sending the door rattling down and plunging the garage into darkness. He really should replace that light bulb. He suddenly froze in place, cocking his head to listen. Something was beeping, loud enough that he could hear it inside the darkened garage.

J.T. sank into a crouch and slid the pistol from his ankle holster. With care, he silently opened the door to the kitchen. He eased up the three steps, the pistol's muzzle leading. The only sound was the sharp beeping echoing through the empty room. He tiptoed with the stealth of a cat through the kitchen and paused, listening, then continued into the living room. His eyes swept the room, finally coming to rest on the sofa table. It was the answering machine.

Brannon laughed out loud at his own paranoia, shaking his head as he stood. Still, moving from room to room, he checked the doors and windows. They were all secure. Brannon slumped onto the couch, set the pistol on the table, and pressed the playback button on the recorder. Easing into the seat, he jerked back up at the panicky, frantic tone of the recorded voice. It was Doug Chapman. His eyes widened as the shrill outburst filled the room.

"Brannon! Brannon! Where the hell are you? Brannon, this is Chapman, Doug Chapman! They tore my place apart! Ripped it up! I just walked over to the hospital cafeteria for lunch, and dammit! They trashed the lab. Glass everywhere, beakers, test tubes, all of it! Specimens scattered all over the floor. What the hell am I supposed to do now? Come on, you've got to help me! Tell me what I should do, dammit! J.T., you said you'd help!"

Brannon leaned forward, still aghast at the terrified voice. A long pause followed, then Chapman continued, more composed.

"They missed the stuff though, J.T. They missed it. Assholes probably didn't even know what they were looking for. I found my beach house ransacked the same way. 'Tore all to hell. So look, J.T., I'm outta here. If you want the stuff, it'll be right where I showed you. Listen, you get these sonofabitches. I'll call you in a couple of days. I'm going to my brother's house.

Dammit, I can't even call the cops! Shit! I'll call again. I'm outta here!"

The machine beeped once more, and the tape began to rewind, hissing softly in the still silent house. J.T. was stunned. He listened again, not believing what he heard. Pacing in circles, he spoke out loud to the empty room.

"Doug! Why in hell did you have to say where you're going? Gees, that was stupid! Over an open line! You told them right where to find you! Dammit, fella, you'd better hustle your ass outta there! And check your six."

Brannon's voice trailed off, knowing it was probably too late. That is, unless Chapman was slicker and had more savvy than he had let on. But no, Doug would leave a big trail. Maybe his brother had a different name. And no, that was wishful thinking too. He stood in place as the thought struck him. Well, if they had Chapman, whoever *they* were, then chances were good they had him too.

Brannon's hand cradled his chin in a pensive pose. He was positive there was no surveillance on him when he left Virginia. He was certain of that. He was clean. But, they could have had a team on the Cape, watching Chapman, just for insurance.

"Damn!" He blurted.

J.T. briskly jogged into the bedroom, throwing open the closet door. A small overnight suitcase sailed onto the bed, rapidly followed by several shirts and pants. He needed to do something. And fast. He didn't know what, but knew deep in his gut that now he couldn't safely stay in the house. Tony Spencer was dead because he'd let his defenses down. Well, not him. He just prayed Chapman was smart enough to get as far away as possible. To disappear.

He retrieved socks and underwear from the dresser and stuffed them into the suitcase. He took time to fold a jacket neatly on top. Then, bending over the bed, he paused to consider. He dropped on all fours and grasped under the bed until he felt the handle of the black ballistic nylon weapons bag. It too was thrust up on the bed. On his knees, he unzipped it, and first pulled out a fat five-inch black tube – silencer for the Walther pistol. He stuffed it in his jacket.

Still rummaging, he next found a smaller black pistol bag… a Heckler & Koch P9, 9-millimeter with a seven-round magazine, a shoulder holster too. He dug down for two boxes of ammunition, one .380 ACP and one 9mm. Slipping the holster over his shoulders, he jammed the H&K pistol into the molded leather holster, plus two spare magazines in their pouches.

His hands and eyes again searched the bag… anything he might find necessary. He raised his eyebrows and smiled. He lifted the slender black object slowly into the light with both hands and quiet ceremony. He held it up for an instant, admiring it before unsnapping the retainer band and drawing the handle out of the black leather sheath. Its polished edges flashed even in the pale light.

His Special Forces dagger. Eight and a half inches of thick, razor-sharp titanium steel, double-edged with one edge serrated like shark's teeth. Nasty. On more than one occasion, he'd been caught in hand-to-hand combat in the Laotian mountains, and this knife was all that stood between him and meeting his Maker.

He slid the blade back in the sheath, snapped it shut, and stuck it under his belt. Next, he snatched a small black-handled hatchet, a twin matched to the dagger. Last time he'd tried, he could hit a bull's eye twenty yards away with it. The hatchet also slipped under his belt.

Brannon stored the weapons bag back under the bed and fastened the latches on his suitcase. He walked, near jogged back to the garage and heaved the suitcase into the trunk. One last quick pass through the house to turn off the lights. He backed the Chevelle into the street and pulled away. He grabbed his shoulder holster, ensuring it was secure. Something told him he was going to need it.

CHAPTER 18

Vienna
Northern Virginia

As Brannon's SS-396 turned the corner at the end of the block, he saw the dark blue Camaro. Nice, but he didn't think the new ones looked remotely like the Camaros he once used to love. It was parked tight against the opposite curb just around the corner. Without appearing to notice, he made out two men, maybe three, just sitting. Waiting. They didn't appear to be in conversation.

J.T. throttled past them and turned south on Maple, edging the SS-396 into the left lane. He accelerated to 40 mph. He checked the rear and side-view mirrors. There they were, the Camaro nosing up to turn the corner, also turning south.

Brannon's foot went down, the dual four-barrel carburetors growled, and the Chevelle leaped up to 55 mph. And yet, the distance between him and the Camaro was narrowing. They were staying in the right lane and accelerating rapidly.

Nutley Road was the next traffic light. The Camaro was

about a block and a half back but still moving up fast. As he approached the intersection, the light flicked to yellow.

"Shit!" he muttered, downshifting. The engine jolted and tires screeched, leaving a trail of black rubber and blue smoke. Brannon took the left turn hard and fast, skidding through the turn. He straightened her out and stepped on it. The engine snarled, screaming as he slammed through the gears, opening her up. He anxiously glanced ahead and behind. No cops anywhere.

As the SS-396 hit 80 mph, he smiled, patting the dash. "Good, baby, good," he said, looking back as he crested a small rise.

Brannon's brow furrowed as the Camaro reappeared in the rear-view mirror... hot on it. They had made the turn, leaving a cloud of burning rubber. He whispered "Okay, boys, let's see what you got." J.T. inched the Chevy up to 90 mph, then edged over 100, literally flying over the I-66 overpass.

Now headed downhill, he swung the car first to the right as he approached Lee Highway. He had the green light. At the last second, he swerved to the outer turn lane and came back hard, sailing past a van and a small car and roaring through the turn. Someone's horn blasted behind him. He throttled the engine up again for the long climb up the hill on Lee Highway.

He checked the rear-view again. The blue Camaro ran the light, swerving wildly to miss a pick-up truck. There was no question in Brannon's mind now – these guys obviously wanted to get to know him. In mechanical fashion, his right hand found the seat belt strap and yanked it snugly across his hips.

Brannon downshifted to third and stepped on it. The big V-8 roared like a pride of angry lions and the Chevy approached 100, then 110, 115 mph, racing up the hill toward the circle intersection with Route 50. Cars were crowding the intersection ahead. He saw nothing but brake lights. Damn. Nope, he couldn't go that way! The SS-396 jumped left into the outside turn lane, screeching to a sudden halt.

Several cars in the oncoming lane were bearing down on him. No time to reflect. He popped the clutch, and the Chevy lurched over the dividing median. Horns blared, tires thumped, and the Chevy's rear bumper bottomed out, scattering a hail of sparks. The Super Sport launched into the plaza's parking lot.

Immediately, J.T. jerked the wheel to the right, skimming around the edge of the parking lot to the opposite exit on Route 50. He gunned it on through as that light turned red. An old Buick SUV dug hard into the asphalt as he swung in front. He accelerated down Arlington Boulevard, jamming through the gears. The Chevelle SS-396 responded with the throaty whining of its dual exhausts.

Brannon settled into his seat. The odometer clicked past one mile, then another. He checked the rear-view. He saw nothing. Did he lose them in the circle intersection? Well, they couldn't be professionals. At the next light, Prosperity Road, he eased up on the gas, slowed the Chevelle, and downshifted to swing smoothly through the right turn. The Chevy settled near 40.

He cruised up and down Prosperity Road's gentle roller-coaster hills. This stretch was heavily wooded, no shoulder on either side of the road. He continually checked his mirrors, but saw nothing. J.T. shrugged, stretched his neck side to side. He wiggled down in the bucket seat, allowing himself a small sigh of relief. He took the next right on Route 236, west on Little River Turnpike. The next traffic light, Guinea Road, was red. The Super Sport pulled into the left-turn lane, idling while Brannon waited for the green arrow.

His eyebrows rose suddenly as he heard the engine's loud wail and screeching of tires long before he saw the car in the mirror. The Camaro cut through the corner gas station at the Prosperity light. It burst out through the low hedges that rimmed the lot, scattering branches, dirt, and leaves everywhere. It exploded over the curb, flew through the air and bounced harshly onto the street. It slid in front of east-bound traffic before swerving and accelerating hard to the west.

"Shit." No waiting now. Brannon simultaneously gunned the engine, jammed the stick, and popped the clutch. The SS-396 blew through the intersection. Angry horns blared from every direction as the wide Polyglass tires spun through the turn. A trail of blue-white smoke rose up toward the traffic light. He closed his eyes for what seemed a long eye blink as a white Cadillac sedan brushed just inches from the Chevelle's front end, its horn trumpeting. He made it. Not a scrape.

J.T. ran through the gears, leaving strips of black on the road with every shift of the gears. The smell of burnt rubber inundated the air. The Chevy howled at 70, 80, then over 100, 110 miles per hour down Guinea Road. The speedometer needle fire-walled at 120. In the mirror, he watched the Camaro make the turn about a quarter mile behind him.

"Nope, no amateurs here," he muttered. The SS-396 dashed down Guinea Road, a long thoroughfare winding generally south. He blew through yet another red light. He couldn't remember how many that was now. The SS-396 slowed somewhat for the sharp turn west onto Braddock Road, then throttled up again. The V-8 was bellowing like an enraged dragon. The speedometer was fire-walled again.

He wound up and down the twisting hills on Braddock Road, blurring the long barrier of roadside trees that guarded the George Mason University campus to his right. He could hear horns wailing in the distance – the Camaro was still coming. J.T. needed a couple of short choppy turns to get out of sight, to lose them.

The Chevy veered sharply left, skidding through a turn onto Sideburn Road. A few houses passed and then on the right was another street. He swung back over right, tires squealing as he downshifted hard through third, then into second. He cruised down Portsmouth Road in second, maintaining about 30 mph past rows of upscale Colonial brick homes with manicured lawns.

This wasn't too far from Pete's home, he thought, just a few blocks away. Brannon scanned the street, looking for the right opportunity. There, on his right – no privacy fence, no cars in the driveway. Maybe, just maybe…

The Chevy halted abruptly. Brannon looked up and down the street to be sure no one was observing, then grabbed the wheel with both hands and turned it as far to the right as it would go. He kept turning hard about as he gunned the engine. It snarled back, and the Super Sport leaped up and over the curb, the sidewalk, and then onto the still-green lawn. The light rear end bounced up the lawn. It couldn't help but send clumps of grass and rich brown topsoil shooting out from under the rear wheels.

"Damn!" He ripped around the front edge of the house, pulled along the side toward the rear, and then… as he stood on the brakes, the Chevy slid through the grass to a stop. Two elms and a magnolia blocked him at the back corner of the house. There was no way to get around them and into the backyard to hide! The Super Sport was caught, wedged in the narrow space between two houses. Brannon eased his foot off the brake pedal. He turned off the ignition and twisted his body around to peer out the back window.

What seemed to be at least five minutes, like the slow tick of a clock. Maybe he'd lost them? Maybe they had missed his turn onto Sideburn Road, much less the second one onto Portsmouth? Maybe, ah… but no such luck! He heard the roar of an engine.

The blue Camaro barreled by the house at high speed, moving way too fast for its passengers to spot him.

But would they come back? To be safe, he'd give it another couple minutes. A bead of sweat trickled into his right eye, its salt burning, and he reached up to wipe it. As he did, his eyes caught a movement in the rear-view mirror. It was a slow moving patch of blue.

"Dammit! Who the hell are these guys?!" he shouted to himself.

Noticing the tracks dug into the lawn, the driver of the Camaro pulled to the curb across the street. They had him. A door opened. J.T could see the pistol in the man's hand as he pushed the front seat and jumped out from behind the driver. Instinctively, he ducked as three ear-piercing reports echoed up and down the street. The rear window of the Chevelle shattered, jagged glass slivers blew up and into the front bucket seats.

The first two bullets left neat exit holes in the windshield just under the rear view mirror. Brannon jerked his body sideways against the door. The third round exploded through the passenger seat and into the glove box, spraying splinters of black plastic.

J.T. reached up for the H&K pistol, unsnapping the shoulder holster with a flick of his thumb. He glanced over the headrest, considering his options. The shooter was bending down into the rear seat and pulling out what looked like an AR-15 rifle! Brannon recognized the flared sights at the end of the barrel. A second man had emerged from the Camaro's right front seat and fired twice over its roof. Both rounds thudded into the Chevelle's trunk.

Brannon knew he was mincemeat if the shooter opened up on full auto with the AR-15. He could almost feel the bullets tearing the flesh off his bones. It was Cairo all over again. Only this time, it would probably be for keeps. Unless… a vision of Tony Spencer's body floating in the water flashed through his mind.

No! No fucking way. He would not let it happen to him! He glanced back again. It was now or never! J.T. dropped the pistol in his lap, firing the ignition and revving the V-8 until it redlined. It was screaming. The roar of the engine drowned out all thought. He rammed the gearshift into reverse and popped the clutch. The Chevelle shrieked.

At the sudden sound, the shooter turned his head. The magazine of ammo in his left hand fell to the road as he twisted himself around. The driver saw it coming. He suddenly pushed his seat back and grabbed frantically for the ignition key. The shooter fell to his knees, scrambling to retrieve the magazine.

The Super Sport raced down the grassy slope in reverse, swerving slightly to the right and then the left. Brannon struggled not to overcorrect. The wheels spun furiously, spitting out grass and chunks of topsoil. The shooter with the rifle stood up, feverishly trying to slam the magazine into the AR-15. The Camaro's driver twisted the ignition key to fire the engine, stomping on the gas, but quickly flooding it. The Camaro stalled.

The Chevelle SS-396 went airborne over the curb, heading straight for the Camaro. The man again dropped the magazine and raised the rifle in front of him as if to block the Chevy's onslaught. His mouth was open. If he was screaming, the sound was lost in the bellowing howl of the Chevy. The shooter on the other side of the car was pumping round after round into the trunk of the Chevy as it charged toward them.

The SS-396 thumped hard onto the street surface, shooting out sparks. It rammed into the side of the Camaro with a sickening crunch. Metal, side-stripping, glass, and plastic furiously blasted away in all directions with the impact.

The side door slammed with a violent thud into its metal jamb, snapping the shooter's legs just below the knee. He shrieked in terror, but his anguish was cut off midstream as the top of the side door crushed his chest. He folded like a towel, half in and half out of the rear seat.

As the Camaro rolled over from the impact, it sheared off the fire hydrant on the sidewalk behind it. The shooter on the other side, his hands in the air, disappeared beneath the rolling blue hulk. A thick gush of water burst up through its interior and broke the windshield out, bending it over the hood. The lifeless form of the driver was impaled on the center hub of the shattered steering wheel, a stream of blood spreading down his chest.

As the Chevelle's crumpled rear end settled against the smoking underside of the Camaro, J.T. looked back through the rear window. The Camaro's ignition had fired. Its rear wheels were now spinning with an eerie high-pitched whine. Sparks streamed down like fireworks from the engine compartment. The battery was crushed, shorting out the electrical system.

Brannon threw the Hurst speed shift into first gear and again gunned the V-8. The Super Sport slid sideways as it spun away from the Camaro. She roared down the street and around the corner. Brannon could smell the pungent odor of gasoline. He barely had time to ponder whose tank had ruptured before he heard the answer.

A muffled detonation caused him to swivel in the bucket seat in time to see a bright red-and-yellow fireball erupt from the street behind him. It rushed upward, filling the air with the following thick black smoke of burning petroleum. The blast rushed through the Chevelle's blown-out rear window. He hunched over the wheel as pieces of glass broke from the window's edges and blew into the back seat. He stomped the gas. The SS-396 tore down Portsmouth Road.

J.T. nursed the battered Chevelle up to Route 50, then back east toward the District of Washington. He needed to disappear. Both tail lights were surely out. He hoped no police cruiser would spot it. Today though, escaping what could have been sure assassination, he had the luck of the Irish. After only twenty minutes, he was entering the city of Rosslyn and cruising down Wilson Boulevard. The Hyatt Arlington was just ahead. That would do nicely.

The SS-396 turned left onto the entrance ramp of the underground parking garage just past the hotel's main entrance. He grabbed a stub from the ticket meter and breathed a soft sigh as the wooden gate swung down behind him. The Chevy wound its way down the ramp to level P-3, the third sub-floor. Brannon backed her into the first vacant spot he saw. He turned the ignition off and unsnapped the seat belt. He leaned back into the seat, collecting himself, not moving a muscle. Minutes passed into an hour.

The sweat on his forehead dry, his hands steady again, J.T. exited the Chevelle and walked across the cement floor of the garage. He took the elevator to the lobby, walked through to the Side Cafe and Lounge and found a booth. He'd been there before. In what seemed like no time at all, he went through two beers, then a plate of grilled pork chops. J.T. then began the task of focusing on the situation.

He was shaken. He was depressed. He was certain he was now not only a threat to Chapman, but most probably to Pete Novak as well. The kicker was that he had become the target of the same Agency he had served so loyally for so many years. He couldn't remotely imagine what in hell could be so damned important that this rogue unit of assassins, the JOG Squad or whoever the hell they were, had a charter to eliminate anybody who got too close. That meant anybody and everybody not cleared for access. And, it applied even to fellow Company colleagues, even inside the borders of the United States!

This was too unbelievable. Beyond a doubt, his pursuers were convinced he knew something, something that was clearly forbidden for him to know. Like Tony Spencer, maybe even like Doug Chapman by now. But more importantly, he was certain he was now a danger to the one man he respected and cared about so much. He had to find some way to fix it. He knew he could, but it would require radical measures. Perhaps it was time for radical measures. First, he needed rest.

Brannon returned to the underground parking garage and the car. He locked the doors, climbed onto the rear seat, and brushed off the splinters of glass. Exceptionally quiet here. His pursuers whacked, it was most likely safe enough for a short nap.

His mind was a blur. What was it that he knew, without even realizing it? Was it the truth about Yezhovich? The projects, MAJIC, the deep black sister project to Blue Book that Carolyn had mentioned? UFOs?

What could be the relationship, if any? Or maybe, was it Maria Dean? Distraught, dying, that's what Tony was desperately trying to pass on. It had to be Maria Dean. It all kept coming back to her. She was the key. Pete Novak would know that much by now.

It all made his head hurt. He knew he needed some serious rest to be able to think straight. J.T. pulled his coat over his shoulders and stretched his legs out as far as the short space would allow. He drifted quickly to sleep.

CHAPTER 19

St. Antoine-Abbé
Canada

Scores of dead brown leaves scattered from the curb as the large wheels of the bus rolled to a stop. The late afternoon sun reflected hard and bright off the maple leaf motif painted on its side. The engine's clattering suddenly ceased, and the hydraulic door opened with a weary sigh. Passengers slogged down the metal steps one after another, shrugging their shoulders and stretching as they dispersed.

Though the small town of St. Antoine-Abbé lay only fifty miles to the south of Montreal, it had been a two-hour trip. Stops at every town along the route. The sun was already slipping behind the line of trees on the hills overlooking the town. A man in a greenish-gray parka was the last to exit.

As he stepped onto the sidewalk, Laszlo looked up into the fading light. He drank in the fresh Canadian air. For a moment, his face twisted in a grotesque smile. Oh yes, this was so sweet. He was close. He could almost smell the stench of the beasts. And, he knew what he had to do when he found them. He'd kill them. Yezhovich had shown him the way. Yezhovich's own dreams had given him a pathway to Laszlo. In the strangest of ways, they were comrades.

Well, just a few more days and Laszlo would be there. He'd have them. The crooked smile contorted his face as he strolled away from the bus and up the street, peering into the shop windows. The bus lurched away with a loud roar, disrupting his reverie. He adjusted the strap of the stuffed hang-up bag slung over his shoulder and stepped off the curb.

He paused in front of the *Mountain House*. Its bright windows brimmed with colorful outdoor clothing, hunting gear, and camping equipment. He pushed through the door. It was warm inside. The inviting smell of freshly brewed coffee wafted from the long glass-topped counter to his left. A hefty, big-shouldered man with disheveled hair and a thick red beard stood behind it, pouring a steaming mug. He glanced up at the new arrival.

"Bonjour, monsieur! Can I help you? Come, have a cup of hot coffee! A croissant too! Both are fresh!" His voice boomed through the large showroom. He motioned to him with his hand.

Laszlo's stomach rumbled. He was starved. The coffee and croissant sounded great. The strange expression had left his face. He was himself, Laszlo, again.

"Why, yes! Thank you," He couldn't remember his last real meal.

"Monsieur, if you would like sugar and cream, they are right on the counter there. Perhaps a croissant? Fresh this morning! Help yourself, please." He pushed the straw basket across the counter.

"Butter and jam? Also, right here." The shopkeeper poured another large mug and set it down, pointing.

"You arc vcry gcncrous, mon ami. Thank you vcry much."

Laszlo took a bite of the croissant and sipped at the hot coffee. Very good. He smiled.

"Now then, how may I help you today? You are new here, yes?" The red-bearded man was munching his own croissant. Crumbs feathered his beard.

"Yes. I'm just passing through, really. I'd like to talk with you about... "

A loud clatter from the back of the store interrupted him. Laszlo turned instantly toward it. So did the shopkeeper.

"What are you doing back there? I told you, if you need to get something up high, I will help you." he blared, moving quickly from behind the counter.

"Hey Pops, sorry! Sorry, man! It's okay, don't get all bent outta shape, Pops! Takin' care of it now. It's cool."

The voice sounded male, but it had a weak, whiney tone. Laszlo could make out two long-haired people milling about in the rear. It was hard to tell from a distance whether they were male or female. They had knocked a camping pot on the floor and set it back on the shelf.

"I'm sorry for the disturbance, monsieur. They call me *Pops*! These long-haired punks are rude. A pain in the ass. Usually, we only see them in summer, but these two have been in and out all day long. They never put anything back in its place! Pains in the ass, that's what they are! But that young man there, let me tell you, he's an especially nasty one, very nasty." He moved back to the counter and picked up his coffee mug again.

"So, how may I help you? I am Louis... please, call me Louie."

"Okay. Thank you again. Well, I am a Louie also – Louie Montesson. Please, call me Louie as well!" The diversion had given Laszlo time to think. He laughed and stuck out his right hand. The brawny shopkeeper grinned at the coincidence. He shook hands with a firm grip.

"Then, you shall be Louie Number One! What do you need, Louie Number One?"

"Well, Louie Number Two," They both laughed again, this time together. "I am going to visit my brother in Bakers Narrows up in Northwestern Manitoba, on a lake whose name I cannot pronounce."

"Oh, I know. Everything in Canada is named after the damn Indians! Only Quebec has kept its identity! God bless Monsieur le General Montcalm for that!" Louie raised his coffee mug in salute and spoke with the fervor typical of French descendants in Quebec.

General Louis Joseph de Montcalm had been King Louis XV's soldier–pioneer in claiming new lands for the King's New France, a *new* France in the New World. But the Marquis lost it all to the British in his defeat on the Plains of Abraham outside Quebec City in 1759 by General Wolfe. Both generals were killed in battle, a very unusual event historically. Since then, Quebec's inhabitants longed for a separate, sovereign political identity.

"Oui, God bless Le Marquis de Montcalm and keep him in the Lord's grace. So, yes, excuse me. What is it you need to bring on this journey to see your brother?"

His outburst had drawn the attention of the two long-hairs. They were meandering closer to the front of the store and the counter. The man appeared very curious.

"Already, I feel that you are a man to be trusted, Louie Number Two. My brother has found, well, he wrote me that he has found gold on his land. Gold. He's now beginning to mine it. He has had too many unwelcome visitors and, well, he has only one helper. He is afraid."

"The bastards. Probably long haired, do-nothing hippies

like those two over there! 'Never working a day in their lives. 'Just stealing from others and screwing each other to death." He shook his head in disgust."

"Louie, I want to bring him two weapons. A rifle, something semi-automatic at least. Maybe a carbine. And of course, a good pistol. Can you help me?"

"Are you a resident of Quebec?"

"No, sadly I am not. I empathize with your feelings about Quebec, though. Perhaps someday I will be able to come back and… "

"I see. That poses some difficulty. But maybe, can I trust you also to do something? Can I have your word on it, Louie Number One?" He leaned over the counter, near whispering the last words. He gave a wink.

"Of course you can. Just tell me what." Laszlo leaned forward as well.

"We will pick something out for your brother. I can sell firearms to other Canadians. I will give you two registration cards. You must promise me that your brother will fill them out and mail them to me. Can you promise me that?"

"Of course. Robert will fill them out the day I arrive. I promise you. Thank you so much. You are a gracious and generous man. He raised his mug and shouted, *Vive Quebec!*"

Laszlo smiled. This was superb. It was shaping up even better than he had hoped. Glancing over, he saw that the two long-hairs had moved even closer.

Louie Number Two turned and reached for the rifle racks behind him. Without hesitation, he pulled down a short-barreled carbine. "Monsieur, I think this is perfect. It is a spin-off of the M-1 carbine, rapid-fire semi-automatic. It has a 15-round magazine, .30 caliber. No jams with this one. Yes? You like it?"

"Yes, this will do perfectly. And, a pistol?"

"I recommend a powerful handgun, you know, in case the rifle does not do the job. The shopkeeper winked, grinning again.

"Yes, of course."

"Good, then like this one here, a Smith & Wesson Model 19. Combat Magnum, .357 caliber. Six-inch barrel. Highly accurate. A lot of stopping power. It will bring down a mountain lion, mon ami! And, an angry mountain lion, at that! A black bear too. Nickel plated. I will throw in two boxes of ammunition for each! Usually, I give only one!"

"I like it. I'll take both. Thank you. You are a generous man, Louie Number Two."

"Well, I can see you are a good man. I should have more customers like you," he said. He jerked his head in the direction of the two long-hairs, then back again.

"Let me see, the carbine is $675 and the revolver $550. You may have both for $1,100. How would you like to pay for these?"

"Will you accept U.S. currency? It's all I have."

"But of course! You are paying in cash then?" A look of mild surprise slid across his face.

"Yes. There you go. That should be $1,100. Once more, my friend, thank you for your generosity." Louie Number One began peeling off $100 and $50 bills.

"Okay. Let me get your change, and then I will wrap them up in heavy paper for you." The shopkeeper strode to the register at the end of the counter.

The long-haired male's eyes bugged wide open at the wad of bills. He then looked at Laszlo's face in surprise. He nudged the young woman away from the counter and back to the wall displays and spoke rapidly in a hoarse undertone. With his other hand, he pawed at some blue jeans on the shelf.

"It's him. Baby, it's him!"

"Who?"

"That's Csengerny. No doubt about it. I'm positive. Did you see that wad of cash! The sonofabitch is loaded. This is our ticket, baby! All that damn money! Guns too. Shit, we will be able to go anywhere and have anything we want!"

"This guy is the traitor from the photo they sent you?"

"No doubt about it. It's him all right. Just stay close, baby. Stay close and do what I say. Okay?"

Her bright blue eyes met his, darkening as she frowned. She didn't like the look on Terry's face. He sometimes did terrible things. And, she didn't like to be around when he did them. But Terry always took care of her, always. She nodded solemnly.

At this particular moment, Terry represented the Russian SVR's last chance. Moscow Center had decided that if they couldn't catch Laszlo, they'd kill him rather than let him fall into the CIA's hands. Terence G. Simmons, as Terry's forged driver's license read, had been assigned for the last five years to the SVR's Illegals Section.

Terry's real name was Dimitri Kolenko, a sleeper. A deep cover mole. Dimitri's only mission was to live out his life in Canada as he chose. That is, as long as he remained within an arm's reach of the hydro-electric generation facilities near Montreal. If hostilities ever seemed imminent between the United States and Russia, he'd receive his orders to blow them up at the appropriate moment.

He'd studied the facilities, had the blueprints memorized, and was confident he could execute that mission even in his sleep. There were a hundred other sleeper agents like him across North America and in all walks of life. And, with similar havoc-raising missions that would support the motherland in a time of war. Of course, none of them knew of the others or where they were assigned.

Peggy, a disaffected runaway from Maine, eventually discovered who Terry really was. She loved him anyway. Terry kept her in clothes, food, and cocaine. She would never leave him, never betray him. Yesterday, Terry received an emergency activation message along with a photo. It was a picture of Laszlo Csengerny, a traitor to Mother Russia.

The Moscow Center's best guess was that Laszlo was somewhere in Canada. They'd identified the flight from Paris. Terry's mission was simple enough – find Laszlo. Then, terminate him with extreme prejudice. Now, due to sheer luck, the target stood just yards from him. Terry could smell his reward already. He kissed Peggy's neck and moved her down the aisle.

The shopkeeper returned with the change and began wrapping the weapons. Once or twice he glanced at Laszlo, noticing his features. He finally decided to speak.

"You look like a fighter, *mon ami*. Did you fight in the ring?"

"I'm sorry?"

"Excuse me for being so personal. But you have a boxer's nose. It looks like you've broken it several times. The scars on your right cheek. I just thought, you know, that maybe you were a prize fighter?"

"Yes, you're right. I tried it when I was young. I wasn't very good, pretty bad actually. The scars are the remains of an old birthmark I had under my eye. In my last fight, my right eye, well, I almost lost it. My right cheek was all torn up. But, I don't miss that birthmark either!" he chuckled.

"Well, what do you do now?" Louie noticed the long-hairs were leaving.

"I teach foreign languages, European mostly. Latin derivatives, and German, of course." He smiled, shoved the package under his left arm, and reached across to shake hands.

"Monsieur Louie Number Two, you will always be *number one* in my book. Thank you for everything."

"Thank you too. Here, don't forget! Please take the registration cards and give them to your brother. Good-bye, my friend!"

"Mon ami, I will. Goodbye!" Laszlo spoke over his shoulder as the door creaked open. It was growing dark now.

CHAPTER 20

Frankfurt
Germany

Pete rose at 6:30 a.m., showered, shaved, then grabbed coffee and a roll at the cafe off the lobby. The hotel was a nice place, grand actually. Nordheimer's car was on time with the same crew arrangement... one driver and a shooter. In Europe, precautionary measures like this were now standard operating procedure.

No one spoke during the fifteen minute ride. A cloak of gloom had settled on the Frankfurt Center. Three of their own were dead, murdered. That kind of thing hadn't happened in a long time. Pete could feel the tension, even in the car. He tried to ignore it.

Upon reaching the old brick building, Pete was ushered inside and then directly into an elevator being held for him. The shooter was never more than a step behind him. As the doors closed and the lift moved, Pete put out a hand to steady himself. The elevator seemed to be going up, then down, then up again. It was disorienting. He looked at the display panel and saw no numbers, just color codes. It had maybe twenty buttons, far more than the building could possibly have floors. The display lit up, the colors rotated as the elevator slid smoothly up and down. Pete smirked. This was pure spook and a little much. It probably served a purpose, such as disorienting the occasional uninitiated visitor to the Center. But still it was a little much.

When the elevator finally stopped, Pete followed his guide down a long hallway. His coat was courteously snatched from him. Bill's office, on what Pete guessed was the southwest corner of the building, boasted a panoramic view of Frankfurt. Pete was impressed. The Frankfurt Center was the focus of all European operations. While the Station Chief sat in a nice cushy office in Berlin, Frankfurt was the nerve center. It was an honor to be selected to run it. Bill Nordheimer knew that. That's why he took the job. It wasn't often that Berlin Station told him what to do… usually the other way around.

Nordheimer was working at his desk, his jacket off. He looked up and smiled. Bill stood, came around his desk, and shook Pete's hand, smiling.

"Well, Pete, good morning. Let me give you an official welcome to Germany." He reached toward a display panel by the large, multi-line telephone set and pressed a button. Seconds later, a woman entered carrying a tray with a silver coffee service and a plate of croissants. She placed them on a coffee table between two easy chairs and smiled pleasantly.

"Thanks, Nancy. Nancy, this is Pete Novak from Langley. Pete, this is Nancy Winston, my executive secretary. Nancy's been at the Center twelve years. Her husband works down in our tech analysis shop. Good people. I'm lucky to have Nancy here. She really runs things."

"Nancy, I'm pleased to meet you. Now we know why Bill's reports are so well done." Pete smiled at her. She was attractive, forty-ish or so. She returned the smile and shook his hand gently, then glanced at Bill and left.

"Pete, have a seat and fix yourself some coffee. Before we get started, I'd like to have Charlie Collins, my deputy, and a couple of his folks come in. They'll give you a run-down on how we're organized, overview of operations, what's going on, you know."

"'Sounds good."

The briefing went on for nearly three hours, a veritable parade of briefers, all of them specialists from different functional areas in the Center. It was a dog and pony show in the best of bureaucratic traditions. Pete struggled to hold back the yawns. Next came the tour of the facility, highlighted by the Technical Analysis Division – some very talented people who took care of electronic gadgets and other wizardry. The *black bag* guys.

Lunch with Bill and Charlie followed in the Taunus Room, named after the mountains to the west of Frankfurt. All small talk. Charlie stayed only twenty minutes, excusing himself after what looked to Pete like a nod from Nordheimer. It was a little after 1:00 p.m.

"How'd you like the show?"

"Impressive. You've got a lot of good folks here. You've accomplished a lot, and you should be proud of it, Bill."

"Thanks, I'll convey your appreciation to all of them. Pete, now that's out of the way, whaddya say we cut with all the bullshit niceties? Doc Kriegel called and told me you were coming over. He didn't elaborate other than to say you'd do the talking, talking for *him*, that is. So tell me, what can I do for you?"

Wild Bill set his glass of ice water down and pushed his chair back from the table. He clasped his hands in his lap and smiled. He assumed the junior man across from him would be a tad stunned. But no, Pete was prepared. He'd heard that a quick shift of gears was pure Wild Bill. He was known for taking the offensive early, capturing the high ground quickly. It was a nice position to negotiate from, if negotiating was what you were up to.

"That's fine with me, Bill. Why don't you fill me in on the latest? The shooting, the Laszlo Csengerny business. Where are we?" Novak didn't even blink. He came back in a monotone voice. He flipped his leather-bound notepad up on the table and jerked a pen from his jacket.

Surprise flitted across Nordheimer's face at Pete's bland response. He eyed Novak warily before continuing, placing his palms on the table.

"Where are *we*? *We* are still collecting on the shooting, but there's nothing new, not really. As for Laszlo, he's gone. We had him covered, but one of our men got knifed in the Hauptbahnhof, uh, the train station. We... "

"Excuse me, Bill, he's gone? When did this happen?" Pete shook his head, dropping the pen on the pad in front of him.

"Pete, let's take this down to my office. My notes are there." Nordheimer stood abruptly. He rose, turned, and left the room, leaving the door open for Novak to follow him.

It was obvious Wild Bill liked being behind his desk. He sat higher than any other chair in his office, surrounded by a virtual fortress of polished mahogany. Nancy appeared with a fresh cup of coffee. He set it on his blotter after taking a sip.

"We had him, Pete. He was leaving his apartment in Dörnigheim. We picked him up and surveilled as usual, very discreet. We took him all the way to the Hauptbahnhof. Two of our guys suddenly dropped off the air. We found one of them lying at the bottom of some concrete stairs on the lower level, missing some front teeth. The other was in the restroom, knifed... twice, in the abdomen and in his right kidney. He's at a hospital downtown. He'll probably lose the kidney."

"Gees, I'm sorry to hear that. What else? What do you think?"

"The SVR owns this guy, at least until yesterday. Our local intelligence tells us the Russkies are frantic. They're looking for him too. They even flew 50 agents in from their Luxembourg center. It's weird. After the shootings, I don't know who's doing what anymore."

"Just when did you become aware of all this, Bill? When did you report it to Langley?"

"Look, Pete, I don't like your tone." Nordheimer facial muscles tightened. His voice dropped, reverberating from deep in his chest.

"I only…" Novak struggled for a breath, staring at Nordheimer.

"Don't talk down to me. As for reporting, I sent a message to the Langley Ops Center by FLASH precedence yesterday. If you don't already know that, fella, it looks to me like someone purposefully kept you in the dark. Obviously, they wanted you over here anyway. What does that tell you, huh? Laszlo's off the continent. He had to have driven to Paris. Flight scheduling at the Flughafen told us he'd hopped an Air Canada flight from Paris to Montreal. He's gone."

"Gees! *He must have driven to Paris*? How the hell do you lose a guy on the Autoroute to Paris? It's gotta be a seven-hour drive on a six-lane highway."

"I told you, we lost him here," he growled, his ears burning red. "*In* Frankfurt. *In* the Bahnhof. It was just minutes before we realized something had gone wrong. Laszlo could have gone anywhere after that. We know he didn't take a train because there were no departures for another thirty minutes. So, what words of wisdom do you have for me, Novak? And, just what the hell does Langley think someone like you can do over here?"

Bill rose and stomped to the window behind his desk. He

looked out, trying to stem the anger bubbling up, then jerked back to face Pete. He leaned over the desk and set his clenched hands on the surface before the dam burst.

"You have no damn idea what I… see that poster on the wall? *Terroristen*! Terrorists! That's what's on my mind every minute of every hour here. Not just the domestics, but Al Qaeda, ISIS, all the other Islamic spin-offs. American lives are at stake every day here. You getting the picture, Novak? You don't have a clue. And, I don't need some damn adolescent desk jockey breezing in here and telling me how to do my job? You got that?"

Pete sat motionless. He just glared up at Nordheimer. He didn't deserve this shit. He was sent here to do a job. He spoke firmly.

"Yes, Mr. Nordheimer, I got that. But I don't think the Director does, nor does the DepOps. So, why don't you pick up that phone and tell them the same thing. Short of that, *Mister* Nordheimer, you stay out of my face. I have a mission to perform. I can perform it with or without you. And, I won't take one iota of your interference. Now, you got that?"

"Damned bunch of snotty-ass kids they got at Langley today! You little bastard!" Nordheimer fumed, looking ready to explode into a million pieces.

"Oh, go to hell. You've no reason to treat me this way. If you won't work with me, don't want me here, then back the hell off and call Washington. I've been instructed that I'm speaking for the DepOps. He told you that himself. So, Mr. Nordheimer, I need to get on with business." Pete startled even himself. After all, this was the Director of the Frankfurt Center, Wild Bill Nordheimer. He shook his head and began to rise.

"Dammit! I don't believe this! The lack of respect. You hold on a damn minute! Just sit tight and make yourself another cup of coffee. You're not going anywhere!"

Wild Bill's hand slammed down on the phone, striking several buttons at once. Half the lines in Frankfurt Center rang, echoing down the hall. Nordheimer's face contorted.

"Dammit! Damn fucking phone system!" He picked up and dropped the receiver, then with an effort pressed a single button.

"Yes, sir?" Nancy's voice responded on the intercom.

"Nancy, get me Kriegel on the phone! Langley Center, now! Go FLASH precedence! Now, Nancy!"

A flustered "Yes, sir" came back again. Nordheimer dropped into his chair, struggling for control.

Nordheimer's eyes bore down on Pete between attempts to gather himself. He'd chewed up and spit out guys like Novak his whole career, and he could still do it.

The intercom buzzed. "Mr. Nordheimer, Dr. Kriegel's holding on Line 2. I can... "

"Doc... " Wild Bill jerked up the receiver.

"Yes, Bill. Good to hear your voice. What's up? Pete get in okay?"

"What? Oh yeah, he's sitting here in front of me. Look, Doc, I know you probably think highly of Novak and, yes, I've got a mess to clean up over here. I've had 'em before. You know that. But this little puke's coming in here, waltzing in on my turf, telling me to go to hell, and I don't... " His voice rose steadily as he looked at Pete.

"Pete Novak told you to go to hell? My, my. Well, look, Bill, take this direct from me. If Mr. Novak told you to go to hell, rest assured I'll check the regulations for you, but I'm pretty sure you don't have to go. Not just yet anyway." A soft, intervening chuckle notched Wild Bill's blood pressure up again.

"Real funny, Doc. Look, I'm telling you... "

"Negative. On this one, you're not telling anyone anything. Get that straight. Bill, I think a lot of you, but you had your chance. If I were you, I'd be real cooperative, and I'd work real hard to lower my profile on this. Fact is, William, if you screw up anymore or make things more untenable than they already are, I'll have your White-Anglo-Saxon-Protestant ass on the next Pan Am flight out of Frankfurt. And I do mean permanently. I want Pete Novak to get any help from you that he needs. Anything. You read me?" Doc's voice was stern. His usual jocularity vaporized.

"But Laszlo's gone, Doc. He's already gone. I sent a message." Nordheimer paled.

"Yes, I know that, and we've notified the RCMP, the Royal Canadian Mounted Police counterintelligence folks. They're hot on it. Nevertheless, I want you personally to ensure that Pete is up on everything at your location. We'll need to pick this thing up at our end now, and we need someone here who knows absolutely everything you know. The clock is ticking."

"Yes, sir. I'll take care of it. Bye, Doc." Novak nearly fell off his chair to witness Nordheimer toe the line. That was a first.

"Bye, Bill. Give Susie a hug for me, okay?"

"Yes, sir. You bet."

It was over. Nordheimer set the phone down slowly, staring at the blotter on his desk. He sat back in his chair and glanced at Pete, his face emotionless.

"Pete, if you and I can, let's try to put this behind us, shall we?"

"Sure thing. Water under the bridge. What now, Bill?" Pete managed a smile, but he still had goose bumps from witnessing a clash of the titans.

"Bill, I've gotta hit the restroom."

"Yeah, me too. Come on, I'll show you where they are." Nordheimer rose and they walked down the hallway in tandem.

Minutes later, refreshed and eager to put the previous hour behind them, they sank into their chairs back in the office. Nordheimer had cooled down; Pete looked at him in anticipation.

"Well, let me give you a thumbnail sketch on the history of this thing."

"Thanks, Bill."

For the most part, it was a rehash of what Pete had already read in STALKER – the initial discovery of Laszlo, their surveillance, and finally, the shootings and stabbings. Pete allowed Nordheimer do his thing. After about twenty minutes, Wild Bill asked if Pete had any questions.

"Who are the dead men, yours or ours?"

"Yours. There's Nick Potter and Bob Kaminov. Both of them were detailed to the Center here, along with a few others, to follow up on STALKER, the Laszlo operation, specifically. And, identifying the SVR as the handlers, we knew then we had a hot one – something strategic."

"Strategic?"

"Yes. The signals were clear. Pete, I only had limited oversight on this. Potter, Kaminov, and the rest were pretty much on their own."

"Really? On *your* turf?"

"You know… that ain't my style. I don't warm up to that kind of arrangement. I'm pretty vocal and I know what people think of me, the *Wild Bill* stuff and all. But when the DCI himself calls me and says to back off, I back off. I gave these guys logistical support, tech stuff, everything. Sure, they worked with my surveillance teams, but they were off on their own a lot too."

"I see. I didn't know that."

"The JOG is a fairly new concept, but I'm surprised you weren't briefed on this."

"JOG?"

"Joint Operations Group, *the JOG Squad,* as our guys call them. A real composite bunch, all disciplines, including some bad-ass, snake-eater, Spec Ops types. Control is buried in Clandestine Ops at Langley somewhere. These guys have the highest authorities, if you know what I mean."

"Sanctions?"

"You got it. I haven't had a briefing on the program yet. Ten of them were here."

"All right, thanks. How does Yezhovich fit in?"

"He doesn't. We believe the sonofabitch was a traitor. At least, everything we've seen points that way."

"A Company man... "

"Hell no, Yezhovich wasn't Company. He was detailed. We had him doctored up with identity documents to look like one of ours. Yezhovich was an Air Force tech puke."

"So what does that mean?"

"Yezhovich was a real brain in composite materials, powdered metals, metallurgy, that kind of stuff. He was working with the highest high-tech stuff, the blackest of the black programs. The crown jewels, the real damn jewels. Well, it was our responsibility to watch him. He was over here working with the Germans and... "

"Working with the Germans? Bill, if this stuff was so black, the program or whatever it is that Laszlo got into, then why were we working with the Germans?"

"Oh hell, we share some of the stuff at the low end. It's good for our allies, you know. They're happy for the crumbs. Of course, they don't know they're only crumbs, so it keeps them off our backs. Lessens their snooping. That's why Yezhovich was over here."

"And the connection with STALKER?"

"Well, Yezhovich ran into Laszlo, or Kurt Kalmbach as he was documented here, or maybe Laszlo ran into Yezhovich. And they fused. Unreal. We don't know why. We picked up on a courier and the courier led us to Laszlo. Surveillance of Laszlo turned up Yezhovich. From that point on, it was simply wait and see."

"Was Tony Spencer here?"

"Pete… how do you know Spencer?"

"So, he was."

"Yes. He was with the JOG team here. My understanding is he requested to leave."

"Why?"

"I honestly can't tell you. I wasn't in his chain of command."

"Spencer's dead too."

"I see. I didn't know that. That's too bad. Strange, but it really doesn't surprise me. This particular subject is embedded with things that are strange."

"Then tell me. Why shovel dirt on Yezhovich? Why still claim he's ours?"

"Only way to keep it under wraps until we knew more. The last time I checked we're responsible for foreign intelligence overseas, right? We couldn't take the heat, not now. I can see the headlines: *CIA Proves Once Again It Can't Find Its Own Ass With Both Hands!* You know that's how the media would play it. This has been a lousy eight years for us. There'd be too many questions. That's what would happen if we colored Yezhovich as some Defense Department civil servant or anything else other than our own."

"Come on Bill, you haven't suffered any."

"Hey, don't get me started again. The rank and file always takes it in the ear. It ain't gonna happen that way this time. It ain't necessary. The DCI, senior staff, if those guys ever get shoved out, they just go back to their law practices, their CEO and chairman of the board jobs. Not the rank and file. They lose big time, every time. This is all they know."

"Okay, if you say so. I just don't see it as an excuse for a cover-up. It's always worse in the end. Let's get off this, Bill. So, it's the technology end that tore this open? What made Laszlo break away? Why'd he run? Why Canada? How's that fit? The Russians are hot on him too, so much so they're killing people?"

"I never said that, Pete. We really don't know who's killing who, but my money is on Laszlo. The guy's a psycho, a nut case. Prone to violence. And, maybe something else too."

"I'll give you a qualified 'maybe' on that, Bill. I'm not convinced yet. Why would anyone get so heated up over some damned technology, over whatever this stuff is, to go start a killing spree?"

"Because it's only the surface, that's why. Yeah, the technology is hotter than hell. Damn deadly stuff, but wonderful stuff too. You know, we will prevail on any battlefield. We will hold the *high ground* forever. It's that profound and in a way, beautiful."

"Profound? Where's the revelation?"

"It's profound. You can bet on it. It's not just the technology, Pete. It's where it all came from. That's the essence of it."

"I don't get you. Where it comes from?"

"Pete, do you know what composites are? Or what makes up a radar signature?"

"Only in a conceptual way. I'm not a technician."

"Ever heard of... Stealth?"

"Some, not much. So?"

"I see. What about Tonopah, Groom Lake, maybe?"

"No, I only faintly recognize those words. Heard them somewhere. Tonopah sounds Indian."

"Right. Well, then I guess brilliant pebbles, smart rocks, particle beams, directed energy, and pulse detonation engines are also out."

"Honest, I don't... no specifics... but, what's the context for those things?"

"Gees, how in hell could they give you this assignment without briefing you fully? I'm sorry but I can't tell you. I can't give you anymore, mainly because I don't really know more, not for sure. I know some of it. Regardless of what I told you, this is truly the abyss. The abyss, dammit. You don't need to know and you don't want to know either. So, don't try to get there."

"I see."

"And this Laszlo stuff is frightening on its own. Yezhovich too. I mean it. In a way, I'm glad Laszlo's out of here. If the medical stuff is factual, then… "

"I'm lost, Bill."

"Damn, I'm so way out of bounds here. Then again, maybe it's the right thing to do. You seem to be dedicated, determined – not to mention that Doc Kriegel thinks you're the greatest thing since cornflakes. I'll give you a little more. However, know that it's much more than you are authorized to know."

"Thanks in advance, Bill."

"Right. You know we've had Laszlo in custody before. Some time ago."

"Yes. I've read the STALKER profile."

"Good. This guy was then and continues to be tormented by dreams, violent, horrific nightmares. It's blown him off his rocker. Army MI had him for nine months. They never understood that part of him, other than it seemed related to crazy stories about the death of his parents."

"Yes, I know."

"They took medical specimen samples from him, ah, blood serum, urine, stuff like that."

"Doesn't surprise me."

"Well, all that stuff went to Walter Reed. Walter Reed doesn't throw anything away when it comes to research. They still have dried blood from Laszlo. And now, from Yezhovich also."

"Okay."

"The bottom line is we know a lot more now about blood and about cellular structure."

"For instance?"

"For instance, DNA mapping. There's a match with those specimens from Walter Reed's research center and fluids from Laszlo's apartment here. All of it confirmed at the National Institutes of Health in Bethesda."

"All right. And?"

"This guy's DNA is unreal. And I mean *un-real*. They say Laszlo has RNA chains within his DNA structure that we can't identify with anything in known science. Not on this planet anyway. His nightmares may come from something else entirely. All theory right now. But guess what? They know now that Yezhovich has some of those very same RNA chains. They think that's why the two of them fused. Speculation at this point though."

"Bill, what in hell are you telling me?" His head felt like it was going to explode.

"Good God, Pete, I can't tell you anymore. I'm way over my head. You're not cleared. Go home, forget this shit. Let somebody else take over. Obviously, Tony Spencer couldn't handle it. He's dead. You may not be able to handle it either. And there's the JOG. My guess is they're protecting this project at any and all costs."

"What project?"

"Drop it. No more."

"I want you to know you're scaring the hell out of me, Bill. But... thanks for telling me what you could."

"Fact is, fella, I shouldn't have told you any of it. I'm not authorized to do that. Pete, I see a lot of me in you. My younger years, I mean. I had your job once, you know."

"I do know. So?"

"So, there's probably some Company folks that would like to see some hot shot like you screw this up, especially something big like this. They'd love for you to be the sacrificial lamb."

"Who?"

"Like I said, I've said enough already."

"Okay, I understand that. Thanks for telling me what you have, Bill. One more thing and we'll call it a day."

"Yeah?"

"What were the weapons involved in the shooting? Calibers? Any matches on ballistics?"

"Yes. Kaminov and Potter were both shot twice, chest and head, very professional. Both were 9 millimeter rounds, full-jacketed hollow points. What's more, my tech folks say the same pistol killed both."

"Yezhovich?"

"That bastard was shot four times in the chest with a .45 caliber. He had a hole in him the size of the Lincoln Tunnel. A mess. We had no matches with anything previous. We sent it off to the FBI ballistics lab. 'Haven't heard back yet. Too soon maybe, but I'm not holding my breath for any big breaks there."

"Yezhovich was shot with a .45 caliber. Four times in the chest? Doesn't that say something?"

"Not to me, it doesn't. Still could be the same assassin. Just a different weapon."

"There may be two sets of killers. You have to at least acknowledge the possibility."

"Yeah, a possibility, but in my opinion it's remote. We need to focus on Laszlo. My money's on Laszlo, a documented, violent wacko. There's a chance you're right, Pete, especially with all these JOG bastards around, but I wouldn't bet on it. Please, seriously, just listen to what I told you and keep your head down.

You want a ride back to the hotel? Dinner? Interested? Let me call Susie and… "

"Bill, thanks. I'll take you up on the ride. Allow me to take a rain check on dinner. I'm bushed, jet lag, I guess. I'd like to come back tomorrow and talk to your surveillance folks, if it's okay?" Pete wanted to give Wild Bill a chance to regain some face.

"Sure, sure. No problem. We'll have you over another time. Tomorrow's fine. I'll have Tom Reinkle pick you up in the morning. He's my surveillance chief. Same time okay?"

"Yeah. Say, what about the JOG types? Can I speak with them?"

"Ah, I'm afraid that's a definite *no*. Sorry. Officially, I'm supposed to act like they don't even exist. Stay away from them, please. If you think it's critical, we can call Kriegel again in the morning."

"No, that's fine. Bill, thanks. I'm glad I got to meet you."

"Same here. Get some sleep and stay out of the brothels downtown!" Nordheimer laughed and shook Pete's hand, chuckling at his own humor.

Nearly an hour later, Pete took dinner in his room at the Intercontinental. It was hard to choose from the menu. The English translations made everything sound delicious. It was the best room service he could remember too. But, the wine did him in. The airplane ride caught up with him, and it was all he could do to get out of his clothes and slip into bed before a deep, dreamless sleep claimed him.

CHAPTER 21

Frankfurt
Germany

Tom Reinkle was in the lobby to pick Novak up at eight sharp. Reinkle was jovial and talkative. He guided Pete through the Frankfurt Center to meet the agents in the surveillance unit. They freely shared their observations of the last few weeks with him. Unfortunately, there were no new insights. The highlight of the morning was a short jaunt out to Dörnigheim where they cruised down Fischergasse past Laszlo's flat.

"Can't go in," his escorts said, a couple of sweep teams were still at work. They were taking apart this and that, looking for any evidence. They didn't want to draw attention with a sudden parade of visitors, especially when Laszlo had kept so completely to himself. Lunch was again in the Taunus Room with Charlie Collins and Wild Bill. This time Charlie stayed long enough for chocolate cake, coffee, and pleasantries.

Nancy called Base Ops at Rhein Main Air Base for Pete and was informed the Special Mission aircraft was still there. It would depart tomorrow morning for the U.S. at 8:45 a.m. local. Pete was assured of his spot on the flight manifest.

After lunch, Pete bid good-bye to Nordheimer who assured him that if anything new developed, Pete would get it pronto... direct from him, Wild Bill. He was a different person now. What a change a royal ass-chewing could make, Pete thought as the elevator doors slid closed over Bill's final wave.

Pete took off the necktie, washed up, and donned his trench coat over the shoulder holster. He'd take some time to see a sight or two. The concierge had recommended the Dom St. Bartholomäus, a beautiful gothic cathedral near the Main River. It was cool, but with the sun still out it seemed a perfect day to play tourist. A taxi was ordered up to the lobby, and Pete jumped in.

The cathedral was beautiful. Its single fat spire sported large, working clocks facing each direction of the compass. He started climbing, determined to reach the top even though his knees began aching halfway up. The view from the spire was stunning. The city of Frankfurt spread out before him. The Main River was to the south and really just a block away.

He noticed a small pedestrian bridge to a strip park on the other shore. People were stretched out on blankets, although the temperature hovered at 60°. Pete was enjoying himself and so he decided to give it a whirl. He skipped back down the winding masonry steps, crossed the courtyard in front of St. Bartholomew's, and cut over to the next street heading for the river.

Novak didn't see it coming. The Mercedes approached at speed from behind him, its rear door opening as it pulled alongside. Pete casually turned his head toward the car, then instinctively moved away from the curb. He heard the scuffle of feet behind him and spun around.

Two men, both dressed in topcoats, had stepped out from

a doorway. Each grasped one of Pete's arms, gently but firmly. Pete struggled to free himself, but the strength of the two men was overpowering. A man stuck his head out from the Mercedes.

"Herr Novak. Please, get in." As the man in the car beckoned, Pete could feel the man on his left reach under his coat and find the shoulder holster. He jerked back Pete's jacket.

"*Schutzwaffen!* Pistol!" He barked.

"*Nehmen-sie dass!* Take it!" The man in the Mercedes paused. He continued in English, "Herr Novak, do not be afraid. I mean you no harm. Please get in. We must talk. Brannon, J.T. Brannon."

"J.T.? Who are you?" His shoulders relaxed, and the men loosened their grip.

"Please get in, Mr. Novak. We're on the street!"

Pete slid into the back seat as the man moved over. The two men who had grabbed him walked away in opposite directions. The Mercedes made a U-turn and accelerated down the street. Two big men were in the front seat. The driver, and probably a shooter.

Novak turned to the man next to him. He looked fifty-something, with rugged features. He was very well dressed. His gray hair was combed back over his head and there was a smell of tobacco about him. The man turned to Pete, smiling.

"Mr. Novak, I apologize for the method but it was quick and it drew no notice. My name is Klaus Reimer, BKA, ah, Bundeskriminalamt. Like your FBI, but maybe a little better." He chuckled softly.

"Who isn't better?"

Both men in front laughed and then caught themselves, but not before Pete noticed. So, all spoke English. Klaus gave the driver a perturbed look in the rear-view mirror. He turned back to Pete.

"Herr Brannon was right. You are able to see things both ways. You're among friends, I assure you. I need to relay some information to you, from J.T." He gestured downward with his eyes and held out Pete's pistol, though his left hand was still wrapped around it. His fingers loosened and Pete took the weapon, tilting it to see that the magazine was in. He reholstered it.

The Mercedes seemed to be heading north. Pete noticed a sign for Senckenberg Allee, but the next minute they curved around a ramp and headed... west. The sign at the ramp had read E-66. Another autobahn, this one to Wiesbaden.

"Okay, Herr Reimer. Please, tell me where we're going."

"Out of Frankfurt. Wiesbaden. A short drive, Herr Novak. Only twenty minutes."

Pete couldn't see the speedometer, but the Mercedes was flying. He grimaced as a second black Mercedes barely skimmed by them before pulling in front. From the feel of it, Pete guessed well over 100 mph. He glanced around the car, but no one seemed to be concerned.

All of a sudden a third black Mercedes roared past them and slipped in front of the second! Two nearly identical black Mercedes were in front of them and four men were in each vehicle. In the blur of such speed, even their license plates looked exactly alike.

Abruptly, as on cue, all three identical limos began a series of high-speed maneuvers – moving up in line, then falling back, passing and shifting position in a well-choreographed mix-up. They were rapidly approaching a large interchange with several overlapping overpasses. Pete scanned for signs, trying to burn the images into his memory... Köln and Essen to the north; Mannheim and Heidelberg to the south; and Wiesbaden straight ahead.

The three Mercedes parted company brusquely: one north,

one south, and Pete's car straight west on its original course, accelerating down the autobahn. It suddenly dawned on him, this was fancy *dry-cleaning*. The old peanut-in-the-shell trick. Which car had the peanut? Pete chuckled to himself at the thought of being the peanut.

After passing several signs for Wiesbaden, they took the exit for Schiersteiner Strasse, toward the *Stadt Zentrum,* City Center. Pete caught some street names as they whipped past, but knew he'd never keep them in order. First, Kaiser-Friedrich Ring, then Rheinstrasse, Wilhelmstrasse, Mainzerstrasse, Humboldstrasse, and finally, Bierstädter Strasse. No way would he keep it all straight. A little way up the gentle sloping hill on Bierstädter Strasse, they pulled over to the curb in front of a building sporting a warm orange glow from its stained-glass windows. The marquis above the heavy wooden door read *Felsenkeller*. It had the warm, beckoning appearance of a German gästhaus, a restaurant.

At Klaus' nod, Pete and the others stepped out from the Mercedes. Klaus guided Pete to the restaurant's front door with the shooter right behind them. The driver stayed with the car. A stocky woman cheerfully greeted them. Her brown hair was streaked with gray, pulled back in a knot at the back of her head. Klaus and Pete were seated in a cozy corner, the shooter at a table near the door. Klaus asked for two beers, which almost immediately appeared on the table.

"Herr Reimer, you talked to J.T.?"

"Please call me Klaus. May I call you Pete?"

"Yes, of course. You spoke to… "

"No, I didn't. A mutual acquaintance called me. He's with the German news bureau, the *Deutsche Tages Schau*, in Washington. J.T. asked him to call me. Herr Brannon is very concerned for your welfare. He said to tell you, 'It does not look good.' I have names of three men who are dead.'" Klaus pulled a piece of paper from his pocket, nonchalantly dropping a hand over it as the woman again approached.

"Want to order?" she said in a cheery German voice.

"Two beef filet stews and when you have time, another two beers."

She nodded and walked away.

"You'll like this. The food here is superb. Not too many people. This place was once an old brewery, excellent beer. The gästhaus is still run by the same family." He took a long swig, smacking his thick lips.

"Thanks, this is fine. Klaus, who are the dead men?"

"Nick Potter, Bob Kaminov, and Jon Yezhovich. You know them?"

"No, never met them. We're in different work areas. But I knew the names already."

"Also, then. A man named Tony Spencer was murdered. No question about it. J.T. said to emphasize that this was a sanctioned hit. It was very professional and very cleverly executed. He said to tell you it was *good ole boys*. Do you know what this means?"

"I think I do. Yes, Klaus, I do." Pete's eyebrows raised. The words put a chill in him, a look of dread flitting across his face.

"Good. J.T. also said that when Spencer was dying, he tried to tell his son something. Spencer must have known he wasn't going to make it. He said the same name over and over. He was in shock, but kept repeating the name. A woman's name, Maria Dean. Or Mary Dean, maybe even Marie Dean. The son did not understand the meaning or the context, but heard the name clearly, or so he said. Herr Brannon is convinced this Maria Dean person must be critical to determining who killed Spencer, and perhaps to all of this. He said, find Maria Dean, and you'll have the key."

"Maria Dean?"

"Yes. Or Marie, maybe other variations on Mary. He said further that traces were run against all Company databases. All was negative. No known references to a Maria Dean."

"Thanks."

"Also, there is no person here in the American or British communities with such a name."

"How can you be sure?"

"Trust me."

"Then, thanks again." Pete smiled.

"You are welcome. Lastly, J.T. said you should come home as soon as possible."

"I'm leaving tomorrow, morning or afternoon. Klaus, I want you to know I trust J.T.'s opinion, but sometimes… "

"And trust him you should, Pete. Without question. There is no better man. None. Herr Brannon does not make friends easily. Apparently, he cares about you a great deal. You should trust him with your life," Reimer interrupted.

Reimer left no room for discussion on the subject. They must have been very good friends. Anyway, Pete didn't want to argue. He'd had enough of that on this trip. The comment *good ole boys*, rather than *Ivan*, was enough ice water for one evening. Brannon would never voice such an opinion unless he was very sure of it.

So, the Company must be killing its own. Despite where Nordheimer refused to go on the subject of the JOG, Pete could read between the lines. But would they risk assassination even in the continental United States? That was exceedingly dangerous. Who was friend… who was foe?

Klaus didn't miss Pete's change in demeanor. Before they could continue, a younger woman arrived with their salads. Klaus gestured to dig in, and Pete was again very pleased with the German cuisine. The entree was even better than at the Intercontinental.

Klaus commented on how good the beef tournedos were, but that was the extent of their conversation during the meal. When Klaus ate, he ate. Pete glanced briefly at the table by the door. The shooter was gone. In his place sat the driver, who was now wolfing down his own dinner.

Klaus only set his knife and fork down when the plate was empty. He wiped his lips and smiled, seeing that Pete was cleaning his plate as well.

"*Das schmeckt?*" he asked. "I mean… was it good? You liked it?"

"Outstanding, Klaus. Thank you!"

"Coffee?"

"Sounds great. Please."

The young waitress approached to collect the plates. At Klaus' request, she left but quickly returned with two coffees and two small goblets of Asbach Uralt, a fine German brandy.

"Pete, do we… does my country, have anything to worry about with this Kurt Kalmbach and Yezhovich, or anything they may have been doing together?"

"Klaus, how, what do you know of the relationship between these two men?" Pete's eyes widened over the edge of his coffee cup.

"I myself know very little. It's not my particular business. But colleagues of mine know enough to be concerned. They're with our BND, Bundes Nachrichten Dienst, our federal intelligence service. From what they know about this matter and our electronic warfare program, *Reggenbogen*, Rainbow, they're very concerned. What shall I tell them?" Reimer took a long sip without taking his eyes off Novak.

"Honestly, Klaus, at this point your friends probably know more than I do. I simply can't, ah, there may have been a problem a good number of years ago with our handling of an interrogation camp south of Munich. Army Intelligence held Laszlo there. But, I just don't know about now."

"No? Okay. I understand you are a man to be taken at his word. That's enough for me." He finished his brandy in another long swallow.

"Klaus, how do you know of Laszlo and Yezhovich?"

"Pete, very little goes on in Germany these days that I or the BND do not know. This is not still *the good old days* as you say. The days of German subservience to the great American plan are over. We always, how do you say it, *check our six*? Yes, that's it. We always check our six, enemies and allies alike. It's good business. Surely you must do the same."

"Yes. Yes, we do. I see. I'm sorry I asked."

"No problem."

Reimer's eyes glinted in the orange light of the tavern, narrowing, boring into Pete's. The very ticking of the clock seemed to slow with the intensity of his scrutiny. Finally, he nodded as if satisfied.

Klaus slowly pulled a neatly folded square of paper from his suit pocket. Inside that appeared to be another paper, a copy of a photo on paper. Glancing around the room, he gently set it on the table and pushed it across.

"Pete, do you know what this is? Have you seen it before?"

"Ah, I can't make it out, Klaus. No, I don't recognize it. What is it?"

The photo looked to be a copy of a copy, and of poor clarity. It was murky, foggy, but he could make out a thin, dark shape in the center. It looked human, but almost too frail to be so. The image was too difficult to discern.

"This is a copy from the original photo. But the original is no better. I was hoping you could tell us." Klaus frowned.

"Where does it come from?"

"Yezhovich's apartment. We got to it first. It was hidden behind a baseboard directly behind his bed. Obviously, it must be sensitive."

"If it is, it's lost on me. It's too densely foggy or something. I don't know." Pete set the photo down.

"No?"

"It's so blurry – it could be anything. The dark shape, the form in the middle, could be someone, a person. It appears human anyway. Whatever it is, ah, maybe a monster coming out of a dark, misty night on the moors. I just don't recognize it. I doubt that it's anything." He grinned, shaking his head

"Perhaps, Pete. But then… why hide it?" Reimer looked to the table by the door. The driver was attentive and nodded his readiness. He rose from his seat and walked to the bar, apparently to pay the bill.

"I would agree with you, Klaus. Sure, why hide it? I just don't see anything at all in the picture that I recognize. The dark shape in the middle looks… I just don't know. Maybe something from a Stephen King novel. May I keep it?"

"Yes, keep it. Maybe it will help you. Pete Novak, you are a pretty good guy." He leaned over the table and extended his right hand. Pete took it and shook it firmly, a big grin on his face. As they stepped out of the gästhaus, the shooter immediately left the car and walked up to Klaus.

"*Müssen sprechen!* 'Need to speak with you!" The man moved a few steps away, obviously anxious.

"Excuse me, Pete. Just a moment."

The driver spoke in a low voice, his gestures animated. The only words Pete could make out were, "im radio von Frankfurt." The shooter pointed up, then down the street. Reimer nodded and walked back, motioning Pete toward the car. As they lurched away from the curb, Pete heard the distinct scrape of metal on metal in the front seat. The shooter was checking his pistol. Reimer reached over and lightly grasped Pete's arm.

"Pete, I don't wish to alarm you, but we may have a problem. While we were eating, my men received a radio transmission from Frankfurt. My team has detected a surveillance at your hotel. They have already determined it's not SVR nor terrorist-related. I think… "

"Your team?"

"Yes. I put a surveillance teams on your hotel in the event I missed you on the street today. They're very good. Also, Horst saw a dark gray BMW make two passes up this street, past the gästhaus."

"And you think?"

"Impossible to know for sure. It may be nothing. Your own people may simply be trying to localize you for your own protection. They may be concerned. Pete, you should know though, that if they followed us here, they are very good. I think you should not return to your hotel. We'll manage to get your things later. We'll go to the Arabella Hotel on Lyoner Strasse. Nice but smaller, much lower profile. We keep a couple of rooms there, safe houses, you know. Horst will stay with you until morning. Then we'll get you to the air base or back to Frankfurt Center. Wherever you want. Okay?"

Pete nodded in agreement. He turned away as the passing streets blurred by and stared without focusing, not knowing what to think. His right hand slid slowly up under his coat until it felt the hump of the Walther pistol. It was reassuring.

CHAPTER 22

St. Antoine-Abbé
Canada

His feet pressed to the curb, Laszlo's eyes swept up and down one side of the street, and then the other. Nothing caught his attention, nothing to be concerned about. Across the street, the small ticket office for Quebec Transport Lines was lit. He needed to buy another ticket, so he stepped off and crossed the broad street, not missing the two long-hairs sitting on the bench outside.

"Hey man, sir, did I hear you say you were going to Manitoba? Peggy and I are going that way. We can get you there a lot faster than any bus. Wanna ride with us? It won't cost you anything. We'll be happy to give you a lift." The young man with the dirty blonde hair stood up smiling, striving for nonchalance.

Laszlo looked at the ticket office again and then back at the long-hair. This might be even better. He had sensed it in the store and decided to let them see the money. Yes, this might do perfectly.

"When are you leaving?"

"Right now, sir. Okay with you? I'm Terry, and this is Peggy. You're, uh, Louie?" This time he spoke with a broad grin, pulling his companion up by the shoulder of her woolen shirt.

"That's right. Just call me Louie. You sure you two have room for me?"

"Hey, you bet. Come on, I'm parked over by the corner. Let's hit the road!" Terry turned, dragging Peggy with him. Terry was even more confident now. The target was going to be easy. Peggy was not so sure. She noticed Laszlo's broad shoulders, his muscled hands. Under the coat, it was hard to tell, but he looked in pretty good shape to her.

As they walked across the street, a car pulled abruptly in front of the ticket office behind them, its tires screeching to a halt. The side of the vehicle screamed in large white letters, *R.C.M.P.* The driver and a man from the back seat briskly walked into the ticket office, pushing their way through the door with authoritative gusto. A third man stayed behind in the right front seat. In the dim glow of the interior light, he appeared to be scanning a large map unfolded in front of him.

"What's RCMP, Terry?"

"Royal Canadian Mounted Police. The RCMP. Cops. Bad asses too. Looks like they're in a hurry. They gotta be out to bag somebody. Come on, let's split!"

He yanked open the door of an older model Ford Explorer SUV. It was pretty beat up, both inside and out. Laszlo glanced at the rear bumper. Even with the grime, the sticker stood out: *"Satan's Coming and He Ain't Happy!"* These two must really be a pair. The engine roared to life. Laszlo could tell it was at least a big V-6. It sounded in fairly good condition, despite its appearance. They pulled away from the curb and made two or three rapid turns through the small town.

In no time, the Canadian night and dark woods closed in on

them. No street lights. Near pitch black. Laszlo was confident they were heading west, maybe northwest. He couldn't be positive. It was difficult to tell without the sun, moon, or a clear look at the heavens.

They passed over a succession of small to medium-sized bridges at a place called Coteau-du-Lac. He was sure they were traveling in a westerly direction. He soon noted a small sign welcoming them to Ontario... so, they were leaving Quebec. Terry had the radio on loud, some heavy metal station from Montreal. The static on the weak signal made it even more annoying to listen to.

"You're heading due west?"

"Yeah, gotta go west first. These roads will get us up to Highway 117. That will take us north, and then northwest all the way to Manitoba. Don't worry, Louie, we'll take care of you. Louie, do you mind if Peggy gets in the back with you? She's dead tired. She can stretch out a little back there. Maybe she can get some sleep, you know?"

"Sure, no problem. By the way, I'd like to pay you for taking me along. At least gas and expenses. Does $200 sound right to you?"

Laszlo slid left against the door as Peggy crawled over the seat. She swung her ass in his face as she backed down, then turned to him and smiled before scooting to the other end of the bench seat. She began taking off her boots and socks, all the while staring at Laszlo with those big blue, catty eyes. Peggy wiggled her toes at him, smiled and snuggled up in the corner.

"Hey, no, no money. We're going that way anyway. 'Glad to have you come along. We're fine."

Terry stared at the road ahead. No, he didn't want $200. Hell no, he was going to have all of it. Every damn penny. The guns as well. And, he would soon have the SVR reward money too.

They'd declare him a hero. Old Louie here was on his last trip anywhere... Terry would see to that. Damn traitor. He gripped the wheel and began whistling along with the radio.

Two hours went by uneventfully. The road was poor. Monotonous thuds of bumps under the tires were enough to put anyone to sleep. Laszlo's eyes were closed, but he was far from dozing. He was keyed up, trying to listen, sense everything in the car. Terry still whistled to the loud music, occasionally checking the rear-view.

His eyes squinted to Peggy. She had managed to work her bare feet up against Laszlo's right thigh. Testing him, she pushed lightly on his leg with her toes. Laszlo didn't move. She glanced up and scanned Laszlo for any response, then took off her jacket and balled it into a pillow, then slid further down on the seat, stuffing it behind her head. She turned on her side, facing the front seat back. Minutes passed. Feigning a yawn, Peggy stretched her legs out. Her right foot slid slowly over Laszlo's thigh and settled into the cavity between his legs. Her eyes were closed, but she grinned mischievously.

Terry whistled away. The music blared. Laszlo was motionless. Peggy wiggled her toes into his crotch, pushing against his genitals. Laszlo still didn't move, but Peggy could feel she was getting the desired effect. She purred. She slid her other foot under his thigh.

Abruptly, Laszlo snorted and sat up, as if waking from a deep sleep. She pulled back, surprised at the sudden movement. A frown of disappointment flashed across her face.

"Where are we, Terry?" he avoided any glance at Peggy who had curled up in the opposite corner. Her knees were pulled up to her chest. She glared at him. The two of them were doing their damnedest to keep him distracted... loud music, Terry's whistling, and Peggy's sexual teasing.

"Oh, a little over two hours out of Montreal. Not that far, Louie. We'll pull over in an hour or so. I don't like to drive past midnight. We usually sleep in the Explorer when we're on the road. Is that gonna be okay with you?"

"All right. Look, I can pay for a couple of rooms. I don't mind."

"Nah, why waste your money? It'll be fine, just comfy. I can take the front if you want. We'll push down the back seat, and you and Peggy can have that. Or vice-versa. Doesn't matter to me."

Terry looked in the rear-view mirror at Peggy and winked. She stared back at him, then looked away. He fiddled with the tuner button on the radio, trying to pick up Ottawa. The signals were stronger, and he quickly found a station he liked. The heavy metal blared louder. Peggy swung her legs off the seat. She stared out her window into the dark forest blurring by.

They'd turned at the last intersection, more of a wide fork to the right than a turn. The road signs now read Route 323. Laszlo knew they had been on Route 148 for quite some time. His mind's compass told him they were now going north again. His attempt to memorize road maps on the airplane had not been all that successful. It had run together on him, a blur of squiggly lines and unfamiliar route numbers.

Another half hour, and a second turn convinced him of the change in direction. They were now on Route 364, heading west. Another left turn onto Route 323, heading south. They were making a big loop. Laszlo saw a narrow blue sign flick past. It was set back from the road, almost overgrown with twisted vines. *Lac Papineau á Gauche…* Lake Papineau to the left.

The night enveloped the Explorer in a blackness deep as a cave. There was the thinnest sliver of moon barely peeking over the horizon, a dim glow. And, the faint light of stars. Laszlo felt he had to say something, lest Terry think he was totally ignorant.

"Say, Terry, what's up? Where we headed now?"

"Oh, just finding a place to park. Not far from the main highway. I've been out this way before. There's a spot up here on the right near a big lake. It's not as cold as it often is at this time in the fall. Maybe it'll be nice enough to take out the sleeping bags. Sometimes you can hear loons out on the lake in the morning. You'll like it."

Terry slowed, turning the wheel hard. The SUV bumped onto a dirt road. Just minutes later, they saw the lake glimmering through the trees. A large clearing was ahead. The Explorer swung into a grassy spot not fifty yards from the water. As they made the turn, the headlights swept over the lake in an eerie, other-worldly view.

They climbed out and breathed deeply of the crisp air. Chilly at the least. The place was deserted. Way too late for casual camping, but there could be some hunters around. This was good weather for hunting.

"Well, it's gonna get too cold, I think. Louie, I'll take the front seat and you can have the back."

"No, you two take the Explorer. If you'll loan me one of your sleeping bags, I'll be just fine out here. Cool clean air, forest and all. Let's do that. It'll be great."

"Okay, if you insist." Terry looked at Peggy as he spoke. She shrugged back.

They all had a great desire to relieve themselves, so nodding to each other, they quickly scattered into the brush. Three hours of sitting in the car had pushed Laszlo's last mug of coffee down to where it begged to be released. Heading south along the lake's edge to avoid the undergrowth, Laszlo came across a strip of cleared forest.

He guessed the clear patch was some fifty yards long, maybe thirty yards wide. In the dim light, the landscape appeared creepy, mysterious. Only a few of the largest trees were still standing. All around him were rows upon rows of pointed, stake-like trunks of smaller trees, sheared off about one and a half feet from the ground. Only their jagged spikes remained, giving the impression of a gigantic pin cushion, the needlelike tips sticking upward.

Laszlo swiveled around to take in the surreal sight. Turning to the lake, he noticed several black humps appearing to sit on the water's surface like tiny islands. Not far from shore. Beavers! This was the work of beavers.

The creatures had trimmed this strip of woods to build homes in the water. The lake was probably teeming with them. Scenes like this were probably repeated all around the lake area. Still, it was an odd, almost grotesque sight. Laszlo stepped delicately between the sharp stumps, working his way back into the trees. In the brush, he found a comfortable enough spot and more than enough dead leaves to clean up after his business.

The beaver clearing wasn't far from the camp site, but he took his time getting back to the car. Though his instincts told him they'd wait until much later to move on him, he cautiously scanned right and left as he walked. He saw them upon reaching the grassy area. The interior light was on in the Ford. Terry and Peggy were in the back spreading out some blankets. They climbed off the tailgate when they saw Laszlo approaching.

"Hey, Louie. Where you been, man? We were about to send the Mounties out to find you! Come on, come get your sleeping bag. We're bushed. You gotta be too, ain't you?" Terry laughed. Laszlo could make out a faint smile on Peggy's face.

"Yeah, I'm tired too. I was just looking around. There's a lotta beavers out here. A whole bunch of them!"

"Oh yeah? Well, show me, man, 'cause I only see this one

here! Hah hahhh! Yeah, show me where the other beavers are! I'm ready!"

Terry gave Peggy's shoulder a shove and doubled over with laughter. He was beside himself, giggling, arms flailing. He stumbled in a half circle around Peggy. He was so amused at his own wit he could hardly get the words out. Peggy just smiled without speaking, shaking her head. She glanced at Laszlo. Her eyes had a far-away look. He wondered if they'd downed some drugs.

"You okay, Terry?" He turned his head back to the long-haired male who was still rambling around, chortling at his own humor.

"Hey, couldn't be better! 'Wired for sound, man! You want some?" He pulled out a plastic zip-lock bag of a white powder. Cocaine.

"No thanks. I'm beat enough. I want to get to sleep. How about that sleeping bag?"

"Right here, Louie old man!" Terry leaned back on the rear gate, reached in, and yanked out a rolled-up bag. "Sure you don't want the back of the SUV here with Peggy? She'll warm you up where you need it most."

Tossing the bag in Laszlo's direction, Terry stood behind her, his hands on her waist, swaying her body back and forth in front of him. Peggy's eyes drifted across the ground and eventually found Laszlo. She stared with her baby blues directly into his, a leering smile on her lips. With some difficulty, Laszlo wrenched his eyes away from her. It was hard to look away. Peggy was attractive, sensual.

"Ah, no, really. I'll be fine out here with the sleeping bag. Thanks."

Laszlo stepped forward and grabbed the bag. Something in the back of the Explorer caught his eye… the tip of the M-1 carbine's black barrel! The masking tape on his package was torn off. Laszlo felt a rush of adrenaline sweep through him. This was getting dangerous. No doubt about it. Both of them were weird. How could he possibly get to the guns now? He now knew why the drugs. These two were prepping themselves… getting themselves high to kill him.

"Hey, suit yourself man. You can always climb in later if it gets too cold. She's warm enough and sweet enough for two. Right, baby?"

Peggy jumped as Terry grabbed her buttocks, but she managed another beckoning leer at Laszlo. These two were really gone, soaring.

"Say, Louie, where you gonna be if we need you for something? In case we gotta split early or something. Sometimes I get a craving for an early breakfast." Terry leaned on the bumper and pulled Peggy onto his lap.

"Probably over there a little to the south. No more than thirty, forty yards."

"Thirty, forty yards? Shit, don't go too far, man! There are wolves here that range further out in fall and winter. They get hungry and move south. Don't let 'em get you. 'Bears too sometimes. Don't get too far away, Louie. Okay?"

Terry peered at Laszlo over Peggy's shoulder as he spoke, his hands sliding up and down her thighs. Terry took his deep cover role as a wandering hippie seriously. He had come to like the adventure of cocaine. He certainly liked screwing western sweeties like Peggy. She seemed never to get enough of it anyway. But tonight, he knew he'd be earning his pay. Terry's smile left his face, sizing up Laszlo's build, thinking he might not be that easy after all.

"Sure. I'll see you in the morning. You two sleep tight."

"Hey, you betcha, man. You betcha. Sweet dreams now." They rolled backward into the rear of the SUV and pulled the gate up behind them. Laszlo could hear Peggy giggling already. The Explorer was bobbing up and down on its shocks before he got totally out of sight.

Laszlo stepped out a large circle about forty yards south of the Explorer. He wanted to know where every depression in the soft earth was, every dead log, every protruding rock, every obstacle. He dropped the sleeping bag in the middle of a small open area. He laid it out where a dim shadow from a nearby craggy maple stretched across it. The tall, leafless tree was between the bag and the lake. It would be difficult to see, yes, difficult to be sure of what was there.

This was the best spot he could pick. It was about quarter of one in the morning. He felt he had only an hour and a half, maybe two. If they had half a brain between them, they would come for him then – in the dead, still hours of the early morning.

Laszlo crawled into the bag and strained to see the Ford but a spread of low undergrowth was between them. Perfect though, if he couldn't see them, they couldn't see him either. He'd give himself a half hour or so to get warmed up, then he'd have to leave.

Laszlo left the zipper on the bag open and settled himself on his side, facing toward the Ford SUV, his back to the lake. Somewhere far off on the other side of the lake, he heard the faint, ghostly howling of wolves. Terry was right about the wolves. He snuggled down and did his best to rest, but with his eyes open.

At almost twenty to two, Laszlo stretched, then rolled out of the bag. It had to be down to twenty degrees. No wind though.

That was lucky for him. Lying flat on his stomach, he slipped off his parka, rolled it up, and stuffed it into the sleeping bag. After zipping it up, he crawled away through the cold, damp leaves to the south. Ten yards away and still on his belly, he scrambled sideways into a thicket of scrub brush. He curled up to stay as warm as possible, watching and listening. The minutes crawled by.

The frigid air was becoming unbearable. His cotton shirt was no help at all. The hands on his watch inched past two o'clock, but nothing was moving. No sound. Laszlo shivered. His fingers and toes were going numb. Now two fifteen. Still nothing.

It was nearly two thirty when he heard the crisp, cold snap of a twig. Laszlo couldn't judge the distance but it seemed close. He unfolded his body, stretching out along the cold ground as quietly as his stiff muscles allowed. Another slight snap. He steeled himself for the onslaught.

Laszlo raised his head ever so slowly until he could just peer over the branches of a leafless bush. Laszlo strained to see in the dim light. Dead ahead was Terry, moving like a cat across the ground. Terry was cautiously closing in, first one step, and… a pause. Then the other leg reached out warily. He had what looked like a shovel, a camp shovel, not the carbine. Terry must have decided that rifle shots would attract attention. In the dead of night, they would be heard across the entire expanse of the lake. Escape might be difficult. Terry decided the shovel was the best option.

Laszlo turned his head slowly, eyes nearly popping with the strain. No Peggy. He peered into the night toward the Explorer. There, that was her leaning on the rear bumper. Peggy left the dirty work to her boyfriend. He turned back to Terry, now just a few yards from the sleeping bag. He had settled down on his haunches, poised for the kill. Clenched in his right hand, the shovel rested on his shoulder.

Terry's head swung back and forth, trying to make sense of the form in the bag. If possible, he wanted to crack Laszlo's skull with the first blow. Laszlo smiled. He had picked the spot well. The dim light and faint shadows made it difficult to be sure. Finally, Terry inched forward. He raised the shovel above his head.

Terry leaped, his arms plunging downward. The sharp edge of the camp shovel sliced through the bag, shredding it. The bag collapsed. Terry realized much too late that the bag was empty! He swung around, raising the shovel again, but Laszlo was on him.

With every bit of strength he had, Laszlo punched the long-hair square in the face. Terry's head snapped back, his hair flying. He staggered sideways. The flat of the shovel smashed into Laszlo's left shoulder. He groaned but kept coming. He grabbed Terry's long blond hair, jerking his head down as he thrust his right knee quickly upwards.

"Arghhh, shit! You prick!" Terry shrieked as his face slammed into Laszlo's knee. The cartilage snapped in his nose. He fell backwards. Then came the revelation. Laszlo's eyes bulged as Terry yelled, "You asshole!" – But he said so in perfect Russian. Terry was Russian! Probably SVR to boot! Startled, Laszlo shoved him away. Terry stumbled, then hit the ground hard on his back and rolled to his side.

Terry struggled to get up on all fours. As soon as his bloody, sneering face lifted, Laszlo's right boot swung up, catching him full in the mouth. The force of the kick flung Terry up, over and onto his back. Laszlo twisted Terry's now unresisting body around and secured him in a half-nelson arm lock.

"My apologies, comrade Terry."

Laszlo's ears perked. His head jerked up at the sound of Peggy running, her boots thudded across the clearing into the low brush. She fell with a crunch at least once. She screamed Terry's name, then the pounding footfalls resumed.

Laszlo glanced behind him into the dark forest. He pushed Terry through the woods and along the lake's edge as fast as he could. Terry was as hard to manage as a drunk. He had nothing left in him.

Peggy was catching up. The sounds of her frantic running were close, too close. Laszlo was afraid to look back. She saw them, and raced faster, tearing through the brush and low tree branches. Just as they reached the beaver clearing, Terry fell. In a last ditch effort, he spun on his knees and thrust his fist into Laszlo's groin.

"Over here, baby!" Terry yelled out frantically in Russian, forgetting for a fleeting moment that Peggy wouldn't understand.

Laszlo pitched over Terry's shoulder and screeched in pain. He forced himself ahead on all fours. He crawled further south into the clearing. He wound his body between the stake-like trunks. He had to put some distance between… Terry grabbed him by the neck and yanked him up, his fist landing a glancing blow on Laszlo's right ear.

Laszlo sank down with the blow, but forced himself to rise back up with all his strength. His left fist punched deep into Terry's abdomen. Terry wheezed hard, the wind knocked out of him. Laszlo stepped forward to finish Terry off with his right fist, but his heel caught the edge of a stump. His ankle twisted and Laszlo tumbled sideways. His head slammed into the ground, barely missing the chiseled stump of a sapling.

A sliver of an instant later, the loud blast of a gunshot reverberated across the lake. Laszlo lay motionless, staring up at his adversary. There was a dull thud as the .357 magnum round slammed into Terry's chest. His body lurched violently backward, staggering, his arms flailing as he tried to regain his balance. He went limp and fell, disappearing behind a cluster of pointed stumps.

"Terrryyy!" Peggy shrieked.

She stood frozen, suspended in motion. The Smith & Wesson revolver wobbled in her extended right hand. A look of sheer horror transformed her face. She took one step forward, then another, immobilized by disbelief. Laszlo pushed up to his knees, breathing hard from exertion.

Peggy turned her head toward him. Her eyes were wild. Her face was twisted, contorted. He heard the bullet snap through the air above him.

"You fucking bastard!" She screamed, leaping forward and burst into the clearing toward him. Both hands were on the revolver's grip, thrusting it out in front of her as she ran. She fired once. The bright yellow blast exploded from the barrel. Then, another shot. She was still running. Three bullets were left. She was only fifteen yards from him. Laszlo rose to run, but he knew it was futile. Peggy would be on him in seconds.

Peggy stumbled. Laszlo was on his feet ready to run, but he stood rooted, unable to move. One of her shoes had caught a stump! Her momentum carried her forward, sailing through the air as if in slow motion. Peggy's mouth and eyes wide open in fright. The pistol glinted faintly as her arms flailed, one hand bracing in front of her for the fall. She landed barely ten feet from him with a dreadful look of panic on her face. She came down hard.

The razor-edged point of a sapling's stump drove straight through Peggy and erupted on her back. She was impaled on the stake, groaning deep in her throat. Stunned at the horrific turn of events, Laszlo stepped cautiously toward her.

The stake had struck at least one artery. A large inky stain on her shirt streamed rapidly across her back. She raised her trembling head, gave Laszlo one last look with her blue eyes. Her head dropped forward. It was over.

Laszlo knelt down and loosened her fingers curled around the revolver. He stuck it in the waist band of his pants. He stood and grabbed her shoulders to pull her off the stump. He grunted with the weight of her body as he rose, nearly dropping her when she suddenly gasped! Laszlo turned her over and set her gently down on the ground.

Peggy's head rolled to the side. Her eyes were wide open but staring at nothing. He shook his head. Such a waste for her to end this way, in a cold black night deep in the Canadian forest. He placed her hands by her side. He watched her for a moment before turning away, and looked back, but Peggy never moved.

Laszlo searched for Terry. He found his body in a crumpled heap behind a group of stumps. At that moment, a piercing sound rang through the night. He jumped, spinning to face the lake. Wolves again. It was impossible to tell where they were, but their howling was louder, agitated. The pistol shots, the screams, and scuffling had definitely caught their attention. They sounded closer.

CHAPTER 23

Lake Papineau
Canada

A shiver surged through Laszlo. A gut wrenching fear gripped him like an icy glove. He was alone now. He looked across the clearing beyond the ring of trees and into the blackness. He began to tremble. He was certain they were there, lurking behind the trees, deep in the shadows. Tall, slender figures. They'd followed... all the way. Waiting for him. Their eyes watched his moves.

Laszlo grabbed the sides of his head, trying to push the thoughts from his mind. He spun about, his eyes bulging, straining to see and straining to hear. Nothing. No sound. One could never be sure. The beasts were so clever that way. He pulled out the revolver, gripping it tight before turning to Terry. Laszlo breathed deep and hard.

He squatted beside the long-haired Russian and pressed his fingers against his neck. No pulse. The impact of the magnum round had left a gaping hole in the left side of his chest. Laszlo rolled the man's hips to the side, searching for a wallet. He pulled everything out, examining each piece in turn.

A New York driver's license listed his full name as Terence George Simmons. Laszlo tossed a credit card in another name, probably from a previous victim. Finally, he found a gas card in Terry's name. That was good. The wallet had no more than fifteen dollars. Terry had been basically broke. Cheap Russian bastards... a hell of a way to earn a living.

Laszlo rose to his feet. He ran as hard as he could, legs pumping, the revolver swinging in his hand. He paused only to pick up his parka. His chest heaved – he gasped for breath. Leaning against the Explorer to steady himself, cold sweat wiggled its way down his forehead. He rummaged through the Ford and found another zip-lock baggie, brown leafy stuff, most likely marijuana. He tossed it out the rear gate along with the bag of white powder. He couldn't have that going through customs, not with drug dogs around.

Laszlo next searched for tape or rope and found duct tape in the glove box. Just what he needed. It took him only minutes to tape the carbine and revolver under the chassis. Once as secure as he could make them, Laszlo closed the doors, rolled the windows up, and drove quickly out on the lake road.

He thought again of the wolves. They would come quickly after hearing all the clatter. So much for Terry and Peggy. Fresh kill for the wolves. He sighed, pressing hard on the gas. Laszlo back tracked to Route 148, turned west, and pushed the Ford up to 60 mph. He knew the Mounties were somewhere behind him. If he guessed right, they would expect him to cross over into New York somewhere south of St. Antoine-Abbé or perhaps on a gamble, back east by Lake Champlain. He doubted they would look for him this far north or west.

Now though, once again there was another chess piece on

the board, the SVR. How many of them? Would more come? His Russian masters weren't interested in talking, just killing. He had to get across the border and into the U.S. They wouldn't chance going for him there. Never.

In less than an hour, Laszlo saw signs for Ottawa and the bridge over the Ottawa River into the city's center. He checked his watch. It was minutes shy of 4 a.m. Route 148 turned into Route 50, a major four-lane highway. He slowed to 55 mph, and at the signs took the turnoff for the bridge.

Downtown Ottawa was brightly lit, but the streets were empty. After only a few minutes on cross streets, he spotted a sign that read *Route 16 South, Ogdensburg, New York, 52 miles.* If he poured on the gas now, he might make the border before daylight.

At 5:20 a.m., Laszlo crossed the blue-green waters of the St. Lawrence River. The bridge was a wide one, and the Explorer was surrounded by trucks of every sort. Loaded with produce, most were headed for the New York markets, hoping to arrive before morning's light. Ahead, only two U.S. Customs agents stood at the checkpoint by the far end of the bridge. Horns blared and drivers shouted, impatient to get their perishable cargo on its way south. The line started and stopped.

Laszlo drummed his fingers on the steering wheel, near nauseous from the smell of exhaust. Sweat dripped into his eyes. The mid-size white truck in front of Laszlo finally jerked to a halt at the checkpoint. A Customs guard approached the cab. Laszlo heard a heated exchange ensue. The guard stepped angrily towards it, his hands raised. The truck rolled through the checkpoint.

Now it was Laszlo's turn. To his surprise, the Customs guard was still looking over his shoulder at the white truck now leaving the bridge and shaking his head. He took one quick glance at the Explorer and with a sweep of his hand waved it on through. He'd made it!

Laszlo followed Route 37 south along the St. Lawrence until it intersected Interstate 81 and continued south for another hour and a half. Exhausted, hungry, he steered the Ford into a restaurant at the interchange with I-90, the New York State Thruway. He pulled the SUV to the far end of the lot and stumbled around to the passenger side. After glancing about the lot for any onlookers, he bent low to pull the weapons from underneath the car. Laszlo threw them on the rear seat and tossed his parka over them.

Leaning against the door, he caught the cold morning wind in his eyes and face. It was bracing. Renewing. He walked briskly across the lot toward the restaurant, straightening his clothes and stuffing his shirt down in his pants. All the way smiling. A cup of coffee, a meal, some gas, and he would be on his way.

Forty-five minutes later, Laszlo was making his way back to the Explorer when his knees weakened. His legs quivered. A heavy queasiness heaved his stomach. It was three days since he'd had a night's sleep. First, the long flight across the Atlantic, then the nauseating bus trip, and topped off by the sleepless strain of last night. The deaths of Terry and Peggy. It was all catching up with him.

He sank into the driver's seat, then inched over and stared at his reflection in the rear-view mirror. He was pale as a corpse. Twisting around to look in the back, he noticed the curtains rolled up and tied with cord along the side and rear windows. Laszlo needed sleep and needed it badly.

Climbing over the front seat, he flipped the rear seat down, and dropped the curtains. He squirmed out of his parka and threw it into the corner. A piece of paper drifted from a pocket. Laszlo snatched it and opened it, staring at it intensely, his hands shuddering. It was the photo Yezhovich had given him in Frankfurt, a copy of which had so puzzled Klaus Reimer and Pete Novak. Only this one was an original print. It was the proof Laszlo's SVR handlers had wanted so desperately to get their hands on. It was also the proof he himself needed, the culmination of years of torment.

The form of the creature was clear despite the thick, murky mist. The Americans sheltered it, protected it. They were actually working with the foul-smelling beast in order to wreak their own evil havoc on the world. Bastards. Yezhovich had told him everything. After all these years, Laszlo would finally have a chance at vengeance. He would destroy the wretched demon. No one would stop him now. He tucked the photo into his shirt pocket. His head dropped back to the floor. Sleep overtook him.

Hours crept by. Suddenly, the phone rang. An eerie, wavering ring tone that filled the SUV. Phone? Laszlo startled awake. His eyes were blurred by sleep, and the Explorer filled with a pale gray, unnatural glow. After a moment of fumbling, he found the receiver and lifted it to his ear.

Laszlo's face went white. His lips curved downward, and his eyes widened. The voice echoed from the darkest, deepest corner of his mind. It was Grandma Margo! She called his name, begged him to let her come in. Laszlo answered, his childish voice so sleepy and confused. Then suddenly she was there in the SUV, her heavy form lying next to him but turned away.

Grandma Margo sobbed from the depths of her chest. He reached over her, trying to hold her, to comfort her. She shrugged him off and moved yet further from him, still wailing. Then slowly, she rolled over toward him. A terrible stench followed. It was a choking, horrid stink. He gasped for air. As her face turned toward him, empty sockets for eyes and grinning teeth gaped mockingly!

Decayed, rotten flesh hung in tatters from Margo's face and arms. Her boney fingers reached for him. She smiled and called him. Laszlo kicked at the corpse, screaming at the horror. He scurried backwards on the Explorer's floor as rapidly as he could. He heaved. Then, in an instant, she was gone. A sudden silence enveloped him, thundering in his ears.

Laszlo's hands reached out to probe where she had been. Nothing. Empty space. Without warning, the car slammed sideways, tossing Laszlo flat on his back. The Explorer shook violently, its side curtains swinging wildly until they finally broke from their rods and clattered down over him. He shuddered uncontrollably and covered his eyes against a sudden, searing light. The light seemed even brighter as outside, then a thick wall of darkness suddenly engulfed the Explorer.

Terrified, Laszlo began to push up on his elbows. He gasped in horror. Bizarre faces of the horrid monsters that had pursued him now pressed against the windows. Dozens of hideous faces with horrid slanted eyes and fang-like teeth completely surrounded the Explorer. Long-fingered hands pounded the glass of the windows, cracking and peeling bits away. Their ghastly shrieks assaulted his ears. The demons, determined to get at him, kept punching the glass. The windows continued to crack.

More faces... human, Terry and Peggy, their eyes glaring with hate. Laszlo could see their mouths were open, screaming at him, but he could hear nothing over the tumultuous uproar of the creatures. The claw-like fingers of the demons snatched at their hair, pulling them backward into the night. Terry and Peggy disappeared into a void. The beasts had them.

Through the din, Laszlo heard his name called... it was the most gentle of voices. He swung his head around, his eyes seeking her. They filled with tears. She called to him again, her voice soft yet so full of fear. Was it... could it be? He reached out pleading for her, but the creatures' grotesque dance paralyzed him.

His parents, Katka and Semmi, stood smiling at the rear window. They were posed just like in the photo on his nightstand. The photo he so often pulled close to his chest and wept when he could no longer stand the pain. They still loved him.

Dreadful boney hands grabbed his mother and father. They jerked them away from the Explorer toward the blackness. Laszlo shrieked as Katka's soft brown eyes, her loving face disappeared in the night. Gone in an instant. Overwhelmed with despair, Laszlo cried out in anguish as the banging on the windows and roof continued.

Then a new sound snapped his eyes to the tailgate. Two clawed hands pried it open at the top and were pulling it down. Laszlo shoved himself against the seat back as far as he could go. Ever so slowly, the window inched open. More hands appeared from the abyss outside the vehicle. More terrifying faces.

A long, slender arm bolted in and gripped Laszlo's left ankle. The beast had his leg. Its skinny fingers wrapped around it, long, pointed nails digging into his flesh. He howled. Another hand reached and grabbed his other leg. They pulled him toward them. He clung to the seat back, kicking and flailing. He flung his body abruptly upward in a desperate attempt to break their hold. His skull slammed into the ceiling. His vision blurred. Everything spun around him. He lost focus. Laszlo felt himself tumbling, sinking into unconsciousness. The inside light dimming, he was soon lost in the emptiness.

Laszlo blinked his eyes open. A warmth engulfed him. He saw the Explorer's domed ceiling light above him. He dripped with sweat. His right hand swept upward to wipe his brow and he stared in disbelief. His nails were smeared with blood, bits of skin and hair hung from the fingers. In the throes of his nightmare, he had gouged himself, badly. Deep rips in his ankle burned like hot irons.

Laszlo sat up. He struggled to catch his breath. The curtains were still drawn but the car was filled with a warm, heavy glow of sunlight seeping in the seams. A sudden banging on the right rear window made him jerk. He cautiously lifted the curtain. Two young kids, a boy and a girl, were peering in.

"Hey, mister! You okay? What's all the racket in there? You want me to go get my Dad?" the boy asked. The two kids looked to be in both shock and awe by Laszlo's contorted face.

"No! Go away! Everything's fine! Just fine. Leave me alone!"

The kids ran swiftly away, laughing. Laszlo dropped back on the floor, staring at the ceiling. Soaked in sweat, his ankle oozing blood, the nightmares were viciously increasing. They would never release him.

CHAPTER 24

Interstate 40
Lebanon, Tennessee

S irens wailed. Lights flashed through the thick haze. It was difficult to see. The soupy fog that collected every autumn morning in the Cumberland River Valley hadn't yet burned off. Tennessee State Police Lieutenant Skip Kenny was grim, and the weather wasn't helping his mood any. His breakfast had been interrupted and for a lousy traffic accident? Damn new recruits.

"Sir, it's something I think you should see!" the young officer had whined, his voice cracking with emotion. Kenny smirked as he rolled down the window. He let go with a spurt of tobacco juice that dispersed in the air behind them. He wiped his mouth with the cuff of his sleeve. Today would be a lesson. He'd teach 'em to interrupt his breakfast for a damn routine traffic call.

As the cruiser drew closer, the lieutenant spied a bunch of cruisers up ahead. County deputies and city cars, even two rescue vehicles. The place was lit up like a carnival. Well hell, it just could be something big. His white cruiser pulled off the road behind a row of six patrol cars. Their flashing lights ricocheted off trees standing like ghostly sentinels at the edge of the embankment.

Sergeant Billy Marks ran up the steeply sloped hill as soon as he glimpsed the cruiser. He immediately recognized the sleek Chevy belonging to the Commander of Tennessee State Police Barracks 16. The passenger door swung open, and two chocolate-colored lizard boots planted themselves on the ground. Skip Kenny's huge frame squeezed through the door.

He saw Billy coming toward him and nodded. Kenny kicked at the dirt, staring down the hill. He could make out what looked to be the rear end of a gold Ford LTD rammed between some trees at the bottom of the hill. Sheriff's Deputies and city police milled around it. Lieutenant Kenny turned and stooped down in the window, facing his corporal.

"Hey Joey, go ahead and get the camera out of the crime scene kit in the trunk, will ya? Let's get our own photos this time. You know how slow those slack-offs down at the city lab are in getting this stuff out to us!"

"You got it, Lieutenant. Get right on it." Eager to please, the young corporal was soon digging through the contents of the black-boxed crime-scene kit. He found the camera and jogged down the hill, the camera dangling from his hands.

"Hey Joey! There a fresh battery in that thing? You did check it, didn't ya?" Kenny shouted, already knowing the answer.

"Ah, get right on it, Lieutenant!" The corporal stopped so suddenly his boots skittered another foot or two in the dirt. He shrugged, turned, and ran back up the hill past the lieutenant.

Get right on it? Kenny thought. Right. That kid would lose his ass if it weren't attached. Corporal Joey needed a lot of work before the lieutenant turned him loose on the good citizens of Tennessee, an awful lot of work. He started down the slope, picking his way carefully to avoid scratching his polished boots.

As he reached the LTD, a man wearing a dark gray suit and sporting a pair of rubber gloves climbed out of the front seat. He peeled off the gloves, grinning as he turned to face Kenny.

"Well, Skip, took you a while to get here, didn't it? You are happy this morning, aren't you." The man was still grinning as he dropped the discarded gloves into a plastic bag.

"Hell, I'm happy as a puppy with two peters. Don't go changing that by giving me any of your shit, Robert E. 'Too early in the day to listen to your belly-aching. I was smack-dab in the middle of breakfast over at Dolly's. What we got here anyway?" Kenny turned away to spit, but the forensic examiner stopped him in his tracks with a stern shout.

"Skip, dammit, don't you dare! Don't even think about spitting on my crime scene, Lieutenant! You do, and I'll have your ass on the State Attorney General's rug before you can whistle Dixie. We're still collecting evidence here, Skip. Get that tobacco crap off'a my crime scene!"

Kenny's eyes bugged out. His eyebrows raised in despair, desperately seeking a spot to release. He held his bulging mouth and ran off into the trees. Moments later, he strolled back from the woods, wiping his chin with his shirt sleeve.

"Skip, you ain't changed a lick. That's a nasty damn habit, you know, and you need to get rid of it. 'Cost you one wife already!" Bob Lee, the forensic expert who everyone in the fine state of Tennessee called *Robert E.* for reasons that were obvious, doubled over at the sight of the lieutenant with his chin dripping brown juice.

"Dammit, Robert E., let's not get personal, huh? Some friend you are! Making me spit in the woods! I could'a got bit in there by a damn snake, a copperhead or something. You never know."

"Well, if you did, it would'a killed the snake for sure! No doubt about that! All right, come on over here, Lieutenant, and I'll show you what I've got."

The forensic examiner was still chuckling as his old friend walked back to the vehicle. Robert E. grabbed Kenny's arm, and together they poked their heads into the vehicle. Bright red, co-agulated blood was splattered all over the driver seat, dash, and steering wheel. They backed out and stood together.

"Find a body?"

"Nope." Robert E. shook his head.

"Okay, then what do you think is going on here?"

"Well, first of all, this ain't a one-car accident. The passen-ger side, from front to rear fender, is all banged up. We have some scrapes of burgundy paint. I'm gonna Fed-Ex some of the scrapings overnight up to the FBI lab along with the blood and tissue samples for chemical and spectrographic analysis. That'll give us the make, year, and model of whatever was ramming this LTD. Fresh skid marks are all over the road for the last ten miles on I-40. And, there's two sets of tire treads up there on the hill. Looks like somebody pulled over to take a look, most likely whoever had a hand in it. We're finished with the tire molds and I figure… "

"Tissue samples?"

"Yeah, minimal though. Some skin off the face. Banged the steering wheel pretty good. There's a lot of blood. But, that's consistent with moderate face or head injuries."

"Thanks. How do you know the other tracks weren't already up there?"

"Because they go right over the LTD's tracks."

"Who found it?" Kenny nodded.

"A county deputy, Mike Paulson. He's over there. Your guys have already talked to him." Robert E. pointed to the group of men still mulling around, chatting in front of the vehicle. "Run the plates yet?"

"Yep, and that was interesting too. 'Got 'em back pretty

damn quick for an out-of-state check. North Carolina plates and they're registered to a Douglas Theodore Chapman from Kitty Hawk. I understand that's out on Cape Hatteras. The county folks out there called after they found out we were making a trace on Chapman's car. Seems this Chapman fella's been missing… hasn't showed up for work in a couple days. Didn't call anyone, leave a note, nothing. He's a coroner and a forensics examiner. They say his office was ransacked."

"No kidding, another forensics puke. They're all over the place, ain't they? Shit, I bet he ain't got half your personality though, Robert E."

"Touché, Skip. Anyway, this guy's office, lab, and his house out on the beach were all tore up. Investigators don't know what to make of it. They're looking at some of Chapman's recent cases, hoping that might bear some fruit. From what they said and from what I see here, I'll make a sophisticated, wild-ass guess that somebody's chasing this Chapman fella. If they followed him all the way out here, they're pretty damn serious about catching up with him, too."

"You mean you think they don't already have him?"

"Don't think so. Not from what we've found. Somebody left a trail through the woods and a good amount of blood too. He's running. Tracks go north to the river. I think somebody was trying to run him off the road and finally succeeded. But it looks like Chapman survived. I don't think they came down here."

"Why's that?"

"Well, for one thing, Deputy Paulson says that when he got here, only one set of tire tracks came down the slope, no footprints. A passing car might'a scared 'em off. They might've thought he was dead, too. From the looks of the car, he had to be doing seventy, maybe seventy-five. He's lucky. That big old LTD engine and frame saved him. That's my wild-ass guess, anyway."

"Sounds good to me. How long ago do you figure?"

"Well, from the looks of the blood coagulation, I'd say two, maybe two and a half hours. Engine was already cooled down. Not much more than that though."

"Okay. Look, thanks Robert E., you've always got the answers. I'll take it from here. Bob, please keep me posted on the lab results, okay? It could help." Kenny thrust out his arm and shook hands firmly.

"You'll be the first one I call, Skip. I promise. Lunch this week?"

"Sure, call me. We'll go over to Dolly's. I didn't exactly get my weekly ration of grease this morning. I must still be at least a quart low!"

They both laughed. Lee clapped a hand on Kenny's shoulder, and Kenny waved to the officers still with the LTD. He turned back up the slope.

"Hey Billy, Joey, let me see both of you up at the car! Now... please!"

"Joey, get on the radio and call Lt. Benson over at Barracks 15. Tell Mack I need six or seven cars and at least fourteen troopers over here as quick as he can get them to me. And tell him that I know I owe him."

"Yes sir, Lieutenant. You got it. I'll get right on it!"

Joey climbed in the Caprice. In seconds had the airwaves crackling. Kenny pulled Billy toward the trunk of the Caprice.

"Billy, call the dispatcher. Get the mid-shift guys and their cars out here. Wake 'em up, call 'em in from the grocery stores, whatever. I want I-40 and every intersecting road north of here to the river blanketed like new snow in December. We're looking for a burgundy vehicle of some sort. I want two officers in each car. Shotguns. Everybody in Kevlar vests and full tactical loads. Tell them to pull over any suspicious vehicle and check them out thoroughly. Got it?"

"Yes, sir. This thing's that serious, huh?"

"Right now, I'd say so. Whoever Douglas Theodore Chapman is, chances are good he's still alive. I want to keep him that way. He's one of us, Billy, a forensic examiner. This thing has the stink of a hit all over it."

"A hit? Here in Lebanon, Tennessee?"

"That's what it looks like. Yep, right here in Mayberry. So get on the radio and, hey, wait… call Barrister and tell him to get his dogs out here. And fast, like now. Don't let Tommy Lee give you any shit about it either. Tell him I'll throw his moonshine-running ass in jail for a month. In fact, do that first, all right? We absolutely have to find this Chapman guy."

"You sure you want Barrister's dogs, not the county blood-hounds? Ole Sheriff Janson's gonna be pissed when he finds out we didn't use his dogs on something this big!"

"Billy, just do what I told you. Tommy Lee's dogs can find any-thing. If it's on the face of the planet, they can find it. Those damn county dogs are useless as hen shit on a pump handle. They couldn't find Sheriff Janson's fat ass and that's bigger than half the county."

The lieutenant shook his head, turned, and watched the dark stream splatter on a tree trunk. He walked to the edge of the hill and stood in the wet grass, staring over the miles of forest slop-ing gently to the Cumberland River. The fog was burning off. Sun would be out soon.

Skip pulled a can from his rear pocket, opened it, and without looking rolled a pinch of the dark tobacco between his fingers. He stuffed it into his right cheek and grimaced. He slipped off his hat, wiped the inside band with his handkerchief, and settled it back on his head. Kenny fixed his vision once more out across the valley, hands on his hips.

"Billy, I want to get to this guy before whoever did this does. Let's just do it, okay partner?"

"Yes, sir." Sergeant Billy Marks was gone in an instant.

CHAPTER 25

Langley Center
Northern Virginia

P hil O'Donnell stormed through the first-floor cafeteria, flipping aside chairs as he wound his way through the tables. At 10:30 in the morning, the place was empty. He could see Mark Bennis through the glass doors ahead. Mark was sitting at a picnic table with his back to the building and huddled over a cup of coffee. O'Donnell shoved open the doors and stalked up behind him.

"Hi Phil, I tried to… " Bennis turned to greet him.

His face as red as an Irish setter, O'Donnell cut him off. His big mouthful of straight white teeth were grinding in an angry scowl. He bent to within inches of Bennis' startled face.

"Just what the hell is going on, Mark? You see the headlines in the Washington Post yet? *Drug War Erupts in Suburban Virginia Neighborhood*? You've got this whole fucking thing going down the toilet. Shit! This had better be good, Mark, so start talking!"

O'Donnell backed off a foot or so, but still hovered with his back hunched up. His arms were straight at his sides, his hands balled into fists. Bennis, his face white as a sheet from the close-quarter verbal assault, pushed himself backwards against the table.

"Yeah, Phil, I saw it. Take it easy. I've got it covered. We underestimated Brannon, that's what happened. But media went the way we wanted it, Phil."

"Excuse me? We underestimated Brannon? And in Suburban, almost rural damn Virginia? A nice high-rent neighborhood a stone's throw from a major university campus? Members of two opposing black gangs? From downtown D.C.? In an open shoot-out? That's bullshit! You've got shit for brains, Mark! Who the hell is gonna buy that? That story won't last three days, not if the FBI or DEA takes a good look at it anyway. Oh, and the three idiots you hired – what were their names, Rosen and Wilkins and, excuse me, Weinberg? Your brain's melting, Mark! The bastards weren't even black!"

"Take it easy. Gees, who's melting down, anyway? Those guys *were* black when I saw them! Crispy critters, nothing but charred bones. We weren't far behind. We caught up and tossed an incendiary device in the Camaro. What was left of them was blown to pieces over a half-block area. They're nothing but lawn fertilizer now. The second car got there almost immediately and retrieved the tech stuff. We're okay, Phil." Bennis stretched out his hands.

O'Donnell glared back at him. He wasn't having any of it. As far as he could tell, things were deteriorating at the speed of light.

"You're clueless, Mark! If you don't get this fixed, and fixed real soon, you're gonna see what the inside of a prison looks like. You may wanna do that, but I don't!"

"Phil, calm down. We can work this together. Have you reported to Tanham yet?" It was the first time Bennis had seen O'Donnell scared, really scared.

"No, dammit! Why the hell do you think I came here? To see if you had anything helpful. As usual, you're clueless. I don't know why the hell I left this to you. I thought you had more smarts than this. Now the whole damn thing's caving in!"

Frustrated, O'Donnell sank down on the picnic bench opposite Bennis. He threw his hands up hopelessly. He turned away to face the woods.

"Phil, what do you plan to tell Tanham? You need help with that?"

"Help? From who… you? Gimme a break! And look, I don't want Tanham taking any more of a hands-on approach than he already has. He's getting cold feet. He's worried. I can tell. He'll dump the whole damn thing if I let him. No, I want to keep John Boy in the background. I'll take care of this myself, and when I do, I'll have Tanham's damn job too!"

"I know you will. I know… "

"Mark, you don't know shit, and you keep proving it over and over. The JOG thing's totally screwed up. Hell, they couldn't even contain Laszlo on the continent. And Nordheimer's expert surveillance teams couldn't keep up with Novak either. And, Novak's not a field agent!"

"Hey, Novak had help, serious help from somebody. The JOG in Frankfurt said that those guys, whoever the hell they were, were pro's."

"Listen to you. *Whoever the hell they were?* What do I have to do, draw you a picture? That's even worse. Probably German intelligence, who knows? But then tell me, how does Novak suddenly go and hook up with a bunch of German intelligence types? We don't even know who they are, much less what they know or why they're involved!"

"Phil, please, it's just a matter of time. Give me a chance."

"No, you're out of time. You missed Laszlo. I don't give a

damn what excuses the JOG has. They're supposed to be the best. The fact is, Laszlo Csengerny is extremely dangerous. They should have localized him, then wasted him at the same time they blew Yezhovich away, the lousy traitor. That's the only bright spot so far... Yezhovich can't do any more damage. Then you missed Brannon. Your idiot temporary hires got themselves blown away and on the front page of the Washington Post! Where the hell are you hiring these guys anyway, down at the unemployment office?"

"Phil, I... "

"Stop! You missed this guy Chapman too. Who knows where that's gonna go."

"Well, the guys said they're pretty sure he's dead. His car was totally destroyed."

"Listen, I don't bet on *pretty sure*. It keeps me awake at night. What about Chapman – can he tie the JOG or us to Spencer's death?"

"We didn't find anything down there. But he does know something. He called Brannon back and as much as told him so."

"How do you know that, a tap?"

"Of course. Brannon's place is wired as well. We had it covered."

"Don't give me any more of that. Nothing's covered. I want Brannon run down, and I don't care how many contractors it takes to do it. Brannon's got to go. Make sure you get the right assets to do it this time. Brannon's resourceful. He's as good as everybody says he is. Brannon's killed more men than anyone in the Company could care to count. Send a team down to get the details on Chapman as well. I want to know... is he dead or not dead? If he's not dead, then make him dead. And, fast."

"Okay."

"As for Mister Csengerny, hell, we don't even know if he's

still in Canada. Call our Domestic Contacts Division, the DCD. That's a legitimate step to take and we'd be expected to use them in a situation like this. Have them cover the border crossings and ports on the Great Lakes. They don't need to know why. Send a couple up to Cleveland to be within arm's reach for whenever we localize him. I want that sonofabitch dead and buried within the week. He's too close.

"We'll press on it."

"Mark, if Laszlo gets to Denver… gees, this whole thing will be on Channel 4 News. We can't move Mike now. We only have the one environmental system, so we're stuck. This stuff has got to stay under wraps at any cost. Damn, if the Russians even get a twinkling of this, who Mike really is, those paranoid bastards will pre-empt. And we'll respond. The entire planet will go up in thermonuclear smoke. We need more time to field the system. Mike is still critical to that. We can't just come close… this ain't horseshoes."

"All right. You want me to put Company types on this?"

"Hell no! Use your head. One of our guys might go and develop a conscience. It's *no* to that, and I don't want any more Keystone Cops, either. Like I said, get the best contractors you can. Lastly, and this is the most important part – Novak's got to meet with a terrible accident. We can't count on him being the naive golden boy anymore. The Yezhovich and Spencer thing, you know how damn dangerous that information is. They were U.S. citizens. We could lose our asses."

"Good God, Phil. Pete Novak? I don't…?"

"Nordheimer went well beyond his authorities with Pete Novak. The JOG told me they're certain of it. JOG will take care of Nordheimer. Novak… damn, Brannon must have found some way to get to him and spin him up. That would explain how Novak got the very capable foreign friends so quickly. Pete

Novak may just be the most dangerous man on the playing field right now! He'd get Kriegel and the DCI to put us away in a heartbeat. End of the JOG. End of you. End of me. No, I want Novak floating face down in the Potomac. It's gotta look good, credible. A criminal thing, a robbery, or something."

"I still don't…"

"What? You still don't know? You'd better know. Novak is the man who can send your ass to prison. You're too cute and too stupid to go to prison. You wouldn't stay anal retentive for more than a month!"

"What the hell does that mean?"

"It means you'd best get on the move, Mark. Fast, professional, and closely coordinated. I want a clean sweep. Within the week. No holds barred, no witnesses. This *is* in the nation's best interest. And, we're the ones carrying the flag here. Don't forget it."

"I'll take care of it."

"Right. I'm counting on you. Your pretty wife is counting on you. Your kids are counting on you, too. So get your ass moving! I want you to brief me by close of business tonight on what you've got lined up."

"Will do." Bennis rose from his seat. He left, not looking back, and leaving behind a cold cup of coffee.

CHAPTER 26

The Hyatt
Rosslyn, Virginia

Brannon woke to the sound of car engines revving. He wondered why he was shivering. It was freezing in the basement lot. Yesterday seemed like a bad dream. But he felt the glass crunch under his elbows and knew it was real. His eyes drifted mournfully over what was left of his car. The rear window was gone. The back seat was riddled with more bullet holes than he cared to count. They had lodged into the front bucket seats, some in the dash. The speedometer and tachometer were both splintered. He wondered if they'd work at all.

He sat up, scanning the garage. No one in the immediate vicinity. It was a hair before 7:00 a.m. The rush hour was in full swing throughout Washington. J.T. opened the door and groaned as he crawled out. His muscles ached from the cramped quarters and the cold air. Brannon stretched out on the cement floor to check out the car's underside. There was no leakage, not a drip.

"Good girl," he muttered, patting the side panel. Next, under the hood. From what he could see in the garage's dim yellow light, there was no damage in the engine compartment either. Remarkable. He closed the hood and walked to the rear, cringing. A mess. Fifteen, maybe twenty neat little bullet holes riddled the trunk lid. Both tail lights shot out. And, of course, the rear window was all over the back seat. He caught his reflection in a side window. Other than two days' growth of beard, he didn't look so bad. He knew a toothbrush and some toothpaste would help. So would breakfast.

J.T. stepped off the elevator on the lobby level and made a beeline for the concession store. He caught a few stares from the business-suit types milling around, waiting for their day of Washington politicking or lobbying to begin. He ignored them.

After brushing his teeth and washing his face in the restroom off the lobby, he straightened his clothes and headed to the restaurant. A cheerful waiter handed him the day's *Washington Post* and poured his first cup of coffee. Before he could even raise the cup to his lips, his eyes widened at the headlines in front of him. The burned-out Camaro, still smoking and flipped over onto its roof, filled the front page. The fire made it almost unrecognizable.

Brannon scanned the story… something about rival black gangs from southeast D.C. engaged in a chase and shootout in Fairfax, Virginia, near George Mason University. The mayor had made his usual comments reaffirming intentions to quell gang violence for the millennium.

"Goodness gracious, this is weak, guys. Real weak. You gotta be able to do better than this." He whispered, suppressing a laugh. But a somber look swept over his face as he recognized the reality of the situation. He needed to act, but do what, and how?

It was a hearty breakfast. His fork played with the scrambled eggs as he tried once again to piece it together. However, just like before, he kept coming down the same path. The Maria Dean and Yezhovich stuff stifled him. Yezhovich was a traitor. And, according to Carolyn, his being a blabbermouth got him in trouble long before he went to Europe. What was it? Oh yeah, NICAP, the National Investigations Committee on Aerial Phenomena. He'd never heard of MAJIC, but he'd heard of Blue Book because it was actually published in the open. Blue Book was an Air Force report that took a lot of heat in the press as being a cover up on UFO sightings.

UFOs? What the hell could be stranger than that? Brannon shook his head. He couldn't make much sense of it. It was almost nine o'clock when he paid the tab. He walked purposefully to the lobby pay phones. His first call was to Virginia National Bank in Vienna, Virginia. That done, he dialed a number to Compton, a little town on the edge of Breton Bay. Compton sat at the southern wedge-shaped peninsula of Maryland's western shore, a stone's throw from Chesapeake Bay. A deep-throated male voice answered.

"Coastal."

"Is Cat there?"

"He's in the hangar. Hold on, I'll get him."

J.T. heard the soft *clunk* of the phone being laid on a hard surface. Coastal was short for Coastal Air Transport, CAT, a small regional air transport company, six or seven helicopters. Bobbie *Cat* Garvey, sole proprietor of the company, was an old friend of Brannon's from his Special Forces days. Like Brannon, Bobbie had been trained as an assassin. His nickname, *Cat*, belied his prowess. He used it to name his company after he came back to the 'States in 1973.

"Yo, Cat here. What can I do for you?"

"Cat, this is Brannon. How're things?" A long pause followed.

222

"Brannon? J.T. Brannon, you old bastard! Gees, what're you up to? No good, I bet!" Cat laughed, his voice suddenly booming over the phone.

"I need a favor, Cat, a big one."

"That's the only kind of favor you spooks ask for, Brannon... big ones. I bet national security depends on it too, right?"

"Cat, I need your help. The Chevy is all shot up, but I think she'll make it out there if you tell me you can help."

"The Super Sport, shot up? Shit, who'd you piss off now, the President?"

"Company."

"Whoa, you serious? You get on somebody's shit list all of a sudden? What's going on?"

"Honest, Cat, you don't want to know. But, you're the only one I could think of."

"Hey, you know better. Hell, I'd love to pay those bastards back a few favors anyway. You know how I felt about you going to work for those assholes to begin with. Can you get all the way down here? Will the Chevy make it?"

Concern thickened Cat's voice. Garvey would never forget how Brannon had pulled him out of several deteriorating fire fights. J.T. saved him from certain death on at least one occasion that Cat could think of.

"That's a *yes* and another *yes*."

"What is it that you need from me?"

"Well, what's one of your Bell choppers go for these days?"

"One of my UH-1s? A lease? How long do you need it? And hey, since when can you fly?"

"No lease. I'm buying."

"You're shitting me, right?"

"No, I'm not. We can talk about it when I get there. Will $100 thousand cover it?"

"That'll do for the right bird. Nothing fancy. Where we going?"

"That's good, because that's how much I've already wired to your account at Chesapeake National Bank. I need to get to the Outer Banks in North Carolina. Manteo Airport down on Roanoke Island. Can one of your birds make it down there unrefueled?"

"Shouldn't be a problem. The way I've configured these babies, all my Bells can go 350 miles without a shot of gas. It shouldn't be more than 250 down there. I'll look at the charts, though, and I'll bring my swimsuit just in case. That is, I assume you want me to go with you? Or do you have your own pilot?"

"No, it's you and me again, Cat. Just like old times. I can't thank you enough. Please know that."

"As far as I'm concerned, J.T., you're blood kin. Get down here safe. Ah, before you hang up, I need to ask... I know it's a silly question, but do you want me to file a flight plan? You know, that little legal requirement of the FAA's."

"Yes. Do it."

"Yes? That's rich. Now you really got me confused. What's up your sleeve?"

"See you in a couple hours, Cat. Thanks again. Get two Hueys fueled up."

"Two... hey, I thought you said one? Brannon, you've got me going... "

There was a click on the line. J.T. was gone. Cat slowly set the phone down, shaking his head. He stuck his hands in his jeans pockets and walked pensively out of the small office. Standing in the pale autumn sunlight, he looked up and saw a long line of Canadian geese heading southeast to the eastern shore. This time of year, the sky was crowded with them. The eastern flyway ran right down the peninsula. They were a beautiful sight. Garvey turned and strode across the clearing to the left of the office and called out for his right-hand man.

"Mason! Come on out here!"

"Yeah, Cat, what ya need?" A middle-aged man in grease-splattered coveralls appeared from the hangar with a wrench in his hand.

"Start fueling birds Four and Six. Then call Frank. He probably tied another one on last night, but tell him I want him here within the next two hours. Two hours, no later. I might need a second pilot."

"Sure. What for?"

"Never mind *what for* this time, Mason. I don't know yet myself."

"Okay, boss. Harry and I'll take care of it."

"Thanks."

Cat walked back to the office, turned and stared through the large windows toward the field of Bell Aircraft Hueys, all sitting patiently on their cement pads. He'd fallen in love with them during his Spec Ops days. Hueys had plucked him out of many nasty situations. They were like angels from heaven and always just in time. He'd learned to fly them himself. Now they were both his family and his life.

J.T. couldn't think of anything crazier to do, so he did it. Instead of turning south out of the Hyatt's garage, he swung left and headed down the hill straight for the Francis Scott Key Bridge. Just before the bridge, he dropped the Chevy down onto the George Washington Memorial Parkway, going north. It took him right by the Company's front door.

225

The Chevelle roared on up the parkway past the exit for the Agency and in minutes merged into eastbound I-495 Beltway traffic. An occasional glance in the rear-view mirror kept him satisfied – no tails. Then again, it was difficult to single out any suspect vehicle in four lanes of heavy traffic.

This JOG squad outfit probably had half the world out looking for him by now. The Chevy bored down the beltway. At the Route 50 exit off the Beltway, J.T. swung west toward Annapolis. He jumped off at the interchange with Route 301 South towards the Southern Maryland peninsula. An hour later, he was on Route 5, the last long leg of his journey south. The rear-view showed nothing. He breathed a sigh of relief and settled down in the seat.

CHAPTER 27

Breton Bay, Compton
Southern Maryland

The SS-396 swung off Route 243 just north of Compton and bounced down the dirt road toward Breton Bay. The woods on both sides of the dusty road were thick with oaks and scraggly Carolina pines. After three quarters of a mile, he could make out the clearing ahead. He passed a large black-and-white sign strung between two trees: *Coastal Air Transport, Private Property: KEEP OUT.*

The Chevelle swung into the grassy clearing as the road broke away from the surrounding forest. It bounced to a stop in front of the small brick building. The door opened and Cat Garvey walked out. J.T. jumped from the battered Chevy.

"Brannon, you old sonofabitch! How you doing, partner?"

Cat ran up, engulfing him in a huge bear hug. Brannon's face broke out in a broad grin. He hugged Cat just as fiercely. Cat was so damn tall and strong he nearly lifted Brannon off his toes.

"Gees, it's good to see you, Cat! 'Been too damn long. Shame on us for not seeing more of each other." They eased off, still sporting broad smiles. Cat threw his arm around J.T. and pulled him toward the office building.

"You're right about that. Shame on us. You're here now, though! Let me show you my set-up. Care for a cold beer?"

"Thanks. 'Sounds wonderful."

Cat pulled two beers from a fridge against the wall and pointed to a small table in the back. The two men sat talking in wooden chairs behind the counter. Cat shook his head in disgust several times as J.T. explained the situation. Tony Spencer's death hit him hard. His eyes glazed for a moment as he envisioned Tony standing with them and getting ready for a mission in front of their choppers.

The three of them were quite a team back then, that is, before everything went to hell in a hand basket. Body bags and more body bags. Cat knew he still had that photo somewhere. He wiped his nose with his big right hand and shook his head to focus on Brannon's story. Cat turned to the window at a sudden clatter. Both men stood to see Frank Halley's old Jeep swerve across the clearing, sliding to a stop just a few feet from the SS-396.

"Who the hell's that?" Brannon leaned over the counter to make sure the Jeep hadn't hit the Chevy.

"That's Frank Halley, one of my pilots. He's probably the best on the East Coast."

"Really?"

"Oh, don't let what you see out there bother you. Frank's a little nutty. He ties it on a lot. Lost his wife to colon cancer two years ago. She went fast. Frank went fast after that too. Down the toilet. He hasn't been totally sober since. But J.T., I wouldn't trade him for a squadron of those little puke helo pilots coming out of Fort Rucker now. Frank's damn good. 'A little crazy, that's all."

"If you say so. This is your show and I trust you."

"Hell, the way I see it, you ain't got any damn choice, you old dinosaur!"

Cat leaned back in a huge belly laugh. He grabbed Brannon's arm to pull him out the door. Frank Halley staggered up to greet them.

"Frank, meet J.T. Brannon." The two shook hands. "Frank, you okay to fly?"

"Just gimme me a set of coordinates, Cat. Give me a vector," Frank's his eyes rolled.

"You sure you're okay? We need you on this." Brannon didn't like what he saw.

"Cat, haven't you given this guy the skinny on me? Look, *Brannon* is it, this is as sober as you're gonna see me. I take a lot of pain killers, right, Cat?"

"Right. He takes a lot of pain killers. Okay then, let's get into the hangar. I'll brief you on the flight. I filed the flight plan with the FAA, so we know they'll be watching us. You're manifested, J.T."

"Good. Thanks."

"Hi, Frank. Cat, when do you want me to get outta here and take the van to the recovery strip?" Mason had walked up as the three men neared the hangar. He tipped his baseball cap in Halley's direction.

"Like I said before, as soon as you're sure Frank's ship is off. As soon as he's off."

"Sure, Cat. I just forgot, that's all."

"I want you off this air patch and down at the recovery strip when we get inland. If Mr. Brannon here is correct, there may very well be a shitload of unfriendly people crawling all over this place tonight. You don't wanna be here when that happens. After tonight, we're all gonna take a vacation and disappear for a couple of weeks, with pay of course. So, just take it easy."

"Okay. Thanks, boss." Mason turned and jogged off to start pre-flight checks.

"While we're at it, J.T., you want to move the Chevelle?"

"No, leave it here. I've got the keys. If they want to bust her open any further, that's their business. And yeah, I'll tear their fucking hearts out if they do."

"I'll be happy to help you with that myself. All right, let's take a look at the charts."

They leaned over a big wooden table groaning under a sea of maps. After 20 minutes, they were sure they'd covered everything. It was almost two o'clock when all of them walked out of the hangar and toward the Hueys. The sky was slightly overcast.

"J.T., go ahead and jump in the right front seat in ship 6-3-0. Frank, remember to give me exactly five minutes. Five minutes. Then I want you on the water behind me, skimming and killing fish. And I do mean skimming, Frank, real low, 30 feet. Under the radars."

"Got it, Cat. Go on, get the hell outta here." The two men exchanged grins and a thumbs-up. Mason ran toward Cat and ship 630 for takeoff.

"Rotate!" The turboshaft engine on ship Six fired, and the massive 24-foot blades began to move. Mason ran to the front, then the back of the ship, then came back up front. He raised both fists with their thumbs up. Cat saluted him, smiled, and the 40-foot chopper rose from the ground. Mason turned his back to the sudden assault of blowing sand.

Cat swung the Huey slowly over its pad to the south, lifted her up and forward. She burst over the grassy field and cleared the tree line in a steady climb. In minutes, they reached Breton Bay, still climbing to the south. The opposite shoreline of Virginia's northeastern tip was in view on the horizon.

As chopper number Six crossed the midline of the Potomac

River, chopper number Four eased off its pad. It too turned south. Mason waved good-bye as Frank's Bell chopper disappeared over the trees. The white company van ripped out of the Coastal Air Transport grounds three minutes later with Mason at the wheel, racing for Route 243.

An hour later, number Six had crossed the Chesapeake Bay and was passing over the tip of Virginia's eastern shore. The Bay Bridge-Tunnel was in sight just to the south. Cat held the Huey steady at an altitude of 800 feet as they cleared the last strips of beach and headed out over the deep-blue water of the Atlantic Ocean. Gorgeous. Smiles bridged the space between them.

"I see why you love this, Cat."

Garvey eased off on the power, slowing to about 100 miles per hour and dropping some altitude. Fifteen minutes later, he turned to Brannon, who was just beginning to enjoy the flight. Cat nodded and then eyed the overhead instrument panel.

"Mr. Brannon, sir, would you mind flipping the overhead switch above you for the radio-telephone. Put it on speaker, please. Please do so smartly, Mr. Brannon."

"Yes, Captain, will do. You have the Com, sir." Brannon reached up to flip the two switches. Their microphones were hot.

It didn't take long for them to draw attention. The voice sounded young. He was courteous but firm. His voice snapped over the speakers and echoed throughout the interior.

"Craft bearing 165 degrees south-southeast, this is Oceana Naval Air Station, Virginia Beach. Please identify. You are two hundred feet below minimum altitude. Identify. Is this Blue Crab 6-3-0? If so, be advised Blue Crab that you are off your registered flight plan. Please respond."

"Roger, Oceana. This is Blue Crab 6-3-0. I know I'm below minimums, but I have a power problem. Please open a corridor for me at this altitude, bearing 170 degrees south. I appreciate the assistance and thanks in advance."

"Negative. Negative, Blue Crab. No can do. Too much traffic in this quadrant. Initiate climb to minimum altitude or come in. Can you make Norfolk International?"

"We've got a power problem? Oh, that's great! How serious, Captain Garvey?" J.T. looked at Cat with his microphone still on and to his lips.

"Serious, Mr. Brannon, serious." Cat was smiling.

"Oceana, this is Blue Crab. No, I can't make Norfolk. We're too far southeast. I must be spitting oil somewhere. Maybe a ruptured line. Pressure is dropping off rapidly. I'm losing airspeed. Request you provide another vector. Over."

"Negative, Blue Crab. No other vector available unless you can make Cherry Point. Can you make Cherry Point MCAS?" The voice now sounded anxious.

"Cat, what the hell's going on? We're down to 550 feet! Shit, this ain't funny! Can we make… " Brannon was getting fidgety.

"Oceana, Blue Crab! Look, I have smoke coming from the turboshaft, repeat, I have smoke! Damn! Acknowledge! Oceana, acknowledge!" Cat's voice was agitated. He looked to the rear of the fuselage and saw smoke seeping into the tail section. The engine was starting to whine. Brannon also turned to look back, then to Cat, shaking his head. His fingers slid down along his side, gripping the seat cushion.

"Blue Crab, this is Oceana! "I'll… wait… no, we will begin… ah…"

The young man's agitation was cut off midstream. In an instant, he was off the frequency. Another voice immediately took over. This one, again male, was much deeper, more authoritative.

"Blue Crab 6-3-0, this is Norfolk Naval Base, repeat, this is Norfolk Naval Base. We have you on scope and have assumed operational control from Oceana. Report your air speed and altitude. Repeat, report air speed and altitude. Acknowledge smoke. What is your assessment of situation? Do you see fire, repeat, do you see fire? Norfolk out."

"Read you, Norfolk. Thank you. I gotta tell ya, this is ruining my day. Air speed is down to 70 miles an hour. Not too much flux left in the throttle. My altitude is, well, I'm passing through 400 feet now. Do you read?" Cat pushed the stick forward, pointing the rotors more fully into the wind. He tried to squeeze as much extra distance out of the ship as he could.

"Read you loud and clear, Blue Crab. Let me have your condition. Bring your ship to a new heading of 270 degrees east, repeat, turn to new course 270 degrees east. I'm opening a corridor for you. I have a corridor secured at your current altitude. Do you see fire? Norfolk out."

"Fire? I don't think so. Probably just the… uh-oh, wait a minute. Gees, that's affirmative, Norfolk. I have fire! Repeat, I do have fire! Looks like it's spreading along the, whoa…engine's gone, Norfolk! My engine's gone! This is a May-Day. Repeat, May-Day. Request surface air rescue. We're going down, Norfolk. Blue Crab 6-3-0 is ditching. Preparing for crash. Blue Crab out."

The loud whir of the Turboshaft engine was suddenly gone. Garvey looked at Brannon, both grimaced. Smoke crept through the fuselage and into the cockpit.

"Blue Crab, Norfolk! Blue Crab, reply! Do you copy? I am vectoring an Orion aircraft to your coordinates. They will guide you in. Can you bring… "

"Come on, Captain, we're down past 100 feet! Shit, the water's coming up fast! Do something, dammit!" J.T. cut off the controller's voice. His fingers were now scrunched white around the edge of his seat.

"Blue Crab, Norfolk. Your co-pilot is breaking up your transmission. Give me... "

"Help us! Please, help! Save us!" J.T. yelled. At this, Cat raised his eyebrows, glaring with a frown at Brannon. He shook his head, thinking – *There he goes again, Brannon, always for the dramatic.*

"Blue Crab, give me your situa..."

The radio-telephone suddenly cut out. Blue Crab 6-3-0 dropped off the radar scope. No blip on the screen and dead silence on the frequency. The controller paused for 10 seconds, straining to hear something through the static. He opened the frequency again.

"Sea Snake 1-2-2, this is Norfolk. I've lost Blue Crab. Our radar doesn't look below 100 feet altitude. He must have gone in. Reported ditching. Do you copy?"

"Roger, Norfolk. I have Blue Crab's last coordinates. We're working a vector as we speak. We should be on station in 8 minutes or so. Request you prep an SH-3 back-up to extract any survivors. Request a Sea King out here. Over."

The P-3 Orion Pelican banked steeply, climbed, and the four Allison turboprop engines screamed out their reluctance. The pilot brought her around to vector 310 degrees northwest, shoving the throttles full forward. The Pelican would have turned home in less than an hour anyway. Her patrol shift of maritime surveillance along the Mid-Atlantic coast was just about finished for the day. The four turboprops roared as the Navy Commander firewalled the throttles, pushing her airspeed to 270 miles per hour toward Blue Crab's last coordinates.

"Norfolk, this is Sea Snake. There is some smoke aloft. Repeat, we have sighted smoke aloft. Could be from a crash. Do you copy, over?"

"Roger, Sea Snake. Continue transmission."

The pilot quickly closed the distance. He dropped altitude and brought the ship down for a closer look. Within 300 feet of the water, he spotted debris.

"We're over the crash site now, Norfolk. Gees, she's gone. Must have gone down fast. There are *no* survivors in sight. Repeat, no survivors in sight. Rough seas out here. I'll do another pass. I don't think there's any need for an SH-3 out here, repeat, negative on the Sea King. There's absolutely nobody here. Lots of big breakers, six footers. Ice cold water too now that the Gulf Stream's moved out. Whoever they were, they wouldn't last long. Let me swing around again." Like a huge bird of prey, the Pelican swooped down again.

"Nope, that's a negative. No need for surface air rescue. Please acknowledge." The pilot climbed another 500 feet bearing east, preparing to sweep the area one last time. The P-3 swung down once more like a seagull aiming for a fish.

"Roger, Sea Snake. Acknowledged. For the record, please describe the debris."

"A piece of a rotor fan is still floating, but no, it's going under. Some cushions. Also maybe a piece of the fuselage, tail section maybe. We got a pretty good-sized oil slick and what looks like a couple of jackets. No raft. Repeat, no raft in sight. Acknowledge."

"Roger, acknowledged. Damn! I'll turn the Sea King around. You sure you don't need them to come and take a closer look?"

"Negative, Norfolk. There's nothing here to see. They're gone. Suggest you notify the Coast Guard. A cutter might be able to scoop up something in a couple of hours, but in these seas, I seriously doubt it. I'm dropping a locator beacon in any case. Notify FAA yet?"

"Negative, Sea Snake. I'll attend to that post haste. Return to base and get some coffee. Sea Lion has launched and is up and on orbit. Thanks for the assist. Norfolk out."

"'Sorry we were too late. That's a shame." The pilot shook his head and turned to his co-pilot, covering the mike with his hands before he spoke.

"Damn civilian pilots. Amateurs, all amateurs." He raised the mike.

"Well, Norfolk, coffee sounds good. Save some for us. Returning to base. Sea Snake out." The pilot made one last pass with the Orion, still saw nothing, and swung into a new course of 290 degrees northwest to Norfolk.

CHAPTER 28

Operations Watch Center
Headquarters CIA

The trainee grimaced. On his first-ever shift, he wanted to get everything right. Nervous, he turned to the Senior Duty Officer at the middle desk two rows behind him.

"Sir, line 23 please, it's the FAA. We have a personnel action report, sir, a probable deceased officer. You want me to take it?"

"No, Fred, thanks, I have the line. Good afternoon, Langley Center. This is Officer Peterson. How can I help you?"

The duty officer's features reflected his experience. His gray hair was thinning rapidly. His face had the weathered look of too many years of extreme stress, like so many operations agents who had stayed out in the field too long. His brow furrowed as he took down the details. Cory Peterson knew J.T. Brannon well.

Peterson quietly laid down the phone. He pushed away from the desk and swiveled his chair toward the smoked-glass wall behind him. He reached into a back pocket for a handkerchief. Brass-rimmed bifocals dropped into his lap as the handkerchief covered his face. He sighed deeply. Reaching behind to the desk, he groped until he grabbed the pad of notes. Despite the rush of emotion, his hand was steady as it settled the glasses back into place.

"Randy."

"Yes sir?" The reply came from a desk off to the left.

"Take the post, Randy. I have to make a few notifications. Back in a couple of minutes."

Peterson walked heavily to the communications area behind the Operations Center. His right hand hung limply down as it swung with his stride, ruffling the pages of the notepad as he walked. The green phone was just ahead on the main console.

"Jack Riley, Personnel. How can I help you?" The Chief of Personnel picked it up on the first ring.

"Jack, Cory Peterson. I have the Watch in the Ops Center. I've got some bad news. We need to start the notification chain. A deceased officer. FAA called not two minutes ago."

"Who is it?"

"It's J.T. Brannon. Know him?"

"Well, I've met him, but I guess I know his reputation more than I know the man himself. He's been around a long time. I thought I'd get him retired this year, but he insisted on staying on. He's been pulling security escort duty. Pete Novak's man, I believe. How'd it happen?"

"Helicopter crash at sea. This afternoon, between 3:00 and 3:30 p.m. FAA says the pilot reported an engine problem, then smoke and fire. They went down pretty fast. A Navy Orion assisted and confirmed debris at the crash site. They found a piece of the tail section, a section of rotor blade, and some stuff from inside, you know, cushions, jackets. Big oil slick too. There were no survivors. I understand the seas were pretty heavy. Only two people manifested on the flight, the pilot and Brannon. The pilot was a Robert Garvey, owner of Coastal Air Transport, a small regional outfit down in southern Maryland. Their flight plan was filed for Compton, Maryland, south to Manteo, North Carolina. Damn! What a way to go!"

"You know, ah, *knew* him well, Cory?"

"Oh yeah, I've known J.T. quite a while. Brannon's the kind of guy who would have wanted to go down fighting. You know, a gun blazing in each hand. He was an old field operations war-horse. Jack, I really don't think there's any next of kin. J.T. was divorced a long time ago, no kids. You know how that is. Please keep a handle on this for me, will you? I'd like to get to the funeral. They'll surely bury him over in Arlington and well, that's where Brannon should be. Shit! Hard to believe he's gone. J.T. was getting to be an institution around here. Anyway, thanks in advance, Jack."

"I'll keep you informed, be glad to, Cory. Take care and thanks for the call. You gonna call Kriegel?"

"Yeah, soon as I hang up. Bye, Jack."

"Bye."

"Dr. Kriegel's office." Joyce Cowan's brisk voice answered,

"Joyce, good afternoon. This is Cory Peterson. I'm the SDO today down in the Ops Center. Is Doc in?"

"Well, he'll be at his desk in about twenty seconds. He's just coming back with the afternoon's fourth cup of coffee. He says he's charging his batteries! I'll connect you."

"Kriegel here," Doc's business-like tone was marred by him sipping at his coffee.

"Doc, this is Cory Peterson on watch down in the Ops Center."

"Yes, Cory. How're you doing? What's up?"

"Sir, I just got off the phone with FAA Center. They have what they believe is reliable confirmation regarding the death of one of our officers in a crash at sea. A Navy Orion confirmed crash debris at the site, but found no survivors."

"Who is it, Cory?"

"J.T. Brannon, sir."

"Brannon? Oh no. Are you sure?"

"FAA and Navy both say they're sure as they can be. A flight plan was filed for Compton, Maryland, to Manteo, North Carolina. Sir, I believe that's down near... "

"I know where it is, Cory. Go on."

"Okay. Only two persons manifested, Brannon and the pilot, a Robert Garvey. There's an old personnel file on Garvey. We tried to vet him, recruit him sometime back. Well, the Orion reached the site about ten minutes after impact. A lot of debris. They said it was commensurate with what they'd expect to find. Heavy seas, cold water too. FAA says the Navy told them that if the crash didn't kill them *and* if they got out of the chopper before it sank... oh, it was a Huey that crashed, sir. The bottom line is that it would have been a near-miracle if they lasted more than a couple of minutes in the six-foot breakers and freezing water. I'm sorry, Doc. I liked him a great deal myself."

"Thanks, Cory. Well, I did too. However, there's more than a few though that didn't feel that way. They wanted to see him go. J.T. was from another era, one with far different requirements and fewer constraints than we have now. Not that that's bad or good, worse or better, just a different time and place. You know what I'm saying?"

"Yes sir, I do. Is there anything else you'd like me to do?" Peterson's voice was thick, near strangled. J.T.'s death was just starting to sink in.

"No, not that I can think of... uh, did you call Jack Riley?"

"Yes sir. First call I made."

"Good work, Cory. No, I guess that's it. Boy, this is bad news. Pete Novak's gonna take this hard. Cory, do you have any information about why Brannon was going down to the Outer Banks?"

"No, sir. Don't have a clue. Would you like me to check on that?"

"No, that's okay. I'll handle that at this end. Cory, thanks for the briefing and the good work. You take care now."

"Yes sir. Thanks, Doc." Kriegel hung up and settled back in his big leather chair, a grim look on his face. He shook his head and reached for the intercom.

"Yes sir?"

"Joyce, see if you can get in touch with Pete Novak. I think he stayed over in Frankfurt an extra day, but I really don't know where he is at the moment. Try the Frankfurt station, Bill Nordheimer first. He may even be in the air by now. I want to speak with him myself. See if you can get a line on him, okay?"

"Yes sir. I'll try Frankfurt first. Anything else?"

"No, please just stay available until you've located Pete. Joyce… the bottle of Cognac, the Rémy Martin. Where are we hiding it these days?"

"It's in the sitting room, sir. Center door on the bookcase. Shall I get that first?"

"No, no. I'll get it. Thanks."

"Yes sir." Joyce set the receiver down. She knew the Rémy Martin was reserved primarily for late afternoon guests in the sitting room. However, Doc also reached for it in situations he found emotionally difficult.

Word of Brannon's demise spread rapidly through Langley Headquarters. Some were deeply saddened at the news. Some didn't know J.T. Brannon. Others couldn't care less. But Mark Bennis and Phil O'Donnell hid their smiles and sat huddled in O'Donnell's third-floor office. O'Donnell was highly pleased with the turn of events. He wanted to make sure the next 48 hours were carefully managed to optimize the situation. First off, he didn't trust Brannon, not even in death.

"Mark, two things… first, move the resources you had on Brannon to Laszlo, Chapman, and Novak, especially Novak. We need to be ready when he gets back. Things are turning our way. I don't want to blow the opportunity. I want all three of those targets terminated. Fast. Second, I want you personally to hook up with the Navy. Get every detail on that crash, the text of every radio transmission the Huey made, the radar indicators, everything. Obviously, Brannon planned to rendezvous with Chapman. I want to make sure that this is genuine. Validate, validate. By the way, what's the latest on Chapman?"

"Nothing yet. They're still trying to locate him. Hospitals, morgues, stuff like that. They're still on it. Phil, I want to tie this up as much as you do. Both Spencer and Yezhovich were done spic and span and this will be too. By the way, what did the Canadians tell you when they called?"

"The RCMP hasn't found Laszlo, but they have picked up his trail. They said it took a helluva lot of back-tracking. It looks like Laszlo went south from Montreal to some dink town called St. Antoine Abby, and on a bus yet! He bought a rifle and a revolver, an M-1 carbine and a .357 magnum! Our man Laszlo's loaded for bear! They got a report about a hunter who found two dead bodies, a man and a woman, up on Lake Papineau. That's west from Montreal, not east or south. Anyway, this guy and the girl – one was shot, and the other one was *speared* or something. They said it was pretty weird. The dead guy was a Terrence George Simmons. He had a long record, mostly petty crime stuff. The really big thing is that the RCMP counterintelligence folks have identified Simmons as one Dimitri Kolenko. We've since verified that. Kolenko was assigned about eight years ago to the SVR Residency in Luxembourg. No shit! Dimitri here was a Russian agent."

"Wow. So, they're still hunting Laszlo."

"Kolenko must have moved over to their illegals section. There was a composite picture of Laszlo in Dimitri's front pocket. That means that yes, those assholes are still after Laszlo. No ID on the girl. But preliminary checks by forensics, get this, show fingerprints on a wallet they found next to Kolenko's body match ones the JOG got from Laszlo's apartment in Frankfurt. No matter how wacked up everybody thinks this guy Laszlo is, he's already killed two people on this side of the Atlantic. Kolenko owned a vehicle, a Ford Explorer. The RCMP's out looking for it, but I think the bastard's already in. Laszlo got over the border, and he's heading west to Denver. Heading for you know what. We've got to nail that sonofabitch and fast!"

"You tell all this to Tanham yet?"

"No, but as soon as you get your ass outta here and doing something useful, I will. Get hustling, Mark."

As Bennis disappeared around the corner, O'Donnell grabbed his notes and hustled down the hall to see John Tanham. So far, he had kept Tanham in the dark, at least on the big stuff like Spencer, Yezhovich, and Chapman. Tanham would have gone ballistic if he'd known the truth. Maybe not Yezhovich, but he'd never buy into terminating Spencer or Chapman, much less Brannon or Novak. He wouldn't approve that no matter how much the project or the entire research and development operation were threatened. John Tanham didn't have the guts for the tough stuff. He was weak.

Laszlo was a different story though. Tanham wanted Laszlo

dead and gone as much as anybody. So Phil kept him informed. It'd be interesting to hear what Johnny thought about Brannon. O'Donnell didn't know where Tanham stood on Brannon. He didn't necessarily like him, but Tanham had never bad-mouthed him either.

If it all worked out right, O'Donnell would come out as the hero who'd successfully kept the biggest, best secret in the modern world – *secret*. He'd be viewed as the real brains behind the JOG concept, the STALKER project, and in Special Projects itself. The new top gun. He'd shove Tanham aside.

Yes, with Novak out of the way, there seemed to be no limit to what the patriot, Phil O'Donnell, could achieve. He'd be on his way up the upper rungs of the Company leadership ladder. What a picture. He was grinning broadly by the time he reached the end of the hall, but wiped it off his face as he reached out to knock on Tanham's door.

CHAPTER 29

Special Air Flight 712
Over the English Channel

Pete Novak took a mild sedative after dinner on the plane. He was more fatigued than he could ever remember, but he wanted to make sure he slept so he'd be as fresh as possible when they landed. After two hours in the air, Special Air Mission Flight 712 was bucking strong head winds and had yet to cross the southern tip of the English coast. By then, it was all the steward could do to wake him.

"Mr. Novak. Wake up, sir. You have a FLASH call on our communications desk." "What, what's that?" Pete heard him but couldn't quite comprehend the words.

"Here, sir, put this cool towel on your face. It might help." Something cold and wet met Pete's fumbling hands.

"Did you say a call? Where are we?" The chill of the wet cloth wiped the grogginess from his mind. He raised the seat back and felt his shoeless feet touch the floor.

"Sir, we're nearly across the Channel. The jet stream's not going our way – we've got horrendous headwinds. You have a call on our communications desk. You need to come up front to take it, sir. Okay?"

"Sure, thanks. I was really out," Pete stood up, a little shaky. The steward took his arm.

"You want your shoes, sir?"

Pete looked down and chuckled at his socks. "No, I'm okay. Do you know who it is?" "It's a Dr. Kriegel, sir, Langley Center. They went FLASH precedence on the call, cut off our navigator's phone call to his wife midstream. Must be important."

"Ah, I guess so. Sorry about that."

Novak's face grew concerned. He hated phone calls in the middle of the night. They always seemed to bring bad news. The apprehension was worse away from home than in his own bedroom. Sarah chided him for being such a worrier. He tried hard to put her and the girls out of his mind when he was overseas, but it hardly ever worked.

Novak knew in his heart that Sarah, even so smart, loving, and caring as she could be, was terribly naive about the dangers of the street. She would never consider calling on J.T. for help. Pete knew that. On many a night, he'd whispered a prayer in their direction.

"Sir, just flip this switch when you're ready to speak. Would you like us to leave?" The lieutenant stood in the dimly lit corridor by the communications desk. He handed Pete the headset.

"That might be a good idea, if you don't mind. Can you give me about five minutes or so?"

Pete pulled the short swivel seat up to the desk overflowing with communications gear. He stared at the electronics. The entire wall in front of him flickered with colored lights.

"Sure thing, sir." The lieutenant closed the door to the comm desk.

"Pete Novak," he said with some hesitation.

"Pete, this is Doc. How are you?"

"I'm fine. Dead tired, but I'm fine. Sarah and the girls... "

"Yes, don't worry, they're fine, Pete. I spoke with Sarah yesterday afternoon, told her you'd be a day late." Novak closed his eyes and let go a deep sigh of relief.

"Pete, that's not why I called. 'Didn't know where you were. Neither did Frankfurt."

"Nordheimer knew I was leaving. Why didn't you talk to Bill?"

"Nobody's talking to Bill Nordheimer right now. The man's in a coma."

"What? How? What happened? I just saw the man yesterday."

"They think it was a stroke. Massive. It happened at his desk, right in the office. They rushed him to the hospital in Wiesbaden. But, they say the doctors aren't confident he's gonna make it. Susie's not taking it well. Everything's in a tizzy back there right now."

"Damn. I can imagine."

"Right."

But Doc's voice was hesitant, not in character. Pete's chest tightened again. There was more. His hands dropped, clenched and then fidgeting in his lap.

"What else. What is it, Doc? Tell me."

"Pete, I felt I had to call you. You deserved to know as soon as possible."

"Know what?"

"Pete, it's J.T. Brannon. I'm sorry. J.T. died today. He... "

"Ohhh... gees, no. God, not J.T. Are you sure, Doc? Is it positive? When, how? How'd it happen?" Pete felt as if a searing poker had rammed through his chest. He slumped over the desk. Pete folded his arms around his stomach, afraid he would be sick.

"Pete, please, take it easy. I wouldn't have called if I weren't sure. It was a crash at sea, a Huey helicopter. There were no survivors. Brannon was on his way down to the Outer Banks in North Carolina. I hate to ask you at a time like this, Pete, but do you know why he was headed there? "

"The Outer Banks? When did this happen?" Novak tried to collect himself amid the million thoughts that flooded his mind.

"Today, about… "

"Today? Well, I don't know. I asked J.T. to go down there last weekend to check on something. Wait a minute, Doc. Hold on."

Pete pushed the microphone down, stood, and shoved open the door. He waved at the steward and lieutenant in the galley, who immediately stepped forward. Novak laid his hand on the nearest one's shoulder.

"Is this line secure? Are these transmissions encrypted?"

"No, not this line, sir. We have a secure comm line, sir, but not the one you're on. The call came in on the open line." They looked at each other, eyes asking.

"Okay, thanks."

He waved his hand at them and turned back to the desk. The lieutenant and the steward retreated slowly, looking over their shoulders at Pete. Pete adjusted the microphone again.

"Doc, I can't tell you any more on this line, but look, I'll need to see you in the morning. I need you to block a couple of hours."

"A couple of hours? Pete, I'm supposed to brief the National Security Council."

"Doc, please believe me, the most important thing you can do tomorrow morning is listening to what I have to tell you. Now with this, I mean J.T.'s death, there's no doubt in my mind. Not anymore. Trust me, it's of the utmost importance. Say, between 8:30 and 9:00. That'll at least give me time to wash up, that is, if this damn thing ever lands. The head winds are nasty. We're not even across the Channel yet. Deal?"

"All right. I'll be waiting on you. Pete, I'm sorry about Brannon. I didn't want to call, but I knew you would want to be first to know. I thought maybe you'd have some time on the plane to think it all through."

"Doc, I know you, and I know that you care. Thanks for calling me. I just can't fathom how, ohhh… I just can't believe it. Look, Doc, I'll see you in the morning. Thanks a lot. Bye."

Pete backed the stool away, barely able to stand. His stomach heaved. A rush of heat washed over his neck and head, his eyes filling with tears. Nausea wracked him so suddenly he almost didn't make it to the tiny bathroom across the aisle, tossing off his headset in route.

He fell through the door and flung himself over the commode. The lieutenant glanced up the aisle and dropped his cup. He dashed up the narrow corridor with the steward just behind him. Pete couldn't hold it in. His hands gripped the edges of the bowl as his guts wrenched again and again. Finally, his head bobbed up for air. He was still spitting and gasping, all of it mixed with tears. The young lieutenant stood behind him holding the door open, his face pale with concern.

CHAPTER 30

Andrews Air Force Base
Maryland

Hours passed. Dead tired and unspeakably depressed, Novak looked at his watch as Special Air Mission Flight 712 touched down at Andrews Air Force Base. It was just after four o'clock in the morning. His head swam from trying to make sense of it all. The murky and mysterious photo Klaus had given him... what in hell was that supposed to be? Then this woman, Maria Dean. How did she fit in, assuming she existed? No one could find traces of her, not in Europe and not in the Company.

And now, J.T.'s sudden death. Pete had lost all sense of it. He turned to the window. It was still pitch black outside except for the blue runway lights. He heard the pilot reverse the thrust on the powerful turbofan engines as the aircraft screamed down the runway. A helicopter bearing the silver and blue of the Air Force settled down on a pad adjacent to the parking ramp. The pilot had ordered it, at Novak's request, for the jump over to Dulles. There would be no Company chopper this trip. Pete wanted Air Force transportation as far as he could take it.

The plane squealed into its parking slot, stopping with a jerk. Novak reached across the empty seat and grabbed his shoulder holster, examining it to be sure the pistol was still in it. Standing up was difficult. His bones were stiff. He managed to slip the loop of the shoulder holster over his head, then donned his jacket. As he stumbled forward, the steward appeared from the aft storage compartment with his bags. Pete stuck his head in the cockpit and thanked the flight crew. They smiled, waved, and wished him good luck.

The helicopter was just a short walk away... its rotors turning, waiting on him. The pilot waved to him from the side door. A crewman helped him climb in and reached out for his bags. The roar of the turboshaft engines and whirring rotors drowned out any attempt at conversation, so Pete just stuck out his hand. The steward grabbed it. The crewman moved up to close the doors as the steward backed cautiously away. Pete sank into his seat, buckled his belt without thinking. He stared into the wall ahead as the chopper rose off the pad.

The jaunt to Dulles was short and unremarkable. The Potomac River and the rolling hills of Virginia swam below as black shadows yet untouched by the light of dawn. After slipping the Sikorsky down to the helipad, the pilot saw Pete safely down the steps, saluted, and immediately lifted off for the return trip to Andrews. Novak saw the baggage handler had also gotten off the chopper, and he was glad to see the man reach down and grab his bags. The way he felt, he couldn't have carried them 50 feet.

Passing through the lobby minutes later, Pete hesitated momentarily by a bank of pay phones near the check-in counters. Maybe he should call Sarah, but his watch reminded him it was still only five o'clock in the morning. No, it would be a bad idea to wake her and the girls. He'd catch a cab.

Novak stepped through the glass doors into an eerie twilight. The lights along the ramp were still lit, but the sky was turning a muddy gray to the east. A porter hailed a cab that had been sitting just down the ramp. The bright yellow cab screeched to a halt just inches from Novak. The porter tossed Pete's bags in the trunk as he climbed wearily into the back seat.

"Where to, sir?" the driver asked politely. He had a strong Mid-East accent. Pete guessed he was either Iranian or Pakistani. Washington seemed to be filling up with them. And, so many of them seemed to be driving cabs.

"You know where Fairfax City is?"

"Sure. It's no problem."

The yellow Chevy Caprice lurched away from the curb and shot down the ramp. Pete was shoved into the seat from the acceleration. Every one of these guys has gotta be a NASCAR driver, he thought. The cab veered around a bend into the south-bound exit for Route 28.

Pete longed to sink back and close his eyes, but the driver's rapid turns kept him off balance. Then, he had a second thought.

"Driver?"

"Yes, sir?"

"Do you know how to get to Vienna?"

"Oh, yes. It's no problem. I go the same way, Route 66. You want to go there first, maybe?"

"Yes, please. And hey, let's try to get there at something less than the speed of light,

okay?"

"I'm sorry? Speed a light? I don't... "

"Just take it a little easy. Slow down. Okay?"

"Oh yes, sir. It's no problem. We go slower," he apologized, turning his eyes back to the road ahead.

The driver blushed visibly. He eased his foot off the gas. Pete managed a slight smile and dropped his head back against the seat. His eyelids sank down and he soon was lost in the hum of the engine and the steady bumping of the wheels. The driver continued down Route 28, turned onto Rt. 66, and soon headed north on Chain Bridge Road.

"Sir? Where now? Where to go now?"

The cabby's voice was insistent. He'd given his passenger every minute of sleep he could, hoping to make amends for his driving. This one, he looked so tired, maybe sad too... it was something. The cabbie took it easy and kept an eye out, both on Pete in the rear-view mirror and for bumps in the road ahead. This one needed his sleep.

"What? Oh, okay, where are we?" Pete's eyes opened abruptly. He rubbed the sleep from his eyes.

"We are close to Vienna, on Chain Bridge Road. It begins to be Maple Avenue here. So where do you want me to go?"

"It's a little street just ahead, just after Lawyer's Road. The next left. There's a blue building on the corner. You'll see it in a couple of minutes."

Pete looked down at his watch – almost twenty to six. The morning traffic had begun. It would be a good half hour before it was in full swing.

"Thank you, sir. I will find it. It's no problem. Here you go. We find it. No problem. What number you want, sir?" The cab swung into the turn.

"Number 313, on the left. There it is. Pull up to the curb, please."

The driver complied, and the cab eased over as Pete stared at the dark windows. He squinted at the street ahead, then looked out the rear window to the traffic passing down Maple Avenue. Nothing in view to cause alarm. No suspicious cars, no movement.

"Okay, go ahead and pull into the driveway."

"Yes sir. No problem." The big Chevy swung up the gently sloped drive and sighed to a stop.

"Please wait, can you?" Pete opened the rear door. He walked around to the side as the driver rolled down his window.

"Oh yes, sir. It's... "

"I know – *It's no problem!* Thanks. I'll be a few minutes, so you might want to turn off your engine. Keep the meter running, though... it's no problem!"

Pete smiled. The driver chuckled, shaking his head as Pete approached the front door. He turned the ignition off, rolled up the window, and sat back in his seat with his eyes closed.

Pete reached into his back pocket and pulled out his wallet. It was still tucked behind the charge card. A spare key. He'd carried it nearly six months now, ever since Brannon told him he'd be honored if Pete would keep it, just in case. Pete had agreed with honest reluctance, but now he was glad he had it.

The front door opened easily. He stepped into the blackness and reached under his coat. Pete curled his fingers around the grip of the Walther pistol, groping on the wall with his left hand. The switch flicked at his touch, flooding the room with light. Pete gasped at the sight. Furniture was toppled. Books were flung about, pages ripped out. Lamps lay on the floor amid broken glass and shredded lamp shades. The place looked like a tornado had burst through it.

He picked his way across the rubble and toward the kitchen. It was the same there. Cabinets had been emptied onto the floor. Dishes smashed. Boxes were scattered and food crunched underfoot. The stench of soured milk was thick. The refrigerator was open, its contents strewn over the floor. Pete stepped over the debris and slammed the door shut.

He went from room to room, his anger rising as each

chamber presented one violent mess after another. The mattress in Brannon's bedroom had even been upended and pushed up against a wall and sliced open. Stuffing hung out of it and lay in clumps on the ripped sheets. Finally, Pete made his way back to the living room. He turned off lights as he went, and then sat heavily on the edge of a wooden cocktail table. His head dropped into his hands. So, it had to be true. J.T. was dead, whether from foul play or an accident, he was gone.

And someone, or several someones, had taken the opportunity to rifle through all Brannon owned. Probably this JOG squad. They must be desperate. The sharp ring of a phone blared suddenly, echoing through the quiet house! Pete was startled to his feet, heart pounding, pistol in hand. He swung around and tiptoed cautiously back to the kitchen. The wall phone rang insistently. Pete reholstered his weapon and reached out to pick up the phone.

"Hello?" he asked, looking at his watch… six o'clock.

"Hey J.T.! Where the hell you been, boy? I've been trying to get you for the last two days. So today, I thought I'd wake you up at the break of dawn! J.T., you there?" A long pause before Pete gave it a shot.

"Yes. Just tired, you know. Rough night." He spoke low from deep in his throat and in a hoarse whisper, hoping the exhaustion in his voice would help, too. It did.

"Well, ye best get up now, sailor, and face the morning! Wind's up and it's six bells, mate! Hoist the jib, raise the mainsail! Say J.T., this is Captain Brent Mason, your own private harbor master down at Colington. Remember me?"

"Of course, Brent. I'm sorry. How you doing?" he replied in the same hoarse whisper. Pete was puzzled, but struggled to pull off his charade. He leaned against the wall.

"How am I doing? I'm fine. It's you who's gone and

disappeared! You still interested in that sport fisherman out of Patuxent, Maryland? The *Moon Shadow?*"

"Absolutely. What can you tell me?"

"Okay. Well, Gary Allen, the captain of the *Jackie Mae*, the Coast Guard cutter down here, has really had his hands full lately. He's been out to sea for days chasing a couple of suspected drug boats that were trying to run in here from across the Stream. He's sorry for the delay, but he got exactly what I asked him for. The *Moon Shadow* is registered to a Mark W. Bennis of Falls Church, Virginia. I have the address. Do you need it?"

"Mark Bennis? Ah, no, that's okay. I know the guy. Anything else?"

Bennis! Pete moved over and flopped into a chair at the kitchen table. This was way too close to home. He was bewildered and at the same time seething with anger.

"Nope. If I recall, that's all you asked for, mate."

"Brent, look, I can't thank you enough."

"Oh, don't mention it, mate. If I ever need something I think you can get me, don't worry, I'll be sure to call. You take care now, you hear? May you have calm seas ahead, fair winds at your back, and all that."

"Same to you, Brent."

Pete sat as a statue, holding the phone, until he realized the harbor master had signed off. Enough time had apparently passed since Mason met Brannon to cloud his memory of J.T.'s voice. Pete felt lucky, then again, not so lucky. Now he knew where to focus, but if Mark Bennis was connected with Tony Spencer's death, this was getting scary.

This thing had to go higher, much higher. Bennis was too low in the pecking order. He would never act on his own, especially if it meant assassination of a fellow officer. He had to have orders from above. Sanctioned hits against the Company's own, and on sacred domestic turf of the United States? What was going on? A struggle among the Company's leadership?

Pete shook his head. This was bad news, and he'd been probing into places he shouldn't be. Was it a set-up? No way. They'd never get it past Kriegel. He knew in his heart Doc would look out for him.

Pete pushed himself up on the table and walked through the ruins of the living room. The gray light of dawn was seeping in through the curtains of the large bay window. It gave the room and all the wreckage a ghostly appearance. He left the house, locked it behind him, and fell back into the soft cushions of the cab's rear seat. His mind still in turmoil, he told the cabby to drive back down Maple Avenue, south to Chain Bridge Road, Fairfax City, and home.

CHAPTER 31

*Novak Residence, Fairfax
Virginia*

Pete paid the cabby in his driveway and gave him a generous tip. The man left sporting a big smile, waving as he backed out of the drive. Pete picked up his bags and paused, looking up at the house. He couldn't see any lights, but it was ten to seven. He knew the girls would be up in minutes if they weren't already. Today was a school day.

He trudged up the three steps to the porch. It was a big one, inlaid with red Spanish tile and dotted with potted plants. Pete thought the whole thing would look weird on the front of a white colonial house, but he had to admit it turned out beautifully. Sarah loved it. The comfortable rattan furniture they put on it every spring was already stored in the cellar. With the cold weather, the plants had taken on an ugly brown look. Sarah was behind in her pruning.

Easing the storm door open, Pete unlocked the heavy wooden front door. He took his shoes off inside and tiptoed across the expansive slate foyer to the Persian carpet runner leading to the kitchen. Whenever he returned from a trip, he marveled at the beauty of his home. Sarah came from a wealthy family up in the hunt country of Potomac, Maryland. It was a land apart from the bustle of Washington. There were long white rail fences with horses and riders replete with English tack cantering alongside them.

Sarah's father was a senior partner in a prestigious Georgetown law firm. After the marriage, they insisted on helping the newlyweds furnish their new home. Since the girls were born, Pete was happy to see her parents spending time on their grandchildren instead of always buying some new thing for the house. They were good people all right, just filthy rich good people.

Pete stepped into the kitchen and leaned his bags against the wall behind the table. He could hear water running upstairs. The girls would be washing their faces and brushing their teeth. He began to spoon some instant coffee into a cup. He caught the sound of whispers, then small footfalls tiptoeing down the stairs. Pete set the cup down, strode back across the tiled floor to the doorway, and poked his head through.

Susie and little Joanna stood in their nightgowns ten steps up. Joanna still had a toothbrush in her mouth. They'd heard the shuffling. When she saw her daddy, the toothbrush bounced onto the carpet. Her eyes lit up, and her mouth turned into a big toothy grin. Then she shrieked in her little-girl voice.

"Mommy, Daddy's home! Daddy's home!"

The giggling girls stampeded down the stairs and nearly bowled him over as he squatted to meet their hugs. Sarah appeared at the head of the staircase in her bare feet, tying on a robe. She could barely make him out with the girls all over him.

"Pete! Did you just get in? I didn't hear a thing! Welcome back, sweetheart!" Sarah came hopping down the stairs to him. Susie clung to him as he set Joanna down. Sarah met him with a full embrace and a very warm kiss.

"Oh Pete, it's so good to see you! I missed you so. But… gees, you look terrible, honey. What have you been doing? You look like you haven't slept for a week! Come on into the kitchen and let me fix you something. Take off your tie and sit down. Okay, girls, Daddy's home. Now you both go up and finish. You'll be late for school. You can see Daddy later. Go on now!" The girls, still shrieking with their delight, tore up the stairs to their bathroom. Pete followed Sarah into the kitchen and slumped into a chair.

"Thanks, doll. I could use a cup of coffee. It's good to be back. More than you could ever imagine."

"I'm not kidding, Pete. You look like hell. Bad trip?" As Sarah dumped the instant out of the cup and put some fresh grounds in the pot to brew, she kept glancing over to Pete. He looked the worst she'd ever seen him.

"I need to tell… "

"Look, why don't you get cleaned up and come with me to the White Flint Mall? We can grab lunch there and then drive over to Mom's."

"I can't."

"Of course, I'm sorry. You look dead tired. Tell you what, I'll pop a bagel in the toaster for you, then go up and freshen the bed. You can sleep to whatever time you need to."

"No, Sarah, it's not that. I've got to clean up and go in. I'm on Doc's calendar for 8:30 this morning."

"Then call and cancel, Pete. You look horrible, like the living dead. I mean it. There is nothing so damn important it can't wait a couple hours."

"What I need is… " he hesitated, then spoke again more softly, "Sarah, please come over and sit down. I need to talk to you. Come here, please."

Pete motioned. Sarah looked at the coffee pot. She set the

package of bagels on the counter before turning to him. A look of concern strained her face as she sat and gazed into the tired eyes and weary face of her husband. Pete got up and stepped quickly to the doorway, looking and listening. There was no sign of the girls. He returned to his chair. Watching him only made Sarah more anxious.

She was totally unnerved to see Pete's eyes filled with tears. As he rubbed them, smearing his face, Sarah began to feel a weight crushing her chest. What was wrong? He looked so devastated. She didn't know what to expect, what to think. She felt she must break the unbearable silence. But Pete suddenly sighed, speaking first.

"Sarah, honey, J.T.'s dead. He's dead." A tear streamed from his left eye. He wiped it away, but more followed. Sarah's expression melted from anxious to grim and then finally, to sad. She slipped off the chair and walked on her knees to Pete, wrapping her arms around his legs. She laid her cheek on his knees.

"Pete, when did this happen? Was J.T. with you in Europe?"

"No. If he had been, he'd be alive today. J.T. stayed here. He died in a helicopter crash going down the coast to North Carolina yesterday. There's more too. I wish I could tell you, but I can't. Something is going on that's very wrong, Sarah. I've got to try to find out what it is and set things right. If I can, that is. But, I've got to try."

Pete straightened up in his chair. Sarah stood and placed a hand on his shoulder. She had never made a secret of her feelings for Brannon, but right now she wished she could take back all the things she'd said about him. Pete genuinely liked the man, perhaps even loved him. Pete had never had a brother to bond with. J.T. was the next-best thing. She knew that. The girls treated him like family. She knew in her heart though that she was sorrier for Pete's sake than anything else. The two men had a strong friendship going, and her attitude hadn't helped. She knew that too.

"Pete, I'm so very sorry. J.T. was a good man, and you two were good friends. Please believe I know that, Pete. This other thing you mention, is it connected? Dangerous?"

"Thanks, sweetheart. About the other issue, I don't know yet. I can't tell you anything more. Just trust me to do what I believe I must. I need your support on this. After I see Kriegel, I'll know more. This matter that I had to go so urgently to Europe on is big, really big. And it just got a lot bigger. I don't want the girls to know about J.T., not just yet. We'll find the right time and place... later."

Sarah nodded in agreement.

"Good. I'm going upstairs to wash, shave and get a clean shirt. Can you pour me some coffee and toast a bagel?"

"Okay." Sarah sighed in resignation. She hugged him, but she wasn't happy. It was not knowing anything that really got to her. Now Brannon was dead. She hated the Company for the walls the Company erected between her and the man she loved, the father of her children.

Less than 10 minutes later, Pete frowned at the large mirror, struggling with the knot on a new tie. Succeeding, he tromped out the door and down the steps, flopping into his chair at the kitchen table. It was 7:30. The girls smiled at him over their bowls of corn flakes. Sarah set his coffee and bagel in front of him, and sat down with a cup herself. As he took the first sip, he noticed the world globe on chair next to Susie.

"Susie honey, what's with the globe? School?"

He sipped again, peering at her over his cup. Susie was in the fourth grade. She loved every minute she spent in school. He and Sarah were happy about that because Joanna was having a terrible time adjusting to first grade. She just couldn't stay at her desk. Mayhem was often the result. Sarah did her best to help her make the transition, but it was a struggle. So, Susie was indeed a bright spot in this regard.

"Yup, that's right, Dad. I gotta make a report to the class today on all the oceans and seas. You know, where they are and all. I'm going to tell them about the North and South poles. About the Arctic and Antarctica, the equator and stuff. I learned a lot."

"Sounds like it. Wish I could be there. Please tell me tonight how it went. A deal?"

"Oh sure, you bet." Susie paused, smiling mischievously. "Dad, do you know what the meridian is? Don't tell him, Mom."

"*The* meridian? Oh, let me see now, hmm." Pete set his cup on the table and stroked his chin. "Do you mean the Prime Meridian? Or, just any meridian?" His 10-year-old sweetheart was testing him.

"Oh darn it, he knows, Mom. Well, I guess I mean the Prime Meridian. Are all the longitude lines called meridians, Dad? Our teacher calls them longitude lines."

"Well, that's correct too. Meridian is actually technically correct, but most people I know call them longitudes too. So, what's the Prime Meridian, sweetie?"

"I know that. That's the one with zero degrees. The first one, you know, the one that goes through Greenwich, England."

"Very good! You are getting smart on this stuff. Okay, so where does the Prime Meridian go on the other side of the earth?"

"I know that, too! It goes through, I mean *between*, Russia and Alaska. The international date line is there also." She was grinning again.

"Wow, Susie. I am impressed!"

"Daddy, what's a mariadean?" Little Joanna burst in, dropping her cereal spoon on the table with a clunk.

"It's a meri-dian, honey, say meridian, not, maria dean...

Maria Dean?" Slowly, Novak straightened in his chair, his face suddenly solemn. His eyes focused on something far away.

"Yeah, so what is it, Dad?"

"Did you say *Maria Dean*, sweetheart?" A thousand-watt light had just gone on in his head. His eyes opened wide. Joanna immediately noticed her father's demeanor change and lost her smile.

"Yes, Daddy, is that bad? I'm sorry. I didn't know." She frowned as she spoke, but her father's eyes were still far-away somewhere.

"Ah… no, no, sweetheart. It's not bad."

He turned back to Joanna, still looking over her head to the wall and beyond. Maria Dean. In his mind, he saw the words form and evolve. Maria Dean. Maria Dean. Meridian. No one could find Maria Dean anywhere. This was why – Maria Dean was Meridian!

"Say guys, excuse me, please." Pete jumped up, reached across the table, and swooped up the globe. He ran from the kitchen. Abruptly, Susie slumped back in her seat. She dropped her spoon into the cereal bowl, splattering milk across the table.

"Heyyy Dad! Come back here! I need that for school! Mom, do something! I need that for school!" She ran after her father. Sarah leaped from her chair and followed Susie. Little Joanna brought up the rear. What a cool new game – chase Dad!

Pete had plopped down on the sofa in the living room where the light from the now-bright morning poured through the picture window. He spun the globe, found the Prime Meridian, and followed it carefully through England to Greenwich. His finger traced it through France, Spain, Algeria, and West Africa. Then through Antarctica and back up the other side of the planet through the broad expanse of the far Pacific. Finally, it crossed the Bering Sea east of the Kamchatka Peninsula, and returned to the Arctic. Nothing stood out, nothing jumped out at all. He leaned back in the sofa, totally puzzled, oblivious to Sarah, Susie, and Joanna staring at him.

"Gotcha!" Joanna jumped onto his left leg. Pete jerked back to reality, nearly leaping into the air.

"Pete honey, what are you doing? Please be a good boy and give Susie back her globe. That is, unless you want to go to the fourth grade today and give that report yourself?"

"Nothing, you know, out of the mouths of babes…" he held the globe out to Susie and pulled her close to him, smothering her in a hug and kissing her forehead. He then lifted Joanna onto his lap and gave her a kiss too.

"Thanks, darlings. I know you don't understand, but you may have just helped Daddy a lot today. And, I want you to know I love you very much." He squeezed them both.

"All right, girls. Daddy's regained his sanity. Now, you two go up and brush your teeth. We don't want the dentist to find any cavities." Sarah's eyes were still opened wide.

Susie set her globe down by the front door, and she and Joanna ran up the stairs. Sarah stood in the living room looking at Pete and nearly beside herself. What could she make of this?

"Pete, I'm worried. Really, are you all right?" She sat down beside him, snuggled her head against his shoulder and kissed the side of his neck. He turned to look his loving wife straight in the eyes.

"Yes, I'm okay. Really. I know I must seem to be acting strange, but I'm okay."

"Strange? Oh, I wouldn't say that. How about *from another planet*? I think what you need is sleep, lots of it. You're a zombie. You want some more coffee?"

"Sure, thanks. Pour it for me, will you? I need to check on something upstairs. I'll be right down." He trailed his hands along her arms as he stood.

"No more globe snatching?" She asked with a weak smile.

"No more globe snatching. Promise." He crossed his heart with his hands, then leaped up the steps two at a time. Sarah shook her head and headed for the kitchen.

Pete ran into his study and pulled the dictionary from the shelf. He leaned over the desk. Leafing through the pages. There it was, *Meridian*. He was fairly sure of what he was looking for. His finger traced through lines of type until a sub-definition buried in the paragraph jumped out at him – *the highest stage, the peak of development of something, its meridian*.

He whispered the words to himself, "Maria Dean, Meridian. Had to be it. There is no Maria Dean. Meridian… that's what Tony Spencer was trying to say! But Tony was dying. He was in shock from the venom, maybe hallucinating. He couldn't get it out right. Meridian."

Pete straightened up. He remembered himself sitting back in Nordheimer's office in Frankfurt. What had he said? Pete squeezed his eyes tighter, straining to bring the words up from his memory. It was *something strategic*. Yezhovich was FTD – Foreign Technology Division. Once the U.S. got its hands on a piece of foreign weaponry, a Russian fighter, surface-to-air missile, these guys examined every inch of it. They examined and tested it to death, flew it, found out how it worked. Then, they determined its vulnerabilities. The research team incorporated the knowledge into an emerging weapon system to counter it.

So, how did this fit in? Had the Russians made another great technology leap, like the eyebrow-raising, decades ago Sputnik launch in 1957? He doubted it. It had to be something else, something on our side, not theirs. Something extremely advanced, maybe even… startling? Then this Laszlo fellow enters the scene. Laszlo was the linchpin, the foreign agent who successfully cultivated and co-opted Yezhovich. In so doing, he gained knowledge, and who knows what else, about this advanced whatever-it-is.

Nordheimer had also said *Yezhovich was an Air Force tech puke, knowledgeable in composite materials, metallurgy. He was involved in high-tech stuff, in the blackest of the black programs.* The blackest of the black, the biggest of the big secrets. Pete strained to remember, *yet this stuff was only the surface, the tip of the iceberg. It was the stuff that would allow us to prevail on any battlefield!* That was it.

There had been something else though, something that had really caught his attention. What was it? It was at the end of their conversation, the cruncher. *It's profound!* Bill had said, "Profound." A technological revelation? Yes, that was the word he'd used, *profound.* Then finally, *It's not just the technology… it's where it came from.* Nordheimer's demeanor had also transitioned noticeably in the telling of it. Wild Bill was afraid of it. Bill was worried, no, frightened. He had told Pete too much.

And now, Nordheimer was in a coma. Coincidence? Pete doubted it. So, the technology was not just *profound*, but where it came from was even more startling? From where? Meridian, that's where. Yezhovich had told all and he was shot to death, probably by us, most likely by the JOG squad.

Even if this were so, why would Laszlo run? Why did he break from his own? Why leave the fold and run into the cold? Laszlo Csengerny would have been hailed as a hero. He would have been showered with gifts from a very thankful Motherland. Laszlo had somehow co-opted Yezhovich and compromised Meridian… without a doubt the biggest secret the U.S. has, maybe the biggest ever. So then, why run?

The answer eluded him. Pete felt in his gut that it was crucial to the puzzle. Laszlo was a man on the run, both from the SVR and the Company. Or maybe, was he running? Was it possible that he was on a search, a hunt of his own? Was there something about Meridian that Laszlo would risk all, absolutely everything, even his life, to find?

Pete had meticulously studied the STALKER profile. Laszlo was a tortured soul. He had been physically and mentally brutalized. He was continually plagued by dreadful nightmares, so horrible that they left even hardened Army MI interrogators on edge. He'd been terrorized all his life by dreams of demons ever since his parents died.

Laszlo was sick, perhaps insane. Grief, fear, hatred, and brutality had paralyzed his psyche. Bill Nordheimer said there might be something *unreal* about Laszlo's DNA, RNA, or whatever. *Something not identifiable in known science.* The bad dreams may come from *something else entirely.*

Pete felt close… the answer was buried here somewhere. An image began to form in his mind's eye. It jumped out at him… Klaus Reimer's murky photo – the strange, and not-quite-human creature. Klaus said his colleagues discovered it in their search of Laszlo's apartment. Pete's eyes opened wide. No, no way. The answer was right there in front of him the whole time, but Pete's mind had refused to acknowledge its presence.

It was certainly startling enough, but too wild? Certainly profound, but too mad? The photo's foggy image of something almost, but not quite human, filled his head. He glanced to the wooden cross mounted on the wall above his desk. For several moments his staring eyes couldn't leave it.

"Oh, God. My Lord." He turned and faced the window. His eyes focused somewhere out over the trees in the backyard, then drifted up toward the vastness of the sky above. And far beyond. "My God."

CHAPTER 32

Oak Trail Motel
Logan, Iowa

The windows of the Ford Explorer were dripping with a thick icy dew. It sat crouched under a leafless oak outside room number 12 at a small motel just a few miles south of Logan, Iowa. The Explorer now bore Iowa plates instead of its original New York plates. Laszlo had stolen and then switched plates in nearly every state, figuring it would help keep the intelligence types off his tail. He'd also stuck to the secondary roads, stopping only in smaller towns.

These were towns too small to have a police force of their own, relying instead on a county sheriff. Laszlo had taken State Route 30 most of the way across Iowa. By then, he was entirely exhausted. The thought of a warm bed and a hot bath seemed worth the risk. The $59 dollars he'd paid for the room didn't put much of a dent in his cash.

The air in Logan this early in the morning was still, heavy with moisture. Not a breeze. Laszlo sprawled across the bed, trembling from the aftermath of the night's hellish nightmare.

They were at the window peering in at him, or trying to, at least four of them. He could see the shadows of their legs in the crack of light beneath the door. This time, while they didn't come in, they moved about outside all night. He was covered with sweat. His fingers were curled around the barrel of the rifle at his side. The butt of the .357 magnum revolver stuck out from under his pillow.

If *they* came for him again, and he knew they would, he would be ready. He couldn't remember when he'd last eaten, yet he really felt no great hunger. His gaunt cheeks sported four days' worth of stubble. The black circles around the sunken pits of his eyes gave him the look of a ghoul, freshly resurrected from the grave.

Laszlo had lost at least twenty pounds. The concept of time had melted away for him. Days turned into nights. Nights turned into hell. And, hell rolled back into days. He slept only two to three hours at a time because of the need to stay somewhat alert. He could never escape them. Laszlo wore the wild-eyed stare of a lost soul desperately in search of peace.

Peace for Laszlo was something that still lay ahead... west. Where he would end it. He would soon cross over the Missouri River into Blair, Nebraska. Then, further west.

Laszlo's face twisted in a grotesque smile. He was so close now. He could smell the rotten stench of the beast. A beast that did not know of its coming demise. And, would not sense that Laszlo was now the hunter.

CHAPTER 33

Langley Center
Northern Virginia

Through the smoked-glass windows on the third floor, Phil O'Donnell watched Pete Novak's Durango cruise down the main drive and pull into the lot. His face paled into a blank stare.

"Mark, Novak just pulled in. Take a look. First there were six, and then there were two. Yezhovich, Spencer, Brannon – all kaput. Chapman too. All that's left to clean up are Pete Novak and Laszlo Csengerny. This is getting better by the minute. We'll have this secured. So, fill me in again on Chapman." He turned to Bennis, who had perched on the edge of the desk.

"The team in Tennessee said they confirmed his death. They're on their way back now. He died shortly after the crash."

"But you said they didn't see the body?"

"No. There wasn't a body to see. They talked to a Sgt. Marks, with the state police down in Lebanon. Marks told them he'd been at the crash site, was involved in the search, and he saw Chapman's body. Marks linked them up with the state police lieutenant who was in charge of the case. His name was Skip Kenny."

"And?"

"Lt. Kenny said they didn't find Chapman's body until two days after the crash. He was near the river, out in the sun for two days, and starting to ripen. The hounds wouldn't go near him because he was so ripe. The coroner had a hell of a time with the autopsy, but they eventually ruled it an accidental death. Kenny said Chapman must have been fatigued or something when he went off the road. After the crash, he wandered off into the woods, most likely in shock, disoriented. Cause of death was a bunch of things… internal bleeding, a ruptured spleen, broken ribs, and a punctured right lung. A few other things too that didn't necessarily contribute to his death. I couldn't get a copy of the coroner's report though. It wasn't ready yet. Due to the state of decomposition, they cremated the body. They've already sent it back to North Carolina at the family's request. There was no corpse to see, Phil."

"Well, not exactly prima facie evidence, but I guess we're stuck with it. What family did Chapman have? I thought he was divorced. What does he have, brothers, sisters, what?"

"Don't know. I didn't think about it. Someone back there wanted a funeral. An aunt, uncle, who knows?"

"Check that out, all right? Not a priority, but don't let it slip through the crack. You've got a lot bigger things to take care, like the guy who's walking in the front door," O'Donnell jerked his head toward the window.

"I know. Novak's gonna see Kriegel?"

"Probably. It doesn't show up on the daily calendar, but 8:30 to 10:00 a.m. is blocked, and it's 8:15 now. Gotta be Novak, his just getting back from Europe and all. Kriegel must be hot to hear what he's got to say."

"Can you cover it?"

"Have to. We need to know. I can do it from a distance, discreetly. We gotta catch up, especially the part where he disappeared with the German Intel types. Who knows what the hell he's aware of now. He ain't cleared to know and Kriegel can't approve that access by himself. This project has sanction authority for unacceptable risks of compromise. Ah, Mark, as of 8:30, I want you signed out on leave for a few days. Just list "out of area." This needs to be good, no traces left behind. Your best effort. I'll hang here and see what's up with Novak, any last-minute changes, whatever. I'm already packed myself. Tanham's ready too, but he doesn't really know yet what for. Laszlo's gotta be real close by now. But we haven't spotted him or heard a peep. The bastard's good at disappearing. We know he's coming though, and exactly where he'll reappear. This'll be a one-two punch. It's looking good."

"See ya and good luck." The door closed behind Bennis.

"Shouldn't have to rely on luck, asshole." O'Donnell muttered as he reached into his right desk drawer for his Colt .45 pistol. He shoved it into his shoulder holster. Next came two extra seven-round magazines, which he dropped in the side pockets of his sport jacket.

He threw the light switch off and locked the door. He wouldn't be back for a while. When he returned and the dust had settled, he'd have to think of an appropriate ending for Bennis as well. The man had no finesse, and he was incredibly stupid to boot. But, first things first.

Pete walked into Doc Kriegel's office a hair before 8:30. Joyce Cowan stood up when she saw him, reaching for a cup and saucer in the bureau behind her.

"Coffee, Mr. Novak?"

"Yes, Joyce, please, if it's no trouble. Thanks."

"No trouble. Please have a seat." She walked into a little

nook of a side office and returned with a steaming cup. Pete took it with careful hands and settled himself on the leather couch against the wall.

"Doc in yet?"

"He's on his way back from the Director's office to explain why he wouldn't make the Security Council meeting this morning. You're first on the schedule. Anything else I can get you?"

"No thanks, this is great." Pete picked up a copy of *The Atlantic* from the cocktail table in front of him. Before opening it, Kriegel came in the front door. Pete stood.

"Morning, Doc." He extended his hand.

"Pete, good to see you. You all right?"

Doc searched Pete's eyes. Doc was good at that. He could tell who had their armor on and who didn't. Pete had lost J.T. Brannon just the day before. From their phone conversation yesterday, Doc knew something else was seriously wrong too. He cared deeply for Pete and he wanted to spare him unnecessary pain. He felt he hadn't done too well on that count. The STALKER thing in Europe must have gone further awry.

"Yes, I'm okay… just tired and, you know. Thanks for asking."

"Good. It's my job to ask. So, what do you have that's so hot the National Security Council has to take a back seat? Don't get me wrong though. I don't mind missing those damn meetings as often as I can. In a way, thanks!"

Kriegel grabbed Pete's arm and moved him toward his office. He patted Pete on the back. Pete may have said he was all right, but Doc knew him too well. His eyes told a great deal.

"Well, in that case, you're welcome. Doc, what I need to talk… " Doc again dropped his hand on Pete's shoulder as he turned back from his doorway.

"Joyce, absolutely no calls, please. If anybody gets curious, tell them I've gone down to Analysis. Okay?"

"Yes, sir."

Doc closed the huge wooden door to his office. The red light above the door frame flashed on. *No admittance.* Pete sank into one couch as Kriegel faced him from the other. As usual, a coffee pot and a plate of cookies were spread out with the bone china service on the cocktail table between them. As Pete opened his mouth to speak, Doc cut him off again.

"Pete, before I forget, I have to ask you something. I want to hear what you have to say, but let's begin with this. Do you know or have you heard of someone named Douglas Chapman?"

"No, I'm pretty sure I haven't. Who is he? Related to STALKER?" Pete raised his cup. He'd take the first one straight black. He needed the brace.

"He might be, I don't know. He's a coroner down on the Outer Banks, Cape Hatteras. But never mind, he… "

"A coroner from Cape Hatteras? What else, Doc? Tell me the rest."

Pete set his coffee down and sat erect, eyes piercing. Doc looked around the room a little apprehensively, and Pete wondered at that. He continued, but his voice dropped. His face showed concern.

"Well, after I spoke with you yesterday, I got a call from FBI Headquarters. They wanted me to come over pronto, at 6:00 in the evening yet. They said they couldn't come here to discuss what was on their minds. So I drove over and met with Don Burroughs. Don's an old buddy. He's a big-wig now with the Bureau and a deputy director for violent crimes."

"Yes?"

"Don said they have a guy on ice over in Tennessee, one Douglas Theodore Chapman. They've got him in a safehouse down there. They're sitting on him while they check him out. Chapman specifically asked the Bureau to try to get J.T. Brannon

275

to him. He had Brannon's home phone and even a number for one of our "hello" phones. That part checks out, and that's of some concern in itself. But this guy tells the Bureau that the CIA has made attempts on his life. That we ran him off the road on the interstate near Lebanon. What's more, Chapman says he can prove beyond a reasonable doubt that Tony Spencer was assassinated. That's the word he used, 'assassinated'. As you can imagine, I was flabbergasted... "

"Chapman's right. Spencer *was* assassinated. Brannon was certain of it, and I'm sure of Brannon. J.T. went so far as to get that information to me in Europe via the German service. Chapman must have been J.T.'s inside source."

"Damn, Pete. German Intelligence? Bad. That still doesn't mean Tony Spencer was murdered, much less that we did it even if he was. Think about what you're saying. Spencer was retired. Here, in the United States? A domestic sanction? Look, J.T. was a good man, but he was also way overdue in hanging it up. He was getting a little wacky – you've got to agree with me on that."

"I not only do *not* agree with you on that, but I resent the comment as well. That man forgot more about field operations than half of those working for you will ever know. Doc, this is what I came here to tell you. What's more, Kaminov and Potter may have been killed in a shooting match with the Russians, but not Yezhovich. Somebody else did that, probably this JOG squad bunch."

Pete paused, his face red, realizing he needed to get hold of himself. He slid back from the edge of the sofa and shrugged.

Doc jumped up so suddenly the china rattled on the coffee table. His eyes narrowed, his ears turning a fiery red.

"This *what*? Pete, how in hell? You're not cleared, dammit!" Just what the hell do you know about JOG, and *how* do you know it?"

Flustered, Kriegel paced between the cocktail table and his desk. Doc was frazzled. This was a new experience for Pete. He had never seen Doc so utterly beside himself. Kriegel turned, glaring, his arms crossed tightly across his chest.

"Pete, you just don't know. I apologize for not being able to fill you in before you left, there was no time. This is so close-hold. What else do you know?"

It took Pete only a few seconds to decide whether to disclose it. A hundred possible outcomes raced through his mind. All right, he'd go for it all, find out if he was right. It was now or never.

"All right, Doc. Tell me about Meridian."

His eyes mirrored fear as a look of stark horror seized Doc's face. Kriegel turned white as a bleached bed sheet. Pete felt his hair stand on end. Gooseflesh prickled his skin from head to toe.

"What the… no! Stop, no more! Not another damn word!"

The room fell dead silent. Pete pushed back into the seat cushion at the sight of Doc, eyes crazy and bulging in disbelief. Doc lowered himself slowly onto the armrest of the couch, be-wilderment replacing the alarm on his face. He sat stone-faced. His eyes seemed to bore through Pete to someplace beyond.

Kriegel stood again, raising his index finger to his lips and keeping it there. Casting his eyes at the ceiling and walls, he walked a full circle behind the couch. He occasionally glanced at Pete and shook his head, as if in remorse for a dear friend who'd unexpectedly died.

Pete couldn't think. His brain seized up. Finally, Kriegel moved to his desk, sank into his chair, and slowly picked up the phone, all the while keeping a wary eye on Pete sitting frozen on the couch.

"Joyce, this is urgent. See if I can get the 'Tank'. And, imme-diately, if not sooner. Then call Sam Sorenson. Tell Sam I want him to come up to the Tank. Five minutes. No more. Tell him it's urgent. Get back to me, please."

Doc's voice was flat, emotionless. He set the phone down and stretched his arms out on the desk. His eyes wandered about the room, occasionally stopping on Pete before continuing. It seemed eons before the phone rang back, Joyce confirming his requests. Doc stood up and Pete with him. Pete's knees were weak. The exhaustion, the lack of sleep, the terrible news about Brannon, and now this.

Boy, he'd really gone and done it. He'd hit the nail square on the head with Meridian. But he'd also driven that nail into the largest raw nerve Kriegel had. He tried to lock eyes with Doc, but couldn't bring himself to do it. He felt like a schoolboy who'd been scolded and sent to stand in a corner. Doc walked past him without speaking. Pete followed lamely behind.

CHAPTER 34

Langley Center

The Tank at Langley Center was on the second floor in the new building. The whole *new* headquarters building was constructed more vertically than the old building. The entire structure was encased in a metal-glass alloy cube. A low voltage current running through the cube caught any and all electrons. As a result, there were no emanation concerns whatsoever in Langley's new building. Completely secure.

Nevertheless, on rare occasions the Agency felt a need for even further security measures. Therefore, *the Tank*. It was the securest of secure rooms, a deep black compartmented facility, intended for the most sensitive of discussions. It was a strange sight to anyone seeing it for the first time. A giant cube of glass and Lucite walls, floor, and ceiling eight inches thick. No phone, no communication lines, no electric wiring went either in or out.

The light inside the Tank shone through from the fixtures of the even larger room in which it was positioned. Air-flow ductwork and acoustic baffling were transparent. The table and chairs inside were also transparent and of ultra-thin, composite material. There was but one door. Once inside, it sealed itself with the hiss of an airlock. Serious stuff.

Dr. Sam Sorenson was the Science Advisor to no less than the DCI. Sorenson was a double PhD, a doctorate in mathematics and another in quantum physics. He was a legend among his brethren in the scientific community. A universally accepted myth around the Company held that Dr. Sam could raise the IQ of a crowd of people just by walking past them.

Sorenson was beyond brilliant. Sorenson's impending involvement left no doubt in Pete's mind that Meridian was as big as he'd assumed. At the moment, he leaned toward assuming it was in fact far bigger than anything he could have possibly imagined.

Kriegel and Novak marched through the halls without speaking. Pete stayed a step or two behind his mentor. At the vaulted entrance door to the Tank area, Kriegel picked up a phone on the wall and called the monitoring crew inside. He then stepped back and pressed his forehead into a screen above the phone… a retina scanner. Pete jumped at the sudden loud buzz. It was immediately followed by the metallic clanking sound of the electronic deadbolt pulling away.

Doc pushed open the gray steel door and he and Pete stepped in. They passed a monitoring station where three technicians intensely watched the control screens in front of them. Their job was to monitor and determine the origin of every stray electron wandering through the outer room. In the center of the room, the huge glass and Lucite Tank glowed luminescent from the bright lights hanging overhead. A surreal, almost unearthly sight.

Pete looked at the walls of the outer room where no less than 10 cameras continually swept across, stopping only to hover briefly over the surface of the tank. Toting a clipboard, the Tank's chief engineer approached Kriegel. He greeted Doc warmly, ushering both of them to the Tank's door just as Sorenson entered the vault behind them. The engineer then led them into the Tank where all three seated themselves at the long table. The engineer waited patiently until he received a thumbs-up signal from the monitoring station, then stepped outside. The door sealed behind him.

At that moment, Phil O'Donnell was buzzed into the Company's physical security office on the first floor. He'd been there several times before to continually cultivate his good friend, Lou Pantusco, chief of physical security. Probably 50 monitoring screens lined the walls, each reflecting a different view of the headquarters and its wooded grounds. There was a security technician for about every five screens. A hefty bearded man turned from the center console and strode toward O'Donnell. They shook hands briskly.

"Hello Phil, you old bastard! What're you up to? Usually, it's no good!"

"I need a view, Louis."

"Of what, Phil, the White House bedroom this time? Well, you know you need to go to the NRO for that!" Louis threw his head back and laughed.

"No, Louis, the Tank."

"The Tank? Hmm, why?"

"Come on, Louis, cut the bullshit. You don't need *why*! Do I get you Redskins tickets every year right on the 50-yard line, just above the helmets? Now you're giving me this kind of shit? Come on! It's legit."

"Gees, lighten up, Phil! What the hell's the matter with you? I'm just kidding. You got a hair up your ass today or something? You can have a view anytime, you know that. Come over here. You know I can't give you audio though, right? Not in the Tank." He grabbed Phil's arm and pulled him toward the farthest bank of screens, away from his security controllers.

"All right, thanks. I'm a little uptight today, that's all. 'Didn't mean to jump on you."

"Okay. Sit down here. Hey, wait a minute. That's Doc Kriegel, Sorenson too! For crying out loud, Phil, don't get my ass in a crack. You sure you need this?" Louis leaned over and punched some buttons on the center keypad. Moments later, a view of the Tank filled the screen.

"I wouldn't ask you otherwise, Louis. It's been a while, is this the zoom control?"

"Yeah, that's it. Up is zooming *in*, back is going *out*. There's side to side, left to right. You got ten minutes, no more. I don't wanna know about this, and you were never in here. Ten minutes, Phil. Not another second." He slapped O'Donnell on the shoulder and turned to walk away, frowning.

"Yeah, yeah. Thanks, Louis."

Phil was captivated by the screen. He zoomed in on the three people gathered around the table. The camera angle and the thick glass walls of the Tank distorted the picture somewhat, but it was almost as good as sitting at the table with them. He watched their lips moving, and a toothy grin spread over his face.

"Gotcha," O'Donnell murmured.

"Dr. Sam, thanks for coming on such short notice. I appreciate that. I really need your help with this." Kriegel spoke first.

"I figured as much. You're not one to spook at the drop of a hat, Doc. 'Glad to help if I can. Good to see you again too, Pete. Come by and visit the labs when you have a chance. I'd like to show you around. So, what can I do for you?"

"It's Meridian, Sam."

"Whoa, excuse me? Look, even that program nickname is classified. You know that. It's got a special access requirement to boot. Young Pete here isn't cleared. I think we need to regroup. Let's you and I talk outside."

"There's no time for that, Sam. I'll take full responsibility and back-brief the DCI. You have my word. I promise, please."

"It's not a question of *please* or *promise*. With all due respect, Doc, even you don't have the authority to accept full responsibility. Not this program. You know that too. I really think you and I should... "

"Sam, we may very well have a couple of unauthorized sanctions on our hands. And, inside the country, no less! It looks like it revolves around Meridian. The program itself may be in serious jeopardy. I need your help on this."

"Sanctions?"

"Sam, Meridian is a must-know access program with termination authority, sanctions, embedded in it. That authority is NSC-based. A compromise means the gravest national security consequences. Strategic consequences. Remember? That's why we created the JOG."

"Oh yes, I understand. Just so many big words used to describe murder. Murder on approval. How do you folks refer to it? A *termination operation conducted under the auspices of competent authority* or some other bullshit. It's the taking of another person's life, the assassination of human beings. That's all the more reason why you should listen to me. Only the NSC can approve Pete's access, no one else, not even the President."

"Oh stop, don't give me editorials from back issues of the *Bulletin of Atomic Scientists*! I sent Pete on an urgent mission to Europe, and he came back infected. That is indeed my responsibility. He needs an immunization. An overview, that's all. Then, I can send him out to cut this thing off... fix it. Help me?"

Sorenson looked at Pete, then back at Doc. He liked Kriegel. Doc had brought a new sense of integrity to the Company, something very badly needed. He shifted his weight in the chair and folded his arms.

"All right, but only on the condition that you and I create a joint memo for record afterward. Acceptable?"

"A joint memo? Gees, I thought you were a scientist, not a damn bureaucrat."

"I'm a scientist who's learned to survive in a bureaucratic jungle, and in front of Congressional Subcommittee interrogations. That's my bottom line. Deal or no deal?"

"Oh, all right, deal. Thanks."

"Pete, how'd you learn of Meridian?" Sorenson opened.

Pete cleared his throat. Sanctions, terminations, assassinations… for compromises of this program, Meridian? Well, he guessed that's what he was at this point – a compromise. He had opened Pandora's Box, and he was scared.

"Tony Spencer said that word with his dying breath. He was murdered, in front of his family. Bill Nordheimer gave me a sketch of something very advanced. Now Nordheimer's in a coma. My question is this… is Meridian what's in the photo the Germans gave me."

"The Germans? The Germans know about this?" Sorenson's face paled.

"That was my first reaction, too." Doc added.

"No, I don't think so. They gave me a photo they found in Yezhovich's apartment. They searched it. Don't ask me how they managed that under our noses, but they did."

"Photo?"

"This."

Pete reached into his pocket and pulled out the photo Klaus Reimer had given him. He laid it on the table. Doc picked it up, looked at it, then handed it to Sorenson, who frowned.

"Must have been Yezhovich, he had more than enough opportunity to do this." Sorenson nodded and turned back to Pete.

"So this is Meridian?" Pete asked.

"Yes." Kriegel and Sorenson answered near simultaneously."

"Well, what is it?"

"Please let me start, Sam. Then you can jump in. Pete, the very bottomline is that it's about an EBE. An extraterrestrial biological entity. In scientific vernacular."

"Really? Since when?" Pete asked, dripping sarcasm.

"Since more than fifty years ago. Yes, Meridian is based on our EBE. This phenomenon has quite a history to it."

"Come on, you're serious. Both of you?"

"Yes, we're serious. This is science, Pete. Empirical, provable reality, not fiction." Sorenson answered matter-of-factly.

"Fifty years ago... why still so secret?"

"Well, first of all, the technology. It's astounding. Mike's the first live one. He survived the crash in upstate New York and now he's... "

"Mike?"

"Mike is Meridian, our EBE. He's been working with us ever since. You might say he's a defector of sorts."

"I don't believe this. So, it's Mike. Just one of the guys... Doc, Dr. Sam, this is too much."

"Listen closely, Mr. Novak," Dr. Sam interrupted. "This is scientific, physical reality. Mike exists. He's the genuine article. The technologies he's shown us... we still don't understand the overall engineering. We can grasp the theory, but the physical engineering itself? Beyond our comprehension. We examine it every which way, test it, yet, it's so difficult to understand. On the other hand, it appears amazingly simplistic."

"You're doing a quantum leap on me here. You're talking about space flight now?"

"Rest assured that Meridian, Mike, and what he's doing for us is fact, proven fact." Sorenson continued as Kriegel sat back, smiling.

"Can you tell me what you *do* know? Where's Mike from?" Novak resigned himself to hearing them out.

"What we know as Beta 2 Reticuli, that system or pretty close to it. Do you have an inkling as to where that is?"

"No."

"Then it doesn't really matter, Pete, does it? It's light years away. Let's move on to the crafts. As I said, this is real. The vehicles are nuclear in function. They've mastered cold fusion. They have limitless power generation along with what we think is some form of electromagnetic propulsion, EMP. The larger ships, ah, we don't have one of those, the mother ships. They must travel well beyond light speed."

"Come on!" Novak had trouble moving into the realm of Flash Gordon.

"They must be, or we'd see them coming sooner. Faster than light is very probable in their propulsion technology."

"Faster than 186,000 miles a second? Einstein's theories proved nothing could really go faster than light. I don't... "

"Well, Dr. Einstein *did* think it was theoretically possible. Just not in our reality, but then Einstein didn't know about Meridian. He never had the opportunity to reach out and touch it. See it fly. Pete, it's like passing your hand through water, like a small waterfall. Approach the speed of light, and space folds in front of you. Time too. Like the water in the waterfall you put your hand through. The craft slips through it. There is no question for us now about flying faster than light. However, the concept of folding time itself, the fourth dimension... that may actually support even more radical proposals despite what Mike tells us about his origins."

"What could be more radical than what you've told me already?"

"There is at least a theoretical possibility, theoretical now, that Mike may in fact, be *us*. Mike says they've been coming here for thousands of years. Or, perhaps they've always just been here. Could be they're us."

"Us?" Pete was lost.

"The future us – splitting the fourth dimension. Trashing $E=MC^2$. Time travel."

"H.G. Wells. I see. Gentlemen, may we have a brief break. Just a few minutes. I desperately need to use the restroom?" Pete offered a weak smile. Now, it was the Morlocks and the Eloi. His disbelief was obvious.

CHAPTER 35

The Tank
Langley Center

Five minutes later, as they once again seated themselves, the three men eyed each other across the table. Sorenson was actually relishing the confrontation. The short break had allowed his mind to wander. Here in front of him was an unbelieving student who saw nothing but fairy tales.

A vision of earlier days in an undergraduate physics lab ran through Dr. Sam's mind. He wanted to say, *No, my son, this is science and I'm going to teach you. It is science and it's here now. So listen up and believe.* But instead, he merely confirmed Pete's sarcastic assessment.

"You've got it. Approach the speed of light, surpass it, and like in *The Time Machine*, space folds, time slows, and you slip right through it. And, you do it with little to no aging."

"It hurts to think about this." Pete sat back in his seat bewildered, lost in the tangled forest of theoretical physics.

"Join the club. We've had the same feelings. We've got more than one ship, uh, ASC."

"ASC?"

"Alternative Space Craft, ASC. An acronym. We have this desperate need in government to label everything within our own vernacular. We have them. We fly them. We put their alloys under our electron microscopes. And yet, we don't really grasp it all."

"Other ships, ASCs? Any other aliens, I mean EBEs, too?"

"Yes and no. Yes on the crafts, but no other *original* EBEs. We've had one ship since 1952. The crew of three died in the crash. That was our first shot at an autopsy... all three. We found similarities but some remarkable differences as well. On the ASCs, we've made good progress in the area of flight controls, vectoring of thrust, and chemistry of the alloys. Super thin and tremendously strong. Hardly any radar profile, which explains a lot of our tracking difficulties. In fact, we're well along in constructing a fleet of completely invisible ships ourselves. Think of it."

"Hard to fathom. This is where Yezhovich came in?"

"That's right. Dr. Yezhovich was one of our top researchers in composites and alloys. We sent him to Europe because we planned to share some of the low-end technologies with our European allies, especially the Brits. 'Too bad about him. Why he did what... except, well..."

"Except what?"

"Yezhovich, Laszlo and Mike all have some similarities in their DNA, ah, RNA chains. I really can't go further on that, Pete." Sorenson frowned.

"Pete? Can you understand?" Kriegel leaned onto his elbows.

"I guess I have to. If this is real, it explains a lot, except Tony Spencer, maybe J.T., and who knows who else. Company people. It doesn't explain that."

"Pete, you and I have to talk about that later. If what you say is true, those involved will face justice. Honestly, I can't fathom that being the case. We'll talk about it." Sorenson looked at Kriegel with a concerned frown. Kriegel returned Dr. Sam's glare.

Pete didn't reply. "Did I hear you correctly? We fly these ASCs?"

"Yes, we have flown them, and we still do," Sorenson responded. "We have a program involving some of our best test pilots. When we harness the power of pulse detonation propulsion, we'll build what's already in the air to replace the SR-71. Mike's given us the design on a platter."

"These are the technologies that will ensure we prevail on all battlefields." Doc said.

"That's what Bill Nordheimer said. Where in the world can you risk flying these craft?"

"We operated out at Groom Dry Lake for a while. That turned out not to be an optimal site. 'Way too visible to overhead satellite surveillance. We've had to move from the Tonopah Test Range, Area 51, Nellis North, as well. That's where the others were." Doc said.

"What others?"

"EBE's. They're at a new underground site in Northern New Mexico. Assisting us with design, test, and evaluation."

"You said there weren't any others."

"Not exactly. No other *originals*. Mike's the only original EBE. The other four in New Mexico are offspring. His. Mike's." Sorenson chimed in.

"We're sure his name is Mike, not Michelle?" Novak's face wrinkled with his lack of understanding.

"They're hermaphrodites, Pete. Mike has male and female chromosomes. Without getting into the details, let's just say that Mike can raise a family all of his own if he so chooses."

"Hermaphro... never mind. Even accepting what you're

saying, I still can't see what makes us shroud this thing as we have? We've made technological breakthroughs before."

"Pete, think of the social, cultural repercussions that might follow. A revelation that could fracture the very foundations of the world's religions. What would happen if we suddenly announce to the world we're engaged in communication with aliens? To some, EBEs might seem supernatural beings. Think of the upheaval."

"That argument holds no water."

"I know your father and mother schooled you in the Bible. Tell me how you reconcile this with your Christian concept of, say, Genesis? Tell me that?" Kriegel stared at Pete.

"My concept of God and Creation vis-à-vis Genesis is bigger than that."

"Go on, Pete. How so?" Dr. Sam's eyes sparkled. He leaned forward, grinning.

"I'm not convinced God stopped creating just because He'd finished with life on earth. He didn't stop with our sun. Creation didn't stop with our planet, not with our solar system, not with our galaxy. And not with the universe. So why stop with life on earth? For me, it's possible that the Seventh Day hasn't yet come nor is God at rest. I believe the process of creation is still ongoing."

"Of course it is! How else do you explain the new suns, supernovas, new pulsar systems with planetary systems revolving around them, blue-red quasars that move away from us with the ever-expanding limits of the universe? The Lord's creation is ongoing. God is still at work!" Sorenson smiled from ear to ear, sat back in the chair, and folded his arms over his chest.

"Gentlemen, I doubt the larger part of the world's population would be so willing to amend their concept of God as you two are." Doc frowned.

"I see. Doc, what you really mean is there's something else, something you and Dr. Sam haven't mentioned. What is it? Dr. Sam, you agree with me. What else scares you about a possibility for public disclosure?"

Kriegel looked at Dr. Sam, who was also frowning at Pete. Pete's eyes focused on Sorenson's expression. He was right. There was another piece of the pie.

"I give up, Sam. He knows just about everything anyway. Should we go further?"

"Doc, I have the depressing feeling we're digging our own graves here. Well, Pete, many years ago when we were well into developing a strategic ABM system, we ultimately realized that we lacked the technology and engineering know-how to build what would represent the most effective, perhaps even perfect, ABM system."

"And that would be?"

"Space-based ballistic missile defense... constellations of maneuverable satellites in of varied orbits. And, with weapon systems that could destroy enemy ICBMs either as they were launched from their silos in the boost phase or in mid-course flight through exospheric space, even launched from nuclear ballistic missile submarines."

"I see. Meridian has changed all this? It's possible now?"

"Yes. Mike has helped us with the engineering. It appears highly effective. We may be able to go directly from test to fully operational status within a few years. Imagine."

"What kind of weapon systems would these satellites use?"

"A mix of platforms... in order to handle different targets. Laser systems for one, powerful lasers with rapid-aligning bore sights, hydrogen fluoride lasers, those in the invisible light spectrum. Also, a mix of particle-beam, directed-energy, and kinetic-energy weapons."

"Dr. Sorenson, other than lasers, I don't even understand the term of the other weapons you mentioned." Pete slumped back in his chair, confusion taking over again.

"We didn't either, at first that is. Right now, still developmental, but well on track to operational status. Pete, with such weapon platforms in orbit, if anything moves on the face of the planet or in the air above it, we will be able to see it and we will be able to kill it. From space. End of story. So, what other questions?" Dr. Sam smiled in the asking.

"So, our overriding fear must be that a disclosure about us building these advanced systems might be destabilizing? Raise a threat of pre-emptive nuclear strikes?"

"No doubt about it, really. The Russians would indeed consider a first-use, pre-emptive attack. All of this is extremely dangerous. Doc, I have a 10:00 meeting with the DCI that I shouldn't miss." Kriegel alerted at the comment.

"I have one more question, somewhat philosophical. Pete laid his hands on the table, palms down.

"Really? Shoot." Sorenson looked at his watch.

"Why would Mike, this EBE you say we have in our custody, offer us such an advantage in weaponry? Why help us fly the ASCs, school us in their systems, build our own fleet? Is he an American patriot? Further, why is he working with us at all? He's a sort of… defector? What's in it for him?"

It was Sorenson's turn to slump back in his seat, his hands folded in his lap. He looked suddenly unhappy, perhaps even fearful. He replied in a low, restrained voice.

"This boy of yours leaves no stone unturned, Doc. I guess I might as well jump off this last bridge like I have every other. We have our necks stuck out so far it's not funny."

"I know. Pete, Mike's helping us because he's *Pro-Life*." Kriegel's voice was resigned.

"Pro-Life? Is that supposed to be humor?"

"No joke, Pete, Mike is helping us because of what he says is coming. It's coming, he just doesn't know *when*." Sorenson replied.

"What's coming?" Pete searched their faces for the answer he really didn't want to hear.

"Mike says, like humans, all EBEs are not alike. Other planets, other civilizations, some are not as friendly as his. Earth is an attractive planet. We have abundant resources, many forms of life. Mike says that at some point, earth will be in very great danger. We're pretty much a defenseless lot against Mike's kind of technologies. It would be no contest at all."

"You're talking about an invasion from space? Shit! I'm losing my mind!" This final step was one Pete couldn't take.

"No!" Kriegel barked, "You're not! Dammit, we're talking about the ultimate battle here! You know, the big "A" word, Armageddon! Lord help us, you asked for this, Pete. Now stand the hell up and take it. Be with us. Help us." Doc settled back in his seat, his eyes blazing. He was flushed. Pete blanched. Sorenson broke in.

"Mike's dying, Pete. Although there's an extremely short gestation period, he barely survived having the offspring he did. Mike's it. He says it's like a cancer, common in his species. Their planetary atmosphere is very easily penetrated by cosmic radiation, gamma rays. It's killing him. He wants to help us be as ready as possible before he dies." Sorenson explained.

"I see. All right. So tell me, how will Meridian's space based defense systems help against these alien ships?"

"Mike is certain they simply won't expect it. Our constellations of varied weaponry will be ready to greet these folks when they come out of light speed. They won't be prepared for the barrage. That's the plan. It's the only one we have, but Mike is confident it will work."

"We just don't know when." Pete shook his head at his own words. This was a big leap. Yet, these two well-educated, extremely intelligent men at the table talked about it so matter-of-factly. It had to be real.

"That's right. We just don't know when." Dr. Sam repeated.

"Meridian is not really about the Russians and deterrence at all. It's about this ultimate battle, fending off this massive invasion at some point in the future."

"Essentially. However, there are tremendous benefits for us now, though, both strategically and tactically, until that future time reveals itself." Kriegel remarked.

"Where are you keeping Mike?"

"Sam, I can take it from here. Thanks so much for coming. You've only got five minutes to make it up to the Director's office."

Sorenson stood and reached across to shake hands, first with Doc, then with Pete. He turned to the Tank's sealed door, then spun around.

"Doc?"

"Yes, Sam?"

"Screw the joint memo.

"Thanks, Sam. Thanks a lot."

"You too."

There was a great hissing, and the door popped open. They watched until Sorenson disappeared through the outer room's vault door. Their eyes locked again.

"Pete, let's finish outside. In the quadrangle... give our legs a stretch."

"Sounds good."

CHAPTER 36

The Quadrangle
Langley Center

Doc Kriegel and Pete Novak pushed through the cafeteria's glass doors and stepped outside. There was a breeze and a stiff chill. Novak folded his arms over his chest.

Lou Patusco switched the coverage for O'Donnell to the quadrangle. Again, no audio, just video. As Pantusco walked away, Phil toggled in on Kriegel and smiled.

"Well, looks like we won't stay out here too long. Nippy. On your last question, Pete, we moved Mike some years ago." Kriegel turned back to Pete.

"Where?"

"Denver."

"Denver? What base?" Pete's curiosity had sparked again.

"No base. That's why this Laszlo thing is so serious. We're hanging out with this."

"No base? Remarkable. Where then?"

"West Denver. A place called Wolf Creek Canyon. There's

an old pharmaceutical manufacturing building nestled up in the foothills. One road in or out. We've renovated it, put in some discreet security systems, sent people in – mostly science and engineering. We left it with an open appearance. It actually couldn't be safer, sitting so open. But if we dramatically increased security, more than just a few would take notice. That's the Catch-22. That's where you have to go. Soon. Pete, tell me about these killings."

"Tony Spencer *was* murdered. No question. J.T. found out, probably through Chapman. And, more confirmation yesterday."

"How so?"

"On my way home from the airport, I stopped by J.T.'s place. I don't know why, really. Anyway, his place is torn apart. Then I took a call on his phone."

"That was risky."

"I know, but I took a chance. The guy didn't recognize my voice, thought I was Brannon. A Captain Brent Mason, a harbor master down on Colington Island on the Outer Banks. He was getting back to J.T. on the registration of a boat that was down there, a sport fisherman. It's linked to Spencer's death, I'm certain of it."

"Who was it registered to?"

"Mark Bennis."

"Shit. Maybe you do have something, Pete."

"There's no question in my mind."

"Tell me about Laszlo. What made him break away from the Russians and run? Come over here... and armed? Why?"

"I'm not positive, but I'll tell you what I think. Laszlo is one sick man, mentally. Unstable. He's had a tragic life. Have you read the complete file?"

"Only summaries written by people who have."

"For some reason, he's always had physically violent

nightmares. Army MI agents caught him. They toted him off to the Bavarian Alps, beat the living shit out of him for nine months. Injected him with sodium pentothal, broke his fingers, hands, and did about every brutal thing to him they could. Even so, Laszlo drove them all batty with his nightmares, screaming in the middle of the night. I believe that Yezhovich's photo triggered it for him. He went over the edge. He's disturbed and dangerous."

"Are you saying he's not really running?"

"Correct. Laszlo's hunting for Meridian, hunting for Mike. Thanks again to Yezhovich, he must certainly know where to find him."

"Right."

"Can't you move Mike?"

"No, the environmental system we constructed for him was transported out to the site with him. It's the only one we have. Mike designed it himself. As I said, we can't create too much activity out there or people will suspect something's going on. We can't go briefing another 100 security types into the program. The NSC sits on top of it and doesn't react quickly. You've got to get out there. Intercept Laszlo."

"A special environmental system? Is that why this photo's so murky."

"The environmental room made it tough to photograph. Mike requires blue light and humidity, lots of moisture. It's all pretty eerie, really. Can you get out there in the morning?"

"Have to. I'll fly out first thing."

"Okay. There's more you need to know. Even Dr. Sam doesn't know this. He doesn't need to know. There's more to Laszlo than meets the eye."

"Is it about his DNA?"

"Damn. How in hell could you know that too?"

"Nordheimer said something about it, but I didn't understand."

"Pete, if Mike's being truthful and we have no reason to doubt he is, then they've been visiting here for thousands of years. They only stopped coming when they felt they'd be influencing early civilizations too much. Some humans saw them as gods. The EBEs didn't intend for that to happen."

"Yes?"

"Mike said they lost some. Not all of them went back. After not finding the runaways for weeks, they considered them dead. Fact is, they didn't die."

"And this has what to do with Laszlo?"

"Mr. Csengerny has RNA chains that match up with Mike's. Sounds crazy, but it's a medical fact. He may actually be a descendent. Also, as Doc Sorenson alluded, so did Yezhovich. They think that's why he bonded with Laszlo and helped him. It was in his genetic make-up to do so. Nuts, I know."

"Then his nightmares…"

"They may be organic to him. His mind has interpreted them as monsters from his subconscious, if you will. It could be that he was going to have these bad dreams regardless of what happened to his parents. There may be certain events that can trigger them."

"Yezhovich too? Damn. What will happen if Laszlo and Mike do meet?"

"Obviously, we don't know. So, we don't want that to happen. Too many unknowns. We'd like access to Laszlo… help him, and assist our own understanding of what is coursing through his veins and what it could mean for us."

"Could there be others like Laszlo and Yezhovich?"

"Why not?"

"Shit."

"Double shit, actually. You've got a tough job ahead. If you can spare Laszlo, then do so. But if you yourself feel threatened, terminate him. Kill him. I'll give you a map to Wolf Creek. Hard to miss, really. There's a big sign out front, *Paradigm Modeling, LLC*. We'll forward your clearances out there."

"Paradigm Modeling?" Pete remembered the helo trip from Dulles to Andrews.

"Right. Okay, then."

One floor down, the flickering light of the monitoring screens raced across O'Donnell's frozen face. He walked blindly away from the monitor, his eyes glazed over. With full knowledge of Meridian and the assassination link to Bennis, Novak was now indeed the most dangerous man alive. And more so by the minute.

No one in the Company had the authority to clear him for access to the Meridian program. No one. This security compromise was a disaster jeopardizing national security. Further exposure could and would threaten escalation, leading to strategic conflict with the Russians.

That's how he had to play it. The spy Laszlo and the uncleared, soon-to-be traitor Novak had to go. O'Donnell was not going to spend his remaining years in prison. He walked like a zombie toward the exit door, his fingers picking nervously at a loose thread on his jacket. He hardly felt Pantusco's heavy hand on his shoulder shoving him out of the room.

CHAPTER 37

The Novak Residence
Fairfax, Virginia

Pete's Durango bumped over the curb into the driveway. He was pooped. The thought of slipping into their king-size bed was inviting. He could see Sarah's Jeep through the garage door windows. Sarah was home. Susie and Joanna were in school.

As he gently closed the storm door behind him, he saw Sarah. She was bent over the kitchen sink, washing her hair. Pete set his briefcase down, slipped off his shoes, and stepped lightly on his toes into the kitchen. Sure she hadn't heard him, he suddenly reached out for her buttocks and squeezed hard.

"Ahhheee!" Sarah splattered suds all over the counter, shrieking like a banshee.

Pete burst out laughing, backing up as Sarah spun around. She was a fearful sight. Her hair was thick with suds, which now streamed down her neck. Pete howled, hardly able to stand, tottering backwards.

"Pete, you're a dirty stinker! Rotten! Rotten to the core!"

Her bare feet moved forward, brandishing a squeeze bottle of shampoo in her right hand, aiming it directly at Pete. Her scowl changed to a devilish grin.

"Sarah! Honey, don't! Please... my suit!"

The smile was still on his face, but the laugh was gone. He backed up into the wall phone. It popped off the hook and hit the floor with a thunk. It was Pete who jumped this time. A gleeful smile spread across Sarah's wet face. Before she could carry out her threat, a clump of soap suds oozed down into her left eye.

"Ouch! Pete, you're a booger!" she shouted. The shampoo bottle clattered to the floor as she vainly tried to wipe her eye. Her hand was covered in suds and made matters worse.

"Come here, darling. Daddy's gonna fix it." Pete rushed to Sarah's side. He groped behind her for the terrycloth towel by the sink and wiped her face gently. He helped her rinse the soap from her eye.

"You're still rotten and you're still a booger." She lifted her face and kissed him on the lips.

"I just couldn't pass it up. You have such nice buns, honey. I just couldn't stop myself!""Oh I do, do I?"

"Yes, you do. Quite a nice set of buns, if I do say. Ooh, that's so nice." Pete's hands slid down and grabbed her buttocks again, this time giving a gentle squeeze

"So, how'd it go today?" Sarah squirmed away, smiling.

"Unreal. You wouldn't believe it. Totally unreal."

"You always say that. Well, I'm glad you're finally home. It must still hurt, Pete, please let me help. Let me know when you need some hugs and I'll be there, okay?"

"Deal. By the way, I'm not really home yet. I've got to go to Denver. I can tell you that much."

"Pete, you're too tired to go off anywhere. You need rest. Tell Doc to send someone else."

"Sarah, it has to be me. I'm the only one up on this thing right now. Please understand."

"I'm only thinking of you. Is it dangerous?"

"No, I'll be fine. I'm only going to Denver."

"When?"

"I'm thinking it might be better to go this afternoon. I could change the ticket at the airport for another flight. There always something available."

"Pete, that's crazy! You need sleep!"

"I can sleep on the plane on the way out. In the hotel too. I'll be rested for tomorrow that way. Try to understand."

"What's the use? I never win these arguments anyway. Well then, why don't you go pack, and we can have some lunch together at the airport. I'll get back in time for when the girls get home. Okay?"

"Great, Sarah, thanks. Half hour or so?"

"That's fine. The girls are going to be upset, though. You'll have to treat them to something special when you get back. You know that."

"I know. I'll miss their goodbye hugs too."

The 30-minute drive to the airport went fast, as did lunch. There was more hand-holding between them than talk. Sarah could see Pete was preoccupied. He'd found a seat on a United flight to Denver at 2:15 p.m., so they didn't have much time. Pete looked so tired, probably distraught as well. There was little she could do about it. Pete would come to grips with it in his own way. He always did.

Sarah was sorry for Pete, but she knew in her heart she wouldn't miss Brannon staring at her all the time, oddball that he was. There was a measure of guilt stirring through her thoughts too. The man *was* dead. She'd live with it. Sarah and Pete parted company in the airport restaurant with a long kiss, then she headed for the main doors. She didn't see Pete wave as he turned onto the concourse.

CHAPTER 38

Fairfax, Virginia

The girls were home at 3:15 p.m. and as usual, demanding cookies and milk for an after-school snack. Sarah puttered around, lost in her thoughts. She stood at the dining room window, staring into the late October afternoon, her mind crammed with thoughts of Pete. The predicted rain hadn't yet begun, but clouds colored everything gray. The woods beyond the back fence were dark and gloomy.

She'd hung three bird feeders up the day before yesterday on the old silver maple. The winter birds always knew to flock to their yard. The maple stood like a tall, lonely sentinel. As she watched the feeders sway gently in the light breeze, it dawned on her that she hadn't gone back to fill them with seed. There was no time like the present.

She donned a jacket and hauled a sack of seed out to the deck and down the stairs to the yard. After a side trip to the shed for the step ladder, she began filling the feeders. As she climbed down, she noticed two brightly colored Snickers candy-bar wrappers at the base of the trunk. The girls sneaking candy?

But then she glanced up and noticed that some of the smaller branches above were broken, not pruned but broken off roughly.

Sarah again stepped on the ladder and pulled herself up to look at the first limb, about six feet off the ground. The limb's thin bark on top was scratched in places, gouged as well. It couldn't have been the girls. They couldn't climb up this high. She dropped to the ground, and stood puzzled, glancing up the trunk. No, it had to be Pete.

She'd seen Pete up there before. He'd spoken often about hanging a couple of swings from the maple tree. He occasionally climbed up to survey the area. He never did seem to get around to the job itself, though. And, Pete had a sweet tooth too. Yes, it would be so like him to climb up and start chomping on a Snickers, allowing his thoughts to wander.

Sarah scooped up the wrappers and headed for the house. She tied knots at the top of the seed bag and dropped it on the deck against the house. Then she leaned against the railing, puffing from hauling the heavy seed. She gazed around the yard and into the woods. The air was heavy with moisture, but it smelled so fresh on the light wind. The door opened behind her and Joanna peered out.

"Hi, mom."

"Hi, sweetheart. What're you up to?"

"Nothing. Can I have some more cookies?"

"No, you won't eat your dinner."

"Then, I guess I'll stay out here with you."

"That's fine, honey."

"Can I climb down the rope?"

"No honey, you… what rope?"

"Over here, mom. I climbed all the way down yesterday. Watch." Sarah stared as Joanna walked to the corner of the deck by the house. Her small frame began to squeeze through the bars beneath the railing.

"Joanna! No, that's over 15 feet down there! Where'd you get that?"

"I didn't get it anywhere, mom. It's been here. Honest. I climbed it yesterday. Really I did."

Sarah walked to the corner post and knelt. A length of half-inch nylon rope was coiled around the four-by-four support beam that rose up from the cement pad below. Was Pete trying to drive her nuts? First breaking branches in the maple tree, dropping candy wrappers all over the grass, and now hanging a rope from the deck. Well, he might have used it to haul something up to the deck, but he should have taken it off afterwards.

The dangling nylon rope was way too much of a temptation for the girls. Dangerous. She reached over and struggled to untie the knot, but her slender fingers were no match against the thick, tightly tied nylon knot. She planted her hands on her hips. Pete would get a piece of her mind when he got back.

"Joanna, I want you to promise to leave this rope alone until I get it down. No more climbing, all right?"

"Okay. I promise."

"Men!" Sarah took one last look into the yard and shook her head. She entered the house.

"Okay girls, what're we having for dinner? How about a nice spinach and broccoli pie?"

"Bleahhh! Yuk! No! Pizza! Yes! Let's go out for pizza!" The girls shouted in delight. "Pizza, huh? Hmm, not a bad idea."

Miles to the northeast in McLean, rain had already begun to drizzle from the dark clouds clustered in the upper valley of the Potomac. Doc Kriegel sat slumped in his leather chair and glanced at his watch. 5:00 p.m. He'd spent half the afternoon getting back-briefed on the results of the NSC meeting this morning. Time had gotten away from him. He reached out and pressed the intercom button.

"Yes, sir?"

"Joyce, get John Tanham, please. I'd like to see him in my office before he goes home. If he's available, tell him to come up here now."

"Yes, sir." A few minutes passed.

Kriegel's intercom buzzed. "Dr. Kriegel, Mr. Tanham signed out on leave at 1:00 o'clock today. He's out of the area for a couple of days."

"He is? Why didn't he tell me?"

"I don't know, sir."

"That's okay… rhetorical question."

"Yes, sir."

"Then, get me Phil O'Donnell. Tell him to come on up."

"Okay, sir."

Again, Joyce rang back in minutes. "Sir, Mr. O'Donnell signed out on leave around noon. He's out of the area. New York City, they said."

"What is this, National Vacation Week? Well, please check on Mark Bennis for me, ah, don't call him up here, just find out where he is. Then get me Lou Pantusco down in Security. I may need him."

"Yes, sir." A minute later Joyce knocked and walked into his office.

"Sir, Mr. Bennis is out too. He signed out on leave this morning. He's… "

"Let me guess – out of the area?"

"Yes, sir. Do you still want Mr. Pantusco?"

"Is he out of the area too?"

"No, he's in."

"No. I guess… well, I don't need to see Lou right now. Thanks, Joyce."

"Yes, sir. Sir, do you want me to stay a little later? Need me to call anyone else?"

"No, Joyce, that's fine. Say, did you send Pete Novak's clearances to Denver?"

"Yes, sir. I sent them out to Wolf Creek this morning."

"Great. Go along home. See you tomorrow. Thanks."

"Yes, sir."

"Out of the area." Kriegel muttered.

Almost every damn one of them gone. He stood, stretched, and paused in thought. He didn't like it, but he didn't want to overreact either. Pete was a big boy. Doc was still of the opinion that Brannon could be a little wacky. No, he would wait until morning to set his forces in motion. Get it all wrapped up by noon. He slumped onto the couch and poured himself another cup of coffee.

CHAPTER 39

The Novak Residence
Fairfax, Virginia

Full of pizza, the girls were already half asleep, their heads tilting toward one another. Sarah closed the garage door behind the Durango, then shook them gently. She had given the orders before leaving the restaurant… brush their teeth, wash their faces, and change into their pajamas. Then they could watch some cartoons before bedtime. They stampeded upstairs.

The pizza was a good idea. It was nice to be out and around other people when Pete was away. The clock on the oven read 7:00 p.m. Pete should already be in Denver. He might be just having dinner now too. Sarah glanced up at the ceiling… it reverberated with laughing, giggling, and thumping of feet. With a smile on her face, she set off to put things in order.

The girls were in bed by 8:30, drifting off to dreamland in no time at all. Sarah decided to turn in early as well. Pete didn't call, but that wasn't unusual. Everything was traceable, he always said. Snuggled under the comforter, she switched off the lamp on the night stand and turned to her left side with a sigh. Sarah was asleep in minutes.

Shortly after midnight, a lone jogger turned the corner onto Chestnut Avenue and crossed the street. His pace slowed as he neared the white colonial just ahead. He glanced cautiously up and down the street. Not a soul was out, not a light in a window.

A slight drizzle misted the air, dimming even further the pale light of the street lamps. The nearest one was four houses down, casting long black shadows across the lawns. He paused at the foot of the driveway, jogging in place, listening intently. All was quiet. Nothing. The window shades were drawn. No interior lights peeked out.

Catlike, he walked up to the garage doors, pulling a flashlight out of his pants pocket. Gently resting it against the window, he peered inside and gave a satisfied smile. Both vehicles, the Durango and the Jeep, were there. So, Novak was home, just as expected. He hadn't yet left for Denver. His airline reservations were for a morning flight, so the travel office told them. The man backed away from the house. The jogger again scanned the street before resuming his run, disappearing into the mist.

By 2:00 a.m., there was not a single sound of traffic on Ox Road. All of Northern Virginia was asleep. The mist thickened into a light rain that puddled the street. As it eased around the corner onto Chestnut, the tires of the large burgundy BMW hissed on the wet street, but the sound was lost in falling rain. The driver swung hard across the street, turning the headlights off.

He pulled into the curb one house up from the white colonial. The engine cut off and the windows rolled down near simultaneously. Five men inside the BMW sat without speaking, just listening. Minutes ticked by... they neither heard nor saw anything of concern. The man in the right front seat looked at his illuminated watch. He rotated his right-hand fingers in a circle.

The curbside doors opened and four men stepped gingerly out onto the wet grass. The driver remained with the car. They eased the car doors back into their jambs and crept up the sidewalk toward the house. They crouched low, spreading out and swarming rapidly like alley cats across the front yard. The silenced barrels of their automatic weapons glinted in the dim light. They reassembled on the tiled porch, squatting under the picture window.

"Look, this is a burglary, so burglarize. The wife's parents are loaded, so there ought to be a lot of art, silver, and jewelry. Take everything you can carry... cash, wallets too. Everyone inside gets wasted. Everyone. No witnesses. Any man screws this up, I'll kill him myself. I mean that sincerely." The man with the watch spoke in the barest of whispers.

"The kids?" A man crouched in back muttered.

"Yeah, kids too. This has to be clean. A burglary that went wrong – got it? You got a problem with this, tell me and I'll retire your ass right now." He swung the muzzle of his machine pistol around facing rearward.

"No... okay. We do the kids."

"Good. Okay, sweep the downstairs quickly and thoroughly. Move up to the sleeping quarters. We do it in three minutes. Three minutes."

The three masked heads nodded.

"Cut the window."

The man knelt by the small sliding window to the right of the picture window. He laid his machine pistol softly on the Spanish tiles and pulled the cutting device from his jacket. Pressing the rubber suction cup against the window glass just above the window's bolt, he looped one end of a three-inch wire over the plunger and swung the diamond cutter around in an arc. Once, twice, three times around. He pulled sharply on the plunger. The six-inch round piece of glass popped neatly out. Hardly a sound.

He backed away to the edge of the porch, peeled off the suction cup, and set the glass in the flower bed. A second man moved up, his assault weapon slung over his shoulder. He reached through the neatly cut hole with a small can of lubricant. He sprayed up and down the inside of the window jambs. The man with the watch stepped up, gently threw the latch and slid the window up and open. One by one, the four men eased silently into the living room.

In the back yard of the house, a brightly colored Snickers candy wrapper drifted down from the silver maple to the moist grass. A candy wrapper just like those Sarah had found. Crawling down the tree, another man clad in black tactical garb slipped to the ground as silent as a panther. Landing noiseless, he swiftly moved across the backyard to the deck.

He tipped his black cap up, and grabbed the nylon rope dangling above him. He pulled himself hand-over-hand up to the deck and climbed over the railing. He had tied the rope there just two nights ago after discovering how badly the wooden deck stairs creaked. Since then, he had returned each night to sit high in the silver maple, waiting for what he knew would come. Tonight it had come, and he was ready for them.

He knelt outside the kitchen door to check his gear… no firearms, just a long double-edged dagger strapped to his right thigh and a short-handled hatchet on his left. He dug into his pants pocket for his picks, selected one, and placed it into the keyhole to the door's spring lock. His left hand held another pick, which he inserted with a twist. The lock clicked, the door sprung open, and he eased it off the jamb. Showtime.

The four men crouched in the living room until the man with

the watch circled his hand overhead. All rose simultaneously and scattered silently into the darkness of the first floor rooms. One broke off to the right, entering the dining room. His weapon led in front of him. He moved cautiously, feeling his way through and around the table and chairs.

From the kitchen, the man with the black tactical cap swept toward the intruder in a crouch. He whisked along like a large black bat – sensing the placement of every object, every barrier, avoiding furniture with uncanny speed. He slipped forward swiftly and surely toward the target. He'd been there before, many times.

The man in black's only flaw in motion was a slight limp... the damn leg had been killing him for two days, ever since that drunken idiot Frank Halley missed them on his first pass. The rolling waves of the Atlantic battered both him and Cat after ditching the chopper. The icy waters left old wounds in Brannon's legs screaming with pain. But Halley plucked them up, and had then made sure to keep below the radars until they reached the recovery strip.

Without hesitation, Brannon rushed the first man as he emerged from the dining room. The man paused, puzzled by the large shadow moving so quickly toward him. Before he could raise his barrel, Brannon's right arm swung forward, its metallic extension glinting in the dim light from the windows. The dagger's eight-inch titanium blade sliced into the soft white flesh of the man's neck, its razor edge severed the carotid artery, jugular vein and esophagus simultaneously.

Bright red blood, headed for the brain, was suddenly diverted, mixing instantly with a river of dark venous blood from the severed jugular. The man's vision dimmed. He tried to scream, but couldn't. There was no air to be had. The horror and dizzying loss of blood brought him to the carpet floor in slow twisting motion. Brannon grabbed his hair as he slumped forward, easing him silently to the carpet.

Without a second glance, he swept into the living room. Another man… no more than ten feet away. He was moving away from J.T. and toward the stairs. Brannon slipped the dagger into its sheath and pulled out the hatchet. The man stopped in his tracks, trying to pinpoint the sound. He began to spin around, the muzzle of the silenced machine pistol at his hip.

The hatchet struck first. It slammed into the back of the man's neck, chopping his spinal cord. The man's weapon discharged with a loud metallic *chunk, chunk, chunk* spitting out bullets in a wide arc as his arms flailed wildly.

Brannon dropped to the floor as the 9mm rounds burst across the room, shattering the picture window and ripping holes in the wall behind him. The man fell backwards, the machine pistol spurting its last rounds into the ceiling. His body jerked violently before his arms fell limply by his side. Brannon crawled up to retrieve the hatchet.

"Mommy! Mommy! Somebody's in the house!" First one, then both of the girls screamed upstairs. Horrified shrieks. Brannon could hear the tapping thuds of little feet running on the second floor, then heavier footfalls. Sarah.

"Susie! Joanna! Run to Mommy! Quick, girls! Come here!" Mayhem broke loose.

Brannon rolled to his side as a third man appeared from the kitchen. He opened fire with a broad sweeping motion across the floor, the rounds thudding in an arc, sending shreds of carpet and splinters of wood into the air. Brannon froze. There was the chunk of a magazine ejecting.

As it hit the floor, J.T. leaped to his feet. The man desperately tried to slam another into the weapon as J.T. took aim and flung the hatchet with every bit of power in his shoulders and arms. It whizzed end over end, striking the man full in the face. A frantic shriek of terror reverberated through the house. The man's weapon clattered to the floor as his hands clutched at the hatchet imbedded in his cheek bones. He spun about clumsily, groaning and pulling at the handgrip of the hatchet.

The fourth man, the man with the watch, emerged from the kitchen. He fired his weapon point blank into the howling man's back, silencing him abruptly. He shoved the man to the floor with a heavy thump. His machine pistol swiveled and fired a burst in Brannon's direction. It exploded into the lamp on the piano, shattering the glass. Brannon spun left into the shadows.

The girls upstairs screamed hysterically. The leader's head cocked to one side, instantly recognizing the location of his quarry. He sprinted up the stairs, popping out a spent magazine and jamming in another.

"Nooo! Leave them alone! Sarah, quick, hide! Hide yourself and the girls!" Brannon raised his head and screeched at the top of his lungs. Upstairs, Sarah paused momentarily, then pushed the sobbing girls down the hall.

J.T. scrambled across the living room, stumbling over the bodies. He leapt three steps at a time, hot on the man's heels. He reached the second floor just behind the other. The man turned to fire, but J.T.'s right leg kicked the weapon aside. As his foot landed, his right arm swept forward, plunging the dagger deep into the man's right shoulder.

The man screamed in pain and jerked violently, sending the assault weapon sailing over his head. The dagger went with him, slipping out from Brannon's blood-soaked hands.

Brannon kept charging. His momentum carried them both crashing into the master bedroom. Sarah and the girls huddled in a corner behind the night stand. They screamed at the sight of the struggling men, J.T. on top. He could see the assault weapon near the corner of the bed, but he couldn't reach it. Instead, he yanked off the man's black stretch mask. Brannon froze, stunned. It was Mark Bennis!

Bennis seized the opportunity. He punched Brannon squarely in the face and pulled a .32 caliber Beretta pistol from his belt. He thrust it forward and squeezed off three rounds, ripping into J.T.'s left chest and shoulder, the impact thrusting him backward. Bennis struggled to his feet, tried to fire again, but the pistol jammed! He jerked the slide back and forth to clear it.

"You asshole, Brannon! I should have finished you in Egypt when I had the chance! You worthless, fucking bastard!"

Egypt? Cairo? The terrorist safehouse where his leg was nearly blown off? The nightmarish memory rose up in Brannon like a blazing fire. His eyes bulged, rage consuming him. He jumped to his feet.

"You? It was you! Well, that's too fucking bad for you, Bennis, you missed your chance! You ain't getting a second one! Oh, and Tony Spencer said to say hello!"

J.T. reached down for his weapons, but he had none. He screamed wordlessly and rushed forward, knocking Bennis' hand to the side as the pistol fired into the ceiling, then flung away into the darkness. One hand reached down between Bennis' legs, the other grabbed his shoulders. In his frenzy and with every ounce of power he had left, Brannon thrust the cursing Bennis clear over his head and just shy of the ceiling.

J.T. lunged for the window with Bennis flailing his arms helplessly, desperately trying to reach Brannon's throat. It was no use. Brannon's seething rage was delivering the strength of ten men to his arms. With an immense heave, he hurled Bennis crashing through the window. The glass blew outwards, raining around the howling Bennis all the way down to the concrete patio below.

It wasn't over. Someone was bellowing up the staircase. The

driver. He burst into the bedroom, his eyes and the barrel of his machine pistol sweeping the darkness. Brannon's bulky form was outlined in front of the shattered window by the watery glow of distant street lights. The driver knew it couldn't be Bennis.

He opened fire and kept firing. Brannon leaped suddenly to his right, away from the window and into the shadows. But it was too late a move. The rounds exploded across his chest, blowing him backward against the wall.

"Stop it, you asshole! Stop it! Damn you!" It was Sarah.

At the horrific sight of Brannon being shot to pieces in front of her, Sarah shoved the girls behind her. She leaped for the assault weapon still lying by the bed. Sarah thudded hard on the carpeted floor in front of the weapon. She grasped it, pointed it up at the driver and squeezed the trigger, never letting go.

Burst after burst of gunfire hit the man – stitching him like a zipper from his legs to his head. The impacts propelled him backward out the bedroom door and into the hallway. He tumbled down the staircase, smashing into walls to the first-floor landing.

Sarah dropped the now-empty weapon and crawled backward. The girls clutched at her in horror. She peered over the bed. Brannon's motionless form lay in a crumpled heap.

"Jayyy Teee! Jayyy Teeee! Don't, oh God, please don't…!" Sarah screamed. But there was no answer, no movement. The terrified girls clung to her, screaming at the top of their lungs.

In the distance, sirens wailed, growing closer by the second. Sarah could hear the chattering of people outside. She pushed herself up with the two girls huddled about her and looked over toward Brannon. Her face dropped in her hands. She gasped.

There was dark splattering of blood across the wall to the window. Sarah urged the girls out of the bedroom and to the stairs. She glanced back several times to the dark corner where Brannon's body lay, riddled with bullets.

CHAPTER 40

Lakewood
West Denver, Colorado

At Colby's Tavern near the corner of Sheridan Boulevard and Quincy Avenue, Laszlo took another big bite from the sausage and peppers hoagie. He had spent the morning driving all over southwest Denver. He finally hit gold. Two Air Force officers sat in a booth to his left. He had followed one of them for ten blocks after spotting the name, *Paradigm Modeling, LLC*, in large blue lettering on the side of the white Ford Taurus.

After waiting at the glass door entrance a few minutes, he had finally taken a seat at the counter allowing him to easily monitor their movements. It was noontime, the place was noisy and filled with people catching a quick bite for lunch. The officers were almost finished with their meal, so Laszlo signaled for his check.

He felt like a new man today... his energy level peaked. The morning's hot shower and shave had done it for him. He'd checked into a dinky motel on south Santa Fe Boulevard and stayed just long enough to clean up. The energy swelled up within him. He was ready for battle, and he didn't want to waste any more time.

And now here he was, clear across the United States, so close to his quarry. He'd been mentally bracing himself throughout the long drive, building his courage, feeding the hatred boiling within him. Today. Today, he would face the demon and kill it. Kill it just as its kind had killed his parents. Nothing would or could deter him now. A great sense of mission filled him.

Laszlo noticed the movement. The major from the white Ford raised his hand, motioning for the check. Laszlo pulled a ten spot from his pocket and slid it across the counter. He raised his glass and swallowed the last of his cola. With any luck, they'd leave the way they had come, separately. His luck was still running high.

The major seemed to be about Laszlo's size… couldn't be more perfect. The uniform would fit. The two men got up and walked out the tavern door. Laszlo waited further, fingering his glass and watching them through the window. They shook hands, then traipsed separately across the parking lot to their cars.

He rose. Pushing through the door, his right hand slipped under his jacket to feel the Pachmayr grip of the .357 magnum revolver tucked in his belt. He trailed about 40 feet behind the major. The other officer's car backed out of its parking slot and pulled away. As the major unlocked the driver-side door, Laszlo pulled a map from his pocket.

"Excuse me, sir. Could you do me a favor?"

"If I can, sure."

"I can't find the road out to Paradigm Modeling. You know, Wolf Creek Canyon. It doesn't appear anywhere on the map. Can you take a look and show me where it is?"

"Is this a joke or something?" The major eyed Laszlo warily, his disheveled clothes.

"No, major, it's no joke."

Keeping his back to the tavern, Laszlo raised the map slightly so the thick barrel of the revolver protruded from underneath it. The officer's eyes widened. He shrank back against the side of the car.

"Hey, take it easy! I don't have much money on me, but you can have whatever I have! Okay?"

"No, you take it easy, major. I don't want your money. Get in the car. You do exactly as I say or I'll blow a hole in your stomach I can stick my foot through. Understand?"

"Sure. What do you want? Look, I've got a wife and kids!"

"All the more reason you should listen. Reach in and unlock the back door. Now."

"All right." The officer reached into the back seat and popped the door lock.

"Good. Now get in, start the car, and drive. Make a right turn out of the lot."

"All right… just take it easy, mister. Don't do anything stupid."

"Shut your mouth and drive! What's your name?"

"I'm Joel… Joel Bryant." The major steered the car out of the lot onto Quincy Avenue.

"Joel, make a right turn up here on Sheridan Boulevard. Get in the right lane and continue north. Don't turn your head. I'm climbing up to the front seat."

Laszlo pushed the muzzle of the barrel against Joel's right temple as he climbed over into the front seat. He sat back into the corner against the door and lowered the pistol. Neither spoke as the Ford accelerated to 35 miles an hour, heading north.

"Where're we going, mister? I have to get back to work. They're going to miss me."

"Let me worry about that, Joel. Just drive. See this sign coming up ahead on the right? It's a double drive. Pull in and… "

"Hey, that's a cemetery! What the hell? I told you, I've got a wife and kids!"

"And I told you to shut the fuck up! I'll blow your head off right now if you don't! Do what I tell you and you won't be harmed, Joel! Drive, dammit!" Laszlo cocked the hammer on the revolver and pointed it at the officer's stomach.

"Shit! We're going… just don't shoot!"

Joel's eyes narrowed with fear. This crazy didn't want money and now he says he won't hurt him. His hands clenched the wheel tightly as he turned the Ford into the entrance gate of Fort Logan National Cemetery.

"Stop at the guard shack. Don't get any great ideas, Joel. I promise, you'll die first. No matter what happens, you die first. I'll do the talking."

"Good afternoon. What can I do for you gentlemen?" The security guard peered out the window of the gate shack and laid his cigar in the metal tray. Laszlo smiled at the dark blue uniform, not Army green – a contract guard, a rent-a-cop.

"Can you tell me where the World War II section is, ah, Air Force?"

"You mean *Air Corps*, sir, Army Air Corps, right?" the guard smiled smugly… at least *he* knew his history.

"Yes, you're right! Army Air Corps."

"Well, if you're not looking for anyone particular, just drive around that circle you see behind me until you're heading north again. Follow that road straight out to the second right turn. Take it, and you'll be right smack in the middle of all Second World War folks. That's where the Air Corps markers start and continue a ways. Okay, sir?"

"Thanks. Have a great day."

Joel pulled the Ford away while Laszlo watched his side mirror. The guard eyed them until they reached the circle, then he turned back toward Sheridan Boulevard. In minutes, they pulled up to the grass on the edge of the road.

"You've done well, Joel. Now get out."

"What, you said... "

"I said get out, Joel. I know what I said. Don't stop listening to me now."

Joel frowned, shaking his head. His eyes were filled with fear as he pushed his door open and stepped cautiously from the car.

Laszlo took a few steps onto the grass toward a cluster of large oaks. He motioned to Joel, who uneasily stopped in front of him. Laszlo again draped the map over the revolver and ushered Joel behind the big trees.

"Take off your uniform shirt."

"I don't understand!"

"You don't have to understand. Take it off, major." This time Joel complied, and the shirt fell at his feet.

"Good. Now stay turned around and put your hands behind you."

"Look, mister, I'll do anything. Please don't!"

"I have to tie you, otherwise, how can I be sure you won't run off on me? Heh?" Laszlo dropped the map on the grass, reached into his pocket for the roll of cord, and pulled the major's right arm back.

"You're not going to shoot me?"

"I told you, Joel, I'm not going to hurt you unless you make me."

At that, the major's hunched-up shoulders slumped down. He was resigned. He brought his left arm behind his back voluntarily.

"That's it, Joel."

"Thank you."

"You're welcome. Squat down here so you can see this map.

Show me where the unmarked dirt road is that leads to Paradigm Modeling." Joel plopped on the grass. Laszlo spread the map out in front of him.

"That site is a classified, a secure site. No, I can't. I'll be in big trouble."

"Major Bryant, if you haven't figured it out yet, you're already in big trouble. If you don't cooperate, I'll leave your dead body here... ready for burial. I don't have time to waste on you. Are you done cooperating?"

"No."

"Then tell me where it is."

"Drive back out to Sheridan and go north. Take a left turn, west, when you hit Hampden Avenue." Joel sat back on his heels, defeated.

"Good. I see it. Then?"

"Stay on Hampden. It turns into Route 285... Wolf Creek Lake Park will be to your north. Keep going west until you see Route 8 to your right. Take it north. The second dirt road on your left is the one you want. There's a small blue-and-white sign on the left side set back a bit from the road, Paradigm Modeling, LLC. There is a private drive sign next to it."

"Then what?"

"The dirt road will wind around through some foothills and red sandstone rocks for a mile and a half or so. After that, it's finished asphalt road again. You'll see a guard shack there as you round a large sandstone outcropping. There's usually just one guard, contract security."

"Contract guards at a secure facility?"

"Yes, outside. But that ain't what you're gonna run into inside, mister. There's security forces all over the place. They're authorized to use deadly force." Joel couldn't believe he was doing this, but he wasn't real hot on dying here either.

"You let me worry about that. Joel, do the gate guards know you?"

"Not really. There are different guards there all the time. Like I said, though, once you're inside the building, it's all security forces. You won't get past them. No way."

"What happens to the road after it passes the guard shack?" Laszlo ignored his comment.

"It forks. Trucks go off to the right, back behind the main building to the receiving docks. The front entrance and visitor lot are straight ahead. I'm telling you, you can't get past the security inside. They shoot to kill."

"Enough of that, Joel. The front entrance, is that where the access card readers are?"

"How do you know that?"

"Joel, where is your badge, your access card?"

"Hey, this is bad enough. You're not using my card to… "

Laszlo shoved himself to his feet and swung the .357 magnum up, cocking the revolver. The major cowered. He turned away as the gun was leveled at the side of his head.

"God! Don't, please! It's in my wallet, in the billfold! Please."

"Lower your voice, major. Joel, you have one chance, one, to give me your key code. The pin, what is it?"

Laszlo stepped behind Joel, and with his foot shoved him hard, face down into the ground. After retrieving the wallet, he pulled the money out. The card dropped on the grass.

"8-3-2-7." The major sobbed. His mind saw his career being flushed.

"Are you absolutely sure, Joel? 8-3-2-7?"

"That's it, you bastard! I'm toast now anyway! So get the hell outta my face!"

The major had begun to shout and this was unacceptable. Laszlo straddled Joel, revolver in hand. He flipped it around and whacked the major in the back of the head with a heavy thump. Joel's eyes closed.

Laszlo knelt, rolled the unconscious man over to his back, and undid his belt. He pulled off the shoes first, then the pants. He quickly shed his own clothing and donned the Air Force uniform. It took him only a few minutes to tie the man's ankles and drag him behind the furthest tree where he strapped the major to the base of the trunk. As a final touch, he ripped a piece off his already tattered shirt and stuffed it in the major's mouth.

Laszlo drove back the way he'd come and squealed through the cemetery gate onto Sheridan Boulevard without stopping.

"Assholes." The gate guard shook his head.

CHAPTER 41

Paradigm Modeling, LLC
West Denver

The white Taurus went briskly due west on Hampden Avenue. Laszlo knew the inside of the Paradigm Modeling headquarters by heart. Yezhovich had briefed him thoroughly on the interior. He knew exactly where to go.

The major's directions proved true. Laszlo hummed as he turned onto Route 8, a two-lane road cutting north through rough hills. He found the second dirt road as well. He was smiling, almost laughing as he swung onto it. His eyes glittered with a crazed look. Oh, he was ready. He stepped harder on the gas, accelerating with a rush of power.

Dust and rocks spewed out behind him. Ahead of him, the dirt road stopped with a good bump up to the macadam surface. The Ford hit it fast and jolted hard. The front wheels spun upwards, airborne by a foot. Laszlo realized the Ford wasn't going to make the turn. He stood on the brakes as the front end landed.

Tires screeched, sending the car into a rubber-burning slide. The sedan slid across the road. Both front and rear left wheels slipped over the edge onto the shoulder. Miraculously, it stopped.

Laszlo had a death grip on the steering wheel. Sweat beaded his forehead. He eased his foot off the brake and turned the Ford gently onto the roadway. Back in the right lane, Laszlo stopped to collect himself. His heart pounded. He dropped his forehead on the steering wheel and took several deep breaths.

In a sluggish turn, the Ford rounded a bend bordered by red sandstone outcroppings. Straight ahead was the guard gate, and behind it was the impressive blue, white, and glass structure of Paradigm Modeling. It was nestled in a gently sloped valley surrounded by hills of red rock. The massive, three-story building seemed out of place here, almost surreal. It was well hidden from view in all directions, except straight up.

The first floor was a series of 20-foot-high walls of copper colored glass that wrapped completely around the sides. Standing 10 feet or so out from the glass, a row of tremendous white pillars rose up from the concrete to support the blue-faced second floor that stretched out and over the first.

The third level was deeply recessed, a solid wall of white with not a single window. Its top edge was skirted by a ring of surveillance cameras. That was it. Laszlo was headed for the third floor. He noted three helicopter pads sitting in a row to the rear of the facility. One had a chopper squatting on it. He was curious to also see that beyond the building were two immense white geodesic domes and a large dish antenna. Satellite communications.

Laszlo adjusted his flight cap in the rear-view mirror as the Ford rolled ahead toward the gate. On the crest of red rock to his right sat a white blazer with a rack of red and blue lights fitted tightly to its roof. Almost upon the gate shack, Laszlo held up the badge card. The guard checked the license plate as the car approached, compared it with the list on the clipboard, and smiled back.

The guard waved and motioned the vehicle on through. He was in. From a parking spot in the small visitor's lot, he walked casually toward the building. The revolver was carefully wrapped in the coat tucked under his left arm. He noted the cracks in the parking lot macadam, barely able to hold back a smile of pure glee.

Laszlo pushed open the first set of glass doors. Then the second set. The large tiled lobby echoed at his entrance. Not a soul in sight. Directly ahead of him stood an army of telephone booth-like cubicles, a camera scanning the lobby from the roof of each one. A green swirling light flashed over one just ahead, announcing its availability.

Laszlo heard a muted chattering of voices coming from around the bend of the cavernous lobby to his left, but still no one in sight. Without hesitation, he approached the portal, his footfalls echoing. He swung open the door and entered.

The door sealed itself behind him. A small ledge to his left held the access card reader. A small black screen was positioned just above it, a concealed camera. He swept the badge through and punched in the key code, 8-3-2-7. The seconds ticked by, agonizingly slow. He could feel cameras sweeping up his back and over him. He began to sweat as he imagined the pressure of eyes scrutinizing him.

"Come on! Come on, open!" He muttered frantically.

The card slipped from his sweaty palm and fell with a light clatter on the metal floor. He bent over to retrieve it and felt his head swim. They had him… he grabbed the narrow ledge to steady himself when a loud clanking filled the cubicle. Laszlo stifled a scream. The portal door's electronically keyed bolt slid away. The green light came on over the exit door. He pushed. It opened.

Laszlo nearly jogged to the elevators and hit the illuminated *UP* button. He heard it engage somewhere above him, beginning its descent. He looked to his right. Nothing. To his left, a man in a white lab coat down the hall, but walking his way. Two police officers wearing berets stepped out of a doorway at the end of the hallway and glanced his way.

Laszlo moved closer to the elevator and hit the button again. It was laboriously slow. The man in the coat, still several doors away, looked up at him and smiled. The elevator door opened and Laszlo practically leapt in. He spun around, his frantic fingers pounding the button for *Level 3*. The doors slid closed and the elevator started upward.

He wiped the sweat off his face with his forearm, breathing hard. He had expected to see patrols of security police roving in the halls, but so far only those two. Why? Why no security patrols? He glanced at the display panel – *Level 2* blinked on, then off again.

When the doors finally opened on *Level 3*, Laszlo quickly moved into a small, narrow corridor. It was painted pastel blue. He noticed that the overhead lighting here was different, cool fluorescent rather than incandescent. His pace quickened, following several sharp turns that seemed to wind in on themselves.

There it was. The second vault door and badge reader loomed ahead, just as Yezhovich had described it to him. A boldly printed red and white sign was posted to the door: *WARNING. Special Access Required. Use of Deadly Force Authorized.*

Laszlo stepped up to it and once again swept the card. The control board came alive with pulsating lights. He punched in the key code 8-3-2-7 but this time, according to Yezhovich's instructions, he added a last digit, "1". Immediately, he heard metal sliding against metal. The light above the door blinked green, and he pushed through into yet another interior corridor. A short hallway. The door ahead looked to be stainless steel. He unwound the coat, which dropped off his arm.

Laszlo held the .357 magnum with both hands to steady the barrel. His heart was pounding again, his eyes wide. He took a deep breath and swung open a second door. A large desk sat some 20 feet directly ahead, dwarfing the man in a white lab coat seated behind it. Above him were floor-to-ceiling sheets of translucent plastic draped from wall to wall. The temperature here dropped off dramatically. The air was heavy with a clinging dampness.

This was the beginning of the disinfection area. The clean room, lay somewhere on the other side. Laszlo felt gooseflesh rising from both the cool air and the tension that knotted his stomach. The man looked up from his work and rose to meet him.

"Good afternoon, sir. You are?"

"Major Joel Bryant."

"I see. Sir, if you're Major Bryant, you've undergone a re-markable transformation since this morning. Another security exercise? Okay, let me get security for you." He chuckled as he spoke. The man moved toward a control panel bolted on a near wall.

"I wouldn't do that. I'll drop you right where you stand. Move away from the wall. Now! Take me to the demon... the beast."

Laszlo raised his right hand, pointing the handgun directly at the man. His eyes gleamed. He closed the distance between them and shoved the muzzle squarely in the center of the man's chest.

"The... beast?"

"Don't screw with me! I've come too far. Take me in or I'll kill you right here."

The man turned, his hands still raised high above his head. His right arm swept aside the cut-away section of plastic serving as a doorway. Laszlo followed. The plastic-draped hallway was dimly lit. Tubing ran along the walls, punctuated periodically by what looked to be nozzles jutting out. Curious, Laszlo bent his head to look at them.

Without warning, the hall was filled with a cold, wet spray drenching them both from head to foot. As Laszlo raised his hands to shield his eyes from the stinging antiseptic fluid, the man swung around. He struck Laszlo in the side of the head.

Laszlo went backward, but staggered and kept his feet. The man started toward him but slipped on the wet floor. His legs skittered wildly. His feet finally flew out from under him, and he found himself sprawled on the floor in front of Laszlo.

"You damn idiot! Move a finger, I'll blow your gray brains all over this floor. Got it?"

"I won't move! But there is no beast – no beast here."

"Go to hell! Move from this spot and I swear I'll kill you!"

Laszlo stepped over him and continued through the tunnel of plastic sheeting. A silvery light beamed into the hallway through a rectangular window coming up to his right. Peering through it, he was startled to see a three-story-high chamber flooded with fluorescent lighting. He pressed his face against the glass.

Below him were several large, black delta-shaped objects, crafts of some sort, suspended by scaffolding over laboratory equipment. From their triangular-shaped body, the wide yet thin wing-like structures jutted to each side. What appeared to be a windowed cockpit in the forward section answered the obvious question. Flying craft of some sort.

A gigantic silvery disk filled the rear of the cavernous room. It appeared at least 100 feet long, 40 feet in height. It too was suspended with steel cabling and scaffolding. He shook his head in amazement.

Laszlo heard a groan as the man lying back in the hall pushed himself to his feet. He moved quickly off from the window and through the last cut-away door. He was suddenly immersed in a fog of frigid air and mist. Loud hissing from the humidifiers assaulted his ears.

He could hardly see in the dim blue light. This had to be it. He felt his way forward, straining to see in the near-darkness as his eyes adjusted. Small lights blinked on both sides of the cavernous chamber. Bulky machinery of all kinds lined the walls. He inched forward. The light ahead was glowing brighter, more luminescent. He passed under a giant archway.

CHAPTER 42

Paradigm Modeling, LLC

A sudden brightness engulfed Laszlo. Blue light here increased dramatically in intensity. His attention was distracted by the table-like bed, pushed up against the wall. On it was... what was it? Laszlo squinted and edged closer. It moved! Though still some 20 feet away, he could make out the form of the creature.

It appeared thin, fragile. Not at all like the horrible, muscled and ravenous monsters filling his dreams since his youth. It was almost... human. The eyes were large, slanted, Asian. Its oblong head was so large in proportion to the body it was startling.

Laszlo couldn't tell if the demon was aware of him or not. A weird tingling sensation began to engulf him. Had it noticed him? Could it sense his presence without actually seeing him? Would it leap from the platform and tear him apart? Laszlo's knees weakened. He raised the .357 magnum in his right hand.

He moved closer to the creature. Its head turned! Laszlo cocked the hammer with a now-trembling thumb. He was unexpectedly nauseous. Now just ten feet away, his left hand came up to steady the shaking weapon.

In his pounding heart, Laszlo wished his mother and father could see this. That they could watch him slay one of the very beasts that had cut their lives short and made his own filled with such misery. This was for them. He stopped abruptly.

"Not much of a demon, is he, Laszlo? Hardly a monster, don't you think? Laszlo, you know in your heart this is not the demon that took your mother and your father from you. And, can you feel his presence? He senses yours. This is not your destiny, Laszlo." The voice came from somewhere on Laszlo's left, in the shadows. He spun around and scrunched his eyes, peering through the blue mist.

Laszlo stared into the nothingness. He was now confused, terrified. Another demon? Were there more? There must be. How else could this voice know so much about him?

"Who are you? Show yourself, and I'll kill you too!"

Laszlo glanced back at the creature. It hadn't moved, though the gray-skinned head now faced him. Laszlo could feel the creature glaring, probing him. The tingling increased, crawling over him like gooseflesh.

"I'm here, Mr. Csengerny, and I'm no threat to you either. No threat whatsoever."

Pete Novak inched forward out of the blue haze. His right hand had slid back into the pocket of his white lab coat, still wrapped around the Walther PPK pistol. Moments earlier, he'd drawn a bead on the back of Laszlo's head, but it seemed so unnecessary. The man was sick. If possible, Novak wanted to take him alive.

He'd had been here all night, waiting. He'd gone straight to the research facility from the airport. He'd slept on the desk in the outer office, and called off most of the interior security patrols, wanting to avoid a gunfight in the building.

"So there you are. Foolish man. You can't stop me. Why shouldn't I blow a hole in you too? Tell me that before I end this."

"How about the fact that I may know you better than you know yourself. Laszlo, I know what the Army did to you in the mountains south of Munich. I know about the beatings, the injections, all of it. They were wrong and I want to make it up to you. Mike here has nothing to do with any of that. Nothing at all."

"How could you know all this? It's a trick! No, I'm not stopping now! Not now!"

"I just know. I know, Laszlo. And I've come to offer you help. A better life. It's what Katka would want for you, Laszlo. Katka, Semmi, even your grandmother, Margo. If they were here now, they'd want you to put the gun down. Come with me. You have nothing to fear from me." Pete stepped closer, taking note of his glassy eyes and the trembling hands.

"Don't take another step!" Laszlo turned again to look at the creature, now slowly pushing itself up to a sitting position. It looked so frail, sick.

"Don't move, beast!" The muzzle of the revolver swung unsteadily between Pete and the object of his life-long hatred.

"Laszlo, don't! Put the gun down! Mike can't harm you. He's dying! Can't you see he's sick?" At that, the creature turned its head to Pete. His face cocked to one side, suddenly curious.

"Mike, you call that thing – Mike?"

"He's no beast, no demon, no more so than you or I. He's an Extraterrestrial Biological Entity. And to us, he's 'Mike'. He's helping us a great deal. And, he'll help you too, Laszlo. He's no threat to you, me, nor anyone else. Put the gun down, please."

Laszlo turned his head slowly toward the creature. Its long and slender left arm was rising, pointing, pointing at him. Laszlo shuddered in horror.

"What's it doing? Tell it to stop! My parents were murdered! They didn't just die in some damn train accident. I know what I'm saying. The railroad man told me. He'd seen the demons himself."

"He lied. Laszlo, he lied. He was trying to protect the railroad. Please, give the gun to me." Pete came within three feet of Laszlo. His outstretched hand softly eased under the weapon pointed directly at him.

"I guess..."

Laszlo's arm twitched, then lowered. He hesitantly held the revolver out to Pete. Laszlo turned to Mike and cracked the weakest of smiles. There was a sudden recognition. Two more EBEs, smaller but lean and strong in appearance, stepped out of the mist and stood by Mike. They had the same eyes. There arms and torso appeared well-muscled.

Before Laszlo released the pistol to Pete's waiting hands, he jerked it back at the sound of a loud crashing behind them. Pete spun around and Laszlo with him. Two forms walked out of the darkness. The first intruder spoke between gasping breaths. Phil O'Donnell, brandishing a Colt .45 semi-automatic. John Tanham stood by him.

"Well now, this is an honor. The crazed murderer, Laszlo Csengerny, alias Air Force Major Joel Bryant. And look here, wonder-boy traitor Pete Novak. You know, Csengerny, you sonofabitch, that poor major was nearly blue by the time the guards at the cemetery found him. It *is* late October, you know."

At that moment, red lights on the ceiling flashed on, their rotating glare creating an unearthly effect in the dim blue of the environmental chamber. Momentarily, everyone glanced up. From somewhere outside, a buzzing noise penetrated the thick insulation.

"My, my, looks like the security alert system's been tripped, fellas. The cops with their big guns will be here in less than a minute. Drop the gun, Csengerny! Drop it *now*, you bastard!"

Instead, Laszlo smiled, abruptly raised the revolver.

"Laszlo, don't! Don't!" Novak yelled.

Without warning, a blinding burst of flame roared from Phil O'Donnell's .45- caliber Colt pistol. Laszlo jerked violently. The bullet blew him backwards. A spray of blood splattered against the wall a microsecond before he slammed into it. The revolver fell from his hands. It skittered across the tile floor and disappeared into the darkness. Laszlo slid down the wall, leaving a dark smear behind him. His head slumped to one side.

"You lousy bastard, O'Donnell! He was giving up! Giving up, you prick!"

Pete yanked the pistol from his lab coat, but O'Donnell's was already drawn. Another explosion of sound and light. This time Pete found himself sprawled on the floor. His left arm flung behind him and a hot, searing pain burned in the other. The bullet had entered his upper arm, grazing the bone, and passed clean through.

"Says you, Novak. Mr. Peter Novak, you have compromised a highly classified, extremely sensitive national security program, and caused grave damage to the United States of America. You are not even remotely cleared to possess this information. And, you have been caught consorting with an individual whose actions are demonstrably hostile, inimical to the best interests of the United States. You are in serious violation of Title 18, U.S. Code." O'Donnell leered at Pete, his big white teeth sparkling like Chiclets. He paused to savor the moment.

"I also note you still have a loaded weapon in your hand. More than adequate justification for self-defense on my part. Wouldn't you agree, amigo? Adios muchachos, golden boy!"

The echo of a terrifying, inhuman shriek filled the chamber.

Like the screaming cry of a banshee filling the dark void. The men froze, turning toward Mike. He slid off his platform. One long and slender gray hand touched the surface of the bed to steady himself, the other pointed directly at Tanham.

The other two EBEs stepped forward in front of Mike. Mike's dark eyes narrowed into thin black slits as he focused on John Tanham. Tanham turned toward Mike, then back to O'Donnell.

"Phil, stop it! I can't let you do this! This is murder! It's over!"

"Go to hell, John! Nothing is over, not until this asshole's dead. You can spend *your* life in prison if you want to, but not me!"

Tanham jumped forward, knocking O'Donnell's gun hand upward as the weapon's sharp report echoed through the room. The bullet thudded into the ceiling, showering them with shards of drywall.

Tanham grabbed O'Donnell's hand and jerked it toward the chamber's exit. Two more blasts in that direction. Phil pulled the weapon inward, almost wrenching it from Tanham's grip. The two men flung each other around the room in a struggle for control of the pistol.

They slammed each other into equipment stands, knocking electrical monitoring equipment to the floor. Miniature explosions of light and crackling sparks rained around the room. Tanham's feet became tangled in wiring. He tripped, but tenaciously hung on to the pistol. He brought the cursing O'Donnell down with him.

As they toppled, the gun slipped under the grappling men as they slammed to the floor. A loud blast. An instantaneous flash beneath them.

Tanham rolled over onto his back, his jacket smoking. His hands slid to his sides. O'Donnell slowly pushed himself to a sitting position, the Colt in his lap. He smiled. Pete gasped. He instinctively pushed himself backward through the room. He knew he'd be next.

O'Donnell's right hand moved to grasp the pistol, but it slipped out of his hand in a streaming rush of blood. He glanced down, surprised at the warm river of red coursing down his chest. His head nodded sluggishly forward, then backward. O'Donnell's eyes rolled upward. He fell... his skull cracking on the concrete floor.

Tanham blinked and rolled to the side. He managed to pull himself up to his feet and looked down at O'Donnell. The bullet had ripped a piece of his heart which in an eye blink pumped out its life blood. Tanham walked to Pete and helped him rise gingerly to his feet. Mike and the two EBEs still stood by the bed, glancing curiously from human to human scattered around the room. Mike's eyes stopped on Laszlo. A strange sadness seemed to fill his face.

"Pete, you okay?"

"Yeah. It's just my arm. You?"

"I'm all right. Looks like Laszlo's still breathing. There'll be help here in a second."

They could already hear boots pounding down the hallway. Both men walked across the room and squatted by Laszlo's side. He was unconscious. Little red bubbles frothed at the wound's entrance on his chest.

"Looks like a punctured lung. Pete, put your hand here and keep pressing until they can put a compress on it. Maintain the pressure. Okay?"

"Yeah, I can manage that. John, thanks for what you did. You saved my life. You may have saved Laszlo's too. You did the right thing, John. Thanks."

"Thanks for that. I'm afraid it may have been just a little too late for me, though. Pete, you take care now, you hear?"

Novak nodded. Tanham turned and looked back at Phil O'Donnell's lifeless form, then to Mike. He managed a weak smile. Mike stared straight at him. The thin lines that were his lips bent slightly up at the corners, smiling in return. The two EBEs grinned along with Mike.

John Tanham walked off into the dim blue light, the red security lights still swirling above him. He disappeared in the cool dark mist as a group of security officers burst into the room, their weapons at the ready.

CHAPTER 43

Three weeks later, mid-November
Fairfax, Virginia

Sarah handed Pete the last of the suitcases. She watched as he tossed it in the back of the Durango and slammed the rear gate. He winced... the arm was still healing.

"Why don't you round up the girls, honey? I'll get the maps and lock up after you're all in the car." Pete stepped around the SUV and into the garage. He began shuffling through a pile of maps on his workbench. Sarah followed him, her hands twisting.

"Pete, I'm not ready for this. I need to stay here for a while. At home. We shouldn't be taking the girls out of school for two whole weeks. They'll miss too much."

"You'll just mope around the house, Sarah. No, we need to do this. Us, together, okay?"

Sarah's face was haggard from lack of sleep despite the medication the doctor had prescribed. She'd often wake in the middle of the night with nightmares. Pete would open his eyes in the darkness of the early morning to find her gone from bed. He could hear her pacing around the kitchen. He knew she'd been through hell. He'd tried to talk to her about it, but she wouldn't, or couldn't, let him.

Sarah carried the great burden of a private guilt that was crushing her spirit. She'd been out to Brannon's gravesite in Arlington several times a week for the last two weeks. Each time, she brought fresh flowers. It didn't help. Pete knew he had to do something before depression overwhelmed her. Taking this trip together was the best option.

"Pete, I can't. I need time alone, that's all. I can't get… that night is still with me. I need time to sort it all out. Besides, there's no need for you to take two weeks of your vacation time now, in the middle of November. The girls can't afford to miss so much school. Please, let's put this off." Sarah's eyes turned glassy and distant.

"Honey, there is no better time. We're ready. The car's all gassed up. We're packed. Why don't…?"

"What in the world will we do down there anyway? We can't swim. It'll be too cold for anything near the water. There won't be any people around. The restaurants will probably even be closed. We'll be completely isolated!"

"Hey, sounds great to me! That's just what the doctor ordered. We'll concentrate on us, the family. People at the Center have told me that's the best thing about being down there in the fall. There's nobody around! We'll be one with nature and ourselves. Just us and the sea. The girls will love it, no school and we get to play board games every night. Susie and Joanna can't wait. Don't worry about food. Some places are open year-round down there. I know. Trust me."

"Pete, I just…"

"No, Sarah, it's too late to turn back now. We're going. You're going. Give it a try. Tell you what, if after three days you still don't like it, we'll come back. I can get a refund on the beach house for the second week if we decide to leave. What do you say?" Pete pulled her close, his arms wrapping around her. Her head dropped limply on his chest.

"All right. Three days. Remember, you promised. I'll get the girls." Sarah pulled away from him. She walked out of the garage and around to the front door. Pete felt the crushing weight descend again.

Susie and Joanna were actually okay. After a couple of sessions with a counselor in kid-speak, their smiles returned in no time at all. They readily accepted the explanation that J.T. was in heaven with God. There were moments where they occasionally forgot though. They asked when he would be coming over for dinner. Pete found himself praying every night in praise and thanks for the lives of his family. He hoped with all his heart that the violent trauma could be put behind them.

All of them piled in, he eased the Durango down the driveway. They all looked at each other in a brief pause. Pete turned back to the windshield, shifted, and accelerated down the street.

CHAPTER 44

I-95 South
Virginia

T he drive down I-95 to North Carolina was tedious. While the girls played nicely in the back seat, the tension in the front of the Durango was thick enough to cut with a knife. Pete and Sarah hardly spoke. Sarah stared out her window. Lost in her thoughts. Pete in his. He stared out the windshield at the road ahead, but his mind was back in Washington.

A tremendous mess was being cleaned up at Langley. Kriegel was in the middle of a firestorm. The affair had reflected poorly on his ability to handle the big picture. Doc had taken it hard. He was harder on himself than anyone else could be. He was reluctant to let Pete leave for two weeks, but finally agreed. Novak was appointed hatchet man for restructuring people, positions, organization, and missions in the Directorate of Operations. Big changes were in the works.

John Tanham tendered his resignation in lieu of disciplinary action. John was mismatched for his work. He'd known that all along, but had tried to muddle through. He had poorly selected his key people. It backfired on him and tragically so. Tanham moved his family up to New England. He stayed behind only to clear out his office and put the house up for sale. There was no farewell party.

Pete turned down the radio. Sarah didn't notice. He remembered the sight of Laszlo slumped against the wall. Laszlo had survived the shooting with a patched lung. A splintered rib would take some time to heal. The .45-caliber round had hit just high enough to miss any critical organs. Lucky man.

An inquiry panel concluded there was no evidence to prove Laszlo had actually killed anyone. All indications were that the Russians and the JOG deserved the blame. He was offered asylum, and he accepted. Laszlo was recuperating somewhere in the Northwest where he would get all the help he needed. The company psychiatrists thought that with the right therapy, Laszlo could once again be whole.

In return, Laszlo was willing to share his knowledge of Russian agent networks. It was a win-win situation. For the first time in a long time, Laszlo Csengerny's future was a bright one. Mike had requested arranging a visit by Laszlo back to Wolf Creek. Mike knew who Laszlo was. That would be an interesting meeting. The scientific community would be watching closely, and very nervously so.

Doug Chapman was very much alive. Remarkably, his only injuries from the crash were a fractured rib and a broken nose. First, Lt. Skip Kenny and then the FBI took good care of Doug. After the dust settled, they returned him to North Carolina where he quickly retreated to his beloved Cape Hatteras. He was deeply moved by the news of J.T. Brannon's death. Chapman thought Brannon had guts and moral virtue on a par with his greatest screen heroes. It was hard for Doug to believe he would never see Brannon again.

Despite the disastrous confrontation with the SVR, U.S. intelligence recognized the STALKER program as an operational success. It was here to stay. The Company was preparing to load it with more personnel and resources. As for the Joint Operations Group, its mission charter was thoroughly reviewed. Most of JOG's manpower had already been reassigned among several divisions in Operations. Its charter would now be limited solely to Frankfurt and Tokyo, and the new JOG supervisor reported directly to the station chiefs of those offices. That's how it should have been to begin with. That's how oversight functions got way out of hand.

Pete and Doc agreed they had never seen such a cloak of secrecy engulf the Agency so completely and so rapidly. A heavy curtain dropped over every speck of information. Every facet of operations was admonished to secure the complete integrity of the Meridian program which maintained its sanction authority. There would be no further compromises.

Phil O'Donnell and Mark Bennis were buried with honors in quiet funerals. Officially, their bodies had been recovered from a terrible airplane crash in Kenya, somewhere along the Ugandan border. Rumors circulating in Washington mentioned something about a surface-to-air missile. Initial rumblings in the Senate Select Committee on Intelligence threatened an official investigation. Those things died down almost as quickly as they had begun.

"Ah, Pete, weren't you turning someplace along here?" Sarah broke her stony silence.

"Uh, yeah. Let's see, where are we?"

"It's a quarter-mile to Route 58 east. That ring a bell?"

"Whoa, yeah! Thanks, honey! Don't know where my mind was."

"Dadddy! Stop jerking the Durango! Now my coloring's all

messed up. Look what he did, Mommy!" Joanna complained, holding up her coloring book.

"Then tell your absent-minded father to pay attention."

"Yeah, Dad! Pay attention!" The girls blurted in unison.

"Okay, gees! Gimme a break!" he whined, but he was happy for the talk, any talk.

The next hour was a little better. The Durango roared over the Wright Memorial Bridge at almost 2:00 pm in the afternoon. On the Cape side of the bridge, a green Jeep sat in an empty restaurant parking lot. Its two male occupants watched the highway.

Sarah didn't notice the fixed-point surveillance team. Pete did. They noticed him as well. The driver leaned over to pick up the encrypted phone. Pete smiled. Despite the long drive, the girls hadn't yet begged to stop for lunch, thanks to the snacks Sarah had packed. That changed as soon as Pete turned south onto Route 12, Beach Road. The stream of restaurants began to slip by.

"Mommy! Daddy! I'm starved! Let's eat!" Susie blared out first.

"Me too! I wanna eat too! I'm hungry!" Joanna followed suit.

"Pete, there's a nice-looking place coming up on the right. Their sign's lit up. Let's stop!"

"Sweethearts, we're so close now, just a couple of blocks. Whaddya say we go to the house first, throw the bags in, and then we've got the whole afternoon. Maybe even time for some hot fudge sundaes too!"

"Yeah! Ice creammm! Let's go to the house first!" Susie shouted.

"Me too! Daddy's right, Mom. Then we got the whole afternoon! Hot fudge sundaes! Yeah!" Joanna bounced in her seat.

"Listen to Mr. Manipulator over here. Hot fudge sundaes, heh?" Sarah smirked.

"Why sure, honey, you can have one too! Doesn't that sound scrumptious?"

"Yeah, Mommy, you can have one too!" Joanna echoed.

"All right, fine. The house first."

They drove past a sign proclaiming Nags Head Town Limits and continued down Beach Road. Pete passed Windy Cove Road on the left. He then turned sharply into Sea Drift Lane. The Durango rolled past empty houses... driveways cluttered with dead brush, all the window shades rolled down. Tall grassy weeds gave the entire street a forlorn, abandoned look.

"Hey, sure looks inviting, Pete. Real cozy-like." Sarah said, her voice dripping with sarcasm.

"Don't worry, it'll be fine. You'll love it. Wait and see." The girls were both kneeling on their seats, their noses pressed against the windows.

"So where's our house? You'll be in the sand dunes any minute."

"Coming up on our left, next to last house."

The large two-story building boasted wide windows and a wrap-around deck. Another deck on top would provide a spectacular view out to sea. Sarah's eyebrows rose.

"Hey, not too bad, Pete. Looks like we have neighbors across the street as well. Must be another wacky family."

Then to her surprise, Pete turned right. He looked in the rear view, then at the driveway ahead.

"Ah, Pete, where are you going? I thought you said we were on the left. What're you doing?" Sarah turned in her seat with a confused look. Pete pulled into the crushed shell drive behind two identical burgundy Jeeps.

"I know the folks in here. Just a short stop, Sarah. Promise.

Come in, Honey. I'd like you to meet them. Girls, you too. Come on."

"Pete, no. We can meet them later, tomorrow. I'm not dressed right."

"You're dressed just fine. This is a beach house. Come on, don't be a stick in the mud. The girls are coming. You want to sit out here all alone? Up to you, Sarah."

Pete climbed out, stretched, and the door thudded shut behind him. The girls slammed their doors and dashed ahead of Pete to the wooden stairs. Sarah frowned, then reluctantly grabbed her purse and opened the door.

"All right, I'm coming. Wait up."

They started up the stairs together. Pete slipped his arm around Sarah's waist. The girls skipped in front. Sarah abruptly froze. Her hand gripped the banister.

Two men dressed in suits had suddenly appeared at the railing above them. Their sunglasses reflected the stormy sky above. Thin wires crawled from their ears to snake down their collars. They loomed ahead, large and ominous.

"Pete, what's this? What's going on?"

"It's okay, Sarah." His hand caressed her cheek, but she abruptly brushed it away.

"Who the hell's here, the damn president? These guys look like Secret Service. Pete, I don't like this." Despite his assurance, Pete practically dragged Sarah the rest of the way up the stairs.

"Good afternoon, Mr. Novak. Mrs. Novak… girls." A man in a dark navy suit spoke.

He nodded to them individually. Susie and Joanna giggled back, unperturbed. The second man moved quickly to open the front door and stood silently holding it for them. The girls stepped through. Sarah followed, glancing fearfully at Pete over her shoulder. As the door was closed carefully behind them, a woman in a white uniform and nurse's cap immediately appeared in the hallway.

"Good afternoon, Mr. Novak. It's good to see you, sir. Mrs. Novak, nice to see you too. 'Glad you could make the trip. Won't you please come in?"

Sarah stood next to Pete, mystified. A nurse? A nurse who knew who they were, and by name?

"How is he?"

"Doing fine, sir. A little better each day. We were going to wheel him out on the deck this afternoon, but the wind came up. It was a little too much." The nurse turned and walked down the hallway which took a sharp bend to the right.

"Pete, I wish you'd tell me what's going on. You know I don't like surprises like... "

Sarah cut off in mid-sentence as they entered a large room. Massive windows faced out to sea. Another nurse stood at the foot of a hospital bed where a man lay, propped up on several pillows. Intravenous bags dangled from bright metal racks, feeding numerous tubes that dripped into his arms. He looked toward them, raising his head in anticipation.

Yet another woman sitting to the man's right stood up as Pete, Sarah, and the girls appeared. A boy was sitting to the left of the bed, holding the man's hand. Sarah stared at the three of them, confused. She seemed to recognize the man in the bed, but it just would not register. It didn't compute. It couldn't.

"Jayyy Teee! It's Jayyy Teee!" The girls screamed in instant acknowledgement, bolting forward.

They rushed to the bed as fast as their little legs would take them, tears beginning to stream down their faces. They flung themselves over him, hugging him ecstatically, shrieking with joy. The man's big hands rose and stroked their hair ever so softly.

"Ohhh," Sarah whimpered. She gasped, her heart skipping a

350

beat. Sarah's lips quivered as the tears broke. She stood still, but couldn't hold back as the truth sank in.

"It can't be... oh God."

Her knees felt weak. Her hands began to tremble. All the strength in her drained away as her arms fell limply by her side. Her purse thumped to the floor. She wavered, suddenly dizzy. Sarah dropped her face into her hands, then looked ahead again. Pete drew up behind her and steadied her.

Sarah edged forward uncertainly, shaking her head. Taking one tentative step then another. All at once, she left Pete's arms and flung herself toward Brannon. Her hands reached out to him in disbelief.

"Jayyy Teee! Oh, my God! J. T., you're alive, not... ohhh!"

A choking sob wracked her as she fell to her knees by his bed. Her shoulders heaved. Her hands clutched at his chest. Sarah let go. She let go of the guilt, the pain, every ounce of it. A smile wavered across Brannon's haggard face as he slowly raised his hands. He reached out and patted her shoulders, then lowered his head on the pillow as the emotion of the moment swelled over him.

Pete lost it. He stood in the doorway, his eyes brimming with tears at the sight. Barb Spencer and her son walked toward him. They glanced over their shoulders and blinked back their own tears. Pete gave Barb a hug, then took young Tony's hand in his and squeezed hard.

The emotional release overwhelmed Novak. He couldn't take it all in. Lying before him was a man who never had someone to call his own... no one to care for. He had nothing but the Agency and the country for which he had been so willing to give his life. He had no family, no son that he had longed for.

And now, in the space of a heartbeat, J.T. had it all. Surrounded by love. Tears tumbled down Pete's cheeks. He backed into the hallway holding back sobs of joy for the old cold, and not-so-cold, warrior, J.T. Brannon.

Novak groped for the door handle behind him and stepped out onto the deck. The security men turned toward him, but he waved them off. He turned the corner to the east side of the deck, facing the ocean. He leaned into the offshore gusts, wiping his face with his hands. The Lord does indeed work in mysterious ways. Out of such overwhelming tragedy came so much love, so much good.

Of course, Brannon would have been dead if he hadn't been wearing the Kevlar vest. Even so, two 9mm bullets had pierced the vest. Two bullets out of the 10 or so that had struck him. Another round had gone through his right thigh. Three hits. But once more, J.T. Brannon survived. He had saved Pete's family from sure death and made four other men give their lives in the process.

His tears abating, Pete smiled at the thought of how the Brannon legend would grow even more. Then, he realized it couldn't. Officially, J.T. Brannon had died in the helicopter crash at sea almost three weeks ago. He was then officially and ceremoniously buried in Arlington. And officially, it was going to stay that way. But, it didn't matter. Brannon was recovering well. The man with nine lives would have yet another life, a new life and a new identity.

As for Barb Spencer, she could let go of her grief. She could once again love her husband, not that she'd ever really stopped. She thought he'd stopped loving her. But of course, there was no Maria Dean, there never could be, not with Tony Spencer. Tony Jr. had again found his loving mother. Their relationship would remain intact forever.

Pete looked across the waves rolling in, one breaker after another. Unceasing. For a passing moment he wondered whether all waves were unique, like fingerprints, snowflakes, and people. No two alike. He shook his head at the notion. Sarah could now be free from her guilt. She had a whole lifetime to make it up to J.T., as he knew she would, in her own way.

His eyes drifted from the tossing sea to the heavens above. He stared at the sky, the clouds tumbling overhead, captivated by the beauty and mystery. Meridian crept into his thoughts like a shadow. The image of Mike in the environment room filled his head. It was still so surreal. Indeed, the Lord's creation was beyond man's understanding. Pete hoped that if all was true about some terrible day when humankind's very existence would hang in the balance, Mike would have time to finish his work... and God would empower him to do it.

"Oh, what do the stars portend? Caesar asked," Pete muttered, pushing away from the railing. He shoved his hands in his pockets and breathed in deeply of the salt air.

Sarah stepped silently up behind him. She slid her hands up to his shoulders, pulling him toward her. Pete turned at her touch. She looked up into his eyes, smiling through the tears that still ran down her reddened cheeks.

"Oh, Pete, thank you. Thank you so much. You don't know... "

"Sweetheart... well, actually, I think I do."

Sarah drew closer, wrapped her arms around him, and rested her head on his chest. As he pulled her in, something else drew his gaze skyward once more and with a broad smile. A ray of sunlight seeped through the clouds, drenching the deck with light.

The light exploded through the sliding glass doors, spreading across the floor and flooding J.T.'s room with a sudden warm glow. He sat up in his bed, surrounded by Barb, Tony, and the girls. They turned their heads and smiled.

The End

ACKNOWLEDGMENTS

This novel has been rewritten by the author from an earlier work published by an independent publisher in the year 2000 and is hopefully a dramatic improvement. I would like to express my sincere appreciation to Ginny Ruths, Editor, Touchstone Publications, for her craftsmanship in sharpening the writing. I also wish to thank my good friend, John Fraser, for his critical reading of the manuscript and the recommendations he made. Thanks also goes to Tom Inks, Joe Dalton and Tom Owen for their close reviews and offering a multitude of narrative and grammatical recommendations. Thanks to my wife, Trudi, for her constant support and encouragement in my pursuit of writing.

CPSIA information can be obtained at www.ICGtesting.com
Printed in the USA
BVOW08s1750100416

443712BV00001B/38/P